About the Author

N.K. Downing is a debuting author with a passion for writing young adult fiction that is appropriate for anyone of any age to read. Growing up as a homeschooled military kid, she was an avid reader with a soft spot for fairy tales. Currently, she attends Cedarville University, where she is studying Economics and Spanish. When she is not writing or studying for exams, she loves reading the Bible, spending time with her family, and learning foreign languages. The Bible passage she lives by is found in Titus 3:3-7.

King of Corvus

N. K. Downing

King of Corvus

Olympia Publishers
London

www.olympiapublishers.com
OLYMPIA PAPERBACK EDITION

A CIP catalogue record for this title is
available from the British Library.

ISBN: 978-1-80074-571-1

This is a work of fiction.
Names, characters, places and incidents originate from the writer's
imagination. Any resemblance to actual persons, living or dead, is
purely coincidental.

First Published in 2023

Olympia Publishers
Tallis House
2 Tallis Street
London
EC4Y 0AB

Printed in Great Britain

Dedication

To my parents, Jonathan, and Jennifer. Thank you for exemplifying Christ's love and grace throughout my life. I love you so much!

Chapter 1

Philip didn't mean to become king. He didn't mean to betray the people he cared about. He didn't mean to lose everything.

Wiping blood from the silver lapels of his deep purple jacket—the very same jacket worn by the previous king—Philip sank back into the obsidian throne. He ran his fingers over the polished, black armrests. Black spines shot from either side of the stiff back like crow's wings. The dramatic silhouette cast long shadows like talons. Sitting here felt blasphemous, as if he were disrespecting every king who ever sat here before him. Making a mockery of all they stood for. How long had he stood beside this very same throne, unaware of his fate?

Perhaps he should have noticed the signs. It wasn't as if he'd had no warning whatsoever; he simply hadn't thought it would go this far. Hindsight was often a cruel, merciless beast.

Footsteps echoed on the black marble. Never a moment of peace. Philip didn't bother to look up; only one person remained by his side through everything. Only one other person was broken enough to stay with a shattered soul like him.

"It's time."

Philip could no longer delay the inevitable. With a labored sigh, he rose. He'd thought sitting on the throne even for a moment would help reality sink in. It didn't. The crown certainly didn't. The clothing didn't. Why had he been so foolish to think this would?

None of this felt real. Part of him wanted to believe it wasn't. But he knew better. He'd learned that the hard way. In just a short time, his life had gone from normal to… *this.*

It all started with a family reunion in the middle of nowhere. Philip had dreaded the trip for months, but his parents resolutely dragged him along.

"It will be good for you to get out of your room and have some family time." They'd said, *"Don't you think it will be nice to have a break from the city?"*

Though Philip thought the exact opposite, he knew better than to say so. His parents would leap to the chance to lecture him about being disrespectful and ungrateful and whatever else they could come up with in the heat of the moment. He could never win, so it was best to shut up and stay out of sight.

Tugging at the zipper of his favorite grey hoodie, Philip gazed out the window of the car. Endless clusters of scraggly trees lined the highway. Now and then, he would catch a glimpse of a house or barn nestled in the trees, and he would have to remind himself that people *chose* to live out in the middle of nowhere. Disgusting.

This definitely wasn't New York City. They'd only been driving for a few hours, and already, Philip wanted nothing more than to turn around and go back. Despite what his parents said, taking a "break" from the city sounded like a terrible idea. Nothing good could happen in a place where people drove battered pickup trucks and unironically said "ain't."

"Are we there yet?" Philip's little brother, Max, asked for the hundredth time in the past hour.

Suppressing yet another sigh of agitation, Philip released a measured breath. Each passing minute only further soured his mood, mostly thanks to his brother. At ten years old, Max still hadn't learned to shut up. He chattered nonstop the entire ride. His knee bounced with anticipation and glee. Weeks before the trip, he'd packed his suitcase and told everyone how much fun he was going to have at the reunion. Relentless energy and enthusiasm were normal for him, but the reunion trip made him reach a new level of excitement; he practically bounced off the walls like a caffeinated squirrel.

Philip wasn't sure how much more he could take.

To pass the time and block out Max's voice, he popped earbuds into his ears. Listening to classical music always calmed him down and cleared his mind. He cranked the volume up so loud that it drowned out the sound of his thoughts.

"Hey, Philip." Max leaned over and pulled the earbud out of Philip's ear. "Whatcha doing?"

"Nothing," Philip replied, fixing his gaze on his reflection in the window.

"Hey, Philip," Max said, "Do you think we'll see bears or wolves or cobras while we camp?"

"West Virginia doesn't have cobras."

"Oh…"

After a blissful beat of silence, Max spoke again. "Hey, Philip. Maybe we'll see rattlesnakes. My teacher says rattlesnakes live all over America."

Sighing, Philip closed his eyes. Max couldn't just allow himself to be sucked into a movie or iPad on a car trip like a normal kid. No. He *had* to bother everyone at any chance he got.

The rest of the drive was the same. Max tried to get Philip's attention, and Philip ignored him. After a grueling, eight-hour drive, they arrived at the overflowing campsite parking lot.

Their father squeezed the car into a parking spot next to a gigantic, highly modified truck, which took up two entire parking spaces. Philip scowled at the sight of his older brother's car. For some idiotic reason, Marius had decided the hectic family reunion was the perfect opportunity to introduce his new girlfriend to his parents, brothers, and entire extended family. Most likely, it was another of his egotistical attempts to pull all the attention to himself. He always had something up his sleeve to try to shock the family. First, it was dropping out of college, then it was moving to Colorado to become a rock climber. His poor girlfriend was in for a rude awakening.

Long ago, Philip had promised himself he would do everything in his power not to end up like his older brother. He had much bigger plans for his life. He would become rich and successful and respected—everything Marius wasn't.

With a sigh, Philip shook himself out of his stewing. It wouldn't do him any good to show up to the reunion in such a foul mood. He slung his backpack over his shoulder and climbed out of the car only to have his father thrust an armful of camping gear at him.

His father grinned broadly. "We'll have to hike to the campsite, but that's part of the fun. Right, boys?"

Philip raised a skeptical eyebrow; seeing his father excited about a camping trip was like seeing an investor excited about losing money. His father wore jeans and a t-shirt in place of his usual suit and tie. He rarely left his office, and when he did, the last thing he would want to do in his free time was take his family on a hike. Nevertheless, he kept up this act of enthusiasm, apparently hoping it would rub off on Philip.

It didn't.

Irritated as he was, Philip trudged after his family to the winding, tree-lined hiking path that led to the campsite. His back ached from the weight of his backpack, and he could already smell the distinctive odor of nature clinging to his clothing and hair.

To distract himself from his discomfort, he turned his focus to the tranquil nature that surrounded them. While he didn't enjoy the mile-long hike, he appreciated the quiet of the early summer woods. Leaves crunched beneath his feet as he strolled, savoring the calm before the Beltran family storm.

They neared the campsite much sooner than Philip would have liked. Before he could see his family, he heard them. They'd probably scared away every bird within a five-mile radius.

The moment they reached the campsite—which was crowded with tents, picnic tables, and campfires—his parents dropped their camp gear in a heap and plunged into the sea of people. Max followed at their heels like a puppy, eager to soak up as much attention as possible. Dogs and small children darted underfoot, adding to the din of boisterous laughter and adults talking over one another.

Philip lingered in the protective cover of the trees, surveying the chaotic sight before him. Steeling himself, he hipped his hoodie to his throat. It was better to get this over with, like ripping off a Band-Aid. He stepped out from the trees, only to be swallowed by the crowd. People pressed against him on all sides. The stench of body odor and perfume filled his nose. He tensed, but he forced himself to keep walking. A few more steps and he would reach safety near the tents.

Casting a glance to the right, he made eye contact with his grandmother, who waved him over with a thin, wrinkled hand. Just great. Like an obedient grandson, he made his way toward his grandmother and paid his respects. "Hello, Abuelita."

Philip stiffened as his grandmother took his face in her hands and planted a wet kiss on each of his cheeks. "Marius! It's so good to see you! How are you?"

Philip pried himself from his grandmother's grip. He spoke

slowly and evenly, careful to keep the irritation from his voice. "I'm Philip, not Marius."

"Oh." His grandmother's face drooped into a disapproving frown. "Well, when you see Marius, tell him I'm waiting to meet his new sweetheart."

"Of course, Abuelita," Philip answered, though his grandmother had already hobbled away in search of his brother before he finished speaking.

A scowl overtook Philip's face once her back was turned completely. This shouldn't have upset him—after all, this same exchange happened every year—but *come on*. Philip resembled Marius like a crow resembled a pigeon.

Philip was easily the more attractive brother. While he took great care to make sure he appeared as perfect and meticulous as possible, Marius always looked like he slept in a dumpster. Philip kept his dark hair short and neat, and Marius wore his shaggy and overgrown. Philip's face was angular with high, sharp cheekbones. Marius's face was flat and round. Nevertheless, everyone, including their own family, continued to mistake him for Marius.

Inhaling a slow, deep breath through his nose, Philip forced himself to stop dwelling on trivial irritants such as this. In the grand scheme of things, why should he care that his grandmother couldn't tell him apart from his brother? This kind of petty frustration would only keep him from focusing on the important things in life.

As he continued to squeeze through the crowd, he glimpsed his grandmother cooing over Max, whose deceptively angelic face practically glowed as he beamed up at her with a chocolate-smeared grin.

Before Philip could escape the mass of people, someone

clamped a rough hand on his shoulder. He bristled as a smug, familiar voice said, "Still being a pest, Phil?"

Philip whirled to shoot Marius a withering glare. "Don't call me Phil." He snapped.

The response came automatically after enduring sixteen years of Marius's "teasing." His anger subsided momentarily as he realized with surprising satisfaction that he was finally taller than his older brother.

Marius raised his hands in mock surrender. "No need to be so touchy. Anyways, I'm not here to chat. Mom's making me introduce you to my girlfriend," He wrapped an arm around the girl beside him, "Phil, this is Thea, my new girl. Thea, this is my prickly little brother, *Phil.*"

Thea had pale skin, blue eyes, and strawberry blonde hair. She couldn't have looked more out of place among the dark-haired, tan-skinned Beltran family. Thea's freckled face broke into a cheery grin. "Hi! Marius has told me so much about you."

Philip held back an eye roll; there was no way his older brother had spoken a single good word about him. Still, it was nice of Thea to try. So far, she was an improvement from the other girls Marius used to bring home.

"Nice to finally meet you," Philip replied politely.

"I was just telling Thea about your little phone repair thing," Marius said, resting a hand on Thea's slender shoulder. "Her roommate spilled milk all over her laptop. I told her it wouldn't be a problem for you to fix it for her."

Philip stiffened at the mention of his repair business. Marius's condescending sneer made his business sound like a child's lemonade stand. The repair business was his life. He lived and breathed troubleshooting and diagnostics. His work was far from child's play; it was his ticket to greatness. With his

15

experience repairing technology, he could build the skills necessary to become one of the best software developers in New York City.

"I already have plenty of paying customers waiting," Philip protested.

"Like I said, it won't be a problem, *will it?*" Marius's voice held a dark warning tone, and he clenched his fists.

Philip had no interest in causing a scene in the middle of the reunion. Though he was taller than Marius, now wasn't the time to see if he could take him in a fight. Gritting his teeth, he gave a grudging nod. "Fine. I'll take a look at it."

Thea clasped her hands together, oblivious to the tension between Philip and Marius. "Thank you so much!"

With a knowing smirk of victory, Marius steered Thea away. "Come on, Babe. I want to introduce you to my favorite brother, Max."

Thea turned back over her shoulder and waved to Philip. "It was nice to meet you!"

Once they disappeared into the crowd, Philip strangled the drawstrings of his hoodie. Leave it to Marius to walk all over him. Well, in a few years, when he was the successful brother, Marius wouldn't look so smug. Yet again, he forced himself to take a calming breath.

To take his mind off the encounter with his brother, Philip decided to make himself useful. He successfully squeezed his way out of the crowd without being ambushed again and made his way to the edge of the campsite, where his family had thrown their belongings into a haphazard pile. Loading his arms with bags, he cursed at the obnoxious number of books his father had decided to bring. He made a wide arc around the swarm of people as he carried the supplies to the other side of the campsite.

When he was halfway across the campsite, someone let out a shriek. Philip turned towards the source of the noise, but before he knew it, someone crashed down on top of him. Everything he carried clattered to the ground, landing in the dirt.

Reeling back, Philip swore under his breath at the sight of the bright-eyed girl in front of him. Of all the people he could have run into, it had to be *her.*

Adela Beltran was Philip's cousin, younger by only a few months. Philip remembered his cousin as a bubbly, energetic girl who never let any one gets a word in edgewise. Aside from the fact that she stood a few inches taller, she hadn't changed much since the last reunion.

"I'm so sorry!" Adela exclaimed, dropping to her knees and scrambling to gather the scattered items.

Philip heaved a backpack over his shoulder, praying Adela wouldn't try to start a conversation. She was infamous for her endless chatter about anything and everything.

"Hi. How are you? It's been a while, huh? You look taller. I'm taller!" Adela's words came out in a rapid stream.

"Oh… hey," Philip mumbled, wanting nothing more than to be left alone. "Sorry, but I don't have time to talk. I have work to do."

"If you're going to set up your tent, I can help you," Adela said. She scooped up Max's superhero backpack and slung it over her shoulder.

"Thanks, but I'm fine doing it by myself."

"That's okay! I'm sure you'll be able to use the help."

"Really, I'm fine on my own." Philip gathered the supplies and strode away. Adela followed him anyways.

When he reached the area designated for his family's tent, he dumped the supplies on the ground and began to work. He neatly spread out the stakes and rods according to the instruction manual and set to work, meticulously following every step.

Adela didn't lift a finger to help, instead, talking nonstop about her plans for the summer. "—And then, I'm going to the beach to celebrate the summer solstice with my friends. Carlos will be there, and I think he's finally going to ask me out. What's more romantic than the beach during the summer solstice? There's just something so magical about the solstice, you know? I can't wait! If you want, I can call and tell you all about it. Oh! You can join the group chat I started last reunion with all of the cousins. It's hilarious! I don't know if I have your phone number, though..." she trailed off, scrolling through her phone.

With a labored sigh, Philip pounded in the last stake of the tent. He hadn't listened to a word Adela had said in the last fifteen minutes. It was best to simply remain silent and let her ramble.

Even after all her blabber, Adela still wasn't finished. "While we're on the topic of group chats—"

"Philip!" Max hollered, cutting Adela off. He raced towards them as fast as his short legs would carry him, and skidded to a stop, inches from crashing into Philip. "You gotta come see this!"

Philip had never been so glad to see his little brother. Any excuse to escape Adela's relentless chatter was a welcome one. He scraped together a halfhearted attempt at an apologetic expression as he allowed Max to drag him away.

Adela nodded in understanding. "Okay! I'll find you later. You *have* to see this hilarious thing Carlos texted in this other group chat."

Philip pretended not to hear her. Once they were out of earshot from Adela, he breathed a sigh of relief. When they got back to New York, he would need a detox from all human contact.

18

Max led him across the campsite towards a cluster of towering evergreen trees at the edge of the clearing. "I found these really cool mushrooms on a tree over here!"

Frowning, Philip slowed; if his few years in Cub Scouts taught him anything, it was to be cautious around wild plants—especially mushrooms.

"Maybe you should leave this alone, Max," he cautioned.

"But you haven't even seen them yet! They're awesome, I promise." Max stopped at the base of a tree and crouched down. He pointed to a patch of brightly colored mushrooms in hues of pinks, purples, and blues. Each mushroom was barely the size of Philip's thumb. "See? Aren't they cool?"

Philip made a noncommittal noise and lingered at the edge of the tree line, regarding the forest warily. Max waded deeper into the trees, following the meandering trail of mushrooms. "There are more over here by this rock," he pointed out. "These are yellow."

Before Max could go any further, Philip grabbed his elbow and dragged him back into the clearing. "Why don't you find Marius or one of our cousins?" Philip suggested, "I bet there are plenty of people who would be happy to explore with you."

Max kicked at the dirt, scuffing his red sneakers. "But I want to explore with *you*. We never spend any time together. You're always working on your computer job. And now that Marius has another girlfriend, he's gonna spend all his time with her just like he did with his last girlfriend. He didn't even remember our secret handshake today."

Philip opened his mouth to say "absolutely not," but paused to reconsider. Though the thought of spending an entire day alone with Max in nature made his stomach churn, it would be an excuse to get away from the rest of the family. Maybe a simple hike with Max would be more bearable than listening to Adela ramble all day…

Max blinked up at Philip, pleading with round, brown eyes. *"Please?"*

With a sigh, Philip gave in. He cast a glance at the darkening sky. "We can explore sometime this week. It's getting late now, and we're losing daylight. I don't want to be in the woods while it's dark."

"Can we go tomorrow?"

The sooner they could get this over with, the better. "Fine." Philip conceded, "We'll start first thing in the morning."

Max spat on his hand and held it out for Philip to shake. "You promise?"

Wrinkling his nose at Max's spit-covered palm, Philip folded his arms. "I'm not shaking your hand."

"Come on," Max said, "You have to. You don't want me exploring all alone in the dark, scary woods where I could get lost, do you?" He stuck out his bottom lip in a pout.

Philip rolled his eyes at his brother's dramatics. He reached out to shake Max's hand. "I promise."

"Nice try." Max pulled his hand back. "Spit first. It's how they do it in the movies."

Groaning, Philip spat on his hand. It took everything in him not to look at the saliva that glistened on his palm. He grasped Max's hand and shook it firmly, suppressing a shudder.

By dinnertime, everyone knew about Max's grand plans to explore the forest. There was no backing out now.

Philip, who regretted his decision more with every passing second, found a secluded picnic table to eat dinner and catch up on work. This week, he had a lighter load than usual. He neatly spread the broken devices in front of him like a grid. As he ate a too-charred hotdog, he replaced the shattered screen on an iPad.

Mustard dripped onto the sleeve of his hoodie, and he frowned; though he could repair a broken game console with his eyes closed, he couldn't do anything about a mustard stain on his favorite hoodie while he didn't have access to a washing machine. He loathed the useless feeling of not having the ability to fix something.

A *thud* startled Philip out of his thoughts. Adela plopped down across from him and spoke. "The other cousins and I are going to roast marshmallows later. You should join us!"

"Thanks, but no," Philip replied shortly, "I have work to do."

Adela's face fell, but she quickly recovered from her disappointment. "That's alright. If you change your mind, you know where to find me!" With that, she left him in blissful science.

Philip turned back to his work, not sparing his cousin another thought. The satisfying press of a fresh screen protector on a brand-new screen made him smile to himself. While he worked, he allowed himself to relax.

The world around him faded to a dull haze of background noise. Behind him, a few people kicked around a soccer ball. A team of aunts and uncles cleaned up from dinner, taking extra care to lock the food in thick, metal boxes to prevent critters from stealing from them. Little kids darted around the campsite as they played a complicated version of tag that only they understood. The elderly family members gathered around a bonfire to catch up on a few years' worth of family gossip.

As the sun dipped below the horizon, people began to trickle to their tents. Sleeping children were collected and carried to bed. Many of the introverts in the family retreated to their sleeping bags for a break from social interaction. Philip remained at the table, content in his solitude.

The evening faded into a brilliant, starry night. A soft hum of conversation floated up like campfire smoke. The rhythmic blend of English and Spanish was like a lullaby to his tired mind.

When it became too dark to see, he pushed aside his work and stared up at the stars. In New York City, stars were invisible even on the clearest nights. The multitude of stars that glittered above him was like nothing he had ever seen before. He'd heard people describe the existential realization of insignificance when seeing the stars for the first time, but he still didn't get it. The vastness of the universe had no direct impact on him, so why should he waste time contemplating it?

Instead, he cleared his mind and savored the quiet; the world rarely spared him a moment of rest. Closing his eyes, he took a deep breath of night air, which was fresh and cool in his lungs. The difference from the hazy, smog-filled air in New York was stark and refreshing.

What wasn't refreshing, however, was the cloud of mosquitos that plagued the air. They swarmed him, taking advantage of every inch of his bare skin. Though he tried to swat them away, his efforts were futile. Thanks to the mosquitos, the moment was successfully ruined.

Later, as he used the communal bathrooms set up on the edge of the campgrounds, Philip decided he hated camping. A worm inched out of the drain while he tried to wash his face in the frigid tap water. He let out a cry of disgust and sprang back, successfully drawing the judgmental gazes of a few of his older cousins.

Scowling, he slunk to his tent and burrowed into his sleeping bag. His parents and Max were already fast asleep, their heavy breathing magnified in such a small space.

Max stirred beside him and mumbled in his sleep. "Night, Philip."

Philip rolled over so his back faced Max. Failing to find a comfortable position on the uneven ground, he knew he was in for a restless night.

The next morning, Max awoke before the sun.

"Philip?" Max whispered.

Philip pretended to remain asleep.

Max poked him in the cheek. "Philip. Philip. Philip."

"Go away," Philip groaned, pulling his pillow over his head.

"Come on." Max yanked the pillow away from him. "You promised."

"Fine."

Dragging himself out of the tent after Max, Philip was pleased to find they were the first ones awake. At least he didn't have to be sociable at such an ungodly hour. He'd slept in his grey hoodie, but even that couldn't shield him from the chill that cut through the pre-dawn air. Stars dotted the lightening sky, twinkling through the early-morning mist.

He made a beeline for the fire pit, where he knelt to start a fire. Just as his Cub Scouts leader taught him, he crumpled newspaper over a pile of brush and ignited it with a lighter. Once a small flame blossomed in the nest of newspaper and brush, he stacked wood in a strategic tent shape. In no time, the fire reached a steady roar.

While Philip hung a kettle of water over the flames, Max rummaged through the metal containers that protected their food from wild animals. He emerged with a package of marshmallows, but before he could say a word, Philip shot him a grouchy look. "Don't even think about it."

Max returned the marshmallows to the pile as if he were

being forced to part with his most prized possession. He glumly pulled out a banana and a granola bar for each of them and sat down with a huff.

Ignoring Max's dejected attitude, Philip used the boiled water to make a pot of coffee. The instant grounds he found were grainy and bitter compared to the smooth, rich Madagascar brew he drank at home, but without his morning dose of caffeine, he would be a zombie all day.

As he choked down his dry granola bar and overripe banana, his eyes drifted towards the forest where Max wanted to start exploring. An inexplicable sense of dread settled over him. Exploring with Max certainly wasn't a good idea, but it was too late to back out now.

The second he finished eating, Max leaped to his feet. "Let's go!"

"Are you *sure* you want to go exploring today?" Philip tried one last time to dissuade his little brother.

Max planted his fists on his hips. "You promised."

"Fine." Philip sighed. After downing his third cup of coffee, he threw some sandwiches into his backpack and followed Max across the campsite. Max stopped in front of the patch of strange, brightly colored mushrooms. He bounced on the balls of his feet. "We're going on an adventure!"

Philip shook his head at Max, who didn't have the least bit of hesitation as he eagerly plunged into the forest. With one last glance at the safety of the campsite, he trudged after his little brother.

Max darted around the forest, happy as a pig in mud. All around them, the woods were beginning to awaken. Birds sang as they hopped over the damp, mossy ground in search of bugs and worms. Moisture hung heavily in the air, promising a hot, humid day. Fresh dew clung to leaves, flowers, and branches like tiny crystals. The smell of pine needles and wet soil engulfed them.

Soaking in every detail, Max scrambled over boulders and around trees. He stopped every few steps to pick up random sticks he deemed interesting. Soon, his pockets bulged with nuts, stones, and leaves.

Philip trailed after Max, taking extra care to watch his step. After a few minutes, he realized his brother was following a trail of brightly colored mushrooms that grew in a strange pattern over the forest floor.

"Philip, look!" Max exclaimed, pointing to a pink mushroom that grew up the side of a tree. "Do you think we can eat it?"

"Let's not find out," Philip said as he pulled Max away from the mushroom.

A twig snapped behind them. Philip whirled around, scanning the trees surrounding them. He assured himself it was just a squirrel or rabbit, but it was better to be safe than sorry.

"Max, remember to stay close, okay?"

There was no reply.

He turned back to Max. "Did you hear—?"

Max was nowhere to be seen.

"Max?"

The forest remained silent.

"Max?" Philip's breathing sped. His head swiveled every which way as he desperately searched for his little brother.

"Philip!" Max called from a distance. "You gotta come see this!"

Philip hurried towards his brother's voice. A breath of relief rushed from his lungs when he found Max kneeling next to an odd cluster of toadstools that shimmered every color of the rainbow.

His momentary relief quickly melted into anger as he trudged over to his brother. "Max, you can't just run off like that! If we get lost, we could be stuck out here for days."

"Sorry." Max didn't sound the least bit apologetic. "I was just following the trail. I think it ends here." He reached down to stroke the flat cap of a blue mushroom.

"Don't touch that!" Philip snapped, swatting Max's hand away. "It could be poisonous."

"Okay," Max grumbled.

Philip gripped the straps of his backpack and forced himself to take a calming breath. "Look, I know you wanted to have some kind of big adventure, but I think we should get back to camp. It was a mistake to come out here in the first place."

"Are you kidding?" Max whined, "We just got here."

Philip shook his head. Frustration and panic welled up inside of him. "We're going back. Now."

Max ignored him and knelt, reaching towards a green, fan-shaped mushroom.

Philip started forward, prepared to drag Max back to the campsite, but his foot caught on a raised tree root. He crashed face-first into a patch of glittering, purple mushrooms. As he struggled to push himself up, a dizzying haze wafted from the mushrooms, clouding his vision. A bittersweet scent reached his nostrils, and everything went black.

Chapter 2

Philip awoke, sprawled out on the forest floor. The world spun around him. His head throbbed. Black spots danced in his eyes as he squinted against the too-bright sun. Waves of nausea rolled over him when he pushed himself to his hands and knees.

Dragging himself to his feet, he nearly passed out from the rush of blood to his head. His legs moved as if they were made of lead. He stumbled and braced himself against a tree. With a groan, he dug the heels of his hands into his eyes.

When his vision cleared, he glanced around the forest. The mushrooms were gone. The ivy-covered birch and oak trees that had surrounded him had been replaced by towering evergreens. He was completely alone.

What happened? Where was he?

Where was Max?

"Max!" Philip stumbled from tree to tree as fast as his weakened body would carry him. Max *had* to be nearby.

After a frenzy of frantic searching, Philip spotted Max leaning against a moss-covered tree near a wide clearing. He gasped in relief and staggered to his little brother's side.

"Are you all right?" Philip seized Max's shoulders and scanned him for any major injuries. Nothing appeared to be broken or damaged.

Though scratches and bruises covered Max's face, his eyes shone with amazement. "Look!"

Squinting in the bright sunlight, Philip followed Max's gaze to where the trees gave way to a rolling, overgrown meadow dotted with mushrooms and wildflowers. What caught his attention wasn't the beautiful scenery, but the three figures standing in the meadow, just a short distance away. Two of the figures were tall and muscular, while the other was short and thin. Veined, membranous wings jutted from their shoulder blades.

The muscular men had brightly colored skin—one the color of an emerald, and the other the color of a sapphire. The color of their close-cropped hair matched their skin, as did the tint of their wings. They wore immaculate uniforms that bore a golden crest across the chest. Massive swords rested against their hips.

The short, thin figure couldn't be much older than Philip. He looked nothing like the other two men. His youthful face and wide, brown eyes were framed by golden curls. An abundance of freckles scattered across his sun-tanned skin. Clear, sparkling wings extended from his shoulder blades.

Shaking his head, Philip pressed the heels of his hands into his eyes until colors exploded in front of his eyelids. This had to be some kind of dream. Any minute, he would wake up back at the campsite. But when he opened his eyes again, nothing had changed.

"Adrian," the boy addressed the green-skinned man. "Have you found anything?"

"Not yet," the green-skinned man—Adrian—responded.

The boy pressed his lips together. "Keep looking. They have to be around here somewhere."

"Philip," Max whispered, "Are you seeing this?"

Philip gave a slight nod, knotting his fingers in the drawstrings of his hoodie. His mind scrambled to find answers to the questions that flooded him. There had to be some reasonable explanation for whatever this was. Maybe this was a result of some hallucinogen those mushrooms released. Yes. That made sense. Surely this was all a hallucination of some sort.

But the mossy ground beneath his feet was as solid as anything. His eyes watered in the blinding sunlight. Cool, crisp air filled his lungs. No matter what he tried to tell himself, this was all too real to be a dream or a hallucination. Even Max with all his imagination and daydreaming couldn't have thought up something like this.

"This is so cool," Max breathed.

The blue-skinned man's head snapped up, his eyes scanning the trees. Philip's heart thundered as the man's gaze swept over where they stood.

Philip clamped a hand over Max's mouth and pulled him behind a tree. Max slipped out of his grip and peeked around the trunk of the tree. "Do you think he saw us?"

"We have to get out of here." Philip kept his voice low, but urgent. He tried to pull Max deeper into the cover of the trees, but Max shook him away.

"I want to hear them." Max crept closer to the meadow.

"Nathan, did you see something?" The boy asked the blue-skinned man.

The blue-skinned man—Nathan—frowned as he spoke. "I thought I heard something, but it was probably just a bird. Rumor has it, the crows here can talk."

"We have to keep searching." The boy instructed.

"We don't have much time." Adrian interjected, "The barrier spell is weakening. I would give it about ten more minutes before we're on our own."

The boy massaged his temples. "This was a mistake. We shouldn't have come here. What are we going to tell Elliott?"

"We are here under Prince Elliott's orders. He can be angry all he wants. We were just obeying his command." Adrian said.

29

The boy sighed. "The sooner we find these two humans, the better."

Philip inhaled sharply. Logic and reason told him they could be looking for any one. There were billions of humans in the world. His gut, however, told him otherwise. This wasn't a coincidence. These men were searching for them.

He didn't know where they could go—for all he knew, they were miles away from the nearest human being—only that they had to get away from these men as quickly as possible.

"Max, we have to go *right now*."

When Philip tried to pull him away, Max stubbornly dug his heels into the dirt. "Just wait. I want to know what's going on."

"This isn't a game, Max. We have to run." Philip glanced over his shoulder, already mapping out the path they would take.

"*Shhh!*" Max hissed. "I can't hear what they're saying."

Cupping a hand around his ear, Max crept towards the meadow. Philip nearly strangled himself with the drawstrings of his hoodie. Was Max trying to get them killed? They had to get as far away from these men as possible. These woods were unfamiliar, but if they got a head start, maybe they could find help.

Max continued to creep forwards, ignoring Philip's protests. Just before he reached the meadow, a twig snapped beneath his feet. Both brothers froze. The three men in the meadow turned towards where they stood. The boy took a step towards them.

In unison, Philip and Max turned on their heels and sprinted away from the meadow.

"After them!" one of the men hollered.

Philip's heart hammered against his ribcage as they raced through the forest. His backpack pounded against his back. Sweat dripped into his eyes. He darted through the trees, ducking over low-hanging branches and vaulting over fallen logs. His sneakers squelched in the mud as they splashed through a stream.

"Philip!"

He skidded to a halt and whirled around. Max was sprawled out on the ground, trying to push himself up. Before Philip could move toward his brother, Nathan reached Max and hoisted him into the air.

"Philip!" Max shrieked again. He kicked and writhed, but couldn't break out of Nathan's iron grip. "Help!"

Nathan's head snapped up, his sharp, blue eyes meeting Philip's. "There's the other one!"

Adrian appeared at Nathan's shoulder in an instant. Without another moment of hesitation, Philip bolted in the opposite direction. Max's shouts rang in his ears as he tore through the forest. His brain screamed at him to stop and think this through, but his flight instincts won. He didn't have time for the questions that swirled through his racing thoughts.

Adrian was gaining on him with terrifying speed. Philip took advantage of his lean frame as he zigzagged between closely grown trees. Adrian, broad and muscular, couldn't follow, and soon, the sounds of his footsteps faded away.

Darting a glance over his shoulder, Philip couldn't see Adrian, Nathan, or the boy. He slowed his pace, pausing every few steps to ease the pain of the stitch in his side. He fumbled for the water bottle in his backpack and took a long swig. Wiping sweat from his forehead, he leaned against a tree.

Now that he was alone, he could begin to unravel the panicked tangle of thoughts in his mind. Where was he? Who were these people? *What* were these people? How could he have just left Max? What kind of terrible person left their little brother to be captured by strangers?

A snap of twigs startled Philip from his thoughts a moment too late. Adrian barreled into him, knocking them both to the ground. Air whooshed out of Philip's lungs. A green hand clamped down on his mouth, slamming his teeth down on his tongue. The metallic tang of blood filled his mouth.

"Don't try to fight," Adrian commanded into his ear, "Come willingly, and I won't hurt you."

With a gulp, Philip did as he was told. Adrian yanked him to his feet, twisted his arms behind his back, and shoved him forward with the gentleness of an ox.

Philip's adrenaline wore off, leaving him shaky and disoriented. Blood coated his tongue. With each step he took, a painful twinge shot through his ankle.

When they reached the meadow, Philip was forced to his knees in front of the boy, who peered down at him with a puzzled expression. Beside him, Max struggled against Nathan, who still held him in the air.

"Hey!" Philip protested as Adrian tore the backpack from his back. He lunged forward to snatch the backpack, but at the snap of Adrian's fingers, green vines shot from the ground and wrapped around his wrists like ropes.

Adrian, completely ignoring him, emptied the backpack of its contents. He briefly inspected Philip's phone as if he had never seen anything like it, before tossing it aside like junk. He did the same to a broken laptop and an iPad, which Philip had forgotten to remove from his backpack before they left.

Struggling against the bindings, Philip spat blood into the grass. "Stop it!"

"Sorry, kid, but I'm doing you a favor. This forbidden magic has no place here." Adrian shoved the devices back into the backpack and threw it into the tall grass, where it disappeared like a stone in a lake.

Philp grimaced at the crunch of metal against solid ground. In a matter of seconds, several hours' worth of work was reduced to a pile of scrap metal. He bit back another protest; arguing would be pointless. Hunching his shoulders, he shrank in on himself.

The boy before them studied them with furrowed brows. "They're just kids."

Philip scoffed—this boy with his wide eyes and soft face and barely changed voice was calling *him* a kid?

"They're not fully grown?" Adrian asked as if Philip and Max were the strange ones.

"No, they're not fully grown. *I'm* not fully grown," the boy said.

Adrian frowned. "Things are different for you."

"Half-humans age just as fast as full-blooded humans." the boy defended. "I'm only fifteen, and I would look the same as I do now if I was fully human. Well, minus the wings."

Max finally managed to squirm free of Nathan's grip. Before Nathan could seize him again, he fired a volley of questions. "Who are you? Where are we? What are we doing here?"

The boy's eyes softened. "These two don't know what's going on. They deserve to know as much as we can tell them. Nathan, Adrian, release them."

Nathan and Adrian exchanged a look of disbelief. With a spiteful shove, Adrian released his grip on the collar of Philip's shirt. Philip scrambled to his feet, prepared to run, but the twinge in his ankle flared. Pain shot through his leg when he put even a little weight on it. So much for that. Since escape was out of the question, he may as well stay and hear what they had to say. If these men—or whatever they were—could explain things, he wanted answers.

"My name is Dash," the boy said. "To answer your first question, we're fair folk. In the human world, they like to call us fairies, but we find that term rather offensive."

A short, harsh laugh threatened to burst from Philip's lips. Surely this boy was joking. *Fairies?* Seriously? He shook his head in disbelief. This couldn't be happening. Fairies—fair folk, whatever they wanted to be called—weren't real.

Max froze, his eyes as wide as headlights. Any frustration or fear about being captured gave way to amazement like the flick of a light switch. "Cool! I knew fairies were real! I'm Max. This is my big brother, Philip."

"Nice to meet you," Dash said. "I believe we owe you an explanation."

"I believe so, too," said a new voice.

Philip stared as a girl with wide, dark eyes and dark skin stepped out of the forest. Delicate flowers were braided into her curly, black hair, which hung down to her waist like a waterfall. Mud—and something that looked suspiciously like dried blood—stained her flowing, white dress.

The girl's eyebrows drew together as she spoke. "Prince Dash? What are you doing here?"

Philip glanced furtively at Dash. He was a *prince?* That would have been an important detail to include.

Dash's lips parted in surprise. "I suppose I could ask you the same thing, Ella."

"I'm here on urgent business of the elven crown." The girl replied with regal poise.

"What business does the elven crown have on the Island of Corvus?" Nathan demanded. "Outsiders are forbidden from coming here."

"Who am I to question the motives of my queen?" Ella's eyes narrowed. "Besides, you're outsiders as well. Going by technicalities, none of us are supposed to be here."

"Yet, here we are," Adrian interjected.

Philip's head spun as he struggled to piece together scattered bits of information. So, fairies—*fair folk*—were real. This girl, Ella, didn't have wings, and she had mentioned an elven queen. Did that mean elves were real too? How was this possible? Nothing made sense anymore.

Dash held his hands up. "That's enough. We don't have time to squabble like this. There's a more pressing issue at hand. We don't know how these humans got here, but we have to find a way to get them back to their world."

Philip's thoughts screeched to a halt. "What do you mean, *'back to our world'*?"

"We don't have much time to explain," Dash sounded apologetic, "We have to return to my kingdom. This island becomes more dangerous every minute we stay here."

Max glanced around. "This place looks pretty safe to me."

Philip couldn't believe his brother. Was he really that naïve? Had he learned nothing in the past few minutes? Sure, Max was only ten years old, but at his age, Philip had started a repair business out of his locker. Inhaling a deep, breath, he released the tension in his shoulders and unclenched his hands.

"We're safe for now, but we don't have much longer." Dash cast a glance over his shoulder. "Without magic to protect us, the monsters could be here any minute."

Philip's heart squeezed in terror. "What monsters?"

Max's eyes lit up. "What magic?"

"A long time ago, humans lived among us in this world, joined to the other races by magic," Nathan began as if he were

35

reciting verses in church, "But humans possess a strange, forbidden magic that cannot be understood by the other races."

"Humans decided to leave this world and form one of their own where they could forget the magical world and use their forbidden magic freely," Adrian finished in the same recitative tone.

Philip recalled what Adrian had said while rifling his backpack. *This forbidden magic has no place here.* Had he been referring to technology? Was this world somehow completely void of modern technology? A shudder raced down his spine. They had to get home as soon as possible; a world without technology wasn't a world he had any place in.

"Cool," Max tilted his head, "But I'm a little confused. If humans have our own world, how did Philip and I get here? How are we going to get home?"

"That's the problem," Dash explained, "The only way to travel between worlds is to use magic, that kind of magic is forbidden. The King of Corvus hasn't allowed travel between worlds since he ascended the throne. If there is a safe, legal way for you to return to the human world, I don't know of it."

Max's lower lip quivered. "So, we're trapped here?"

"Only for the time being," Dash assured him.

Philip wanted to curl up and never move again. This couldn't be happening. Why him? Why now? This was a living nightmare.

An eerie screech sounded in the distance. Philip's body seized up. Nathan and Adrian exchanged a wide-eyed look of alarm. Dash's hand crept to the sword at his hip.

"We're not safe here," Ella said, scanning the tree line. She gasped and drew back. When Philip followed her gaze, he found the source of her terror.

Five, massive beasts prowled the edge of the tree line. Philip recognized them as manticores. In the human world, a cartoon manticore was his high school's red-and-gold mascot. These beasts, however, were nothing at all like the ridiculous mascot costume.

"Just great," Adrian muttered, drawing his sword, "I'm not really in the mood to be eaten right now."

"This is *not* how I thought this day would go," Nathan added, drawing his sword.

Dash grinned. "Just like old times."

Somewhere far in the distance, a bird let out a throaty caw.

Ella drew a silver knife from the holster against the inside of her thigh. "Why aren't they attacking?"

"They must be toying with us," Nathan said.

As soon as the words passed Nathan's lips, the manticores charged. The first three spread their wings and sprang into the air. Nathan, Adrian, and Dash flew to meet them. The fourth rushed towards Max but found itself facing Ella and her knife.

Philip became acutely aware of his lack of weapons. He cast his eyes heavenwards to send up a silent prayer, but his gaze caught on Nathan and Adrian as they battled the manticores in midair. They both abandoned their swords and gestured wildly like they were trying to signal each other.

Then, the impossible happened.

Thick, leafy vines shot out of the ground and latched onto an airborne manticore's tail. Adrian's hands glowed green as they made wide, circling motions, and the vines wrapped around the manticore until it was tightly bound in a writhing green mass. It plummeted to the ground with an earth-shaking *thud*.

Blasts of water formed from thin air and sprayed at the manticore with the force of a firehose. Nathan held his glowing blue hands straight out in front of him as if he were pushing against an invisible glass wall. When he lowered them, the water ceased, and when he raised them again, the water came back with double the force.

Philip couldn't believe what he was seeing. There had to be some logical explanation. People couldn't just pull water from the air or summon vines from the ground. That was like magic, and magic didn't exist. It couldn't. The odd twist in his chest was just his imagination. The chills that rushed across his arms only occurred because of a crisp breeze. There was nothing phenomenal about this.

Completely absorbed in his panicked thoughts, Philip didn't see the fifth manticore until it was too late. He froze like a rabbit caught in a hawk's sights.

The ferocious, hybrid beast pounced and pinned him to the ground with a massive paw. It had a patchy, wild mane, oversized bat wings, and a curved scorpion tail. Its ribs stuck out of its emaciated body, and its skin stretched too tightly over its gaunt face. Hunger glinted in its glowing, red eyes. Saliva dripped from its serrated teeth as it licked its chops with a forked, green tongue.

Philip flinched as the manticore let out a ferocious roar. Its rancid, acidic breath stank of rotting meat and stung his face. He tried to swallow, but the manticore's paw pressed into his throat, claws digging into his skin.

A strangled gasp of pain and terror escaped his lips as the manticore roared again. His ears rang at the sheer volume of the noise. The manticore reared his head back and brought it down onto his shoulder. Razor-sharp teeth sank into his flesh, tearing it from his bones. White-hot pain engulfed him as if he were being burned alive by acid.

Then, the world around him simply stopped. His vision blurred with tears. All he could hear was a faint ringing. His head

38

spun. His breathing sped. Blood poured from his shoulder. Everything happened in slow motion, yet at the same time, flew by in a haze.

Before the manticore could strike again, a knife plunged into its eye. With a furious roar, it stumbled away. Free of the pressure of the beast's weight crushing down on his chest, Philip sucked in a lungful of air.

Ella ripped her knife from the manticore's eye and dove out of the way as Nathan bore down on the manticore. With one fell swoop, Nathan hacked the head off the manticore's body. Oozing blood splattered all over Philip, burning holes through his clothing and searing into his skin. His vision darkened, consciousness slipping away like thread unspooling.

The next thing he knew, Max loomed over him screaming. "Help! Philip's hurt!"

Hurt. That was a strange word. It didn't even begin to describe the burning agony that coursed through his veins. But, like everything else, his pain began to fade farther and farther away. Everything smudged and softened. The edges of his vision faded. Muffled sounds echoed in his head. The pain that seared every nerve of his body dulled to nothing but shiver-inducing cold.

Ella appeared above him. He imagined her face drawn with concern. Though he couldn't distinguish what she said, the message was clear: this wasn't good.

Ella's movements were slow and methodical. Her voice rolled over him in suspiciously calm waves. Philip couldn't protest as she peeled his hoodie from his body. She stripped away his armor, the very shell that protected him from the horrors of the world. That was ridiculous, of course. It was just a hoodie, and it hadn't done anything to prevent the manticore attack.

He dimly registered Ella wrapping his hoodie around his shoulder like a makeshift tourniquet. The hoodie squeezed his shoulder so tightly that his entire arm went numb.

"—move him?" Dash's voice floated somewhere far away.

"—careful with—" Ella's hands slid under Philip's head.

Philip found himself being scooped into Dash's arms with surprising ease. He had enough sense to resent being carried like a child, but he was surprised that Dash was much stronger than he looked. Closing his eyes, he tried to block out the muddled voices around him. His consciousness faded in and out like a spotty channel on the radio.

A flash of awareness shot through him just in time to hear Dash speak. "We're going to ride griffins."

Chapter 3

"Griffins?" Max gasped.

Philip flinched at his brother's cry of amazement. Why did Max always have to be so *loud?*

He inhaled sharply as an earsplitting whistle cracked through his skill like a spike. Moments later, three shrieks responded somewhere overhead. Risking a glance upwards, he nearly passed out again. In the blue sky above, three beasts circled. For a moment, he thought the manticores had returned to finish what they had started.

But when the beasts landed, they were nothing close to manticores. They were like something from a fever dream. The creatures were twice the size of lions, with stocky back paws that opposed sharp front talons. Feathered wings sprouted from their backs. Each beast had an eagle's head that tapered into a wickedly curved beak. Feathers crowned their heads and blended into thick fur on the rest of their bodies. Unlike the fair folk, griffins appeared in this world just as they were pictured in the human world.

Without hesitation, Dash marched up to a griffin and swung Philip onto its back like he was nothing more than a sack of groceries. If it weren't for Dash climbing on behind him and wrapping his arms around his waist, Philip would have tumbled to the ground.

Mounting a griffin with an unconscious Adrian in his arms, Nathan let out a sharp whistle. The shrill sound was like a knife to Philip's brain. At that signal, the griffins unfolded their wings

41

and took a running start before launching themselves in the air. Philip's stomach lurched as the griffin hurtled upwards. His ears popped from the rapid change of altitude. The steady beating of the griffin's wings pounded alongside his splitting, dizzying headache. He shivered, but Dash's body head did little to warm him.

His vision blurred and refocused every few seconds. Foggy awareness reminded him of his throbbing shoulder and spinning head and numb arm. Below them, the grass bled into a rocky beach. The sharp scent of salt overwhelmed him, and waves crashed in the churning waters. Numb panic seized the back of his mind, but before he could form a cohesive thought, his vision faded completely.

He snapped back to consciousness with the pulse-racing sensation of hurling towards the ground at terrifying speed. When opened his mouth to scream, no sound came out of his raw throat.

"We're landing now. Hang in there." Dash said, pressing his lips against Philip's ear so he could be heard over the wind.

The griffins made a swift, elegant landing on a grassy hill. The moment their griffin's claws hit the ground, Dash scrambled off its back. Without any support, Philip tumbled down after him. Before he hit the ground, though, Dash caught him and set him on the damp grass.

"We can't wait for help," Dash said, rolling up his sleeves. "I'll have to do the best I can."

Philip lay on his back, head resting in Max's lap. Ella and Dash loomed in his vision, both hunched over his shoulder. A wave of nausea rolled over him when Ella undid the makeshift tourniquet. Blood poured from the mangled remains of his shoulder. As much as he wanted to look away, he couldn't.

Dash planted both hands directly on his bloody shoulder.

Philip sucked in a sharp breath as Dash's fingers began to glow a soft yellow. Warmth spread through his body, numbing the pain completely. He could only watch in rapt awe as Dash pieced together the shredded skin, muscle, and bones in his shoulder with the slow, careful precision of a surgeon. Under Dash's touch, the wound slowly closed like metal being welded together.

The world tilted and swayed beneath Philip like a waltz. This couldn't be happening. Dash couldn't be healing his shoulder. Healing was a natural, uncontrollable process that occurred automatically in the body. There was no way to simply *heal* someone like…

Like magic.

Though warmth flooded his body, ice shot through his veins. This wasn't possible. His brain scrambled for some kind of explanation. But no matter what logic said, Philip could feel Dash's every move. He felt his muscles mending together, his cells being restored bit by bit, and the tendons and ligaments re-attaching themselves.

There was no denying it. Magic existed and it was saving his life.

He tore his gaze from his shoulder, focusing instead on Dash's face, which hovered mere inches above his own. Beads of sweat formed on Dash's forehead. His eyebrows wrinkled in concentration. His warm breath tickled Philip's cheek. Only once did he pause to sweep his curly hair out of his eyes, leaving a streak of blood across his face.

Finally, Dash sat back. "There," He panted, "I did everything I could."

Philip eased himself to a sitting position and ran a tentative hand over his shoulder. The newly healed tissue was scarred, uneven, and bumpy like a burn wound, but the pain subsided completely. But as he touched his skin, he couldn't feel the pressure of his fingertips. Frowning, he dug his fingers into his shoulder. Though his nails left small crescent-shaped marks on his skin, he felt nothing. Not even the slightest pressure.

A heavy, void feeling replaced the prickling, burning numbness in his arm. He tried to curl the fingers of his right hand into a fist, but they refused to move. Trying again, he found he couldn't move any part of his arm from his shoulder down to his fingertips.

He shook his head. This couldn't be right. He'd watched Dash heal his shoulder. The pain was gone. The shock had faded. There had to be a mistake.

"Why can't I move my arm?" He rasped. His voice was foreign to his ears. He hated the desperation he heard.

"The damage was too deep for me to fix completely," Dash drew his face into an expression of pity. "I'm sorry. I did everything I could."

Philip's throat constricted. Burying his head in the crook of his elbow, he fought the hot prickle of tears behind his eyes. His dreams were crushed. Without both hands, he would never be able to run his repair business. Fixing things was the only thing he excelled at. It was all he had. His plans for the future, his success, even his happiness rested on his ability to work with his hands. What was he going to do?

Max gingerly touched the scarred tissue on Philip's shoulder. "It's gonna be okay, Philip."

With a shake of his head, Philip pulled away. How could he say that? Things were not going to be okay. They both knew that. Lying and pretending things away would only make things worse. They were lost and alone. They were in an entirely different world. Nothing would ever be the same again. How did

44

Max not see that?

"I'm sorry I couldn't do more. If I'd had more time…" Dash said softly.

"Wouldn't it have been faster to heal Philip on the Island?" Max asked. "Nathan and Adrian used magic there, right? That's how they could blast the manticores with water and strangle them with plants."

Dash's expression curved into a frown as he turned to Nathan and Adrian. "Yes, I suppose we should address that."

Nathan and Adrian exchanged a guilty look.

"Look, we didn't—" Nathan began.

"What were you two thinking? Of all the stupid things! You could have been killed! Your magic could have backfired. The Island of Corvus is cursed. Magic isn't right there. If something had gone wrong, there would have been nothing any one could do to save you. You would be dead, and the manticores would have eaten you, and…"

"We didn't mean to scare you." Adrian interrupted.

"*Scare me?* You should have been scared for yourselves! What would have happened if your magic would have backfired and killed someone? What then? How would you be able to live with yourselves?"

Nathan hung his head. "It was stupid of us. We knew the risks, but we did it anyway."

Dash pinched the bridge of his nose. "I'm sorry for yelling, but there are rules for a reason. The King of Corvus does not take kindly to people who violate his laws. I don't know what I would have done if something happened to you two."

"You're right," Nathan admitted, "We're lucky to be alive. The King had mercy on us today."

"I can't argue with that." Dash sighed.

Philip watched this exchange in a daze. His arm lay limp beside him. Some moments, he thought he could feel the faintest tingling sensation in his fingers, but they refused to move. If he concentrated on the conversation around him, maybe he could distract himself from his devastation.

Ella cleared her throat. "I hate to interrupt this touching conversation, but I must return to the elven kingdom. It is unwise for me to remain here any longer than I must."

"I'm afraid we can't just let you go," Adrian said. "The Sovereign Prince has given us orders to arrest any elves spotted in the fair folk kingdom. Unfortunately for you, this is our territory."

"Wait, you can't just—hey!" Ella's protests were cut off as vines sprang from the ground and bound her wrists.

"What are you doing?" Dash addressed Adrian with a frown, "This is an unjust violation of the treaty between the elves and the fair folk."

Adrian shook his head. "I'm sorry, Your Highness, but we can't disobey direct orders from the Sovereign."

"The elven queen will hear about this," Ella growled.

Adrian shrugged. "Only if you're lucky enough to see her again."

Ella scowled but didn't look particularly surprised.

Dash sighed, turning to Philip. "Can you stand?"

"I lost my arm, not my legs," Philip muttered indignantly, struggling to his feet. Dizziness washed over him. Dash rushed to support him when his knees buckled.

"Careful," Dash said, "You lost a lot of blood. You should take it easy for a while until you can regain your strength."

Take it easy? Was he joking? Did he seriously expect Philip to relax after everything that's happened? Until he and Max were

46

safe at home, Philip vowed not to let his guard down for a single moment.

This proved to be more difficult than he'd thought—especially since he couldn't even stand on his own. His cheeks burned with embarrassment as Dash helped him onto the back of the griffin. Most of his weight rested against Dash, who supported him without complaint.

"It's a short ride to the palace, and you'll get a good view of the city on the way," Dash said.

The griffins took to the air once more. Endless meadows filled with lush grass and vibrant wildflowers replaced the waters beneath them. Even with significantly more consciousness, Philip had a difficult time staying balanced on the griffin's back. As much as he hated to admit it, without Dash's steady grip behind him, he would have toppled off and plummeted to his death.

After a while, the meadows gave way to vibrant clusters of villages. White stone buildings inlaid with brilliantly colored stained glass sparkled in the sunlight like precious jewels. Every village shined with pristine fixtures of gold.

The villages gradually grew larger and taller until they were sprawling cities. Soaring, white buildings glittered with stained glass in every color of the rainbow. Fair folk every bit as colorful as stained glass darted over the gold-paved streets. Sunlight beamed through the fair folks' brightly colored wings, casting rainbow shadows that danced through the cities. The fair folk cities shimmered with the strange incandescence of magic.

Philip squinted over an expanse of the nearest city as a shimmering, white light appeared on the horizon. At first, he dismissed it as sunlight reflecting off of glass, but soon, the light became a fixture on the horizon.

Max noticed the light too. "Hey, what's that?"

"That would be the Grand Palace, home to the Sovereign Prince of the fair folk," Dash responded. "It resides in the heart of Hayala, the largest city in Haderra, the fair folk kingdom."

As they drew closer, Philip could discern the details of an iridescent, white stone palace decorated with priceless jewels and golden designs. Elegant turrets and towers stood out from the palace's symmetrical shape like tines on a jeweled tiara.

The griffins landed before the magnificent staircase leading to the palace's entrance. Armored guards drew the golden front doors drew open with a flourish. Colorful fair folk servants rushed to Dash's side. Many of them hovered in the air, their feet inches from the ground. They made quick work of helping everyone dismount and whisking the griffins to the stables.

The servants eyed Philip curiously, and he returned their glances with a stony expression. He was relieved that they left him alone instead of fussing over him like they did to Max.

Dash greeted each servant with a smile and thanks. Nathan and Adrian flanked him, folding their muscular arms over their chests as if they intended to mutilate any one who so much as glanced at Dash with a suspicious expression.

"Welcome back, Your Highness." A servant girl with orange-peel skin curtsied to Dash. Her orange eyes darted towards Philip as she spoke.

"Thank you, Emily. It's good to be back, though I wasn't gone long," Dash said with a smile.

"I'm sorry, Your Highness, but the Sovereign Prince has been waiting for you all morning," Emily hesitated, "I have been instructed to escort you directly to the throne room."

Dash's smile fell into a frown. "This can't be good."

Emily turned on her heel and entered the palace. Dash kept

pace with her and gestured for everyone else to follow. Philip was left alone to limp after them. His head still felt light, and when he entered the palace, his mind struggled to process the sheer splendor before him. A stained-glass ceiling soared high above their heads, allowing the sunlight to bathe the white walls in brilliant hues of color. Ornate gold molding decorated every pillar, every arch, every sconce. A patchwork of gleaming mirrors and imperious portraits hung on the gold-framed walls.

They ascended a grand staircase, made of polished marble. When they reached the top, a pair of guards bowed and drew open a set of golden, ruby-handled doors. Dash breezed through the doors without hesitation. Everyone else followed, but Philip paused at the threshold. Drawing in a breath, he stabled himself and plunged forward.

The golden doors slammed shut the moment he stepped through. He inhaled a sharp breath as he took in the cavernous space before him. Luminous, gold candelabras lined the shimmering, jewel-encrusted walls. A thick velvet carpet made a path from the doors to the base of a raised dais that held an ornate, golden throne silhouetted by a masterpiece of stained glass.

A young man of solid gold lounged on the throne. Everything about him exuded regal superiority, from his haughty expression to his nonchalant posture. Ambient light filtered through his thin, sharp wings, casting golden shadows across the white floors. A bejeweled, silver crown rested on his spun gold curls.

Dash bowed his head and knelt in front of the throne. Nathan and Adrian followed suit. Awkwardly, Philip and Max did the same, leaving Ella the only one standing. She raised her chin defiantly, a burning expression of hatred on her face.

The man glanced up, eyes sweeping over the motley group

before him. His expression hardened when his gaze landed on Ella. The candles around the room leaped to life in an intemperate blaze. Gooseflesh pricked Philip's arms.

"Elestren Daughter of Lillia," the man sneered, "I have to admit, I am surprised elven filth such as you would dare show your face outside of Elvenmar. If I were you, I would show some respect to your superior."

"You are no superior of mine, *Sovereign Prince Elliott*." Ella spat the title like an insult. "Queen Celosia sends her regards along with a message: release our prisoners or you will come to regret it."

Prince Elliott gave a dark laugh. "I do not take kindly to threats from little girls who are foolish enough to venture alone into enemy territory. You come to my palace as a prisoner and have the audacity to disrespect me in such a way."

Ella kept her posture perfectly straight, a vision of defiance. Philip envied her ability to remain calm in a situation like this. "The elves and fair folk are not enemies. We have a peace agreement, and you have violated it. The elven queen demands justice for her people."

"The elven queen will have to be disappointed," the sovereign prince dismissed flippantly.

Before the situation could escalate, Dash intervened, shooting to his feet. "Sire, we have more pressing matters to discuss. Two humans were found on the Island of Corvus. I brought them to you and hoped you could—"

"I care not about what you hoped," Prince Elliott cut Dash off, "Your brother told me he would like a word with you."

Dash froze, his expression filling with concern. "Is everything all right?"

"He sent a bird, as usual," Prince Elliott rolled his eyes, "It is not my place to bother with the details." He tossed Dash a miniature scroll.

Dash unrolled the scroll and scanned it urgently, eyes widening as he read. When he reached the end, he tucked the scroll into his yellow silk jacket and unfolded his wings. "I'm sorry. I have to go."

Elliott dismissed Dash with a wave of his hand. "Don't hurry back."

Nathan and Adrian stood to follow Dash, but he shook his head. "Stay with the humans. Make sure Elestren gets back to her people safely. I'll be back soon." Throwing an apologetic glance to Philip, Dash hurried out of the throne room.

Panic bubbled inside Philip as he watched Dash leave. How could he just abandon them like that? He had promised to help send them home. What were they going to do without him? Sure, he had promised to *be back soon*, but accidents happened. Accidents like finding an entire other world filled with magic, for example.

Max put a hand on Philip's arm. "We're going to be okay."

Why did he keep saying that? Philip shook Max's hand away and glanced at Ella, whose expression remained placid as glass. He turned to Nathan and Adrian, who seemed to be preoccupied with a silent argument. When he looked up at the sovereign prince, he met with gold eyes glaring down at him as if he were nothing but an insignificant worm. Philip shuddered at the thought—worms made his skin crawl almost as much as physical touch.

"Your Majesty, sir?" Max blurted.

Prince Elliott broke his glare away from Philip and narrowed his eyes at Max. "What do you want, human?"

Max's lip quivered at the sudden intensity of the sovereign's attention, but he continued. "How are we gonna get home? Your world is great and all, but I miss my mom." Max blinked innocently, softening his features into a classic, puppy-dog look.

"Hmm." Prince Elliott rolled his eyes, unaffected by Max's manipulation. "I suppose we have to do *something* with you. My little cousin, Dash, is far too trusting." After a moment of consideration, he spoke again. "Guards, take the humans downstairs."

Adrian frowned. "Downstairs, Sire?"

"You heard me."

"What should be done with the elf?"

The sovereign prince's gaze flicked to Ella. "Take her with them. I want her out of my sight. They will be dealt with tomorrow with the rest. And make sure Dash does not find out about this."

"But, Sire—"

"Cease this insolence at once," Prince Elliott snapped, "You heard my orders, now go!"

Nathan and Adrian bowed dutifully. "Yes, Your Sovereignty."

Green vines snapped around Philip's wrists, binding them like ropes. He strained against the vines, but they held fast. The faint sensation of magic twisted in his gut.

"Hey!" Max exclaimed, struggling against his bonds.

Nathan seized Philip and Max, while Adrian took a hold of Ella. Though Philip tried to break away, Nathan kept a firm grip on his injured arm. He quickly discovered the futility of his actions, unlike Max, who continued to fight and struggle.

"Stop it!" Max cried as Nathan and Adrian dragged them from the throne room. "What are you doing?"

Nathan and Adrian didn't respond, their gazes focused

directly ahead. Their boots echoed militantly against the polished floors. The sting of betrayal and anger welled up in Philip, but he could do nothing. He scolded himself for his stupidity. If he hadn't agreed to explore with Max in the first place, they wouldn't be in this situation.

Max peppered Nathan and Adrian with questions. "Where are you taking us? Why are you being so rough? Where's Dash? Would he like you doing this to us?"

"We've been given orders to escort you to the dungeons," Adrian said gruffly. He deliberately avoided Philip's glare.

"But Prince Elliott told you to take us downstairs!" Max protested. He dug his heels into the ground, but Nathan easily hoisted his small body over his shoulder.

"The dungeons *are* downstairs," Adrian muttered.

Nathan and Adrian dragged them down a spiral staircase that descended into gradual darkness. Philip shivered as the cold, damp air pricked at his skin. At the bottom of the staircase, they reached a claustrophobic stone corridor. The top of his head nearly brushed against the low ceiling. Sparsely populated cells lined the corridor. Each held a wooden bench and a tin bucket. He shuddered in disgust, refusing to dwell on the bucket's purpose. Water dripped from cracks in the stone and pooled into murky puddles on the uneven ground.

The dim torches became few and far between as Nathan and Adrian ushered them deeper into the dungeon. Eventually, they reached a wooden door with another oversized padlock, which Adrian unlocked with an iron skeleton key.

When the door creaked open, the musk of waste and sweat was overwhelming. Philip gagged, nearly vomiting at the harsh odor. As his watering eyes adjusted to the darkness, he could make out a small, stone cell crowded with people of all ages.

Children cried. Teenagers muttered to themselves. Mothers and fathers conversed in weary voices. Elders struggled to draw wheezing breaths in the stale air. Every head turned to stare as Philip, Max, and Ella were shoved into the room.

"We're sorry. You just have to trust us," Adrian said. With a wave of his hand, the vines loosened on Philip's wrists.

Max let out a relieved cry and rubbed his wrists. Philip wished he could do the same to his own raw, sore wrists. The best he could do was shake away the vines and try to ignore the pain with every movement.

Without another word, Nathan and Adrian left, slamming and locking the door behind them. Ella released a choked sob, clapping a hand over her mouth as she sank to the ground. Philip blinked at her, surprised by the outburst of emotion after she'd remained so calm. He debated asking her if she was alright, but before he could make up his mind, an unfamiliar voice echoed through the cell.

"Elestren?" A gaunt young man with waist-length, blonde hair approached. His pale face wore an expression of disbelief. After a moment of hesitation, he rushed forward and embraced Ella.

"Is it really you?" the man asked. His pale eyes drank in Ella's tear-stained face.

"Torryn, what have they done to you?" Ella sobbed into the man's shoulder. He clutched her as if he thought she might vanish into thin air.

Turning away from Ella and Torryn's heartfelt reunion, Philip retreated to an unoccupied corner of the cell. His chest tightened with a mixture of anger and despair. He didn't see how things could get any worse. They were prisoners drenched in blood. His right arm hung limply at his side, completely useless

54

for the rest of his life. He had no idea where he was or how they were going to escape. They would have to find a way home themselves; no one was going to help them.

He and Max were doomed.

Chapter 4

Dash drew in a deep breath as he landed in a meadow on the Island of Corvus. Folding his wings behind him, he ran a hand through his curls and glanced around the empty space. He frowned; it wasn't like his brother to be late.

"Hello there," a voice said.

Dash whirled around, heart bursting with joy. A wide grin broke across his face. "Rhett!"

A young man landed behind him and gracefully folded his clear wings. His dark hair gleamed like ink as it hung in a feathery plume over his glittering, violet eyes. Everything about him was sharp; from his angular features and high cheekbones to his slender, elegant frame. His pale skin appeared ghostly white against his purple silk jacket.

In the presence of his older brother, Dash allowed himself to relax. Rhett brought the comforting nostalgia of home and childhood. When Rhett was there, nothing could go wrong.

"You came." Rhett sounded surprised.

Dash smiled up at his brother. "I'll always come for you."

Shaking his head, Rhett began to pace. "You were here today. Why didn't you tell me?"

Classic Rhett. Always direct and to the point about everything. "Elliott said he told you," Dash responded.

"We both know he's a liar."

"I'm sure he just forgot, that's all. He *is* the Sovereign Prince. He has lots of other responsibilities."

Rhett muttered something Dash pretended not to hear.

"I was okay, Rhett. My guards were with me the whole time. I mean, sure, we were attacked by manticores, but we got away."

"Dash," Rhett pinched the bridge of his nose. "You could have been killed. You have to be more careful."

"It wasn't a big deal—"

"That's enough," Rhett snapped. "I'm your older brother. My job is to look out for you. If you don't let me do that, I can't protect you."

"I don't need you to protect me all of the time!"

Dash regretted the words as soon as they left his lips.

Rhett stopped pacing, looking stricken.

"If you want to protect me," Dash softened his voice, "you can focus on keeping the monsters here on the island. Yesterday, the elves stopped a wraith on the western Haderra border. They're not happy, and Elliott isn't making things easy for any one."

"I'm doing the best I can." Rhett flexed his fingers. The corners of his mouth tugged down into a pensive frown, and a crease appeared between his eyebrows.

Dash knew that expression. Something was definitely wrong. "Is it your magic?" He asked tentatively.

"I'm fine," Rhett insisted too quickly. The bite in his voice made Dash's heart wrench with compassion. Rhett always hated discussing his magic.

"You don't have to pretend."

Rhett pressed his lips into a thin line and avoided Dash's gaze as he spoke. "My magic is fine. You don't have to worry."

Dash folded his arms across his chest. "Lying to me will only make things harder."

Irritation sparked in Rhett's eyes. He flicked his wrist, summoning a handful of purple fire. As Dash watched, Rhett formed the fire into the shape of a small bird. The bird soared into the air and let out a screech before disappearing in a wisp of lavender smoke.

"My magic is *fine*," Rhett repeated, staggering slightly.

Dash caught his brother as his knees buckled. He eased Rhett onto the grass and sat beside him. "Here, let me try something."

Pressing his fingers to Rhett's temples, Dash ignored his brother's protest and allowed the warmth of magic to well up inside him. His fingers began to glow a soft yellow.

"Dash, wait—" Rhett's protest was interrupted by an agonized scream.

Dash sprang back. He scrambled to his feet, searching his brother for wounds. "What? What's wrong?"

Rhett clutched his forehead, his expression contorted with pain.

Dash moved towards him. "Let me see."

"No," Rhett interrupted, holding up a hand.

"But I can just—"

"Please stop," Rhett's voice was firm and strained, "You'll only make things worse."

Dash drew back, confused and concerned by his brother's sudden onset of pain. Why couldn't he just put aside his pride and allow himself to be healed? But when he saw the angry red marks on Rhett's temples, horror clawed at his stomach. Did he somehow cause them?

"Our magic doesn't mix, Dash. You know this." Rhett's tone was heavy with weariness as if he were explaining something to a small child. "Yellow and purple magic are opposites. Your magic heals, while mine destroys. You can't heal me, no matter how much you try."

Every fair folk child knew how magic worked. Each color of magic had its own powers, and the magical opposites balanced each other out perfectly. The opposites orange and blue allowed control over fire and water. Red and green connected the user with animals and plants. Yellow and purple healed and destroyed. The balances created harmony and peace amongst the fair folk.

Dash placed a tentative hand on his brother's shoulder. "I'm so proud of you, Rhett. Every day, you sacrifice your magic to keep us safe. If it wasn't for you, the monsters would have devoured everything in this world and the next. No one would be safe without you."

"You're not supposed to see me like this." Rhett's violet eyes clouded over. "My magic is running out. Corvus is draining me too fast. What happens when my magic is gone? I can't keep all the monsters here forever."

"We'll find a way to fix this. I promise." There had to be something he could do to help. Rhett had done so much for him, and the least he could do was return the favor.

Rhett shook his head. "You can't help me."

His words were like a knife to Dash's heart. "I'll always be here for you, Rhett."

"But what if I'm not there for you? I'm supposed to protect you. How can I do that without my magic?"

Seeing Rhett so vulnerable and helpless was just *wrong*. Rhett had sacrificed everything to give Dash a new life. Rhett was always strong. Rhett never faltered. Not during their turbulent childhood, not during the deaths of their parents, and certainly not now.

"You have been looking out for me, and you always will. Magic or no magic. Ever since Dad died…" Dash trailed off as Rhett's head snapped up.

Rhett's eyes hardened like they did every time Dash brought up their father. He knew how much Rhett hated discussing their parents, but something inside him couldn't resist bringing it up every single time. Usually, he took a cue from his brother and dropped the subject there, but today, he sensed a shift in Rhett's behavior. Something was different today; Rhett's guard was lowered, more vulnerable than usual.

"Why don't you ever talk about him?" Dash asked, daring to venture into forbidden territory. "As soon as he died, you began to act like he never existed."

"That's because he didn't," Rhett said sharply. His guard flew back up, but it was too late to back out. "He left us, Dash. And when he finally decided to show up, he brought us here and got himself killed. He was nothing to us."

"He was something to *me*." The all-too-familiar hollow in Dash's chest ached. The hunger to know more about his parents could never be satisfied. "Tell me something about him. You knew him for months before I did."

"He's better off dead."

"Rhett!" Dash pleaded, "Just one thing. Please. He had yellow magic like me, right?" Maybe with some prompting, Rhett might relent…

Rhett gave Dash a pitying look. "Be grateful yellow magic and blonde hair were the only things you inherited from him."

"What about you? Was he little like you?" Dash knew he sounded desperate, but he wouldn't be able to muster the courage to bring this up again later.

"The only thing we had in common was a deep hatred for myself."

"Rhett, I—"

"You should go home, Dash," Rhett interrupted.

Dash frowned. "But I just got here. Do you expect me to fly back to Haderra after I've already flown here and back today?

It's not exactly pleasant to fly over so many miles of monster-infested water just to reach a monster-infested island."

"Not Haderra," Rhett said gently, "*Home*. Do you remember what day it is?"

Realization dawned on Dash, as did a spike of guilt. "With Elliott and the humans and the attack, I didn't even think about Mom…"

"Ah, yes. What *are* you going to do about those two humans?"

Dash glanced sideways at his brother. "How did you know there were two of them?"

At that, the ghost of a sly grin crossed Rhett's face. "The monsters tell me everything that happens on this island."

"I'll worry about the humans later," Dash said, "Right now, I should go visit Mom."

A wistful look crossed Rhett's face. "Visit the meadow for me."

"I wish you could come too."

"Alas," Rhett sighed dramatically, "I am trapped on this island until the end of my days, cursed to have monsters as my only companions."

With a grin, Dash shoved Rhett playfully. "I love you."

"I love you too," Rhett flicked Dash's shoulder, "Write me soon."

"I will," Dash promised. Unfolding his wings, he took to the air. The familiar pang of sadness shot through his chest just as it did every time he had to leave his brother alone, trapped on the Island of Corvus.

When Dash disappeared on the horizon, Rhett collapsed in the grass. His head pounded and his body ached, clinging to the last scraps of magic that coursed through his veins. Purple tongues of fire leaped from his fingers involuntarily, devouring the lush grass. It helped ease some of the pain, but it was a far cry from relief.

If everything went according to plan, Dash would be out of harm's way for the next few hours. By the time he returned from the human world, everything would be over.

A few weeks ago, when the elves had approached him about their plan, Rhett had been skeptical to say the least. But the opportunity had been too great to pass up. Everything had just so happened to coincide with the death anniversary of their witch of a mother, who Dash had idolized since infancy. Rhett was confident he'd made the right decision in agreeing to the elves' plan.

The elves must have been truly desperate to come to the Island of Corvus. Asking him to keep Dash out of the way was one thing, but making a bargain with an evil king was another. Rhett cast a glance at the obsidian spires in the distance. Dash always pretended the spires away, acting as if their every movement wasn't being watched. But Rhett knew it still struck a chord of fear in his brother's heart. He would be a fool not to be afraid.

Rhett had seen the elven girl walking towards the palace on Corvus just that morning. In her snowy white dress, she had looked like a lamb to slaughter. Despite the confidence in her stride and the determined set in her jaw, her eyes had darted around, betraying her terror. So long as she'd kept her head on her shoulders, she'd had the potential to make it out of the King's palace alive.

Not many did.

A part of Rhett hoped she had succeeded. She didn't appear

to be a fool betting on a gamble she greatly misunderstood. She might be one of the few to walk away from a bargain relatively unscathed. Of course, everyone wore their scars from a bargain with the King. Hers just might be useful, because if she succeeded, if the elves succeeded, Rhett's magic would be restored to its full power. His magic would be just as it was so many years ago when his life was nothing more than surviving to live another day. He ached for that feeling one more.

Rhett flexed his fingers, watching small, violet sparks leap between them. He studied the dark purple veins in his palm. He could feel the crunch of bones beneath his grip. He could see the monsters' blood on his hands. He took a slow breath, forcing the usual images from his head. It would all be worth it.

Dash would never have to find out the truth. He could *finally* be safe.

Rhett had done his part. Now, he just had to wait.

Chapter 5

They had been locked in the cell for hours.

Philip's back and tailbone ached from sitting on the rough, stone ground. A chill lingered in the air, which stank of waste and unwashed bodies.

To pass the time, Max walked in dizzying circles and sang to himself. Each time he restarted the same song, Philip's eye twitched.

Ella hadn't left Torryn's side for a second. They huddled together in a corner, speaking in low voices. Their introductions had been rushed, and Ella had neglected to explain who Torryn was or how she knew him.

Philip twisted the drawstrings of his hoodie around his thumb. His gaze caught on the small mustard stain from the hotdog he had eaten the night before. It didn't seem possible that less than twenty-four hours ago, a tiny mustard stain had irritated him so much.

An ache lingered at the base of his skull. He had long since given up trying to rationalize this new world. This wasn't a dream or hallucination. Somehow, this was real. They were locked in a dungeon, and there was nothing they could do about it.

Everyone else seemed to have accepted the same fate. The rest of the prisoners kept a sort of routine. They milled about their cells, conversing in low voices until somewhere above, a bell rang six times. Guards delivered a meager meal of stale bread and molded cheese, which everyone ate in silence. When the bell rang seven times, the prisoners broke off into small groups.

Passing around a cup of water, each person recited an unintelligible incantation and took a deep drink. Torryn partook in this ritual alongside everyone else, but Ella abstained. When the bell rang eight times, the guards removed the plates, utensils, and tin cups. Once the guards left, each person curled up on the cold, hard ground and tried to sleep.

Max made friends with a group of young children, who piled themselves in the middle of the cell and fell asleep instantly. He snored louder than the rest of the children combined.

Only a few people remained awake, mostly young men and women who stared into the darkness with hollow eyes. Philip didn't want to know how long they'd been here. Why were they imprisoned? What had their lives been like before they became prisoners? Like him, they must have had hopes and dreams. Like him, the world had ruthlessly shattered any optimism that may have remained. What brought them to this moment, where they sat in a dark, overcrowded cell, morning the life they could have had?

A soft noise startled Philip from his bleak thoughts He glanced up to find Ella, who cleared her throat again and spoke. "Torryn and I agreed that you should know the plan."

"The plan?" Philip asked warily. Of course, they had a plan. Whether it was a good plan remained to be seen,

Ella's eyes shifted. Her gaze lingered on the few prisoners that remained awake. "We'll explain over here."

Philip struggled to his feet, wincing at the stiff creak in his joints. He followed Ella to the corner she and Torryn had claimed. They sat around a series of strange charcoal marks on the stone.

For the first time, Philip got a good look at Torryn. Everything about him was pale, from his skin to his icy blue eyes, to his waist-length platinum hair. He tossed his hair over his shoulder, revealing pointed ears covered in piercings. He sat with impeccable posture and somehow managed to stare down his long nose at Philip, even from a seated position.

"Philip, I know this is confusing and terrifying for you," Ella began, clasping her hands together, "However, I have a plan to escape. If everything goes smoothly, we'll be in the elven kingdom, where we can figure out how to get you and Max home. Trust me."

Philip raised a skeptical eyebrow. He wanted to believe her, but that was a big *'if.'* "How do I know we can trust you? The last people who told me to trust them threw us into a dungeon."

The corners of Torryn's thin lips quirked into a smile. "I like him."

The feeling wasn't mutual quite yet.

Ella gestured to the sleeping prisoners around them. "You should trust me because *they* trust me. Each of the elves in this cell was captured by the fair folk and thrown here to rot without any good reason, just like us."

Philip was still skeptical, and Ella continued. "Recently, the elves received intelligence that Prince Elliott intends to use us as hostages. We don't know what he wants, but we cannot allow him to have any leverage."

"He *will* kill us without hesitation, no matter the consequences," Torryn added in a smooth voice.

Fear clawed in the pit of Philip's stomach. Torryn's cool gaze rested on him, waiting for a show of weakness. Swallowing back the bile that threatened to rise at such a statement, Philip schooled his features into an expression as placid as glass. The expressionless mask brought a strange, familiar sense of comfort. It was the same mask he wore every hour of every day—every *normal* day where he was a normal teenager in a normal world.

"Prince Elliott has caused so much suffering during his reign," Ella said, "I refuse to let him shed more of my people's blood. The pain and heartache caused by Sovereign Prince Elliott will end no matter the cost."

Torryn mimed applause. "Spoken like a true princess."

Philip's eyebrows shot up in surprise. Did he hear that correctly? Surely Torryn was joking.

Ella bit her lip. "He doesn't know yet."

"He doesn't know?" Torryn gave a short, harsh laugh, "Hemnes would tear his hair out if he heard you say that. Too bad we might die before we see him again."

"We're not going to die."

"That remains to be seen," Torryn sniffed pretentiously, "Philip of the human world, I present to you, Her Royal Highness Princess Elestren daughter of Lillia."

Philip blinked, still skeptical. "You're *really* a princess?"

Ella fidgeted with the hem of her skirt. "It's more complicated than that, but yes."

Philip floundered for a response. He hated being caught off-guard with something as important as this. Finally, he muttered, "That would have been nice to know."

Torryn snorted with laughter, which he suppressed when Ella shot him a sharp look. "Apologies," he said, "I have been imprisoned for so many months that I forgot the refreshing, invigorating nature of sarcasm and dry humor."

"You've been imprisoned for so long that I forgot how dramatic you can be." Ella rolled her eyes.

"It *is* one of my finer traits."

Ella shook her head, but couldn't hide her grin. "You're insufferable."

Watching Ella and Torryn's exchange sent a pang through

67

Philip's chest that he couldn't quite place. He stood abruptly, noting the judgmental quirk of Torryn's eyebrow.

"I'm going to get some rest," he announced.

Ella tilted her head, expression taut with concern. "Is everything okay?"

Philip wanted to scream in frustration. Why did everyone keep asking that? Instead, he mumbled a weak dismissal and retreated to the opposite corner of the cell.

If what Ella and Torryn said was true, they would be rescued. If this rescue succeeded and the elves agreed to help, he and Max could find a way home. He hated how many 'ifs' they were gambling on, but what option did they have?

He refused to think about what would happen if this plan failed. Torryn's words lingered in his mind. *He* will *kill all of us without hesitation, no matter the consequences.*

Exhaustion took hold of Philip. He no longer had the energy to care whether he lived or died. Curling onto his side, he pillowed his arm under his head. Though he didn't expect to rest a single minute, sleep found him before he knew it.

Hours later, Philip awoke to screaming.

For a moment, he panicked, unable to remember where he was. His stiff body lay on cold, hard stone, and he couldn't feel his right arm. A dull ache consumed his entire head. He pressed his palm against his forehead, willing the pain away.

Memories of the past twenty-four hours flooded his brain. He recalled the hike with Max. The bittersweet-smelling mushrooms. The manticore attack. Dash abandoning them. Nathan and Adrian betraying them.

Ella's escape plan.

Philip found Ella speaking with a group of elves. For once, Torryn was absent from her side. She clasped an elderly elf's hand in hers and spoke a few words. A smile spread across the elf's weathered face, and her eyes filled with joyful tears. Ella bowed her head respectfully before moving on. Each elf she spoke with received her full attention, and once she finished speaking with them, their eyes glittered with a new light.

Torryn leaned casually against the stone wall, examining his nails. His smooth, blonde hair was draped over one shoulder to show off his ears, which were covered in an array of metal rings and studs. When he glanced up, his gaze settled on Ella. Though he shook his head at her, a small smile tugged at his lips.

Max drummed his hands against his knees, singing an off-key version of their father's favorite rock-and-roll song. The reminder of their family at home made Philip's gut twist. Surely someone had realized they were missing by now. What would their family do to find them? It would take days to comb the entire forest surrounding the campsite. At least it would be easy to explain their disappearance as a simple wilderness accident. Anything was better than the truth, which sounded like something from a fever dream.

A small voice nagged in the back of Philip's head. Was their family searching for him and Max, or were they just concerned about Max? Philip knew these thoughts were irrational and ridiculous, but he couldn't shake the bitter feeling that his family had noticed Max's absence, not his.

"How are you feeling?" Ella approached, startling Philip out of his sulking.

"I'll be fine as soon as I know what's going on," he said.

"The attack started at exactly six chimes of the bell. The soldiers should reach this cell at seven chimes, which will happen in a short while."

Philip let out a breath, relieved that nothing had gone wrong yet.

"Come with me." Ella took hold of his limp arm and dragged him to the opposite corner of the cell. Philip stiffened, uncomfortable with her touch, though he couldn't feel it.

As they passed, a small elven girl gasped and loudly exclaimed, "Look, Mama! It's a real human!"

The girl's mother leaned down to chastise her daughter, but when her gaze landed on Philip, she froze. Her mouth formed a small, shocked 'o'. Philip gave them a canned, tight-lipped smile and turned away immediately.

Ella overturned an empty chamber pot and climbed on top of it. She gripped his shoulder to steady herself as she straightened her spine and lifted her chin. Even standing on the bucket, she barely stood as tall as Philip.

"People of Elvenmar," Ella began, her voice ringing through the tense silence in the cell, "Today, you will be free!"

Murmurs arose from the elves, who looked up at their princess like she was a beam of light in the darkness.

"In a short while, a team of our best soldiers will free us and return us to our homelands, where our friends and families are waiting with open arms. Sovereign Prince Elliott believes he can do whatever he wishes without suffering the consequences, but we will show him and everyone else in this world and the next that the elven people are not to be trifled with!"

The elves roared with approval at Ella's vengeance-spurred words. Wild, uncontrollable energy swept through the dungeon, setting Philp on edge. Their anger at their captors was justified, but unpredictable emotions could put the entire plan in jeopardy.

Ella continued. "Our soldiers will lead you to safety, and I implore you to trust them. Your cooperation is vital to the success of our mission. On my honor as Princess of Elvenmar, I swear you will return home unscathed."

She gripped Philip's shoulder tighter as her balance wavered. "This will be the end of your suffering once and for all."

The elves cheered, energized by Ella's words. From the way they were acting, Philip bet they would follow Ella if she led them off the edge of a cliff.

A deafening crack echoed throughout the dungeon, abruptly silencing the cheers. Everyone froze. In the distance, a bell chimed seven times.

"Remember my words!" Ella called over the ringing, "This is the beginning of our freedom!"

As soon as the words left her lips, the stone ceiling exploded, showering chunks of stone and debris into the dungeon.

Here lies Dash Robert Calloway, beloved son of Maryn Calloway.

No matter how many times he visited, seeing his own grave made Dash's skin crawl. It unnerved him to stare at the spot where he was supposedly buried. Though reading the inscription over and over sent a chill down his spine, it was the only remainder of his mother in this world and the next.

He had been standing at the gravesite for hours. A gloomy, early-morning mist hung over the graveyard, chilling him to the bone, despite the warm summer breeze. It reminded him of the old horror movies his mother used to watch when they were younger. His dead mother who he remembered so little of.

Next to Dash's fake grave lay a much smaller headstone, where his mother's body was actually buried. The short inscription on his mother's gravestone was far simpler than his.

Maryn Elizabeth Calloway. RIP.

Dash wished he had more memories of his mother. When she

71

was alive, she had worked two jobs to feed and clothe him and Rhett. On the rare occasion she had been home, a glass of wine was never absent from her sharply manicured hand.

She died shortly after her oldest son went missing and her youngest son supposedly died. No one questioned what happened to Maryn's strange oldest son, but everyone had mourned her sweet younger son.

Dash squirmed just thinking about it. His father had taken him to watch his funeral, where strangers had lined up to stare at his small casket and his devastated mother. They'd murmured condolences and shaken their heads.

No one could have suspected Dash's death was simply a ruse. Just as Rhett had planned, who would bother looking for a dead boy? When they had disappeared into the magical world, no one even knew to follow.

Bowing his head, Dash knelt before his mother's grave. He summoned a palmful of yellow magic, casting a warm glow onto the cold, crumbling stone. He had never truly known either of the people who gave him life, but at least he had Rhett.

No matter what happened, Rhett would always be there to protect him. He would always offer a ghost of a smile and the wave of a hand, and, like magic, everything would be okay again.

If only Dash could do the same for Rhett.

Coughing into his sleeve, Philip squinted through the thick dust that swirled through the dungeon. Chunks of the stone ceiling were now scattered across the cracked dungeon floor.

A young man dropped through the newly created hole in the ceiling and kicked away the rubble. Dust silhouetted his tall, broad figure. As the man drew nearer, Philip could make out the details of his face. He had a wide jaw and a dimpled smile. His auburn hair hung to his waist like a curtain. Piercings lined his pointed ears and accented the corner of his eyebrow.

At the sight of him, Ella's face lit up.

"People of Elvenmar, I am Hemnes, Son of Freesia, servant to Queen Celosia, Daughter of Camalia," the man announced, "Under Her Majesty's orders, we have come to your rescue!"

A cheer arose from the prisoners as a team of uniformed elves dropped into the dungeon from the hole in the ceiling. While the uniformed elves dispersed among the prisoners, giving orders and organizing everyone into groups, Hemnes turned to Ella.

Before he could take a single step, Ella rushed into his arms and hugged him like she never wanted to let him go. His muscular frame swallowed Ella whole.

"Elestren," Hemnes's voice broke with relief, "Thank the stars you're safe."

Ella laughed against his chest. "I had Torryn to keep me in line."

"Classic Torryn, always bossing everyone around."

Torryn rolled his eyes. "Nice to see you too, Hemnes. Now, can we save the hugging for later? The rest of us would like to get out of here sometime."

Reluctantly, Ella pulled away from Hemnes. She whispered something in his ear and drew him into an empty corner. Hemnes's pierced eyebrows drew together in concern as Ella spoke.

"What's going on?" Max asked, still groggy from sleep.

"We're getting out of here," Philip replied.

"Cool," Max was suddenly wide awake, "A jailbreak!"

When Ella finished speaking to Hemnes, she climbed on top of the overturned chamber pot and cleared her throat. The prisoners immediately fell silent.

Ella projected her voice over the crowd. "Our soldiers will lead all of you to safety, but your cooperation is crucial to the success of this mission. Remain silent, keep to the shadows, and don't lose sight of the soldiers. Am I clear?"

The prisoners murmured their assent, but nervousness settled over them. A tense, anxiety-ridden silence filled the dungeon.

Ella placed a hand over her heart. "May the King grant you safety."

"And may he spare his wrath," the elves replied in unison.

Though the exchange made no sense to Philip, the elves straightened their spines, strengthened with a new resolve. When Hemnes unlocked the cell, the soldiers funneled the prisoners to freedom.

Torryn placed a hand on Philip's shoulder, keeping him rooted to his spot. "We have orders to remain with the princess."

Philip frowned but didn't object.

Once the last prisoner left the dungeon, Ella breathed a sigh of relief and sagged against the stone wall. "Their safety is out of our hands. I must now fulfill my end of the bargain."

Hemnes hesitated. "Are you sure we have to—"

"There's no other way," Ella said firmly.

With a relenting sigh, Hemnes nodded. "Alright. I trust you."

Pushing herself off the wall, Ella assumed a stance of authority. "Torryn, how quickly can we reach the throne room from here?"

Torryn glanced up through the hole in the ceiling. "There's a passageway through the servants' corridors above us."

"Wait," Max interrupted, "Why are we going to the throne room? And why didn't we go with everyone else? We're trying to escape, right?"

Ella nodded. "We're going to get out of here, but first, I have unfinished business with the Sovereign Prince."

Chapter 6

Hemnes peered up through the hole in the ceiling. "How do you suggest we get up there?"

"I don't have any magic on hand," Torryn grumbled, "They took it when I was caught."

Philip frowned; from what he'd seen, magic wasn't something you had on hand like you would a wallet or a pocket knife. No one had mentioned it was possible to take away magic.

Hemnes grabbed the leather pouch he wore on his belt. "I should have enough magic, but the stone might not hold all of us. The explosion weakened the stone more than I expected."

"Well, it's our best bet," Ella said, "Hopefully it will be strong enough to hold us. Torryn, would you go first and lead the way?"

"Oh great," Torryn rolled his eyes, "So if the ceiling doesn't hold up, *I'll* fall through."

"I can go first," Hemnes volunteered, "Once I reach the top, I can help pull everyone up. Besides, I'm bigger than the rest of you. If the ceiling can hold me, it can hold any one."

Philip held back a derisive snort; saying Hemnes was larger than any one else was like saying an ox was larger than a sheep. His sheer height and muscle mass dwarfed everyone in comparison.

Hemnes knelt and opened the leather pouch. He scooped fine, sandy powder from the pouch and sprinkled it onto the stone floor. As he muttered an unintelligible incantation, the stone and debris rose from the ground and formed itself into a crude staircase that led up through the hole in the ceiling.

A wave of nausea rolled over Philip as he watched the impossible unfold before him. A twist of *wrongness* in his gut caused his head to swirl. A bitter, earthy scent wafted into his nostrils, overpowering the stench of the dungeon.

"Wow!" Max stared at the staircase with wide eyes, completely enamored.

Ella and Torryn didn't bat an eyelash at the magic. Hemnes climbed the staircase like it had been there all along. When he reached the top, he peered down through the hole in the ceiling. "It looks safe enough. You guys can come up now."

Max's face broke into a grin as he bounded up the stairs. "This is the best day ever! I love magic!"

Philip objected strongly. This was most certainly *not* the best day ever. In fact, he would argue it was one of the worst. He would have given anything to be safe and sound back home, not breaking out of a dungeon with strangers.

Of course, he didn't say any of this as he followed Ella and Torryn up the stairs. He simply tucked his limp arm into the pocket of his hoodie and tried not to think about the stairs crumbling beneath his feet.

When they reached the top, they stepped onto the cracked stone floor that, just moments ago, was the ceiling above their heads. Torryn didn't wait to see if any one was following before they drew open the room's small, wooden door and led them into a narrow hallway.

The servants' chambers lacked all of the lavish splendor of the rest of the palace. Dim torches lit the empty stone corridors, which were lined with identical wooden doors engraved with strange symbols. Signs of battle littered the abandoned hallways. Brilliantly colored ooze splattered the stone walls like graffiti.

"What's all this paint doing here?" Max asked, examining his sneaker, which was covered in a dripping tie-dye of the colorful ooze.

"That's not paint," Ella explained darkly, "It's blood. Fair folk bleed the color of their magic."

Philip shuddered in disgust, but Max was unfazed. "Whoa! I wish I had colorful blood. Plain old red is just boring."

Despite the blood, the hallways remained abandoned. The eerie silence put Philip on edge. With a shudder, he zipped his hoodie to his throat. Normally it gave him a sense of security. Now, however, the browning crust of blood that covered the grey fabric made his stomach writhe.

Torryn stopped abruptly in front of a golden tapestry the size of a Persian rug. Its extravagance stood out against the drabness of the servants' chambers. The tapestry depicted a semicircle of multicolored fair folk holding a crown above the head of a gold-skinned man. The fraying, top corner of the tapestry hung loose, revealing the curved arch of a door hidden behind it. Torryn and Hemnes unceremoniously ripped it down and tossed it aside.

The door behind the tapestry was short and narrow, embellished with a familiar symbol. Philip recognized the symbol as the golden crest worn on the fair folk guards' uniforms.

Torryn heaved the door open and motioned for them to follow. Philip held his breath as he entered the hidden corridor, expecting to find it covered in blood. Inside the corridor, however, it was pitch-black. He stiffened as someone clamped a hand on his shoulder.

"It's only me," Ella whispered from somewhere behind him.

"We don't have to whisper, you know," Torryn said at full volume.

Feeling around in the dark, Philip grasped Max's arm. As

they stumbled blindly through the corridor, he kept a firm grip on his little brother, afraid he would disappear the moment he let go. Max dragged a hand along the stone wall. Though it caused a horrible, scraping noise, no one told him to stop.

After a few minutes of walking, Philip felt the ground slope beneath him. Just as he gained a bit of momentum, an elbow collided with his gut.

"So sorry," Torryn didn't sound the least bit apologetic.

"Why did we stop?" Max asked.

"This is our entrance to the throne room," Torryn replied.

"Are you sure?" Ella sounded skeptical.

Torryn sniffed. "Are you questioning my judgment?"

A heavy scraping noise echoed through the corridor as Torryn drew a door open. A sliver of light leaked into the darkness alongside a wave of noise. Screams and shouts echoed off the stone, driving a spike of pain into Philip's aching head. The harsh sound of metal against metal rang cut through the din. Surely, this couldn't be the throne room.

"What's going on out there?" Ella asked, sounding worried.

"It's a warzone," Torryn said, "Our soldiers are trying to blast the doors open, but the fair folk guards aren't giving up without a fight."

Light glinted off the knife that appeared in Hemnes's hand. "I have weapons and plenty of magic."

"We have to reach the throne room," Ella said, "If the only way to get there is to fight, so be it."

Without another word, Ella brushed past Philip and plunged into the open. Torryn and Hemnes followed, leaving him no choice but to follow, dragging Max along with him.

When he emerged from the corridor, he froze. The grand hall containing the imperious staircase that led to the golden throne room doors was a mass of chaos and confusion. Elves clambered up the white stone steps, which ran red with blood. They pummeled the barricaded doors with blasts of explosive magic, fair folk perched in the ornate golden fixtures overhead, firing down at them with magic. A team of elves armed with bows and arrows shot at the fair folk high above them, but few arrows struck their targets.

Magic writhed through the chaos, shooting up in spikes of fire, columns of water, chunks of stone, and crawling vines. Explosions burst like grenades, leaving a smoky haze that filled the space. The cloudless blue sky that could be seen through the glass ceilings above contrasted with the vicious image of blood and corpses below.

Philip felt the twist of magic deep in his gut. Waves of nausea rolled over him. Swallowing back the bile that rose in his throat, he forced himself to focus on the golden doors at the top of the staircase. All they had to do was make it to those doors without dying. Simple.

Beside him, Ella's knuckles whitened as she clutched Hemnes's knife. She took a shaky breath and set her jaw. "On the count of three, we break for it. Three…"

Philip tightened his grip on Max's hand.

"Two…"

His heart thundered, and his pulse roared in his ears.

"One!"

They charged into the fighting. Hemnes set the pace at a dead sprint as he wove through the chaos. Philip kept his gaze locked on Hemnes' red hair, determined not to lose him in the fray. He kept a vice like grip on Max's hand as they ran.

Water rained down, plastering his hair to his forehead. He didn't dare release his grip on Max to wipe it away. Cursing the loss of feeling in his other arm, he pressed on blindly.

A vine shot across the floor and wrapped around Max's ankle. Max tripped, busting his lip on the white stone. Philip grabbed the vine and yanked it off of Max's ankle. As he yanked his brother to his feet, a tongue of fire lapped at Max's leg, catching on his pants. Max shrieked and swatted at the burning fabric.

Hemnes reached them in seconds. He tore his jacket off and used it to smother the fire. Throwing Max over his shoulder, he abandoned his scorched jacket. Philip kept pace with Hemnes as they wove through the heavy fighting.

The air was thick with smoke that stung Philip's eyes. Elven soldiers crowded on the stairs. They shouted incantations and hurled powder, which exploded like hand grenades, shaking the doors with the force of impact.

"Stand back," Hemnes commanded, thrusting Max towards Philip. Digging into the pouch at his hip, Hemnes joined the elven soldiers. The explosions he created burned brighter and hotter than any of the other soldiers' explosions. With only three handfuls of powder, he blew the doors open, shattering the barricades behind them.

The fighting around them screeched to a halt. Philip's ears rang with the feedback from the explosions. The solid gold doors warped from the impact and heat from the explosions.

Elven soldiers parted like the sea as Ella ascended the stairs. Despite her dirty, bloodstained dress and her wild hair, she held herself regally, looking exactly as a princess should.

Torryn grabbed a half-conscious fair folk soldier from the ground and hoisted him to his feet, using him as a living shield. None of the fair folk risked shooting at them while Torryn held the hostage.

When they entered the throne room, Hemnes turned and spoke an incantation under his breath. Thick, green vines shot up from the ground and wrapped around the melting doors, sealing them shut. Philip desperately hoped they wouldn't have to make a quick escape.

Prince Elliott sat rigidly on his throne, gripping the gilded armrests until his golden knuckles turned silver. Nathan and Adrian stood on either side of the throne, wielding massive spears. A dozen of the sovereign's guards surrounded the dais where the throne sat. They stood with stiff-backed postures, holding their weapons at the ready.

Before any of the guards could move, Torryn passed the hostage to Hemnes, who held a knife to the guard's neck. He pressed the tip of the knife into the guard's cerulean skin, sending a trickle of blue blood down his chest. "Stay back," he warned, "or the guard dies."

"Stand your ground," Nathan commanded, tightening his grip on his spear.

Prince Elliott rose from his throne furiously. "What is the meaning of this?"

Ella straightened her spine and stepped toward the sovereign. A dozen weapons leveled at her, but she dismissed them with a wave of her hand. "I come bearing a message from the King of Corvus."

Unease rippled through the guards. Some lowered their weapons and backed away, while others cast their eyes heavenward and muttered a prayer. Nathan and Adrian exchanged a wide-eyed glance.

"What business do you have with *His Majesty*?" Prince Elliott's lips curled into a sneer. He glared down at Ella with burning hatred and condescension.

81

"Sovereign Prince Elliott of Haderra," Ella's clear voice echoed in the cavernous space, "you have found disfavor with all the kingdoms in the magical world and with the King himself. You have lied, stolen, and killed in the name of your kingdom, yet you pay no attention to the needs of your people."

The sovereign scoffed. "You come in the name of the King, though you are loyal to the elven Queen? I see through this pathetic ruse. Why would the King send *you*, an insignificant princess, royal in nothing but name?" a sneer crossed his lips, "You are weak. Your queen is weak. She cannot even muster the courage to face me herself. Instead, she sends her expendable little niece to carry out her dirty work."

Ella pressed her lips together, regaining her composure. "My queen sends her regards with the elves we freed from your dungeon. The kingdom of Elvenmar will no longer tolerate negotiations with Haderra so long as you sit on the throne."

The sovereign's face twisted with rage. Philip was struck by the way his features contorted with anger, removing all traces of beauty from his golden face.

"I order you to kill them!" Prince Elliott shrieked at his guards.

Hemnes sank the knife deeper into the guard's neck, just inches from an artery. "If any of you move, I'll slit his throat."

"Stand down," Nathan commanded the guards.

"I said kill them!" Prince Elliott snapped. "Who cares about one guard? I am Sovereign Prince of Haderra. My word is law, and my life holds more value than all of your measly lives combined."

If this comment affected the guards, they didn't show it. Nathan and Adrian exchanged another glance, this one weighted with clenched jaws and flashing eyes.

"This is why the King has sent me," Ella said, "You are unfit to rule. A just sovereign should value the lives and safety of their people above all else."

"Oh please," Prince Elliott spat, "Save your speeches about honor and justice for the King himself. One day, you will learn the weight that sits on the shoulders of a monarch. Sacrifices are never easy, little princess, but they must be done," his tone turned mocking, "This *is* why the King sent you, is it not? I guarantee you, whatever bargain you made with him is for naught.

Ella flinched, and the sovereign continued. "When the tables have turned, you will be the one perched on your throne weighing the value of your own life. Once you have been in my position, you can lecture me as your heart desires," Prince Elliott tapped his chin thoughtfully, "Oh dear. I almost forgot. You shall never have the elven throne, you dirty halfling."

Ella drew in a sharp breath as if the sovereign's words physically pained her. On either side of her, Hemnes and Torryn gripped their weapons, eager to tear the smug expression from the sovereign's face. Anxiety knotted in Philip's chest as the tension mounted. Nothing good could come from this exchange.

Satisfied, Prince Elliott sat back on his throne and steepled his hands. He flashed Ella a mocking smile. "Anything else?"

Ella took a steady breath. "I may never have the throne, but at least my fate will be better than yours. I will die surrounded by people I love. You will die surrounded by traitors. Here is the King's message, *Elliott*."

Before Philip could grasp what Ella meant, Nathan and Adrian turned. With expressions of fury, they shoved their spears into Elliott's body, skewering him with an X through his heart.

Chapter 7

Rhett knew exactly when Elliott died.

He *felt* his cousin's death the moment it happened.

It was a surge of power that started in his heart and rushed through his veins. Purple sparks cracked over his knuckles and up his arms. Rhett couldn't remember the last time his magic had come so easily.

Elliott's death marked the beginning of something momentous. Something that would change *everything*. For the first time in a long while, Rhett smiled.

A horrified silence crashed over the throne room as Elliott's body slumped to the ground. His golden blood poured onto the dais, pooling at Nathan and Adrian's feet. Elliott's golden, unseeing eyes were wide in surprise. Nathan and Adrian exchanged a grim look of resignation; there was no going back from what they had done.

The shock in the room was nearly palpable. Max's eyes were wide as saucers. His lower lips trembled, but he didn't cry. Guards stood frozen to their spots, gaping at Elliott's corpse.

Their Sovereign was dead.

Their Sovereign had been murdered by his own guards, under the order of a mysterious king who sent a young elven girl as his envoy.

The absurdity of the situation almost made Philip laugh. He didn't quite know what to think. Whatever he and Max had stumbled into, they had no part in this tangled web of death and chaos. This wasn't a game he was willing to play.

A shadow passed over the throne room, interrupting Philip's thoughts. He glanced up through the glass ceiling and inhaled sharply. He had half a second to pull Max to the ground before the ceiling exploded.

Shards of glass rained down like hail. Philip shielded Max with his body, gasping in pain as broken glass sliced his skin. Warm, sticky blood trickled down the back of his neck.

The fair folk guards dove for cover. The glass shards cut their skin and embedded themselves into their delicate, membranous wings. Multicolored blood dripped everywhere, staining the glass on the floor like an ornate chapel window.

With a chorus of unearthly screeches, a team of elves mounted on griffins dove through the gaping hole where the ceiling had been.

"They came for us!" Ella's voice broke with relief.

One griffin swooped dangerously close to the ground. Its rider leaned almost completely out of their saddle and plucked Torryn off the ground as if he weighed nothing. The rider swung Torryn onto the back of the griffin and shouted triumphantly.

The fair folk guards scrambled their wits together and realized what was happening. They leveled their weapons and attacked the griffin, hurling bursts of fire and streams of water into the air. Vines shot up from the ground, green tendrils snatching at the griffin riders. A few griffins fell to the ground, completely unconscious.

The elves responded with equal fervor, flinging their magical powder through the air. Upon impact, the powder exploded with different consequences. Some explosions sent jolts of lightning into the guards' bodies, while others caused tornadoes of wind that whirled broken glass through the air.

Nathan and Adrian turned on the fair folk around them. They fought their former comrades alongside the elves, killing them with the same ruthlessness they showed to Elliott.

Screams of pain and shouts of terror crashed down on Philip. His head spun as the explosions shook the foundation of the palace. The twist of wrongness in his chest doubled in the magical chaos. There was nothing logical about any of this. This frenzy made Elliott's murder seem like mercy.

A griffin dove towards Philip, gaining speed as it drew closer. He scrambled out of the griffin's path. At the last second, the griffin pulled up. Its claws raked across his cheek.

Philip's hand flew to his cheek. When he pulled his hand away, he saw dark blood dripping down his fingers. An odd, disjointed calm settled over him. The sight of his blood reminded him that he was alive. He could still feel something other than the wrongness of magic.

The griffin's rider reached for him but missed by a fraction of an inch. Instead, the rider looped around and swung Max onto the griffin's back. They shot into the air, weaving around columns of fire and plumes of smoke.

The grating sound of claws against marble drew Philip from his thoughts. Another griffin swooped down and landed in front of him.

"Need a lift?" The griffin's rider asked. Her dark, angular eyes glittered, and her pale cheeks flushed with adrenaline. An emerald nose ring accented her nose, and, as was apparently common among elves, piercings covered her pointed ears. She tossed her long, glossy hair over her shoulder and shot Philip a dazzling smile, radiating easy charm.

When Philip didn't respond, the elf patted her griffin's rump and beckoned for Philip to hurry. "Hop on!"

Philip obeyed, grabbing the elf's outstretched hand. The leather of her gloves kept Philip's bloody palm from slipping out of her grip. He allowed the elf to pull him onto the griffin's back. Shrieking impatiently, the griffin clawed at the ground until the elf clicked her tongue. At her signal, the griffin took flight. Philip's stomach dropped as the griffin swooped through the air.

"I didn't know they'd be bringing humans in for this job," the elf called over the wind and the sounds of the fight below.

Philip didn't try to speak for fear of vomiting the moment he opened his mouth.

"I'm Treave, by the way," the elf gave an affectionate grin and patted her griffin, "And this handsome hunk is Ochre."

Ochre screeched and shot up through the hole where the ceiling had been. Philip clung to Treave's waist as they flew vertically, climbing higher and higher with each beat of Ochre's massive wings.

"Stop it, Ochre! We're on a mission," Treave laughed, "You can show off later."

When Ochre finally leveled out and settled into a steady flight pattern, Philip found his voice. "Where are you taking me?"

"We're going back to Elvenmar, where we'll meet up with the rest of the army."

Unsure what to think, Philip stayed silent. Whether this "rescue" was a good thing or a bad thing remained to be seen. Dash had abandoned them, and Nathan and Adrian had thrown them in prison and murdered their own—albeit, cruel— sovereign, but were the elves going to be any better?

"You never mentioned your name," Treave said.

"I'm Philip."

"So, tell me, Philip," Treave began, "Why *did* they bring in humans for this mission? The princess didn't mention anything about humans in the briefing she gave. Besides, I thought the King made travel between worlds impossible."

"She didn't mention anything about murder either, but here we are," Philip muttered.

"What?" Treave called over the wind, "Did you say 'murder'?"

"Didn't you see? They killed Prince Elliott."

Treave swiveled her head to gape at Philip. "You're kidding! They killed the *Sovereign Prince of Haderra*?"

"His guards stabbed him as a message from the King of Corvus."

Treave threw her head back and laughed. "He had it coming!"

Philip frowned; murder wasn't a laughing matter, especially when the victim in question happened to be a monarch. Back in the human world, he never cared much for politics, but he knew killing someone as important as Elliott would have grave repercussions.

"I can't wait to see what the fair folk will do. They'll hold a kingdom-wide celebration before his body's cold, especially since the King of Corvus ordered his death."

Philip balked. "What?"

"The fair folk never liked Elliott," Treave explained, "Everyone says he and his hand-picked Counsel of Lords were corrupt. I guess the rumors must be true if the King got involved."

"Who *is* the King of Corvus anyways?"

Treave's expression turned grave. "The King of Corvus is the most powerful man in this world and the next. His magic is unlimited, and his spies are everywhere. Nothing happens without him knowing. He never does anything without reason, and his bargains are infamous."

"You think the fair folk will turn a blind eye to Elliott's murder just because the King of Corvus ordered it?"

"It's happened that way for centuries. Every ruler knows not to cross the King unless they have a death wish. Some rulers received poison with their morning tea, while others found basilisks in their beds. There's a reason the King is the monster parents use to scare their children into obedience."

A shiver shot down Philip's spine; what could a person do with power like the King possessed? To murder without consequence was one thing, but to have such an absolute say over who ruled entire kingdoms was another thing entirely. A pit of dread settled in Philip's stomach. The King of Corvus had prohibited travel between worlds. What would he do to them for breaking his laws, even accidentally?

After a few hours of flying, the rolling meadows beneath them bled into dense evergreen forests. Ochre flew low enough that the tips of the tallest trees scratched against Philip's legs. Philip and Treave sat in silence, each taking in the aerial view.

When a small spot appeared on the horizon, Treave's face broke into a grin. "You see that?" she called, pointing into the distance. "That's Velsailia, the largest city in Elvenmar. It's the most beautiful city in this world and the next!"

Philip raised a skeptical eyebrow. From this distance, the city was nothing more than a smudge on the horizon. But as they drew nearer, his skepticism gave way to amazement.

The city of Velsailia in Elvenmar was nothing like the city of Hayala in Haderra. Hayala was a gleaming city that reached towards the heavens like an ornate tiara set with glass jewels, while Velsailia was a heavily fortified city that rested on a hilltop like an imperious crown of stone.

A thick wall of weathered, moss-covered stone surrounded the exterior of the city. Lush, green trees with tightly woven branches provided a cover over the city's cobblestone streets. Stone buildings lined the streets, only breaking occasionally around wide courtyards. A massive castle sat at the heart of the city, a regal, stately masterpiece of stone and ivy. Its moss-covered spires peeked out through the trees like thorns.

Treave leaned back in the saddle and sighed contentedly. "Home sweet home."

Ochre circled the city as if he were trying to show off its beauty. Once Philip had seen a thorough aerial view of Velsailia, the griffin swooped towards the ground.

They landed just outside the city in front of the wall, which was lined with elven sentries armed with crossbows. Treave gave them a wave, and a few lowered their weapons to wave back.

About two hundred elves milled around the clearing in front of the city. Philip recognized many of them from the dungeon and rescue mission. Automatically, he scanned the crowd for Max, sure his little brother would rush to recount every detail of the flight from Hayala.

Treave dismounted and offered a hand to help him from the griffin's back. He ignored her and swung down on his own. Immediately, his knees buckled beneath him, and he grabbed Ochre's saddle to keep himself from collapsing in the grass.

"It's always hard the first few times," Treave laughed.

Philip shot her a withering look to cover his embarrassment. He regained his footing and brushed invisible dirt from his body. Tucking his limp arm into his pocket, he let out a deep sigh.

"Something wrong?" Treave asked. She pulled a piece of dried meat from the pouch at her hip and tossed it to Ochre, who snatched it out of the air.

Philip craned his neck to see through the crowd. Though he was tall for a human, he realized he was only average height for an elf. "I have to find my brother."

"The princess is over there," Treave pointed to where Ella stood with Hemnes and Torryn apart from the crowd, "She'll know where to find him."

"Thanks," Philip started towards Ella, but Treave caught his elbow.

"Hey," she said, "If you ever need anything, don't hesitate to reach out. I'm here for you." She released him with a pat on the arm and strode away with Ochre in tow.

Philip watched her go for a moment. Her long black hair glinted in the sunlight as she led Ochre through the crowd. The memory of her grin lingered in his mind. With a shake of his head, he scolded himself; he had to find Max and get home as soon as possible. This world was messing with his head.

Squeezing through the crowd, he fought the anxiety that mounted in him. He didn't see Max anywhere. He tried to assure himself that his brother was safe, but he wasn't a naturally optimistic person.

All around him, elves cried and embraced each other joyfully. The once-wilted and depressed elves from the dungeon bloomed like flowers in the sunlight. Their eyes glittered with relief and happiness.

Philip wondered if these elves knew the price of their freedom. Did they know about Elliott's murder? Did they realize the consequences that might have?

By the time he reached Ella, Hemnes, and Torryn, his thoughts were tangled like yarn. Exhaustion set into his bones, and he wanted nothing more than to get Max and go home.

He finally spotted Max hanging from Hemnes's arm like a

monkey. Relief crashed over him at the sight of his little brother, whose wing-ruffled hair stuck out on all sides like a mad scientist.

"Philip!" Max released Hemnes and charged toward Philip, barreling into him with a hug, "I got to ride a griffin! It was awesome!"

Philip clutched his brother to his chest, savoring the press of Max's small, warm body. He was safe. They could finally find a way to go home. They would get out of this world and never have to worry about any of these people or their problems or their politics ever again.

Chapter 8

Dash knelt next to his cousin's corpse.

Elliott's unseeing eyes were wide, forever frozen in an expression of shock. Golden blood stained his mouth and leaked from the four stab wounds on his body. Two on either side of his neck where the spears entered his body, and two on either side of his ribcage where the spears burst through.

If only Dash had been there; maybe, then he could have saved his cousin from this terrible fate. Though Elliott had been unkind at best, he didn't deserve this.

It had been easy to turn a blind eye to what Elliott did behind closed doors. It had been easy to pretend Elliott was trying to be the best ruler possible—that he only wanted what was best for the kingdom. It had been easy to justify Elliott's actions to Nathan and Adrian and convince himself everything was for the best. He hadn't wanted to believe his cousin could be anything less than a perfect ruler.

Only now, did Dash see the consequences of Elliott's actions. If only he had seen his cousin for who he truly was instead of allowing himself to be blinded by an ideal.

Dash knew what Rhett would say. He could hear Rhett's voice in his head. *Elliott deserves this. For everything he's done to us, he deserves this.*

Shaking his head, Dash shoved his brother's cynical words away. Rhett only saw the worst in people. He didn't understand. *He* didn't have to deal with the repercussions of Elliott's death.

With a deep sigh, Dash closed Elliott's eyes and said a silent, final goodbye,

"Are we interrupting?" Nathan's voice echoed softly through the empty throne room.

Dash turned from his cousin to address his closest friends. He tried to keep his gaze away from the mess surrounding him. The despicably bright, colorful blood of Elliott's guards—Dash's guards, now—Dash's people—stained the white floors. The velvet rug stretching from the golden doors to the base of the dais had been kicked aside, too torn and stained to be good for anything but mopping up blood.

"Not at all," Dash dragged his attention to Nathan and Adrian, trying not to let his weariness show, "How can I help you?"

"We need to talk," Nathan said.

Dash pressed his palms to his eyes until colors exploded behind his eyelids. He let out a deep breath on the count of three before he opened his eyes. "What's wrong?"

Adrian held a damp cloth to the massive welt on his forehead that sealed his eye shut. "We wanted to speak to you about Elliott's murder. We were both there."

"Let me heal that first," Dash said, gesturing to Adrian's wound. "It will only take a moment."

With a relenting sigh, Adrian allowed Dash to draw closer and sweep his green hair off of his forehead. Gently settling his fingers over the welt, Dash closed his eyes and allowed the magic to flow through him.

Warmth blossomed in Dash's chest and spread through his veins. The magic coursed through his body and into Adrian's. Dash could feel every cell in Adrian's body. He could sense how they were all supposed to fit together. He repaired crushed capillaries and reduced the swelling, returning the skin to normal as if nothing happened.

When he released Adrian's head, the warmth lingered in Dash's body. The yellow glow slowly faded from his fingers. His body sang, rejuvenated by the use of magic.

"How's that?" Dash asked.

"Much better," Adrian answered, "Now about Elliott…"

"Maybe we should talk about this later," Dash interrupted, "The doctors probably need my help in the infirmary." He tried to step past his friends, but they used their broad bodies to block his path.

"We were there, Dash. In the throne room, we saw who killed Elliott. You have to listen us," Adrian insisted.

"I don't think we should discuss—"

"Princess Elestren ordered it herself," Nathan said, "Her guard stabbed Elliott right in front of us. We were powerless to stop it."

Dash's heart sank. *Of course.* It was the only logical conclusion to the mystery of Elliott's murder. Nathan and Adrian had been the only fair folk survivors of the throne room massacre. They had seen Elliott's death with their own eyes. The elves had staged an entire jailbreak as a distraction to get close to the Sovereign Prince and murder him on his throne. He knew this, but facing the truth was another thing entirely.

Now, Dash would be crowned Sovereign Prince of Haderra.

What was he going to do?

Philip watched as elven sentries drew the heavy, iron gates to the city open. The gates creaked on their hinges, rusty from underuse. Everyone in the meadow turned towards the gates. Many snapped to attention, clapping their fists over their chests.

A tall, broad woman marched out from the city. A chest full

of medals decorated her crisp, forest green uniform, and her knee-high boots shone immaculately. There were strands of white streaks in her red hair, which was braided into a coil that wrapped around her head and hung down her back. Creases lined her aged skin, and deep lines set her firm mouth. She strode forward with posture as stiff as an iron rod.

The elven soldiers saluted as the woman passed, while the rest of the elves bowed their heads in respect. The woman kept her chin raised, hazel eyes trained forwards. When she reached Ella, the woman bowed and clapped a fist over her heart.

"General Rhodes," Ella acknowledged the woman with a nod, "You have served the crown well today."

The general smiled up at Ella. "Thank you, Your Highness. It is good to see you safe and sound."

"Thank you, General. I am afraid we have some unexpected news."

"Oh?"

"Sovereign Prince Elliott is dead."

A shadow passed over the general's face. "This is grave news indeed. Someone must inform the queen of this turn of events."

Ella gave a resigned sigh. "I will tell her myself. She needs to hear the story from my lips."

"Very well, Your Highness." General Rhodes bowed her head. "If you will excuse me, I must address my soldiers."

"You have my permission, General," Ella said.

When General Rhodes turned, her gaze snagged on Philip and Max. Lines of confusion appeared between her eyebrows as she glanced back at Ella. "Your Highness?"

"Philip and Max, this is General Rhododendron daughter of Finnala," Ella introduced, "General Rhodes, this is Philip and Max. They're from the human world."

The general's eyebrows lifted. "I can see that."

Unsure what to do, Philip nodded politely to the general.

Max bounced on the balls of his feet. "I like your hair!"

General Rhodes chuckled. "It seems you have your hands full, Your Highness." With one last bow to Ella, General Rhodes turned away.

Ella watched the general's retreating form. "I suppose we should go…"

"After you, Princess." Torryn gestured towards the city.

Ella squared her shoulders and marched up the hill, flanked by Hemnes and Torryn. Max followed at their heels like a puppy, while Philip trailed close behind them. As they passed through the gates into the city, Philip felt the hawk like stares of the sentries on him.

Philip drew in a breath as they stepped under the stone wall, emerging into a different world. Gigantic, gnarled trees enclosed the city in shade beneath the twisted branches that formed a green canopy over their heads. Lanterns hung from the branches, shining overhead like stars. The lanterns illuminated the wide, cobblestone roads, which were lined with towering, stone buildings.

Elves leaned out the shutter-framed windows to call out greetings to their returning princes. Their expressions filled with absolute adoration as Ella passed. Children darted up to Ella and handed her flowers, which she tucked into her hair. Adults bowed and waved, basking in her presence. Philip supposed it wasn't every day they saw their princess on the streets.

Ella acknowledged the greetings and praises with smiles and graceful waving. Hemnes and Torryn remained statue-like, acting as her guards. Philip did his best to blend in and stay unnoticed while keeping a close eye on Max.

It was much easier to blend in with the elves than it was with the fair folk, though Philip's short hair made him stand out like a sore thumb in a sea of elves with flowing, waist-length hair. His soft, round ears were obvious markers of his humanness. Each elf wore dozens of piercings in each pointed ear, emphasizing the difference between humans and elves.

Soon, the branches overhead gave way to a fortified, stone castle. Moss crept up the lowest stones, and decorative ivy twisted in the cracks between the stones as if it had been instructed to grow there. Balconies and towers sprouted from the castle at random, giving it an asymmetrical silhouette. Through the arched, glassless windows, he saw elven servants bustling through torch-lit corridors.

Ella climbed the mossy, stone staircase that led to the castle's wooden front doors. Elven guards bowed to her and drew the doors open with a flourish. Ella, Torryn, and Hemnes breezed past them with a polite nod as if they owned the place.

Philip hesitated on the steps before hurrying after them.

The interior of the castle smelled like old books and wet wood. A green velvet rug covered most of the stone floors, giving the illusion that the floor was a bed of moss. Tendrils of ivy crept in through the windows and wound around the wooden beams that supported the steepled, stone ceiling. Torches on iron sconces lined the walls, their flames casting a warm glow through the dim corridors.

Ella strode with purpose as she led them through the castle's endless hallways. Hemnes and Torryn relaxed and fell into step behind her. The quiet in the halls provided a much-needed escape from the chaos of the day.

Whatever ease they had in the corridors instantly evaporated when Ella stopped in front of a set of dark wooden doors adorned with an iron knocker in the shape of a griffin's head. Ella lowered her chin and arranged her hair over her ears. Hemnes folded in on himself, hunching his broad shoulders. Even Torryn deflated as his stiff posture gave way to something almost fearful. Exchanging a somber look with Hemnes and Torryn, Ella lifted the knocker and let the iron clang against itself.

In the silence that followed the knock, a heaviness settled over them as if they were about to march into battle. Philip wasn't sure why his pulse sped, but from the way Ella braced herself, he knew nothing good was going to come. Only Max was oblivious to the tension in the air. He tried and failed to juggle two acorns, scrambling after them when they hit the floor and rolled away.

Finally, the doors creaked open, and a young girl popped her head out curiously. Her sparkling doe eyes widened as her delicate face lit up. A silver diadem perched atop her thick, black curls. Glittering jeweled earrings lined her pointed ears. She let out a squeal and threw her arms around Ella.

"Elestren!" the girl cried. "You made it! I missed you more than you could possibly imagine."

A grin broke across Ella's face. "Everleigh! How's my favorite little sister?"

Both girls had curly dark hair, dark skin, and deep brown eyes. But while Ella was graceful and willowy, Everleigh was petite and fragile. Ella had freckles and full lips, while Everleigh had dimples and a tiny smile. Philip decided the resemblance was there, but vague.

Everleigh released Ella and grinned up at Hemnes and Torryn. "Hello! I am so glad to see you all safe and sound."

Hemnes gave a gentle smile as he dipped into a bow. "Thank you, My Lady."

Torryn swept the girl a more elaborate bow and kissed the

back of her hand. "It's always a pleasure to be graced by your presence, Your Highness."

When the girl turned to Philip and Max, her eyes widened even further than he thought possible. "Who are you?"

"Everleigh, this is Philip and Max. They're my friends from the human world," Ella introduced, gesturing between them, "Philip and Max, this is my little sister, Everleigh, the crown princess of Elvenmar."

Taking a cue from Hemnes and Torryn, Philip bowed. "Nice to meet you."

Everleigh giggled. "I had no idea humans were so polite."

Max simply gaped up at Everleigh, too awed to speak.

"Is Aunt Celosia here?" Ella asked.

"As of now, she is occupied in a meeting with the governors," Everleigh said, "She should not take long, but I have instructions to keep you in the throne room until she arrives."

Relief crossed Ella, Hemnes, and Torryn's faces.

Everleigh clasped her hands together. "Linnmon and I have been waiting all day for you to get back. Come! He cannot wait to see you."

At the mention of the name Linnmon, Ella's face twitched into a sour expression. Hemnes and Torryn exchanged a knowing look as Ella's hand curled into a fist, bunching up the bloody fabric of her dress. When Everleigh turned and stepped into the throne room, Ella scowled and muttered under her breath before following her sister.

Philip drew in an awed breath at the magnificently simple throne room. He'd expected the throne room to be like the rest of the palace—a stone, torch-lit room accented with iron plating and wooden furniture. Instead, the throne room was a cavernous space with soaring ceilings and gigantic arched windows that allowed sunlight to flood the room. Another green velvet rug stretched from the doors to the base of the enormous oak tree that grew in the center of the room. The tree's trunk curved and twisted into a throne.

A man lounged on the throne but shot to his feet when they entered the room. He flashed a perfect, cocky smile as if nothing in the world could bother him. He wore a gaudy velvet jacket with cream ruffles around the collar. Running a tan hand through his chestnut hair, he swept into a halfhearted bow.

"Your Highnesses," he greeted, his voice like a purr.

Ella scowled at the sight of him. "Did I miss something, Linnmon? Have you been crowned queen in my absence? You have no right to sit on that throne."

Linnmon spread his arms, inviting Ella into an embrace, which she refused. "Elestren, dearest, I have missed you dearly."

Ella cast a glance towards Hemnes, whose face was like a storm cloud.

Linnmon noticed the look and strolled between them like a weasel among mice. He took Ella's hand and planted a kiss on the back of it. With a frown, he examined her fingers. "Dearest, you are not wearing your ring."

Ella snatched her hand back. "I was on a mission."

"I understand." Linnmon's lips curled into a feline smile. "We would not want you losing the ring before our wedding, would we?"

Chapter 9

Glancing from Ella to Linnmon, Philip tried not to let his confusion show. Ella was engaged to *him*? This slimy elf with his sharp smiles and gaudy outfit had somehow gotten himself engaged to a princess? He was most likely rich. As far as Philip knew, that was how things like this worked.

Ella glowered at Linnmon, but before she could say a word, Hemnes elbowed past him and placed a gentle hand on her shoulder. "Why doesn't Torryn show Everleigh down to the kitchens? Max, you can go along with them too. I hear sometimes, if you ask nicely, the cook will let you sample dessert."

"Cool!" Max exclaimed.

Betrayed and offered as a sacrifice without his consent, Torryn glared daggers at Hemnes but offered Everleigh his arm. Everleigh took it gladly and led him from the room. "The cook always makes the best cakes," Everleigh told Max, "You should try the lavender cake with lemon icing and—" The heavy door closed behind them, muffling the sound of Everleigh's chatter.

Philip's chest constricted as he watched Max leave. There was no way to excuse himself now without appearing rude, but could he trust Torryn to keep a close eye on him?

Ella turned to Linnmon with a steely glare that sent a shiver down Philip's spine. Hemnes stood protectively behind Ella, watching Linnmon with a distasteful scowl.

"I told you to leave me alone," Ella spat at her fiancé, "We may be engaged, but I would rather die than marry you."

The smug expression didn't leave Linnmon's face. "That could be arranged if you so wish. However, need I remind you that the queen herself arranged our marriage? These royal engagements are an important matter, and who are you to argue with her? After all, she only has our best interests in mind. You are the illegitimate daughter of a princess, and I am the son of a marchioness. It would be impossible for you to have a more advantageous marriage with any one else, especially considering your *situation*."

"I'm perfectly aware of my 'situation'*,*" Ella's voice held a twinge of bitterness, "But marrying *you* will never be in my best interest."

A ghost of a triumphant smirk crossed Hemnes's face. His hand rested on the hilt of his sword as if he were ready to use it on Linnmon at any moment. Philip didn't miss the furtive glances exchanged by Hemnes and Ella, and, apparently, Linnmon didn't either.

Ella's fiancé sniffed. "As I said, *I* am nobility, unlike many *other* suitors." Hemnes flinched, and Linnmon continued with a smirk, "Our union is advantageous to the crown. As the crown princess, Everleigh will remain unmarried, as is customary, so you must the position of the royal family through marriage. I have the power to protect you in court and keep you in line. Just picture it," his eyes gleamed hungrily. "If anything were to happen to Everleigh before she can produce heirs, you would be queen, and I will become king."

Ella and Hemnes inhaled sharply.

"You shouldn't say that," Ella warned. Her eyes darted around the throne room. "There is only one king in our world. If I were you, I wouldn't make him angry by blaspheming."

"Yes, yes. We all know the King of Corvus is *always*

103

watching." Linnmon rolled his eyes. "I have no fear for the monster king on the forbidden island."

Ella narrowed her eyes. "You should be. I've met the king myself and have seen the results of his punishment firsthand."

Images of Elliott's skewered body flashed through Philip's mind.

Linnmon flicked an invisible piece of lint off his arm. "Whatever you say, dearest."

The throne room doors creaked open, hinges protesting against the movement. A guard in fine livery entered and announced, "Presenting Her Majesty, Queen Celosia, Daughter of Camalia."

Ella, Hemnes, and Linnmon stiffened immediately, freezing like prey in the presence of a predator. Philip straightened his spine and tucked his limp arm into his hoodie. A column of guards marched into the throne room. They fell into their positions around the throne and snapped to attention.

The queen stepped into the room after the guards. Philip's eyes widened at the sight of her. Tall, graceful, and elegant, the queen floated to her throne. Her flowing, white dress complimented her flawless dark skin and perfect hourglass figure. Her silver eyes glistened under long, dark eyelashes. A small section of her curly, black hair was woven into intricate braids, while the rest hung loose past her waist. A silver crown rested on her head, and its diamonds glittered, casting speckles of light across the ceiling.

Ella, Hemnes, and Linnmon bowed as the queen settled onto the throne. Philip shook himself out of his dazed state and bowed as well.

"Your Majesty, may I just say how ravishing you look on this fine evening," Linnmon gushed, bowing so low that his forehead nearly touched the floor.

The corners of the queen's lips curved into a smile. "Thank you, Linnmon."

"If I may have your exquisite permission, Your Majesty, I regretfully request to leave your superb presence to find my darling fiancé's sister," Linnmon continued, "I promised sweet Everleigh I would take her on a picnic, and it would be disgraceful to keep the lady waiting."

"You may take your leave. Give Everleigh my love." The queen's smooth voice was cool as glass.

With another flourishing bow, Linnmon sauntered from the throne room. Ella glared at his retreating back, her hands bunching in the fabric of her skirt.

"Well," the queen raised her perfect eyebrows and addressed her niece, "It seems you had quite a few complications with your plan, Elestren. I have heard many rumors, and unfortunately, the one about the human appears to be true."

A shiver raced down Philip's spine as the queen's eyes slid to him and narrowed. Disapproval radiated from her in blood-chilling waves.

"This is Philip," Ella said. "He'll be staying here until I can return him and his brother to the human world."

"How is this possible?" the queen asked.

"I have no idea," Ella admitted, "But I'll get to the bottom of this as quickly as possible."

"And what of the rest of your mission?"

"We freed all of the elves in the palace dungeon, just as we planned," Ella reported, "But the King had other ideas about his part in the mission. He ordered Sovereign Prince Elliott's death, and Elliott's guards delivered the killing blow."

The Queen's knuckles whitened as she gripped the armrests

105

of her throne. Philip remembered how Elliot had done the same thing moments before his death. "What could have prompted such drastic action? And why did the King of Corvus become involved in this? The King was not a part of our deal, Elestren." Queen Celosia's tone was sharp with accusation.

"I did everything as you instructed," Ella defended, "You told me to do whatever it took to ensure the success of our mission. The King of Corvus was necessary for securing our position and guaranteeing our victory. Elliott's death was a small price to pay for freeing our people. I found favor with the King, and he granted us safety."

"The King does nothing without inflicting pain and suffering in our lives. He is not to be trusted. How could you be so idiotic?" Queen Celosia snapped. "You were ordered to free the elves and return immediately. I was being graceful in letting you take charge of this mission, and this is how you repay me? By putting is all at risk?"

"There's no risk. I already paid the price. Elliott is dead, and that's all the King asked for. No elf laid a hand on the Sovereign Prince, so there's nothing to worry about. There were fair folk witnesses and everything."

Queen Celosia narrowed her eyes. "Did any one of importance witness this murder?"

"No," Ella cast an uncertain glance at Hemnes.

"Then how can we be sure the fair folk will not blame our kingdom for the murder of their sovereign? I can imagine they will not be quick to admit Prince Elliott was murdered by his people. This could be the opportunity they have been looking for. They could declare war over this if the fair folk choose to blame us. It will be our word against theirs."

"But the King—"

"The King has not interfered in any past conflicts, nor will he do so now. Your foolishness may cost us our peace," Queen Celosia said.

"Please, Aunt Celosia. Elliott was going to start a war regardless. He would have used the elven prisoners as hostages and put you at a disadvantage."

"Do not talk back to me, young lady. I should never have let you become involved in this. You were of more use to me when you simply remained in your room. From now on, you will stay in the North Tower. You will not leave until your wedding to Linnmon."

Ella looked stricken. "No! You said if I completed this job, the engagement would end. I can't marry him!"

"That was before you deliberately went behind my back to involve the Demon King. For this act of treasonous disobedience, you need someone to keep you in line. Linnmon will suffice."

"Treasonous disobedience?"

"Your Majesty, if I may—" Hemnes tried to interject.

"Silence!" the queen commanded. "You have served me well today, Hemnes, but you are dismissed. This does not concern you."

With a reluctant bow and an apologetic glance at Ella, Hemnes left the throne room.

"You didn't have to make him leave," Ella said quietly. "Hemnes is your ward just as Torryn and I are."

"Hemnes knows I love him just as much as I love the rest of my wards." Queen Celosia replied. "He of all people should know better than to backtalk me."

"He wasn't backtalking!"

The Queen arched an eyebrow. "Who are you to speak of such things?"

Ella's eyes welled with tears. "Please, Aunt Celosia. I completed my side of the deal. Don't make me marry Linnmon. *Please.*"

The Queen sighed and sank back on her throne. "I cannot converse with you when you act like this. Your human half is too emotional."

Philip glanced in surprise at Ella, who deliberately avoided his gaze and adjusted her hair over her ears. He wasn't sure he heard the queen correctly. Ella was half-human? But that didn't make sense; she was an elven princess. Then again, hadn't Elliott alluded to her humanness before his murder? What had he called her? *Dirty halfling.*

"Can't I do something else to prove myself?" Ella spread her hands pleadingly, "I can't go back to how I was living before. No one should have to spend their lives locked away. Just because I'm half-human—just because I'm an embarrassment to you—doesn't mean I should have to live in solitude."

Queen Celosia brushed her hair over her shoulder. "You weren't living in solitude. I let Hemnes and Torryn choose to stay with you."

"They want to see the worlds too!" Ella insisted.

"Hemnes and Torryn are grateful to be alive, and it would be wise for you to learn from their example," Queen Celosia shot a pointed look at her niece, "I took you in when no one wanted you. When your father died, when Hemnes's parents were killed, when Torryn's mother sent him away, who took you in?"

"You did," Ella admitted.

"I did," Queen Celosia confirmed. "Without me, you would be orphaned and alone in the human world. Unwanted and unloved."

Philip could almost feel the sting of the queen's words. Ella hung her head, tears rolling down her cheeks. Feeling like an intruder in the conversation, Philip glanced away. He studied a trail of ivy that crept along the cracks in the stone ground. Maybe he was being cowardly, but under the queen's harsh, silver gaze, he almost missed the fair folk dungeons.

Queen Celosia's eyes slid to him. She studied him like someone might watch an ant moments before squishing it. After a moment, she gave a relenting sigh. "I am willing to be generous once more with you, Elestren. I want this human out of my kingdom. Return him safely within two weeks, and I shall reconsider your engagement to Linnmon. If you do not return him after two weeks have passed, you will stay locked in your room until your wedding."

Ella's face broke with relief. "Thank you, Aunt Celosia. I promise I won't fail you."

"I will not be disappointed again," the Queen warned.

"The humans will be back in their world immediately," Ella promised.

The Queen dismissed Ella with a wave of her hand. "I do not wish to see you anymore. Besides, you have quite a bit of work ahead of you."

"Of course," With a curt bow, Ella turned on her heel and exited the throne room. Philip followed close behind, not wanting to spend another second in the queen's presence.

As soon as the throne room doors slammed shut, Ella whirled to face him. He staggered back in surprise at the determination simmering in her deep brown eyes.

"I'm going to get you and your brother home," she vowed, "even if it's the last thing I do."

Chapter 10

Ella led Philip up to the North Tower, where Torryn, Hemnes, and Max waited. They all sat at a circular table in the tower, which was a round room isolated from the rest of the castle. A high, cone-shaped ceiling soared above their heads, and the arched, glassless windows let in a gentle breeze. A braided rug covered most of the stone floor, and multicolor pillows were scattered around like birdseed. Stacks of books littered the room, some tilting too precariously for Philip's liking.

Ella plopped down at the table and shoved aside a stack of books. Hemnes caught them before they crashed to the floor.

"Hemnes told me about your meeting with the queen," Torryn said, studying Ella closely.

Ella nodded. "She wasn't happy about Elliott's death. She thinks the fair folk will take this opportunity to declare war on our kingdom. She made a deal with me: we have two weeks to return Philip and Max to the human world. If we succeed, we'll finally be free. But if we fail, I'll be forced to marry Linnmon."

Hemnes drew in a sharp breath. "But the King banned travel between worlds. Returning the humans directly defies his laws."

"I'm sure he wouldn't mind us bending the rules a bit," Torryn folded his hands behind his head and kicked his feet up on the table, "All we have to do is find a way to open a gateway between worlds, and freedom is as good as ours."

Philip gave a skeptical scoff. In his experience, things were never that simple. If something could go wrong, it did. Besides, where would they even start? How did they go about opening an illegal, magical gateway? Would it take them two weeks to do so? The reunion was only supposed to last a week. Would their family remain at the campsite until they returned? What if the King of Corvus caught them and punished them for coming here in the first place? What if he refused to send them home, or worse, threw them in a dungeon forever?

Ugh. His head pounded, muddling his thoughts. He desperately needed a cup of coffee. Maybe some fresh air would do him some good.

"I'll be right back." Philip rose and left the tower before any one could respond. Though Ella called after him, he didn't slow his pace.

Descending a set of winding stairs, he let his feet carry him through the palace. He had no idea where he was going, but before he knew it, he emerged into a wide, square courtyard that was surrounded by weathered stone walls. Gravel paths meandered through the courtyard's lush gardens like a river through a delta. Strange plants grew all around him, varying from bowl-shaped flowers with midnight blossoms to small trees laden with plump, magenta fruits. Tendrils of ivy clung to every surface like veins. Most importantly, the courtyard was empty.

Philip collapsed on a stone bench and struggled out of his hoodie. A warm breeze brushed across his skin. Flowers perfumed the air, and he took a deep breath. At first, the fragrant, intoxicating scent reminded him of his mother's orchids. His heart lurched at the reminder of home. After that, the smell just made his headache worse.

What was wrong with him?

He'd never felt like this before—so trapped and hopeless...

Things couldn't get any worse; he and Max were trapped in a world full of dangerous magic, and their fate rested in the hands of strangers. On top of everything, his arm didn't work. Everything he'd ever worked towards was for nothing. He had pushed away his family and friends for a dream that would never come to fruition. His lifeline, the only thing that got him out of bed in the morning, was gone.

Marius's words echoed in Philip's head. *You are nothing. You will never be anything but a pathetic wannabe. You will never amount to anything.*

Marius was right. He always had been. Philip was just too stubborn to see it, too unwilling to admit the truth.

A familiar caw reached Philip's ears, dragging him from his thoughts. It was the same caw he heard every day on his walk from school when he passed the crow's nest hidden in the branches of the tree outside his apartment.

He craned his neck to see the small, black crow nestled in the leaves of a tree with purple blossoms. Its beady eyes glinted in the light of the setting sun as it cawed again. Philip tipped his head in imitation of the bird, studying it carefully.

"Hey there." A voice startled both Philip and the crow. Fluttering its inky black wings, the crow launched itself into the air and out of sight. Philip whirled around, coming face-to-face with Treave, who leaned casually against the trunk of a tree with lacy white leaves.

He almost didn't recognize her as the elf who had rescued him from the fair folk; she had traded her forest green army uniform for a billowy white top, deerskin trousers, and black riding boots. Her dark hair draped over her shoulder in a braided coil that hung down to her waist. The emerald earrings covering her pointed ears sparkled in the dim light.

"You come here often?" she asked with a casual grin.

Philip let out a breath. "You startled me."

"Sorry." Treave's eyebrows drew together. "Are you all right? You look…"

Philip imagined he looked awful. With his dirty, bloodstained clothing, messy hair, and the jagged cut across his cheek, he didn't think he qualified as a vision of 'alright'.

"…Terrible." Treave winced as she finished.

Sheepish, Philip scratched the back of his neck. "I know."

Silence lingered between them. Treave watched him with intelligent, dark eyes. Philip looked away, not knowing what else to do.

"What's going on?" Treave asked finally. "Everyone's been asking me about the human I rescued, but I had to tell them I didn't know any more than they did. There hasn't been a full-fledged human in this world for centuries, and now, all of the sudden, there are two of you."

"I don't know," Philip said, "No one will tell me anything worthwhile. All I want is to go home and forget about everything that's happened here."

So I can be miserable for the rest of my life, he didn't add.

"I'm sure the princess is doing everything she can to make sure you get home as soon as possible." When Philip didn't respond, Treave pushed away from the tree. "Come on. Let's get you something to eat. Food always makes things better."

With nothing better to do, Philip stood. "Lead the way."

Treave led him through the castle to another wide courtyard filled with tables, benches, and elves. Lanterns dangled from the trees overhead, swaying in the breeze. The moon peeked through the leaves as knighted dawned upon them.

Had it already been a day and a half since they arrived in this world? Philip didn't want to think about it. Instead, he focused on the heavily spiced aromas that made his mouth water. Heaping plates of foreign food filled the tables. At that moment, it didn't matter whether he recognized the food or not; he hadn't eaten all day.

He received open stares from many of the elves as he followed Treave through the maze of tables. They took a seat at the end of a long table, far enough away from any one else. An elf in a white uniform whisked platters of food and pitchers of drinks in front of them. Treave thanked the elf and immediately dug in, using her hands to eat straight from the platter.

Studying the food warily, Philip hesitated. Would it be safe for a human to eat? Although, if it poisoned him, would it really be so bad compared to his current situation?

Here goes nothing, he thought as he reached for what appeared to be a slice of meat with a green, jelly-like sauce. Steeling himself, he shoved the meat into his mouth. The tart sweetness of the sauce exploded on his tongue, but the taste that lingered after he swallowed burned with spices.

"What do you think?" Treave asked, nodding to the food.

"It's not bad," Philip admitted, "As long as it doesn't kill me."

Treave threw her head back and laughed, a loud, boisterous sound that drew the attention of the elves around them. Philip's cheeks heated at the disapproving frowns they received. He didn't say anything *that* funny.

"You're a very interesting human," Treave said once she finished laughing, "I don't quite know what to make of you, but I like a challenge."

Philip frowned; 'interesting' wasn't a word people typically used to describe him. Was she making fun of him?

Grinning at him, she tossed her braid over her shoulder and winked.

Wait…was she—was she *flirting* with him?

Absolutely not. Philip shoved the thought away the moment it crossed his mind. He never wanted anything to do with girls back home. Now, here he was, trapped in a magical world, thinking a girl—a magical elven soldier, nonetheless—was flirting with him.

He was being ridiculous.

Shaking his head, Philip tried to distract himself from his foolishness. His gaze drifted upwards to the sky, which looked like a painting come to life. It faded from vibrant pink to hazy purple to dark blue with the remnants of lingering stars. Stars were such a simple thing, yet they were almost as foreign to Philip as the magic in this world.

"Do you have stars in the human world?" Treave asked, noticing Philip's gaze fixed on the stars on the horizon.

Philip nodded. "We just can't see them where I'm from."

"I can't imagine a sky without stars," Treave said. "They are the preserved souls of the deceased elves who honored the laws of magic and kept the sacred traditions."

"That's… poetic."

"It's what every elf aspires to. Obeying the laws is essential to gain favor in life after death. If you don't keep the laws, your magic will become tainted and your soul won't be preserved."

"Is elven magic different than fair folk magic?" Philip had witnessed elven magic, but unlike fair folk magic, he couldn't discern a pattern or rule to it. Fair folk could only use a specific type of magic depending on the color they were born with, but that didn't apply to the elves. They could grow vines, move stones, and create explosions with nothing but powder and a few incantations.

Treave's jaw dropped. "They couldn't be more different!

115

Elven magic is sacred, and fair folk magic is unnatural. Elves believe magic is a part of nature that is there for us to care for and use in moderation. We spend our lives following the laws, giving offerings, and learning to use magic the way it was intended. Fair folk believe magic belongs to them. They use it however they want without consequence. It's not the way we elves believe things are supposed to be."

An ironic laugh threatened to escape Philip's lips. Hearing an elf call fairy magic "unnatural" was a cruel joke from the universe. It made sense for each race to have their own views on magic, though he hadn't expected the beliefs to be so opposite. He wondered if the elves were right, though. Back in Haderra, Dash had healed his shoulder using fair folk magic. If it weren't for the magic that the elves considered to be so "unnatural", Philip would have died.

"Elves use specially made powders to help us summon magic from nature, while the fair folk claim they have magic in their blood," Treave continued. "Elves use magic for many different things, while fair folk only use their specific 'color' magic. The only thing we can agree on is that using magic keeps us alive and sane. If someone were to stop using magic, they would lose it completely and either die or go insane. The only race that can survive without magic is humans."

"Lucky us," Philip muttered. If he spent the rest of his life without encountering magic ever again, he would be more than thrilled. Magic got them into this mess to begin with. He didn't know what type of magic brought them here, and he didn't care what type of magic got them out.

"So," Treave propped her elbows on the table, "What are you going to do once you get back to the human world?"

Philip raised an eyebrow at her confidence. "What makes

116

you think we'll be able to get back?"

"Just humor me."

With a sigh, Philip pressed a hand to his temple, where a dull ache throbbed. "I'm going to make a cup of coffee."

Treave's laugh surprised him. This time, the sound satisfied him more than he cared to admit.

"I've always wanted to see the human world," Treave mused, "Before I met you, I imagined everything all grey and withered without magic, but you don't fit that description. So, what's it like?"

"It's not as bright, and the people are less… magical,"

Treave snorted. "Well, *obviously.* But I want to know what your life was like. What did you do for fun? What did you live for? What made you happy?"

Philip faltered. What *did* he do for fun? He spent all of his time working or doing school. He holed himself up in his room and drowned his thoughts out with music. He lived for work and school. He didn't have time for happiness or any other emotions for that matter; he made sure he never had a moment to stop and think about any of it.

Was his life really that mundane? Did he really live for so little?

Why did Treave care about any of this?

Mercifully, he was saved from giving an answer when Max ran up to the table and barreled into him with a hug.

"Philip!" Max cried, "We've been looking for you all night!"

Ella arrived a few seconds later with Hemnes and Torryn in tow.

"Thank goodness," she breathed a sigh of relief when she saw him, "I was worried something happened to you."

Philip furrowed his brows. Why did they care if anything

117

happened to him? "I left less than an hour ago."

"Yeah, but this world has *magic*," Max said, "You could've been eaten by a monster or turned into a pumpkin!" He glanced at Treave. "You could even be a shapeshifter!"

Playing along, Treave gave a devilish grin. "You never know. Any one of us could be a mermaid in disguise, or an ancient monster healer, or a spy for the King of Corvus."

Max tilted his head. "Who's the King of Corvus?"

Treave leaned in and hunched her shoulders like she was about to tell a ghost story around a campfire. "The King of Corvus is an ancient immortal who sees all and knows all. He has eyes in the trees, and his monsters prowl in the dark. And do you know what the monsters eat? Their favorite snack is naughty little children who disobey their parents."

"Woah," Max's eyes widened, but he didn't look remotely afraid, "Can I meet him someday?"

"No one has heard of him for years. Everyone has forgotten what he looks like, but they say he has wrinkled hands with black talons instead of fingernails."

"Cool," Max studied his fingernails, no doubt imagining what it would be like to have talons.

"Actually," Torryn interjected, "Elestren has seen the King. She went to his island to make a deal with him."

Awestruck, Max turned to Ella. "Is that true?"

Ella ducked her head. "I went to the island, but I didn't see the King's face. He stood at a window and kept his back to me the entire time."

Hemnes's face twitched at the mention of Ella's visit with the King. He ran a hand through his long, auburn hair and said, "I think we have more immediate matters to worry about right now."

"You're right," Treave agreed, "I hate to leave so soon, but I have quite a bit of unfinished work. If you'll excuse me, Your Highness," she stood and swept a bow to Ella. Turning over her shoulder, she winked at Philip before she strode from the courtyard.

Once Treave was gone, Torryn collapsed dramatically into her chair, "I haven't had a proper meal in days."

Ella, Hemnes, and Max took their seats as well. When they sat down, the elves around them rose and moved to other tables further away. Philip watched them, noting their upturned noses and furtive sneers.

"Don't mind them," Ella said, gesturing to the other elves, "They're members of the court. They don't particularly like any of the queen's wards, the three of us included. They're not that bad, though."

"Manticores aren't that bad," Torryn deadpanned.

Philip flinched phantom pain shooting through his limp arm at the mention of those monsters.

Max frowned and spoke through a mouthful of food, "But you're a princess. Shouldn't they love you?"

"Both of my parents are dead," Ella explained, her voice hitching, "I'm living here courtesy of my aunt's goodwill, and the court doesn't approve of us, even princesses like me and Everleigh."

Torryn rolled his eyes. "Those bigots are too preoccupied with their precious reputations to go against the status quo. At least my reputation was shattered at my scandalous birth. These court politics can be dreadful if you actually care."

"It must be so hard to be burdened with such a large chip on your shoulder," Hemnes said, shooting him a teasing grin.

Torryn sniffed indignantly and heaped a pile of food onto his

119

plate. "Not all of us can uphold such precious honor and duty."

"I have sworn to follow in my parents' footsteps and uphold their legacy," Hemnes replied.

"At least one of us is a good son," Torryn muttered.

"Can you two stop bickering and eat?" Ella interrupted, glancing pointedly between Hemnes and Torryn.

Hemnes ducked his head like a scolded puppy, while Torryn *hmphed* and tossed his hair over his shoulder.

"This is so good!" Max exclaimed, shoveling two salted rolls into his mouth. His cheeks puffed out like a squirrel.

"The food here is much different than in the human world," Ella said, "It's delicious, but there's nothing better than deep-dish pizza."

Philip raised his eyebrows. "You mean thin-crust?" That was the way they ate it back home. Any alternative was unacceptable.

Ella narrowed her eyes in challenge. "Where in the human world are you from?"

"Queens, New York."

"That explains a lot."

"Where are *you* from?"

Ella lifted her chin proudly. "The beautiful windy city of Chicago."

Philip couldn't hide his surprise. "You're a city girl?"

"Born and raised," Ella paused, "Well, almost."

Strange. Philip felt a sort of solidarity with Ella, a mutual understanding of what it was like to grow up in the city. He'd never had this kind of bond with any one else before. How much did she remember of Chicago? Had she ever memorized the streets of her borough, knowing each alleyway like the back of her hand? Had she ever stood in the middle of the crowded streets, wondering if they would swallow her whole?

Hemnes glanced from Philip to Ella, a small crease forming between his eyebrows. He opened his mouth to speak, but Torryn, apparently bored with the conversation, cut him off with an exaggerated yawn.

"I, for one, am exhausted," Torryn announced, "I have been living in a dungeon for the past few moons, and I am eager to get a good night's rest."

"We should all get to bed," Ella said as she stood, "Tomorrow, we have a long day ahead of us."

They left the dining room and followed Ella through the palace. She led them to a long hallway lined with ornately carved doors. Stopping in front of a door carved with a multitude of birds, she spoke to Philip and Max. "Well, here we are. You two can share this room. My room is right across the hall, and Hemnes and Torryn's rooms are on either side of mine. The three of us normally have the guest wing to ourselves, but we're happy to have more company."

Philip frowned; they were the Queen's wards, yet they stayed in the guest rooms like inconvenient relatives that refused to leave?

Ella shook her head as if she knew what Philip was thinking. "Don't read too much into it. My aunt does the best she can."

When Philip remained silent, Ella turned to Hemnes and Torryn. "Go find some extra clothing that might fit Philip and Max. I'm sure they'd like to change out of their dirty clothes."

Nodding, Hemnes and Torryn disappeared into their rooms.

Ella placed her hands on her knees and stooped to be eye-level with Max. "Why don't you head to your room and see if it's up to your standards?"

Max, who could barely keep his eyes open, gave a sleepy nod. Mumbling, "Okay," he stumbled into their room.

Philip moved to follow, but Ella stopped him. "I wanted to speak to you alone."

"What is it?" He couldn't help his wariness; normally, when people asked to speak with him alone, things didn't end well.

"I wanted to ask if you had any questions. I'd imagine you had a lot of them, and while I can't answer them all, I'll try my best."

In his surprise, it took Philip a moment to piece together a cohesive thought. After a moment of consideration, he asked, "How did we even get here? If the human world doesn't have magic, and travel between worlds is forbidden, this shouldn't have been possible."

Ella's expression turned somber. "That's the problem. I don't know how you got here or how we're going to send you back, but we *will* find a way, no matter what."

Philip wasn't so sure about that. Dissatisfied but unsurprised by the lack of an answer, he chose a different, less complicated question. "Isn't it a bit convenient that everyone here speaks English?"

Ella's somber expression broke into a laugh. It wasn't a mocking laugh, rather a knowing one. "That was one of my first questions too. Everyone in this world is gifted with the magic of universal communication. There are no languages here. It's just," She waved her hands in a vague gesture, "Communication."

Philip frowned, irritated by his lack of understanding. "That doesn't make sense."

Ella didn't seem bothered or annoyed. "When the humans tampered with forbidden magic—technology—they were banished from this world into a world of their own. Part of the punishment was losing any traces of magic they had, including the magic of communication, hence the different languages.

122

Someone with magic can speak to a human, and the human will hear the words in their own language. In turn, the person with the magic will understand the human's language."

Finally, *something* made a bit of sense. Ella's answer was congruent with everything Nathan, Adrian, and Dash explained before. At the very least, Philip appreciated a logical explanation for something that shouldn't exist ordinarily.

Hemnes reappeared moments later with a stack of clothing, which he handed to Philip.

"Thanks," Philip said as he struggled to balance the clothes in his one-armed grip.

Hemnes gave Philip a weak smile. "If they don't fit, Torryn might have something better."

"This will be fine, thanks," Philip replied. Anything was better than the torn, dirty, bloodstained clothing they wore now.

"Thank you, Hemnes," Ella said, "You're a lifesaver."

Hemnes wrapped his arms around Ella and planted a kiss on top of her head. "Anything for you, Elestren."

Before things could get awkward, Philip bid Ella and Hemnes a hurried goodnight, and let them have their privacy. Thankfully, Max had left the door cracked open, allowing him to push it open with his shoulder. The sight of the small, wooden bed in the corner of the room was enough to make the weight of the past day-and-a-half crash down on him. With food in his stomach and exhaustion numbing his mind, he didn't bother with the change of clothing Hemnes loaned him—not when deep, glorious sleep was within reach.

Collapsing next to Max on the straw mattress, Philip fell fast asleep.

Chapter 11

Dash ordered breakfast in Elliott's chambers—*his* chambers now, he supposed.

Sleeping in Elliott's chambers sent a ghostly shiver down Dash's spine, but Nathan and Adrian had insisted. They'd mentioned something about stepping into his role as Sovereign Prince and "making a statement."

Dash didn't think it mattered what room he slept in. Though he wasn't sure how much of a statement sleeping in his dead cousin's bedroom made, who was he to argue with his best friends, who had newly been appointed as his royal advisors?

He *was* the Sovereign Prince, but that didn't change who he was as a person. He always trusted Nathan and Adrian no matter what, and he always would. Royalty or not.

While Dash had spent the night in Elliott's chambers, he hadn't slept a single minute. How could he? His cousin was dead, the kingdom was in turmoil, and everyone had their eyes on him. His first steps as Sovereign Prince would be critical.

Instead of sleeping, he'd hauled books on foreign policy to his chambers and poured over them for hours. He knew little about diplomacy, economics, trade, treaties, or anything else to do with politics; Elliott had made it clear that though Dash was a prince, he was half-human and would never be the Sovereign Prince. Fixing Elliott's mistakes would prove to be a daunting job, but Dash could do it. He had to. He owed it to the people of Haderra.

Dash skimmed a book on government reform as his

breakfast was delivered to his room on a golden tray. When he saw the extravagance of the meal, he gave a small smile.

The heaping tray of lemon pastries, buttered sweet rolls, and fresh fruit made Dash's mouth water. These foods were as human as fair folk breakfasts got. After the equivalent of six years in the magical world, Dash still hadn't acquired a taste for boiled harpy eggs and jackalope sausage with mushroom jam.

"Thank you, Bridget," he said to the servant girl as she set the tray on the only corner of his desk that wasn't piled with books. "Please give Helen my gratitude."

Helen, the palace cook, had always been a motherly figure to everyone she encountered, and today, she prepared a breakfast assortment of Dash's favorite foods.

Bridget dropped into a curtsey, green curls bobbing. "As you wish, Your Sovereignty."

Dash's heart sank at the new formality. He and Bridget had been friends since she'd first arrived at the palace as a chambermaid. It had taken a few years of prodding and pleading, but he'd eventually gotten her to simply call him Dash. Many long afternoons had been spent studying with Bridget in the garden or practicing waltz steps with her in abandoned hallways.

Now, she wouldn't meet his eyes. She bowed her head and folded her hands demurely.

Dash tried not to let his disappointment show. "You are dismissed, Bridget."

Bridget curtsied again and left without another word.

Sighing, Dash plucked a lemon pastry off the tray and turned back to his reading.

This was never supposed to happen. Had Elliott lived a long life and produced heirs to carry along his pure bloodline, Dash would never have been put in this position. A half-human with half an education and no clue how to run a kingdom had no right to be Sovereign Prince of Haderra.

A glob of filling spilled out of the pastry, splattering on the crinkled, yellowing paper of the ancient book. Dash darted a glance at his guards before scooping the filling off the page and into his mouth. The guards paid him no attention.

Giving another sigh, Dash propped his chin on his hands and continued reading.

When he was re-reading a paragraph on social welfare programs for the third time, Nathan and Adrian burst into Dash's chambers. Dash tore his gaze from the words, thankful for the distraction.

Nathan and Adrian exchanged a familiar glance at the sight of him. Frowning, Dash ran a hand through his curls; he'd been friends with Nathan and Adrian long enough to recognize their concern. He could only imagine what he looked like after a night of flipping through pages and pages of endless words, which flowed in and out of his head like the tide.

But everything was perfectly fine.

He could ignore the heaviness of his limbs and the ache of exhaustion under his ribcage. He could heal the dull ache that blossomed behind his eyes. He would push through this day and the next and the next for the rest of his life. He would fix Elliott's mistakes, even if he died trying.

Everything would be alright.

Dash stood, inhaling deeply. He tried to manage a grin, but it faltered as Nathan and Adrian swept into militant bows.

"Good morning, Your Sovereignty," Nathan said.

First Bridget, now Nathan and Adrian... Couldn't they just treat him normally? He hadn't even been officially crowned Sovereign Prince of Haderra, and already, he was tired of the stiff

126

formalities.

He dismissed them with a wave of his hand. "I told you not to bow or call me 'Your Sovereignty,' 'Your Majesty,' or 'Sire'." He took a ragged breath and ran a hand down his face.

"As you wish, Your Highness." Adrian met Dash's glare with a mischievous grin.

Dash sank back in his seat, relieved that Adrian still teased him like normal. He struggled to remember why he'd summoned them. It must have been something about policy or reform or report or… the daily briefing.

"Do you have any news for me?" he asked.

"Well, Sire," Nathan began, ignoring the withering look Dash threw him, "we have received news of riots throughout the kingdom."

"Riots?" Dash repeated incredulously, "But the kingdom is supposed to be in a time of mourning. Why are they rioting?" Protests were one thing, but riots were another beast entirely. What did the people have to riot about? Was there an issue regarding the labor unions? Had the Fair Lords issued a decree against the wishes of the people?

Nathan pressed his blue lips together. "I fear this is a result of a cumulation of issues. Many people believe you should not be seated on the throne of Haderra."

"Oh." This wasn't news to Dash. *He* didn't believe he should be Sovereign Prince. His coronation and gilding ceremonies weren't for ten days, as was customary after the death of a sovereign. Couldn't the people have waited to start an uproar until after the time of mourning passed?

"The riots are getting dangerous. We've sent guards to settle the issues in the most violent areas and we have tripled palace security."

"Are they upset because I'm young, or because I'm human?"

"Both, I'm afraid."

"That makes sense." Dash sighed. "What can I do? Do they want me to abdicate? Who would become the next sovereign?"

"The people don't have any specific candidates yet. Many believe it should go to one of the Fair Lords, while others believe the matter should be put to vote."

"We aren't democrats like those stupid pixies," Adrian muttered.

Dash considered this. He supposed any of the Fair Lords would be a good alternative. The Fair Lords were representatives of each color of magic. Each of them held titles in court and high power in the government. Aside from the reigning sovereign, they were the most powerful fair folk in Haderra. But the problem would be deciding which Lord would become Sovereign. Each color would want their representative to become Sovereign. The rest of the colors would cause an uproar when their representatives weren't selected. If they held a democratic vote as they did in Eabith, the pixie kingdom, the fair folk with green magic would be the overwhelming majority due to the size of their population. Either way, it could be a recipe for disaster.

"What do you think I should do?" Dash asked.

"No matter what you do, people will be unhappy," Nathan said. "Half the people want your bloodline to continue ruling Haderra, human or not. If you were to abdicate, that bloodline would end. These people will fight to keep you on the throne no matter what.

"However, the other half will not stand to see any one with human blood sitting on the throne. They demand that you abdicate within a week of your coronation or be deposed."

Dash took a moment to compose himself. He noticed a paper

cut on his thumb and focused his energy on healing the abrasion. A soft yellow glow spread across his skin as warmth seeped into his finger. There. Much better.

"Why else are they upset?" he asked. "You said there were multiple issues."

"Ah, yes," A royal blue flush blossomed in Nathan's cheeks. "When Elliott was murdered, all of his guards were killed in the throne room, and we lost dozens more on top of that. These guards were draft subjects, self-enlisted, and even a few reserve volunteers. The people are demanding justice for their deaths. They want the elves responsible for the attack found and held accountable for the deaths they caused."

A heavy silence fell over the room. Even the guards lining the walls responded to this claim with the slightest change in expression and posture. Lips quirked into frowns and grips tightened on spears. Dash wondered how many of them wished to see him abdicate and how many of them would fight to keep the last of Elliott's kin on the throne.

The thought that people *wanted* him to be Sovereign, that they would follow his lead, kindled a small flame in Dash's heart. Some of his people believed in him. Nathan and Adrian believed in him. Rhett believed in him.

Dash could not let these people down. An idea began to form in his head. If his people were divided, they would have to be united somehow. Perhaps against a common enemy... This idea might cause more problems than it solved, but it was a risk he was willing to take.

"Nathan, set aside some time for me to visit my brother. Adrian, schedule an address to the Fair Lords as soon as possible."

Nathan and Adrian exchanged a glance. "What are you

planning?"

"Something that's going to change everything."

The next morning, the sun was just barely peeking over the horizon when Philip and Max arrived at the dining courtyard, where they were supposed to meet the others. Sleepy elves milled around with steaming mugs of dark liquid that Philip desperately hoped was coffee. The light of the rising sun filtered through the leaves, casting sunbeams across the wooden tables. Birds perched on the unlit lanterns overhead, serenading everyone with a chorus of unharmonized chirping.

The elves didn't pay much attention to them as they wove through the courtyard towards the largest table, where Ella, Hemnes, and Torryn were already waiting. Ella and Hemnes welcomed them with cheerful smiles, while Torryn groaned and hunched over the mug he clutched.

"Good morning," Ella greeted, "I hope you slept well."

"That bed was so comfy!" Max exclaimed. He wasted no time in stuffing strange meat and bread into his mouth. At least he wasn't a picky eater like most other ten-year-old.

"It's too early to be awake," Torryn muttered.

"You say that every morning," Hemnes said with a teasing grin. Though his hair was braided back neatly and his clothing was immaculate, bluish circles shadowed his eyes.

As they ate, a pounding ache enveloped Philip's skull. On a normal day, he drank three cups of coffee just to get him through the morning. Now, after two days without a single drop of coffee, caffeine withdrawal attacked him with full force.

"Do you have any coffee?" he asked.

Ella shook her head. "Coffee and anything with caffeine is an exclusively human thing. It's highly addictive and damaging

130

to your body, you know."

Philip stifled a groan. Just great. Of course this world didn't have caffeine. They didn't have any modern technology, even something as basic as a faucet or a zipper. It was ridiculous.

"You should try this," Hemnes nodded to his mug, "It's beetroot tea."

"I'll pass," Philip grumbled. He tried to distract himself from the ache in his head by eating something. Though the savory, heavily salted elven food made his stomach turn, he refused to let his nausea get the best of him.

Once everyone finished eating, Ella led them back into the castle towards the library. The hallways of the castle blurred together as they walked. They eventually stopped in front of a set of double doors made of heavy, dark wood engraved with ivy designs. Silver leaf inlaid the engravings, and the ornamented, silver handle gleamed with polish.

When Ella pushed the doors open, the scent of dust and old paper greeted Philip like a familiar friend. The ivy-decorated ceiling soared high above their heads, making room for the gnarled oak tree that grew in the center of the library. Rays of sunshine poured in from the arched windows, casting a halo around the tree's crown of leaves. Countless stories of curved bookshelves formed a semi-circle around the tree, each shelf filled to overflowing with books and scrolls made of thick, yellowing paper.

In a chair beneath the shade of the tree sat Treave, who was examining a long scroll. She glanced up, her expression brightening when she saw them. She swept a militant bow towards Ella, but her eyes remained locked with Philip's.

"Your Highness," Treave said, "What bring you here?"

Ella glanced around the empty library to make sure no one

was around to overhear. "We're here to find a way to get Philip and Max home. I thought there might be something in the ancient texts that could open a gateway without alerting the King. Care to join us? We could use all the help we can get."

Treave clapped a fist over her heart, every bit the dutiful soldier. Philip didn't miss the wink she shot at him. "I would be honored to serve any way I can, Your Highness."

"Well…" Ella placed her hands on her hips, surveying the shelves. "Where should we start?"

They claimed a table under the boughs of the oak tree and set to work, piling the table with stacks of books and mountains of scrolls. Max didn't offer much help as he jumped on one of the couches beneath the tree, trying to grab a branch so he could climb it.

Philip settled at the table and began to skim the book in front of him. All of the books and scrolls must have been written with communication magic because he could read them all. He scanned page after page, unsure what he was looking for. Letters and words whirled through his head like a hurricane as he searched.

Hours passed, and no one found anything. At some point, Ella had curled up on a couch with Hemnes, who twirled a strand of his hair around his finger as he read. Torryn sprawled at their feet, twisting his earrings absently. Treave perched in the oak tree on a branch directly above Philip. Occasionally, she leaned down to grab another book from the towering stacks. Max had taken to making airplanes out of the loose papers that fell out of the books. A servant brought them lunch so they could eat while they searched.

As the day went on, frustration began to mount in Philip. His mind grew number with each sentence he read. Despite this, he continued the seemingly endless search; they had no other options.

Pushing aside a scroll, he rubbed his eyes and rested his head on his hand. They hadn't even begun to put a dent in the piles of books surrounding them.

It was hopeless. They could search forever and never find anything.

As soon as that thought crossed Philip's mind, Ella shot to her feet. "I found it!" She cried triumphantly.

Philip launched out of his seat and squeezed between Hemnes and Torryn to read over Ella's shoulder. She held a heavy, leather-bound book with creamy white pages that were fresher and crisper than the crumbling, yellow ones he had grown accustomed to.

On the top of the page, elegant, swooping handwriting scrawled, *"Maryn, my love, we will be together soon."* Below was a list of objects and simple directions:

An elven ruler's golden vessel
A fair folk ruler's shard of glass
A pixie ruler's sacred boughs
A mermaid ruler's precious armor
A giant ruler's guarded treasure
A dwarf ruler's heart of stone
A human's dying breath
On the island of monsters these items belong,
to open a gateway at the crow's song.

Philip scanned the list again and again, not wanting to believe his eyes. What was this? Nothing on the list made sense except the very last item. A human's dying breath. The air

133

squeezed out of his lungs. Did this mean one of them had to die for the other to get home?

Were the rest of the items some sort of riddle? He had no clue how magic worked but was he supposed to believe these random objects could get them home? Some of these items seemed impossible to collect. How were they supposed to capture a human's dying breath?

This was madness. Absolute madness.

"Philip?" Ella's voice startled him from his thoughts. He glanced up to find everyone staring at him. He became acutely aware of the fact that he had tangled his hand in his hair and was breathing in short gasps.

He met Ella's gaze and winced at the concern swimming in her deep brown eyes as she asked, "Are you all right?"

He forced himself to release an even breath and extract his hand from his hair. "What does any of this mean?" he asked, ignoring her question. "It doesn't make sense."

"We'll have to figure out the riddles, but aren't you relieved?" Ella gestured to the paper. "We found a way to get you home!"

Philip wasn't relieved in the slightest. The coils of anxiety constricted as he snatched the book away from Ella and reviewed the list again. He should be grateful—excited, even. These people were sacrificing their time and energy to find a way for them to get home, but there were too many unknowns and too many 'if''s in the equation.

"How long will it take to find these items?" Treave asked.

Ella pursed her lips. "We have two weeks to get them home. Hopefully, it shouldn't take much longer than that."

Hopefully. Not 'definitely', or even 'probably'. Hopefully. Just great.

"We should start figuring out the riddles," Treave said, "The sooner we figure them out, the better."

Hemnes took the book from Philip. "First is *'the elven ruler's golden vessel'*."

"Whatever that means," Torryn muttered under his breath.

Hemnes set the list on the table, angling it so everyone had a clear view. He made a thoughtful humming noise. "Perhaps the vessel is talking about a ship. The queen has a private skiff, but is it golden?"

From the branches above, Treave shook her head. "All of our ships are wooden. Gold is too heavy and expensive."

They fell into a pensive silence. Ella propped her chin and chewed her lip as she thought. Philip could practically see the wheels turning in her mind. Though he hated to admit it, he would be of no use in figuring out a riddle from the magical world.

Ella's head snapped up. "That's it! We use powder to perform magic. That makes the powder a vessel for magic, right?"

"Of course," Hemnes said, realization dawning on him. "Elestren, you are a genius!"

"One problem," Torryn interjected. "The queen would never willingly part with a single grain of powder."

"Then we'll just have to take it against her will," Ella said.

Philip's eyebrows crept up; Ella didn't strike him as particularly ruthless. He had to respect that kind of ambition, even if it involved committing treason.

Hemnes ran a hand through his auburn hair. "How do you suggest we do that? If we are caught, the queen will never forgive us."

"Torryn," Ella turned to address him, "Do you know which

guards will be stationed in front of my aunt's chambers tonight?"

"I can find out," Torryn said with a smirk.

"Good. We may need to secure a bribe. Maybe you can work some of that charming magic of yours and get them to turn a blind eye while you sneak in and steal a handful of my aunt's powder. You'll be the least conspicuous, and we all know you're the fastest and most cunning."

Torryn heaved a dramatic sigh. "Flattery will only get you so far, Princess." But from the way his icy eyes gleamed at the prospect of stealing from the Queen, Philip guessed that was his version of a vehement 'yes.'

"This could probably be considered treason," Treave said, voicing Philip's thoughts. She didn't sound too concerned at the prospect, though.

Ella waved her away. "This is for a good cause. My aunt will never know."

"I'm not accusing, just commenting. After all, you're the princess. What reason could you possibly have to steal from your aunt?" Treave said with a conspiratory wink. "It would be a shame if some shadowy figure was spotted sneaking out of the castle at the same time, only to disappear before any one could catch them."

A slow grin crept across Torryn's face. "Now, *that* is an idea."

"That could be dangerous," said Hemnes, ever the cautious one. It intrigued Philip to see who played what role in their little trio. "What if you get caught? They would end your career in the army and throw you in the dungeon, even if they had no proof you stole anything."

Treave shrugged. "I'm willing to serve my princess in any way needed." She mimicked Torryn's grin, "Besides, I like high stakes."

Hemnes had a point, but Treave was right. Her idea would keep the guards occupied with a wild goose chase and would make sure they didn't suspect any one inside the castle to be the thief.

It was ingenious.

"Perfect," Ella said, "Now, why don't we work out the details over dinner? I'm famished."

As they walked to the dining courtyard, they continued to discuss the possibilities. Their semblance of a plan fueled the conversation, inspiring confidence in the others. Philip, however, was still wary.

"Which fair folk ruler applies to this list, Elliott or Dash?" Hemnes wondered aloud. "Elliott is dead, but Dash is half-human. Would it still count with either?"

"I hadn't thought of that," Ella said as they took their seats at the largest table. "Maybe Nathan and Adrian would know?"

Philip had mixed feelings about Nathan and Adrian. Sure, they had defended him from the manticores, but they had also thrown him into the dungeons. They'd betrayed their Sovereign, murdering him under orders from a monster king. Could any one trust people who would betray their ruler to such an extent?

Hemnes expressed the same sentiments. "We have to figure this out on our own." He insisted. "Nathan and Adrian will be our last resort."

"They helped us free the elves and kill Elliott," Ella argued as she filled her goblet, "They upheld their end of the deal. I know you don't trust them, but they've proven to be nothing but trustworthy and dedicated."

Unconvinced, Hemnes turned to Torryn for support. "What do you think?"

Torryn rolled his eyes. "I *love* being put in the middle of your arguments."

"Not helpful, Torryn," Hemnes said with a frown.

Torryn shrugged and took a bite of bread. "Not helpful to *you*."

"Nathan and Adrian are cool," Max said. He used his fingers to grab a piece of meat. "On that island, they said they could help get me and Philip home."

Ella shot Hemnes a pointed look. "See? We can at least ask them to help. The worst they could do is say no."

"I could think of far worse things," Torryn muttered low enough for only Philip to hear.

"Are you going to fly to Haderra simply to ask them for help?" Hemnes asked.

"Why not? They might know something about the other items."

After a moment, Hemnes gave a relenting sigh. "When do we leave?"

"You're not coming with us," Ella said.

Hemnes narrowed his eyes. "If I'm not going, then who do you mean by 'us'?"

"I'll go with Philip and Max. You and Torryn need to stay here and cover for me. My aunt can't know about this, or she'll know we're the ones who stole her powder. If she knew, she could have us banished for breaking the laws of magic."

Hemnes pressed his lips together and glanced at Philip with the barest flicker of envy in his grey eyes. Torryn scowled, unhappy with the arrangement as well.

Before either of them could speak, Max asked, "Can't you just explain to your aunt why we have to leave?"

"My aunt kept me locked in the castle for eight years just

because I'm half-human," Ella explained, her eyes filling with tears, "When she finally let me go on a mission, she claims I did everything wrong. She'll never let me leave, even to help you."

Hemnes and Torryn exchanged a glance. A silent conversation passed between them, not unlike how Nathan and Adrian often communicated.

Finally, Hemnes sighed. "All right. I respect your decision. When will you depart?"

"We leave at dawn," Ella said, "But first, we have a vessel to steal."

Chapter 12

Philip waited patiently in a flower-filled courtyard, just as Ella instructed him. He had been sitting on a cool stone bench for an hour, long after the sun sank below the horizon.

The lanterns above him swayed in the breeze, the warm light flickering like a candle. Brilliant, white lilies bloomed in the absence of the sun, heavily perfuming the night air with their sweet scent.

There were worse places to wait.

He peered through the trees to see the position of the moon. When the moon reached the tip of the North Tower's spire, Treave would be in position, and Ella, Hemnes, and Torryn would be on the move.

Philip paced under a tree, twisting a palm-sized leaf in his fingers. He distracted himself with thoughts of the world around him. The cool night air pricked at his skin, and a shiver raced down his spine. Though his knee-high boots were comfortable, he couldn't say the same for the formal outfit Torryn loaned him. At least the too-short sleeves and awkwardly tight trousers distracted him from what was to come.

If they were caught, the consequences would be grave. No one stole from the elven queen without suffering a fitting punishment. The outcome of their entire plan depended on nothing more than distraction and darkness. They could be found out at any moment. He pictured a full elven guard charging in to arrest him. If that happened, would he and Max ever get home? The uncertainty clawed at his brain, circling his thoughts into anxious loops.

He thought of Max, tucked in his bed, sleeping peacefully. Max had begged to have a part in the plan, but the decision to send him to bed had been unanimous. Despite Max's grumbling and complaining and pouting, Philip knew they'd made the right decision in leaving him.

A flash of light caught Philip's eye. That was Torryn's signal. He forced himself to release a steady breath. Letting the leaf flutter to the ground, he paced back to the stone bench where Treave would meet him shortly.

Treave had the riskiest job, but she didn't seem concerned. In fact, it was quite the opposite. At even the mention of danger, a daring gleam had sparkled in her eyes, and her cheeks had flushed with excitement. She was a soldier; she thrived in this kind of high-stakes environment. Philip could easily imagine her perched on the edge of the queen's windowsill, rope in one gloved hand, grappling hook in the other.

When Philip had suggested they use a grappling hook, he'd half-expected them to give him blank stares and ask what a grappling hook was. Thankfully, grappling hooks weren't the sort of technology the elves considered "forbidden magic." He was quickly growing frustrated with the blurred lines of what they forbid and allowed.

A bottle of red wine and two glasses sat on the edge of the bench like the subjects of a still life painting. Mercifully, Ella had thought to uncork the bottle for him before she left with Hemnes and Torryn. Philip carefully filled two glasses and set the bottle aside. Torryn had managed to acquire the wine with suspicious ease. He had to applaud the efficiency, at least.

Shouts arose in the distance. This was it. Treave would be here any minute. His heart thundered. What if she didn't make it?

141

What if she was caught? What if they were *both* caught?

Was he worrying too much?

Seconds later, Treave raced into the courtyard. She tore off her black cloak, and the skirts of an emerald green evening gown spilled out. Had she scaled a tower in that dress? Shaking his head, Philip forced himself to concentrate. He snatched the cloak and shoved it into a bush as she ripped her hair out of its tight braid. For someone who had just raced halfway across the castle, she didn't seem winded at all.

He and Treave collapsed on the stone bench and snatched up the glasses of wine just as three guards burst into the courtyard. Immediately, they fanned out, like dogs on a hunt.

The tallest guard approached Philip and Treave. "Have either of you seen a strange figure run through here?"

Philip tried his best to look surprised and concerned, lifting his eyebrows and widening his eyes just so. "I'm afraid we haven't. Is everything alright?" He was thankful for the dimness of the lanterns that obscured his expression; acting wasn't one of his talents.

Treave casually swirled her wine in her glass, a vision of calm and innocence. "I'm sure we would have noticed something so suspicious." She settled a hand on Philip's knee. "The two of us were just enjoying this lovely evening together."

The guard didn't look convinced. "Search the area," she commanded, "Someone could be hiding in the foliage."

It took all the self-control Philip had to keep his knee from bouncing with anxiety. If the guards found Treave's cloak hidden in the bushes, they would have grounds for suspicion. Would the guards arrest them over a discarded cloak?

Treave's eyes trailed the guards passively, but Philip could see a plan forming in her head. As the guards neared the bush

142

where Treave's cloak was hidden, his heart rate sped. Treave set her jaw and leaned towards him.

"Follow my lead," she whispered, slipping her hand into his.

Treave pulled him in front of the bush where her cloak was hidden. The guards neared them on either side. She reached up and cupped his face in her hands, forcing him to look at her. Her hands were warm and soft.

"Don't enjoy this too much," she said with a grin.

Before Philip could comprehend what was happening, Treave stood on her tiptoes and pressed her lips against his.

He froze. This couldn't be happening. Never in his entire life had someone invaded his personal space so thoroughly. This was a calculated gesture, to be sure. This kiss was only for show. It was a smart, logical move. Surely, the guards wouldn't interrupt their kiss to search a single bush.

Still, he remained frozen, unable to withdraw or lean closer. His brain seized up, refusing to process anything through the shock.

Treave took charge, moving his hand so it rested against her waist. The silk of her gown was cool and smooth under his touch. She deepened the kiss, raking her thin, elegant fingers through his hair. The scent of saddle leather clung to her skin. Her lips tasted like wine.

After a moment that lasted a lifetime, Treave pulled away. Their lips were inches apart, and Philip could feel the warmth of her breath on his face as she whispered, "Worked like a charm."

The guards made a wide arc around them, deliberately averting their eyes.

"Elves are so prudent that a simple kiss will practically clear a room," Treave said with a mischievous grin.

Sure enough, the guards hurried out of the courtyard as

143

quickly as possible, discomfort evident on their faces. Relief washed over him. By some miracle, they were safe. When the guards were out of earshot, Treave let out a laugh. "I didn't think that would work."

Philip managed to press his lips into a semblance of a smile. "Hopefully the rest of the plan works just as smoothly."

"While we're here," Treave sank back onto the stone bench and lifted her glass of wine. "Let's have a toast. To your quest and your swift return home."

"Cheers," Philip clinked his glass against hers.

She took a long sip, studying him over the rim of her glass. She assessed him like a sparring partner might size up their opponent before a fight.

"You look like you're about to be sick," she said finally. "Was the kiss bad?"

"I'm fine. The kiss was fine." Philip's words came out too quickly. In truth, he had never kissed any one before, so he had nothing to compare it to. Books and movies had exaggerated how spectacular kissing was, in his opinion.

"Just 'fine?'" Treave's eyebrows shot up. "I must be losing my touch."

Philip remained silent. He didn't want to think about the implications behind her words. He didn't want to imagine her kissing any one else…

"Come on," she prompted. "What's going on? You can tell me."

When Philip didn't answer, she continued. "Look, whatever it is, everything is going to turn out in the end. You'll be able to do whatever it takes to make things right. I just know it."

Philip snorted derisively. "You barely know me." One kiss didn't mean they suddenly knew everything about each other.

Treave's dark eyes glittered. "When baby griffins hatch, they're adorably disproportionate. They have huge heads, stocky bodies, short legs, and mismatched feet. They spend their first week of life learning to walk, but after that, they have to learn to fly. Their mother takes them to the top of the tree and throws them off. If they don't learn to fly, they hit the ground and die. But, if they do learn to fly, they've just opened their tiny lives to a world of possibilities. Think of this quest as your baby griffin moment. You're being thrown away from everything you've ever known. But when the time comes, you'll learn to fly."

"What if I fail?" Anxiety-filled thoughts raced through Philip's tired mind. He needed a cup of coffee and a full night of sleep.

"Over the years, griffin trainers get pretty good at telling which griffins will fly, and which ones will fall. I'm a fantastic judge of character. Trust me." She grinned and leaned back on her hands.

A faint smile tugged at the corners of Philip's mouth. Usually, he never trusted any one who had to tell him to do so. Despite that, Treave's easy, casual conversation was strangely comforting.

"What will you do while we're off on our quest?" He offered the question casually, ignoring his nagging curiosity.

"I'll have to go back to my post. I'm stationed in a coastal city, but the princess had me brought into Velsailia for the extraction mission in Haderra. Once I'm back in the city, I'll return to my job training griffins for the army. It's a tough job, but I love it. I always have."

In the distance, bells chimed. That was the second signal. Philip tried not to let his disappointment show. Though he was reluctant to admit it, he'd wanted to learn more about Treave and her life in the magical world.

He scolded himself for his foolishness; they had more important things to worry about. By now, Ella, Hemnes, and Torryn would be retreating to the North Tower. If everything went according to plan, they would have the queen's powder in hand. If things *didn't* go according to plan...

"Well, time to head to the rendezvous point." Treave stood up and stretched. She cast a regretful glance back at the wine. "It seems like such a shame to let all this wine go to waste."

Wine? Philip couldn't care less about the wine. "You can bring it along if you want."

"Great! It will be more fun to celebrate with the others."

"If they're not locked in a dungeon cell," Philip muttered.

His stomach churned with dread and worry as he followed Treave to the North Tower. There were hundreds of ways this plan could have gone wrong. Just because they had gotten away with their part of the plan, didn't mean the others hadn't been caught. What would the queen do to them if they were found out? What horrible punishments would she give them?

Treave tried to distract him with chatter the whole way up to the tower. Though he was grateful for her effort, he only half-listened to her stories of growing up on a griffin farm in the elven countryside. He wanted to know more about her, to learn about her life before the army, but his brain refused to focus.

As they reached the door to the North Tower, Philip held his breath, anticipating the worst. Treave strode into the room without hesitation and tossed him a triumphant grin when she saw Ella, Hemnes, and Torryn seated at the round table. They were completely fine.

Philip breathed a sigh of relief. He'd been worried for nothing. Why had he been so worried? In the real world—the *human* world—he rarely worried about things that were out of his control.

He knew what he could control. The things he couldn't control, he left alone. That was the normal way of things. He usually didn't become so trapped in his thoughts that he circled endlessly in 'what if's. Was the stress of the magical world too much for him to bear? Was he going crazy?

There he went again. This too had to stop.

In the human world, he was a normal, logical person with realistic goals and a reasonable means to reach said goals. Now, in the magical world, everything crumbled around him. Nothing was concrete, not even a concept as constant as time. Everything seemed *wrong* here, including his brain.

The sooner they were home, the sooner he would feel normal again.

And to go home, he had to focus on the mission at hand. This quest to retrieve the list of items was his top priority. It was the only thing that should occupy his thoughts.

Ella tossed a small, leather pouch onto the table. Shimmering, golden granules glittered inside the pouch. "This is it. Everything went just as we planned."

They had the first item. They were safe. They were one step closer to getting home. This realization was like a weight lifting off Philip's shoulders.

"We all did it together," Hemnes added.

Torryn stretched languidly. "Yes, yes. We did it. Teamwork and togetherness and all that. Do we get to have some of that wine or not?"

Treave plopped down in the seat next to Torryn and handed him the bottle. She laughed as he took a deep swig straight from the bottle.

"Now *this* is a celebration," Torryn said, kicking his heels up on the table.

Hemnes shook his head. "If you vomit all over the carpet again, I'm not cleaning it up."

"You say that every time,"

"Well, I mean it this time."

Ella plucked the bottle from Torryn's grip. "No one's doing anything stupid tonight. Philip, Max, and I have to leave for Haderra at dawn, and I expect you to see us off."

Torryn groaned, "Why do you have to leave so early? We haven't had a proper night's sleep since Elliott's murder."

The image of Elliott's skewered body flashed before Philip's eyes. He thought of Nathan and Adrian on either side of their sovereign. Murderers and betrayers. What kind of consequences would follow such an act of treason? How had Dash reacted to the betrayal of his closest guards? Did he even know the truth of what had happened?

Ella rolled her eyes at Torryn. "If you're so worried about getting enough sleep, go to bed."

"I agree with, Elestren," Hemnes said, "You'll need all the sleep you can get. You have a long journey ahead of you."

Ella stood and tucked the small leather bag into the pouch at her hip. She gave a triumphant smirk. "Tomorrow, we leave at dawn."

Treave grinned. "One item down, six to go."

That was almost enough to make Philip hopeful.

Chapter 13

The next morning, Philip trudged to the griffin stables with Ella and Max. The sun hadn't yet risen, something he envied it for. His entire body ached as a result of a terrible night's sleep. His head ached with caffeine withdrawal. The heavy pack slung over his shoulder didn't help either. He carried enough food, water, clothing, and blankets to last an entire week. He even wore a sword at his hip, though he hoped it would never have to be drawn. Ella had claimed the excess of supplies was all just a precaution, but he had a sinking suspicion she was wrong.

Treave, Hemnes, and Torryn waited for them outside of the griffin stables with two saddled griffins. When Treave saw Philip, her face broke into a grin. This early in the morning, she looked as if she had gotten plenty of sleep and had guzzled down three cups of coffee. Her sleek hair was pulled into a tight, militant braid, and she wore an immaculate, forest-green uniform. Flight goggles perched on top of her head, and her hands were clad in fingerless, leather riding gloves. She looked like an ace pilot straight out of a movie.

"Good morning!" she greeted.

"No one should sound so cheerful this early in the morning," Torryn grumbled beside her.

"You've obviously never been through basic training," Treave said. "The army doesn't care if you're tired. You can rest when you're dead."

"I'll second that." Hemnes agreed.

Torryn sniffed indignantly. "You two don't have to gang up

on me."

"But you make it so much fun," Treave said with a wink.

Philip's headache pounded, worsened by the sound of their voices.

Ella interrupted their teasing banter, impatient to leave. "Is everything ready?"

"Yes, Your Highness," Treave said, handing Ella the reins of the larger griffin. "Their saddlebags are filled with everything you requested."

"Perfect," Ella replied, "Thank you for your help."

"Happy to serve, my lady."

"Be careful," Hemnes said, taking Ella's hands in his. His face drew into an expression of worry.

"I will. Don't worry about us. We'll send word as soon as we arrive in Haderra."

Hemnes's grey eyes darted to Philip, then back to Ella. "Torryn and I will cover for you as long as possible."

"Thank you," Ella reached up and planted a gentle kiss on Hemnes's cheek.

"Well, I suppose this is goodbye," Torryn cut in, stepping between Ella and Hemnes. He swept a deep, exaggerated bow before pulling Ella into a hug. "Come back soon, Princess."

Philip had to avert his eyes, unable to stomach this much affection so early in the morning. As he turned away, he came face-to-face with Treave. She grinned and handed him the reins of the smaller griffin.

"Thank you for preparing all this," he said.

"Just doing my job." Treave laced her fingers together and stretched like a cat. Small popping noises came from her spine and knuckles. Philip had the sudden urge to do the same, though he knew it was impossible with his limp arm.

150

With some difficulty, he managed to mount the griffin by bracing his arm against the saddle and swinging his leg around. His leg caught awkwardly behind the griffin's wing, but he adjusted himself quickly.

"Not bad." Treave gave an appraising nod. "Try to get a little more momentum when you swing your leg over, and you'll land more smoothly."

"Right," Philip said, grateful he hadn't completely fallen out of the saddle.

Treave reached up and patted his knee. "Remember, this is your griffin moment."

Philip managed a weak smile despite the anxiety gnawing at his mind. He wished he had half as much faith in himself as Treave did.

Once Ella and Max mounted the larger of the two griffins, Treave strapped their packs to the back of the griffins' saddles. Philip worried the weight would be too much for the griffins to bear, but they hardly noticed it.

"Are you boys ready?" Ella asked.

"Yeah!" Max exclaimed.

Philip managed a nod.

"Be safe." Hemnes gazed up at Ella, concern swimming in his crystalline eyes.

Ella smiled down at him and brushed a stray auburn hair behind his pointed ear. "We'll be home soon."

With that, she gave a short whistle, signaling the griffins to take to the air. Philip's griffin launched itself off the ground and soared higher on an updraft. Philip's stomach dropped. He still hated the dizzying, weightless feeling that came with the first few minutes of flying. Gripping the reins as tightly as possible, he squeezed his knees against the griffin's sides. The steady, rhythmic beating of its wings helped him ease back in the saddle. He may as well get comfortable; it was going to be a long ride.

As they flew, he began to lose track of time. The sun crawled higher in the sky, and shadows stretched along the ground. Though the day grew hotter, a slight breeze offset the heat. The griffins flew side-by-side, setting an even pace to the fair folk kingdom.

After hours of trying to distract himself with the passing scenery, he found his mind slipping into a bottomless pit of worry and anxiety. Again, he tried to distract himself, this time, by mentally reviewing Maryn's list. They already had the golden vessel. Next, they would search for the fair folk's shards of glass, whatever that meant. Each of the items seemed to be a riddle or a metaphor of some sort—except for the last item.

A human's dying breath.

To Philip, that item was self-explanatory. A human would have to die to open a gateway. With only two humans in this entire world, he had the sinking suspicion it was meant to be him. Would he be willing to die if it meant Max would be sent home safely? Or would he save himself at the expense of never returning home?

There had to be another way for both of them to get home. Problem-solving was one of the essential skills required to fix electronics. If he looked at this problem like a broken device, he could find a way around this.

He would come up with a solution. He would fix this.

His life depended on it.

The cross from Elvenmar into Haderra was marked by a wide river. On the Elvenmar side, towering evergreens brushed the sky, while on the Haderra side, meadows stretched on as far as the eye could see. Trickling streams crawled through the meadows. The tall, unkempt grasses were dotted with myriads of wildflowers. The meadows sparkled in the midday sunlight, though the morning dew had long since evaporated.

They reached the palace a few hours later. They circled the glistening spires of the palace, before landing on the edge of the cliff. The heavily-guarded palace doors were only a short distance away. Philip studied the palace warily, remembering the horrors he'd witnessed behind those golden doors.

In a fluid, graceful movement, Ella dismounted her griffin. Her hair was coiled into thick braids littered with tiny, white flowers. She wore a loose-fitting white blouse and deerskin riding trousers. Like always, the leather pouch hung at her waist, though this time, it was accompanied by a silver scabbard. Her knee-high boots were polished, and Philip didn't miss the glint of metal as she strapped a silver knife to her calf.

"How are we gonna get in there? Are we gonna sneak in like spies?" Max asked.

Ella shook her head. "We're going straight through the front door." Before Philip could object, she added, "Leave everything to me."

Philip checked to make sure his sword was securely fastened in the scabbard on his belt before they approached the palace. The fair folk guards eyed them suspiciously as they neared the golden palace doors. When they were close enough, both guards lowered their weapons. The first guard ordered them to halt.

"State your name and business."

Ella carried herself like a woman on a mission. "I am Elestren of Elvenmar. My assistants and I come bearing an official message for Nathan and Adrian."

The first guard pursed her green lips. "Commanders Midori and Neibeski are no longer accepting visitors."

"Commanders?" Ella asked, raising her eyebrows in surprise.

"They received a promotion under the leadership of Prince Dash," the guard replied.

"Well, I have an urgent message for the *commanders* from Queen Celosia herself," Ella repeated.

The guard heaved a relenting sigh. "Fine. I will take you directly to the lieutenants' office. If they turn you away, you will be apprehended under the authority of the crown of Haderra."

"Of course, ma'am." Ella swept a shallow bow. "We come with the utmost respect for your commanders, especially during these trying times."

The guard stiffened at Ella's words; Elliott's death was still a fresh wound. It took her a moment to regain her composure, and when she did, all she said was, "Right this way."

They followed her into the palace without another word. Memories of the escape from the dungeons were fresh in Philip's mind. He recognized many of the hallways, which were still in a state of disarray. The brightly colored blood had been scrubbed from the marble floors, and the broken glass had been swept up, but remnants of the battle scarred the palace. Burnt curtains still hung, charred by fire magic. Magically manipulated vines knotted around furniture. Ornate paintings were torn and stained by what appeared to be neon paint, but was most likely fair folk blood.

The guard paid no attention to the damage as they passed. She used her spear as a walking stick, favoring her right leg. A sticky, honey-colored substance covered the tear on her wings. She stopped in front of a set of golden doors emblazoned with an intricate coat of arms. After a sharp rap against the door, she stepped back and snapped to attention.

154

"Yes?" Adrian sounded annoyed as he threw the door open. When he saw Philip, Ella, and Max, his green eyebrows shot up.

"They requested an audience with you and Commander Neibeski, Sir."

"Thank you, Lieutenant Aka. I will be happy to speak with them."

With a salute to Adrian and a glare at Philip Ella, and Max, the guard turned on her heel and marched back to her post.

When she was out of earshot, Adrian ushered them inside. "Get in before someone else sees you," he hissed.

Philip had expected their office to be small but orderly. In reality, the room was large, with a glass ceiling and a picture window that showed a wide view of the city and the meadows beyond. Papers and weapons were scattered all over the room, covering any available surface. Two desks stood in the middle of the room, both piled high with papers, scrolls, quills, and ink.

Nathan glanced up from his work as Adrian slammed the doors shut. His blue eyebrows shot up in surprise. "What are you doing here?"

Ella got straight to the point. "We came because we need your help. We found a way to get Philip and Max back to the human world."

Nathan and Adrian's jaws dropped in tandem.

"*How*?" Adrian asked incredulously.

"We found this," Ella said, "It's our only hope of getting Philip and Max home. All the items on the list are riddles, though, and we need your help to figure them out."

She reached into the pouch at her hip and pulled out a copy of the list. Nathan reverently took it and sank back into his seat. Adrian hovered over his shoulder, inspecting the list carefully.

"*'An elven ruler's golden vessel'*," Adrian read. "What's that

155

supposed to mean?"

"We already found the first item. It was my aunt's magic powder."

"Ugh." Adrian rolled his eyes, "Elves and your ridiculous superstitions."

"Now isn't the time to argue about magic," Ella dismissed. "We hoped you would at least know something about the second item."

"'*A fair folk ruler's shard of glass*'," Nathan hummed thoughtfully, "Do you think it's talking about Elliott's wings and stained glass?"

"What does stained glass have to do with the list?" Max asked.

"Stained glass has been a part of fair folk culture since the beginning of magic." Nathan explained, "It's our way of preserving history and honoring the deceased. The palace has one of the most elaborate displays of stained glass in the entire kingdom."

The image of shattered glass flashed in Philip's mind. Countless years of history and tradition reduced to nothing in a single moment. An involuntary shudder raced down his spine.

"But some of the stained glass isn't exactly glass," Nathan continued, "When the fair folk die, our wings dry out and harden into a glasslike substance. We cut the wings off of the deceased and use them as a part of the stained-glass windows."

Philip wrinkled his nose. They preserved the body parts of their dead as decoration? Each culture had its unique ways of preserving and honoring the dead, but that didn't make it any more disturbing

"So, you think Elliott's wings might be the shards of glass the riddle is talking about?" Ella asked.

Adrian shrugged. "It's the best bet we have. Elliott wasn't exactly a glass collector."

"How would we get a piece of his wing?" Ella asked, "I'm guessing they don't just auction off his dead body for any one to preserve."

"We already burned his body. The wings are the only parts we keep." Adrian said somewhat indignantly, "But his wings will be on display in the center of the city for the ten-day mourning period so people can pay their respects."

Dread stirred in the pit of Philip's stomach. Stealing powder from the queen in the dead of night was one thing, but stealing Elliott's wings from the center of the city where any one could see them was another thing entirely.

Ella looked thoughtful. "Where are the wings kept, exactly?"

"They're displayed in the city's hanging gardens," Nathan replied, "When he died, his wings were preserved in a sealed glass case to encourage the drying process and prevent vandalism. People can view them at all hours of the day, but they're always guarded."

"Hmmm…" Ella tapped her chin. "I have an idea."

Chapter 14

Philip shifted uncomfortably in his perch. A branch dug into his side. The black fabric tied around his face was suffocating. He didn't like Ella's plan one bit, yet here he was.

From his position, he could see the entirety of the hanging gardens at the city's center. Flowers spilled from every available inch of space like running water. They tumbled from pergolas, wrapped around golden sconces, and floated in fountains. Birds flitted through the forest of flowers, chirping happily in contrast to the grave mood. A somber line of fair folk wrapped around the largest marble fountain, awaiting their turn to view the disembodied wings of their dead ruler.

Nathan and Adrian marched through the gardens, bypassing the line completely. They approached the guards on either side of the case and conversed in low voices. After a moment, the guards bowed and stepped aside, just as Nathan and Adrian said they would. While the guards made a rushed apology to the fair folk waiting to pay their respects, Nathan and Adrian opened the display case and removed the wings as carefully as possible. They wrapped the wings in a white cloth and bound them with a golden cord. Though the people cried out in protest, no one stopped them. Who could argue with Prince Dash's new royal advisors?

Of course, their new status as royal advisers was both a help and a hindrance. They couldn't just take the wings and hand them over. No. They wanted theatrics. After all, they had reputations to maintain.

They made a show of marching back through the garden, carrying the bundle of wings between them. Reverent silence fell over the people. Fair folk commoners bowed as the wings passed. A few children threw flowers in Nathan and Adrian's path. A path that led right beneath Philip and Ella's hiding place.

No one saw Ella coming.

With a terrifying war cry, she leaped from a tree and brought her sword down on Adrian. The metal struck his armor with a clang that resonated through the gardens. Though Adrian wasn't hit, he let out an exclamation of pain and collapsed to the ground.

Philip followed Ella's lead, dropping down on top of Nathan. He landed awkwardly, and a twinge shot through his ankle. Still, he managed to bring his sword down, narrowly missing Nathan's head, just as they'd rehearsed.

Nathan sprang back and screamed. "Elves!"

At least he was as good an actor as he said he was.

The somber mood was destroyed by chaos. The once-silent fair folk began to scream and rush towards the exits on the opposite side, eager to escape the "attack." Guards tried to shove towards Nathan and Adrian, but the current of people pushed against them.

Max hid in the bushes below, shouting to rile up the crowd. "They're here to kill us! There are too many of them! Run for your lives!"

Philip and Ella made a show of attacking and disarming Nathan and Adrian. Neither of the fair folk put up much of an actual fight. Adrian's sword nicked Ella's cheek, drawing blood. In return, she faked hitting him on the head with the butt of her sword. He crumpled to the ground, sprawling melodramatically. Both Philip and Ella attacked Nathan, beating him back until he was pressed against the wall. Just as Ella was about to "stab" him, the guards reached them.

She cut the act short and scooped up the wings. "Let's go!" she hollered at Philip.

He followed close behind as she sprinted from the gardens. Together, they wove through the streets, trying to throw the guards off their track.

"After them!" The guards' voices were too close for comfort.

Philip struggled to keep up with Ella. Pain shot through his twisted ankle every time his foot hit the ground. He stumbled too often, tripping over himself. The fastest guard caught up to him immediately and slammed him to the ground. A knife appeared at his neck in a flash. The blade dug into his skin but didn't break the flesh.

"Don't move," the guard growled.

Philip did as he was told. He had no interest in having his throat slit.

"Who sent you? Was it the elven queen, or are you just vigilantes?" the guard demanded.

Philip swallowed but remained silent. What was he supposed to do? This wasn't part of the plan. The guards were supposed to be swallowed by the crowd. He and Ella were supposed to have enough time to escape with the wings. Even if Ella had escaped, that was little consolation. What was the point of attaining the items for the quest if he wasn't with them to return home?

"I asked you a question!" the guard snapped. She grabbed him by the hair and tore the black fabric from his head. When she saw his face and round ears, she balked. "A human?"

Philip said nothing. The guard's grip on the knife went slack. Maybe if he tried to escape now… No. That would be stupid. All he could do was be still and accept his fate.

"Did you catch them?" Relief washed over Philip at the

160

sound of Nathan's voice.

The guard tightened her grip on the knife. "I caught one, Commander Neibeski. It appears to be a human. The other escaped, and their identity is unknown."

"You may release him." Nathan said, "I'll take it from here."

The guard followed Nathan's orders obediently.

Philip scrambled to his feet, careful not to put any weight on his ankle. The guard kept her knife level with his throat. Though Nathan's presence should have put him at ease, he wore a brand mark reminding him otherwise.

"My partner continued the pursuit of the other," the guard reported. "Shall I join him?"

"No," Nathan replied. "Return to your post. I will return shortly with the wings."

"Who will apprehend the human?"

"I will. Commander Midori and I have this all under control."

"No disrespect, Sir, but Commander Midori is unconscious."

"Do as you're told, soldier," Nathan said firmly. "It would be best if you didn't question the authority of your superiors."

Philip swallowed a derisive snort. Superiors? Nathan and Adrian were common guards when he first met them just a few days ago. Their new promotions to Royal Advisors had gone to their heads far too quickly.

Still, the guard didn't question him. She sheathed her knife and marched back to her post. Nathan gripped the collar of Philip's shirt until she was out of sight.

"Sorry about all that," Nathan said, "But this charade is more important than you think."

Philip dusted himself off. "Shouldn't you go make sure the other guard didn't catch Ella?"

"Adrian should have intercepted her by now and relieved the guard of his duty."

"He must have made a miraculous recovery to be conscious so soon," Philip drawled.

Nathan made a face. "Don't be smart with me. *We're* helping you. Without us, you wouldn't be able to complete your little quest."

"Right." Philip sighed. "Can we hurry up and find Max and Ella so we can be on our way?"

"Max is safe and hidden where the guards won't find him. Adrian and Ella will meet us there. Then, Adrian and I will return the wings, and you'll have what you need." Nathan glanced up at the setting sun. "Though, you may want to stay for the night. We have plenty of rooms in the palace where you can stay. No one will know you're there."

"That's up to Ella," Philip said. He followed as Nathan wove through the back streets, heading towards the gardens. Just before he reached the entrance, he veered sharp right into a shaded alcove, where Max hid behind a bush.

"Philip!" Max exclaimed. He popped out of his hiding place and threw his arms around Philip, who shifted uncomfortably in Max's embrace.

His first instinct was to shove his brother away, but he refrained. Max had been through so much the past few days. He didn't deserve to be pushed away again and again.

Adrian and Ella appeared moments later with the wrapped bundle.

"We'll take that." Nathan scooped one side of the bundle from Ella's grasp. "You wait here. We'll be back in a minute."

While Nathan and Adrian went to play heroes returning Elliott's wings to their rightful place, Philip and Max turned to

162

Ella.

"Did you get it?" Max asked.

Ella pulled a long, jagged shard of honey-colored glass from the pouch at her hip. She held it up to the light, which illuminated thin veins that shot through the glass like minuscule branches.

"You did it!" Max cheered.

When Ella had Elliott's wings, she had broken off a piece and pocketed it. That way, when Nathan and Adrian returned the wings, they could claim that the wings were broken in the chase. Philip, Ella, and Max had their item, and Nathan and Adrian's reputations were still intact. It was a win-win.

Nathan and Adrian returned shortly and took them back to the palace. They had to sneak in through the servants' entrance to prevent any one—namely, Dash—from seeing them.

Once they reached Nathan and Adrian's office, everyone released a collective breath. Philip didn't allow his guard to lower, though. He still hadn't forgiven Nathan and Adrian for throwing them in the dungeons. Besides, how could he trust someone who had murdered the very ruler they were sworn to protect?

"What we did today was risky," Nathan said. "You three need to be careful; the other items will most likely be more dangerous and difficult than this."

"What's next on the list?" Max asked.

Ella unfolded her copy of Maryn's list and set it on the table. "*'A pixie ruler's sacred boughs.'*"

Adrian made a face. "'Ruler' is hardly the right word for the pixie president."

"Please put your prejudices aside for now," Ella said diplomatically. "Our priority is figuring out the next clue."

"What does 'boughs' mean?" Max asked.

163

"'Bough' is another word for a tree branch…" Nathan snapped his fingers, "That's it. The Elder Tree."

Ella frowned. "Are you sure?"

"The Elder Tree is the pixie kingdom's most sacred place. The leaves of the tree contain the most powerful magic in their kingdom. It's said that each president is blessed with the power of the tree at the beginning of every term."

"That must be it, then," Ella shook her head, "This list seems to be compiled of the most powerful objects in each kingdom. My aunt's magic powder, Elliott's wings, the Elder Tree's branches…"

How was a human's dying breath the most powerful object in their 'kingdom'? Maybe it didn't count, being that the human world was entirely separate. Either way, Philip couldn't ignore the dread in the pit of his stomach.

A knock sounded at the door.

"That would be supper," Nathan announced, "Adrian and I have a meeting with the Sovereign Prince, but you three stay here and eat."

Steaming platters of food were placed in front of them. Philip was surprised to recognize some of the food on his plate. Never in his life had he been so happy to see a plate of limp, overcooked vegetables.

"You three can thank Dash for our cook knowing how to prepare humanlike dishes," Adrian said. "We'll be back soon. Try not to burn the place down."

They didn't waste time with chatter as they dug into their food. Having only eaten dried fruit and dried meat all day, it was heaven to have their fill of something substantial. Even Max didn't complain about eating his meal without ranch dressing.

By the time they finished eating, Nathan and Adrian still

hadn't returned. The moon was beginning to climb its way into the sky when drowsiness settled over Philip. He leaned back in Nathan's plush chair and closed his eyes. Exhaustion from the day weighed heavily on him. They had flown to Haderra from Elvenmar, found Nathan and Adrian, gotten the pieces of Elliott's wings, and figured out the answer to the next riddle. This sudden burst of progress sparked a glimmer of relief in him. Maybe, just maybe, this quest wouldn't be entirely terrible.

Max dozed in an armchair, snoring softly. Ella sat at Adrian's desk, scribbling a letter to Hemnes and Torryn. The foreign scratching of her quill on the parchment and the occasional clinking of the quill in the inkwell was strangely calming.

Philip had come to realize how much modern technology he took for granted. The technology that was banned from the magical world wasn't just complicated machinery such as phones or laptops or guns or airplanes, but simple things like fountain pens, zippers, light switches, and toilets. Things that most people wouldn't think twice about. Things that people noticed only in their absence.

If—*when*—they returned to the human world, he decided he would be mindful of these things. Technology would not be something taken for granted again.

Ella finished writing her letter and set her quill down. "You know, it's nice being around humans again," she said. "I've been in this world for so long, I've forgotten what it was like in the human world."

"Do you like it here?" Philip offered the question like an olive branch. He wouldn't exactly call Ella a friend, but what she was doing for them was more than he could have hoped for. He would be polite and considerate, even if it meant making small talk.

"It has its pros and cons," she responded. Yet another diplomatic answer from the elven princess. How fitting.

"Such as?"

"Well, the food is much better in the human world, but in the magical world, traffic doesn't exist." A wry smile played across Ella's lips.

The corners of Philip's lips quirked up. "Very funny."

Ella sighed and sat back, the smile evaporating. "The journey ahead of us is going to be especially dangerous. In this world... well, things don't usually end well for people like us."

"People like us. You mean humans?"

"Yes," Ella said. "In all my time living among the elves, I've had to learn this the hard way."

They fell into a heavy silence. Philip knew the probability of things ending badly for him was high. *A human's dying breath.* Hearing the same sentiment from Ella's lips solidified his deep sense of dread and finality. This quest very well could be the death of him.

With these thoughts in mind, he sank into a fitful sleep.

Nathan and Adrian woke them at dawn. Adrian slapped a piece of parchment on the desk.

Philip leaned forward to study it. It appeared to be a map of some kind, punctuated by scribbled lines and strange symbols. On the bottom right corner, *'Elvenmar'* was penned in neat script. A squiggly line divided Elvenmar and Haderra, which was found on the bottom left corner. Above Haderra, an area was labeled *'Eabith.'*

"That's the pixie kingdom," Ella explained when Philip asked. She pointed to the Eabith's southern border. "Those trees mark the boundaries of the Pixie Forest." She traced a finger to the small circle in the middle of the forest. "And that marks the

166

location of the Elder Tree."

A tidy swoop of a line connected a small X, which marked their location on the right side of Haderra, to the circle that marked the location of the Elder Tree.

Philip tried to pay attention as Ella, Nathan, and Adrian discussed the most efficient methods of travel to the Pixie Forest, but his eyes drifted to the very center of the map. The Island of Corvus lay at the very heart of the world. Surrounded by water on all sides, it was secluded and isolated.

It was intriguing.

He and Max had arrived in the magical world on the Island of Corvus. The instructions on the list said to take the items to Corvus to open the gateway. What was it about the island that made it so important and extraordinary? Was it the ferocious monsters that prowled there? Was it the mysterious King of Corvus, the monster king whose very name struck fear into the hearts of the people?

Perhaps this fear should have pertained to him too, but all Philip felt towards this king was a strange sense of curiosity. Did the King of Corvus enjoy having the island all to himself with no one to disturb him? Was it a burden to know everything that occurred in the world? Or was that kind of knowledge powerful and freeing? What would that kind of power do to a normal person, let alone a person gifted with magic?

Shaking his head, he snapped back to reality in time to hear Nathan speak. "—griffins won't go past the Haderra-Eabith border. You may just have to walk."

Ella frowned. "How long will that take?"

"According to Dash's map, it's a three-day walk to the Elder Tree."

Ella shook her head vehemently. "Three days is too long.

There has to be another way."

Philip agreed. They could take a wagon or a carriage or whatever technology-free transportation they had in this world. Surely people didn't just walk everywhere if they didn't have wings.

"Animals won't go into the Pixie Forest," Adrian said. "It's too dangerous for them. It's too dangerous for *you*, but there's no other way. To reach the Elder Tree, you have to go through the forest."

"What's so dangerous about the Pixie Forest anyways?" Max asked. "It doesn't sound dangerous."

"The Pixie Forest is cursed," Nathan explained, "Everything in there is deadly poisonous—the water, the berries, the wildlife. The magic of the forest kills your body, but your mind doesn't die. You're trapped in your own immovable body, but still able to feel pain. Once your body is dead, your mind stays conscious as it rots in your skull."

Philip's stomach churned at the images his mind conjured up. He quickly ran the calculations. According to Ella, they would be stuck in the Pixie Forest for at least two days—four if they had to walk there and back. As long as they were in the Pixie Forest, they would be vulnerable to a horrible death. He was already stuck inside his head enough as it was. The thought of being trapped inside his own body, unable to escape the endless circling of his mind sent a shudder down his spine.

"We should leave for the Pixie Forest as soon as possible," Ella said. "But I only have enough food for two days at most."

Nathan scribbled something on a piece of parchment. "I'll send word to the cook. She can prepare food that won't spoil quickly."

"Dinner was yummy last night," Max added. "Tell her she's

a great cook."

Nathan smiled. "I'll be sure to give her your compliments."

"We'll also need plenty of water," Ella continued, "as well as bandages, ointment, and other medical supplies."

"It won't take long for us to gather what you need," Adrian said.

Why were Nathan and Adrian being so compliant? What did they have to gain from helping them return to their world? Nothing they did made sense. They killed Elliott. They allowed the elves to escape from the dungeons. They helped steal a piece of Elliott's wings. They were giving away supplies like it was nothing. What was their motivation? Weren't the fair folk and elves enemies? Surely, they weren't helping the princess of an enemy kingdom only for Philip and Max's sake. They had helped her with the jailbreak before Philip and Max even knew this world existed.

"Why are you doing this?" Philip asked, unable to help himself. "What do you want from us?"

"We owe it to Dash," Nathan said after a moment. "So many things have happened that he didn't know about..." he lowered his gaze. "Dash wanted you two to get home safely. Adrian and I will do what we can to make sure that happens."

Ah. They were doing this out of guilt. Dash had no idea about the truth of Elliott's murder, did he? He didn't strike Philip as a type to stage a coup such as this. Besides, Dash had been sent away before Elliott's murder. Someone wanted to keep him in the dark about what happened. That made sense considering Nathan and Adrian's promotion to Royal Advisors.

How would things be different if Dash knew the truth?

Chapter 15

Nathan and Adrian gathered all the supplies Ella requested. By the time they were ready to leave, the sun had already risen, though it was obscured by dark clouds. Nathan and Adrian didn't see them off. They simply handed over the supplies and told them not to die.

Ella distributed a sparse breakfast of bread and cheese before they took to the air. Philip fought the nausea that came with his caffeine withdrawal and choked down the food. It didn't help ease the pain. Once they finished eating, they mounted the griffins and began their journey to the Pixie Forest. They spent the overcast morning in silent flight. Grey clouds filled the air, and light rain sprinkled on their cheeks.

Philip began to grow nervous as the northern forests in Haderra thinned out dramatically. The grassy meadows turned brown and sparse. No birds sang, and no small animals bounded beneath them. His griffin became anxious. Its wings began to flap irregularly, and they dipped towards the ground. The griffin's nervous squawks were returned by Ella and Max's equally anxious griffin.

As they drew closer to the forest, colorful trees rose in the distance, starkly contrasting with the grey skies above. They had trunks with bark as brown as dark chocolate and leaves the colors of a sunset, ranging from deep magenta to vibrant orange to pale lavender. Unease settled in the pit of Philip's stomach. Something was wrong with the forest. A place so dangerous wasn't supposed to appear as peaceful as a watercolor painting.

"Are we in the right place?" Max called over the wind.

Ella glanced down at the map. "According to the map, this is the Pixie Forest!"

Just before they reached the forest, the griffins shot towards the ground, landing a few yards away from the tree line. Philip's griffin flicked away imaginary flies with her tail and made nervous clicking noises.

He dismounted and stroked her neck soothingly. "*Shhh*," he murmured.

"What's wrong?" Max asked.

"This is as far as the griffins will take us," Ella said, "We'll have to let them go. They know their way back to the castle in Elvenmar."

Max nodded sagely. "Just like pigeons."

"Sure." Ella cast an uncertain glance at Philip.

He simply shrugged; he'd never cared for the stupid, dirty pigeons back in New York. They simply blinked brainlessly and pecked at crumbs and trash on the street. He much preferred the sleek, intelligent crows that decorated their nests with shining treasures.

Ella unloaded the packs from the griffin's saddles and handed them to him and Max, who strapped them to their backs. Much to his embarrassment, he had trouble securing his own pack one-handed. His cheeks heated when Max had to help him.

"All right, you beautiful beast," Ella said, patting her griffin's flank, "time to go home."

Ella's griffin took to the air with a screech, eager to get away from the Pixie Forest as quickly as possible.

Philip hesitated to let his griffin go. Living in apartments his whole life, he had never been allowed to have a pet. But with this griffin, he could begin to understand the unique bond between humans and animals.

"Are you ready?" Ella asked.

Sighing deeply, Philip gave his griffin one last stroke. "Fly home quickly."

His griffin gave him an affectionate clicking noise in reply, before spreading her wings and taking off after the other griffin.

Philip's heart constricted as he watched her disappear into the horizon. He moved to turn away but paused when he saw Ella's hand resting reassuringly on his injured shoulder. She wore a faint, wistful expression as she watched the griffins disappear into the distance. Philip felt an irrational sense of invasion and a completely rational sense of irritation at not being able to feel the pressure of her hand on his skin.

"This just started to feel real," Ella murmured. "It's only the three of us now. Once we step into this forest, we're on our own."

Philip's heart plummeted; if Ella was nervous, that was cause for alarm.

"But," Ella went on, squaring her shoulders. "We'll find the Elder Tree in no time. We have to. Besides, this walk will give us plenty of time to get to know each other."

Philip shook his head, unable to keep the small smile from his lips. Leave it to Ella to put a positive spin on a potentially deadly situation.

All three of them turned to face the forest together. Ella stood between Philip and Max, taking their hands in hers. Philip savored one last moment of calm before they plunged into the Pixie Forest.

Rhett stood over the corpses of four, dead manticores. Other monsters had come and picked the corpses clean, leaving nothing but broken skeletons. Dried blood stained the lush, green grass, making it appear as shriveled and dead as the manticores.

Four perfectly healthy manticores had been slaughtered, yet there was no evidence that any one or anything strange had been to the island within the last few days.

But Rhett knew exactly what had happened. His brother told him all about the human boys and their daring escape from the monsters. Dash had spared no detail when he recounted the attack.

Footsteps crunched in the bloody grass behind Rhett.

"How nice of you to finally join me," Rhett said without turning around.

"In case you haven't noticed, visiting you isn't the only thing on our to-do list," Adrian sniffed.

Rhett could feel the hostility radiating from Adrian in waves. He held up a slender hand and examined the purple flames that lapped up from his fingers. Adrian's hostility chilled to fear, the common reaction to seeing Rhett's magic in person. It was ironic, Rhett supposed, that people abhorred his magic—the very magic that kept them safe from the unspeakable terrors that roamed this island. No one needed to know he could barely summon a blaze, let alone enforce the barrier.

"You requested a word with me?" Rhett arched an eyebrow.

"We wanted to speak to you about Dash," Nathan said.

Rhett's nonchalance evaporated completely. Though he still maintained his usual cool countenance, it was all he could do to keep the panic from his eyes, his posture, and his voice. If something happened to Dash, he would never forgive himself. "What's wrong? Has something happened to him?"

Nathan shook his head. "Dash is alright, but we wanted to discuss the frequency of his visits here."

"Oh?" Rhett's expression remained placid as glass, but his

173

hands curled into fists at his side.

"We believe Dash should visit you more sparingly."

Rhett's eyebrows shot up. "I hope Dash coming to visit me—his older brother and, as of recently, his only living relative—for advice and comfort isn't disturbing your precious schedule." Nathan and Adrian exchanged a glance, and Rhett pressed on. "Oh, yes. I've heard all about your little promotions to Royal Advisors, your meetings, your schedules, all of it. I know *everything*. Elliott's murder must have been satisfying. You've worked hard to keep this dirty little secret from my brother. But it's cost you, hasn't it? I can see the blood on your hands. You've had to bury so many unfortunate souls that just happened to be in the wrong place at the wrong time. Why, just yesterday you killed that poor guard who captured the human…"

Nathan stiffened, curling his hands into fists. Adrian's face flushed a dark, angry green. Rhett relished in their terror and rage, allowing it to fuel him.

"Luckily for you," Rhett continued, "your little plan just so happens to align with my interests. You won't receive any resistance from me."

This shocked both of them. They froze, blinking at him in surprise.

Adrian was the first to recover. "Dash's meetings with you take up too much of his time," he managed. "He has to fly all the way here and back when he wishes to speak with you. From now on, if he wishes to have a word with you, he will send a bird."

Rhett's lip curled. They all knew Dash would be doing no such thing. Too often people had to rely on ordinary birds to deliver their correspondence, only to have that bird snatched out of the air and killed. Sending a bird was too great a security risk for the soon-to-be Sovereign Prince of Haderra.

"I'm sorry to be such an inconvenience to you," Rhett drawled, "but you can't keep my brother away from me."

"We can and we will," Adrian challenged. "If you know what's good for you, you would tell him to leave you alone."

Rhett narrowed his eyes. "Is that a threat?"

Nathan glanced from Rhett to Adrian with mounting fear. "We don't mean to insult or threaten you," he assured quickly.

Of course not. No one ever meant to insult Rhett to his face. Oh, he was perfectly aware of the things people said about him when they thought he couldn't hear them. He'd heard it all. *Monster. Bastard. Murderer.*

"We will no longer allow Dash to come to Corvus," Adrian said.

Rage boiled beneath Rhett's skin. Who were they to keep Dash away from him? They had no right. He would teach them not to interfere with him. He would make sure they never stepped foot on this island again. He would—

He took a deep breath and straightened his spine. As he exhaled, he forced his emotions away.

"I'm sorry to hear that," he said, calmly resting his eyes on Nathan and Adrian in turn. "Will you at least let me see him for his gilding and coronation next week? It's not every day your little brother is crowned Sovereign Prince of an entire kingdom."

He was pleased to see his quick change of mood and halfhearted attempts at humor unsettled Nathan and Adrian.

"I'm afraid there may not be much time to celebrate our prince," Nathan said.

"And why is that?" Rhett already knew the answer, but was curious to see how much Nathan and Adrian would tell him.

Adrian glanced around hesitantly as if he were making sure there was no one else around to hear him on the deserted island.

"There is a great unrest among our people."

"I should assume so," He replied, "It's only natural for there to be unrest during a change of leadership, especially when the previous leader met such an untimely end." *Untimely indeed.*

"We're doing everything in our power to stop things from escalating, but there aren't enough hours in the day," Nathan explained. "This is difficult on Dash, and we know he values your support, but this is why we need him to stop visiting you. He needs to focus completely on the kingdom."

It was as if they thought Dash visited him to talk about palace gossip.

"My brother chose you two as his royal advisors," Rhett said with as much sincerity as he could muster. "He trusts you to keep his best interests in mind, and I will respect his judgment."

Once again, surprise flickered across Nathan and Adrian's faces. Rhett loved that he could have such an effect on them.

"You will?" Adrian didn't bother to hide the disbelief in his voice.

"Of course. I love my brother more than anything in the world. If anything happened to him, I would be absolutely beside myself." Rhett's lips curled into a smile. "I'm just grateful he's in *such* good hands."

Nathan and Adrian traded a terrified glance. Good. They understood the implied threat.

"Yes. Right. We should probably be going now," Adrian said too quickly. "Thank you for your time."

Rhett inclined his head. "Give Dash my regards."

Nathan and Adrian took to the air, their colorful wings sparkling behind them as they retreated to Haderra.

"Idiots," Rhett muttered once they were out of earshot.

Of all the people in Haderra, Dash had chosen those yes-men

176

to be his royal advisors. Nathan and Adrian had been his best friends since they first arrived in this world. Of course, he would have chosen them. As much as Rhett loved his brother, he wished he could shake him for being so sentimental.

Nathan and Adrian were fools to think he was oblivious to what was happening in Haderra. That he knew nothing of the civil war brewing in his brother's kingdom. That he knew nothing of the "solution" they'd concocted. What did they think Dash talked about on his visits to Corvus? Granted, not all of his knowledge came from his brother. He was perfectly capable of gathering information himself.

Dash told him everything, and, like a good older brother, he gave him the best advice possible. Whether Dash took that advice or not was up to him. It was shortsighted and naive of Nathan and Adrian to believe Dash blindly followed whatever instructions he provided.

They clung to the fantasy that their precious prince was as innocent and complacent as he seemed. Dash could think for himself. Rhett would have it no other way. But if and when Dash came to him for advice or comfort, he would gladly oblige.

After all, what were brothers for?

They had been walking for hours.

Philip's feet throbbed, and his legs ached, but he continued to keep pace with Ella. There would be no rest if they wanted to find the Elder Tree as quickly as possible.

Ella instructed Max to leave a pile of twigs on top of every large rock they passed, so they would know if they were walking in circles. Max was overjoyed to have such an "important" task and took pleasure in frolicking through the leaves in search of any large rocks. The task was pointless, but it kept him busy and he didn't whine about being tired or hungry or sore.

The sun slowly sank below the horizon, turning the sky the color of the leaves overhead. Long shadows stretched across the leaf-covered ground. They had been lucky to avoid any unsavory creatures all day, but Philip feared what might come out at night.

Ella's eyes stayed glued to the map as she walked, and Philip had to yank her out of the way of a fallen log.

"Thanks," Ella said, sparing him a quick, grateful smile before she turned back to the map.

A concerned line was etched between her eyebrows. Her laser-sharp focus hadn't dwindled, despite the monotony of the hike. Somehow, she even managed to keep a lightness in her step that suggested they were simply on a stroll around a park, not a trek through a deadly forest. Concern began to mount in Philip, though, when she became so absorbed in the map that she accidentally slammed into a tree.

"Do you need to take a break?" he asked, half-hoping she would say yes for his benefit as well.

"We have to keep moving," Ella said.

Philip was unimpressed by her non-answer.

When he said nothing, Ella eyed him warily. "As much as I would like to stop, we can't lose our momentum."

"Will you at least let me take over the map?"

"All right," Ella said, reluctantly handing over the parchment.

Philip took the creased paper and scanned it. According to Dash's drawings, the Elder Tree lay northeast from where they stood. If they continued in that direction, they would reach the Elder Tree. Though he didn't doubt Ella, he had a strange feeling about it. Maybe it was just the unease of being in the Pixie Forest, but something inside him whispered that they could wander the forest for the rest of their lives and never find the Elder Tree.

"So, Queens, huh?" Ella said casually. She stretched, her joints popping. "I've always wanted to go to New York City. What's it like?"

Philip gave a half-shrug. "There's a lot of noise and traffic and crowds, and everything's more expensive."

"That's it?" Ella cocked her head.

"You grew up in a big city," Philip said, "You know what it's like."

"But Chicago and New York are so different. What makes New York special?"

Philip took a moment to think. New York was home. When he was little, he would go on school field trips to the Statue of Liberty and the Empire State Building, but he had never been captivated by the tourist traps the city was famous for. New York City lured people in with the promise of glamour and swallowed them whole. But it wasn't all bad. It gave so many people a purpose. A way to wake up each morning and look forward to what lay ahead.

"I like the food," he said finally, "At every corner, there's a different restaurant that serves a different type of food from a different place in the world. The street vendors sell the best hotdogs ever, and there's never a shortage of food trucks."

"That sounds nice."

"And there's nothing like thin-crust pizza with a Coke." Philip couldn't resist a faint, nostalgic smile.

Ella raised her eyebrows in a challenge. "You mean a deep-dish pizza with a root beer float."

"Absolutely not."

Ella looked unconvinced. "Whatever you say."

"Well, what makes Chicago so special?"

179

Ella's expression turned wistful, "I wish I remembered more, but I was so young when my dad died." Her voice hitched.

Philip shifted uncomfortably; his relationship with Ella hadn't reached the level of depth it would take to talk about her father's death. He wasn't quite sure how to react. Did he try to say something comforting? No. He wasn't good with words, and she'd probably heard it all. Should he put an arm around her shoulder? Definitely not. The thought of physical contact made him squirm.

He needed to work on his people skills...

Thankfully, Max saved him from any possible awkwardness by shouting, "There's a river up ahead!"

"Don't drink the water," Ella reminded him. "It's poisonous."

A shiver raced down Philip's spine. He didn't need another reminder of the forest's dangerous nature.

Ella glanced up at the sinking sun. "We should set up camp before it gets too dark."

Finally. It would be a relief to get off his feet. His limbs were heavy and his back ached from the weight of his pack. He just wanted to collapse onto a blanket and sleep—even if they had to sleep on the cold, hard ground under the stars.

When they reached the river, he marveled at how wide it was. So far, they had only passed small streams barely as wide as his foot. But this river would be impossible to cross without swimming to the other side. The last thing he wanted to do was submerge himself into strange, poisonous water of unknown depth. If the water wasn't safe to drink, was it even safe to touch? The river could be teeming with dangerous creatures, and if the current was strong enough, they could be swept under and never resurface.

"We'll have to camp on this side of the river," Ella announced after inspecting the rushing waters.

"This looks like a good spot," Max said, pointing to a small, elevated clearing a few yards away from the river's edge. Dense trees shaded the clearing, and the heavy foliage gave it an enclosed, protected feeling.

Philip shrugged the pack off his back and instantly felt ten times lighter. They unloaded the supplies they needed and spread their blankets in a wide circle around a pile of brush and twigs they could use to light a campfire. As they settled onto their blankets with a dinner of dried meat, bread, and cheese, there was a splash in the river like someone falling in.

Philip and Ella froze and exchanged a glance. Whatever that noise was, it couldn't mean anything good.

Max scrambled to his feet and raced to the side of the river. He ignored Philip's protests as he scanned the water.

The splashing continued to grow louder, though none of them could see anything amiss. Peering into the darkness, Philip thought he saw an inky shape move under the surface of the water.

His pulse raced. "Did you see that?"

"It's probably just a fish." Ella didn't sound certain.

Max, who was closest to the edge of the river, let out an audible gulp. He backed away from the water, eyes wide. "That's not a fish."

Chapter 16

They scrambled away from the edge of the river as a creature emerged from the water. It was a horse with a flowing, midnight mane and a glossy, cerulean coat. Its emerald eyes glittered as it advanced. Its hooves made no sound when they met the ground. Though there was no sign of a saddle or rider, the horse's muzzle was fitted with a silver, jewel-encrusted bridle.

The horse flicked its tail, surveying Philip, Ella, and Max in turn. Its nostrils flared, taking in their scents.

Philip backed away, wary of the horse's unearthly gaze. There was something very *wrong* with this horse. Its movements were too smooth, too silent. Too calming.

The horse turned its eyes on Max, who was frozen in place, his body rigid with fear. His eyes turned vacant, and he stared straight through the horse with an unblinking gaze. He took a robotic step forward. Then another.

"Max," Philip began cautiously, "What are you doing?"

The horse lowered its head as Max approached. His hand stretched out in a jerky, mechanical movement and landed on the horse's muzzle. The moment he made contact with the horse, it let out a bloodcurdling screech. Its eyes flashed ruby-red, and it bared its gleaming, needlelike fangs. Seizing Max in its fangs by the collar of his shirt, the horse swung him onto its back. Max's blank face remained expressionless as stone as the horse reared around and galloped towards the river.

"It's a kelpie!" Ella shrieked, stumbling backward.

"Max!" Philip cried, surging forward.

182

The two of them collided and knocked each other to the ground. Philip's jaw slammed shut as he fell. His teeth snapped down on his tongue. The metallic tang of blood coated his mouth and throat, filling his nose.

The kelpie skidded to a halt just short of the. Its nostrils flared as it sniffed the air. Licking its chops, it whirled to face Philip. It bucked Max off of its back like a ragdoll and snarled at Philip. Pawing at the ground with silent hooves, it charged toward him.

Philip dove out of the way, only to slam headfirst into the trunk of a tree. Pain shot through his skull, and he crumpled to the ground. Ella screamed as the kelpie barreled towards him. He wouldn't be able to get out of the way in time. Grimacing, he braced for impact.

This was going to hurt.

But before the horse collided with Philip, a smaller kelpie leaped from the river and raced towards the larger kelpie. It lunged forward, burying its fangs into the larger kelpie's throat.

The larger kelpie stumbled and fell inches from Philip. It thrashed on the ground, snapping its teeth wildly, but the smaller kelpie didn't relent. It kept a firm hold on the larger kelpie. Emerald blood poured from the larger kelpie's wound until finally, it stopped thrashing. With a final, defeated whinny, its red eyes rolled into the back of its head.

Once the larger kelpie was dead, the smaller kelpie released its grip and turned towards Philip, who clamped a hand over his mouth and nose in a futile attempt to staunch the bleeding. He locked eyes with the smaller kelpie. His heart thundered and the blood roared in his ears. The kelpie studied him with a strange intelligence in its emerald eyes.

With a mix of horror and astonishment, Philip watched as

183

the smaller kelpie changed in front of his eyes. It morphed from a horse-like beast to a petite girl. She couldn't have been more than fourteen years old—at least, fourteen human years. She was short, with a slight frame and brown skin. Her dark hair was bluntly shorn at her chin, framing her heart-shaped face. Her features were tiny and delicate, except for her gigantic, amber eyes. A thin, silver necklace rested at the base of her throat.

Sighing contentedly, the girl stretched. "Much better," she said. "You really should be more careful around rivers at night. The Pixie Forest isn't the place you want to become kelpie food."

Max, who had snapped out of his stupor, gaped at her with shock and fascination. "Who *are* you?"

"Well, you're in my forest, so I should be asking you the same thing."

Philip eyed the girl warily, grateful to see Ella's expression mirrored his own. It proved his assumption that whatever magic the girl used wasn't normal in this world. People didn't just *change* like that.

Max opened his mouth to answer the girl, but Philip clamped a bloody hand over his face before he could speak. Max's expression twisted in disgust, but Philip wasn't going to risk letting his little brother run his mouth to a stranger who could turn into a demon horse.

"You know, I *did* just save you from being eaten by a kelpie, so the polite thing to do would be to introduce yourselves." the girl said with a shrug.

Max's curiosity about the girl overcame his fear. Extracting himself from Philip's futile, one-handed grip, he introduced himself cheerfully. "I'm Max, and this is my big brother Philip. We're humans. This is Ella. She's an elf."

The girl smiled. Her white teeth gleamed in a straight,

184

perfect row. "Nice to meet you. My name is Vinnia. I'm a mixie."

"What's a mixie?" Max asked.

"Mixies are half-mermaid and half-pixie," Vinnia explained. "We're known for our shape-shifting magic."

"Whoa," Max breathed, "that's so cool!"

Ella looked intrigued. "Even I've never met a mixie before."

"We're a rarity," Vinnia said. "Though, even if you have met a mixie before, you wouldn't know it. We never stay in one form for long."

Max's eyes widened. "So, you're not really a kelpie?"

"Only when I have to be," Vinnia said. "Now, what are two humans and an elf doing in the Pixie Forest? You *do* know what would happen if you were to die here, don't you?"

"We know the risk," Ella replied.

"And it's none of your business." Philip cut in before any one could divulge more information. His tongue throbbed with pain as he spoke.

Vinnia turned her gaze to Philip and cocked her head in a birdlike manner. She shot a pointed look at the dead kelpie. "*That* wasn't any of my business, but you'd be dead if I didn't decide to poke my nose into it. It would be a shame if you were to reject my help, only to die out here and suffer forever."

"Your help?" Philip asked skeptically. People didn't just offer help for free. Vinnia wanted something, and whatever she wanted, it wasn't likely to be beneficial to them.

"Yes, I'm offering to help you," Vinnia said. "Wherever you're going, I want to go too."

"Why?"

Vinnia scuffed at the ground. "It gets lonely out here. I've been living on my own for years. I want to travel with others. I want to know what it's like to have friends for a change…"

"Poor thing—" Ella began.

Philip suppressed a groan. Ella was *actually* buying Vinnia's act. Compassionate, determined Ella believed everyone deserved a chance. Right now, though, she was just being gullible.

"Of course, you can come with us," Ella said.

Philip wanted to smack his forehead against a tree trunk. They couldn't let a stranger tag along with them *just like that.* She could be another monster weaving an elaborate trap to lure them into her clutches. Or maybe she was planning on devouring them in their sleep. Maybe she was a malicious pixie trying to trick them into an unbreakable deal. Or maybe… just *maybe*, she was simply a lonely young girl who wanted companionship. Maybe he was becoming paranoid. Traumatic experiences could do that to a person.

"Thank you so much!" Vinnia exclaimed. "You won't regret this."

Philip snorted derisively. Typically, when a person claimed he wouldn't regret something, he ended up regretting it.

Ella gave Vinnia a warm smile. "We'll be glad to have you along."

Philip wanted to list all of the reasons not to allow Vinnia to come with them. Having an extra person would mean smaller food portions, less drinking water, and fewer blankets at night. She would take up supplies and would probably slow them down.

But he didn't say any of that. Maybe he could scare her out of wanting to come with them. Ella said no one came to the Pixie Forest without a good reason. Well, their "good reason" would most likely get them injured or killed.

"We're going to find the Elder Tree," he warned. "Are you sure you want to come along?"

"Why?" Vinnia's expression was incredulous. "Why would

186

you go *there* of all places?"

"We need branches from the Elder Tree to open a gateway to the human world."

Vinnia gazed somberly at Philip, Max, and Ella in turn, as if she were already planning their funerals. This was when she would tell them she changed her mind. This was when she disappeared into thin air, never to bother them again. Instead, she sounded impressed. "I've never known any one who wanted to find the Elder Tree. You're either really brave or stupid."

"Or desperate," Philip muttered under his breath.

"How do you plan on finding the Elder Tree?" Vinnia asked, "Do you have a guide?"

"We have a map," Ella said, offering it to her.

Vinnia wrinkled her nose as she studied the map. "This is all wrong. Everyone knows you can't find the Elder Tree without a guide."

"This map is our only option." Ella sounded defensive.

"I could be your guide," Vinnia suggested after a moment. "I've been to the Elder Tree before. It's only a day's walk from here."

This was too good to be true. Was she seriously offering to take them to the Elder Tree just because she was lonely? Sooner or later, there was going to be a catch.

"You could do that?" Ella glanced at Philip as if to confirm he heard the same offer.

"Sure," Vinnia said. "It wouldn't be a problem."

"Thank you!" Ella's expression broke with relief.

"Don't mention it. And who knows?" Vinnia shrugged, "My skills might be useful in a pinch."

Philip was still wary about allowing Vinnia to come with them, but she was right. Her shapeshifting abilities *could* be

187

useful, especially if she could take down monsters as quickly as she killed the kelpie.

Max gave an exaggerated yawn. "I'm tired."

"Really?" Philip muttered, rolling his eyes. Exhaustion took the edge off his sarcasm. The adrenaline in his system was wearing off, making him jittery and irritable. All he wanted to do was curl up on the ground and sleep.

Instead, he knelt by the kindling with Ella, showing her how to light a campfire. For once, he was grateful to his father for forcing him to be in Cub Scouts when he was younger. Though he could only give instructions thanks to the loss of his arm, Ella was a fast learner. They didn't have matches and had to make do with flint and steel. Primitive.

While they worked, Max and Vinnia settled down and fell asleep. Max drooled while he slept, peaceful and angelic. Vinnia slept in kelpie form. Her breath whooshed out in small whinny-like snores.

The woods were quiet and still in the dark. Insects chirped softly in the trees. Leaves rustled in a cool, gentle breeze.

After a few minutes, Ella succeeded in igniting the tinder, which smoldered beneath the pile of brush. The flames grew gradually until they became an impressive campfire.

"Good work," Philip murmured, keeping his voice low.

Ella looked pleased with herself as she tucked the flint and knife into her pack. "Hemnes tried to show me how to make fire years ago, but believe it or not, he's not a very good teacher. Torryn wasn't much help either..." She trailed off with a sigh. "I hope they're okay without me. We haven't been separated like this in a long time."

Though exhaustion tugged at Philip's mind and body, his curiosity took priority. The three of them had a close bond that

188

only came with years of friendship, but the dynamics were different with each pair. Torryn and Ella teased like siblings. Hemnes and Torryn traded sarcastic jabs like lifetime best friends. Ella and Hemnes had a more complicated connection.

"Did you three grow up together as the queen's wards?" Philip asked.

"Yes and no," Ella said. "Hemnes was the son of the queen's best general. When he was little, his parents were killed in combat, and my aunt took over as his legal guardian. As for Torryn, he was the illegitimate son of a noblewoman and her butler. His birth was the scandal of the decade, but to smooth things over, my aunt offered to have Torryn stay at the castle and 'begin his studies.'"

"What about you?"

Ella shook her head. "I came to live with my aunt when I was ten."

There was undoubtedly more to her story, but if that's all she was willing to share at the moment, it was none of Philip's business. He hated when people tried to pry into his life and he wasn't about to do the same to Ella. Sometimes, it was best to keep things close to your chest until the moment was right.

Ella fiddled with one of the tiny flowers that had fallen out of her braids. The firelight reflected in her dark eyes. After a moment, she spoke, "My mother was the younger of two princesses. She knew the chances of becoming queen were slim, so she lived a very carefree life. The people loved her. She was radiant and innocent and beautiful; everyone says Everleigh is a miniature version of her. One day, she decided she wanted to visit the human world. She knew her parents would never give her permission to go, so she simply packed up and left."

Philip himself had often considered doing the same thing. Of

189

course, that would be foolish and dangerous. No good would come from it.

"Somehow, she ended up in Chicago," Ella continued. "She was young, alone, and lost. Just as she was about to give up, she met a dashing young man who offered to help." Ella gave a small, wistful sigh, "It was love at first sight."

Philip gracefully held back a skeptical snort. There was no such thing as love at first sight, but Ella could believe what she wished.

"She lived with his parents while they dated, and a few months later, they were married. About a year after that, I was born. But when I was a few weeks old, the elves found my mother. They had been searching for her ever since she left. Many believed she had been kidnapped or killed, but no one guessed she would have gone to the human world, married a human, and birthed a half-human child. They dragged her back to the elven world against her will, leaving my dad to raise me on his own."

After a moment, she continued. "He was the best man I ever knew. He worked as a librarian and devoted his life to keeping kids off the streets. He provided them a safe space to go after school and experience the magic of books. He was my hero."

Ella paused, swallowing hard. "But when I was nine, he was in a car accident. He hung on long enough to tell me he loved me one last time before he died in the hospital. My aunt found me and brought me to this world, where I met my half-sister Everleigh, who was orphan too. My mother had remarried a high-ranking officer in the army, but they both died shortly before my dad."

Philip shifted uncomfortably. No one had ever opened up to him before, especially not like this. People didn't share their lives with him. How was he supposed to act in a situation like this?

190

"Because I'm an illegitimate, half-human child, Everleigh will be queen even though I'm the firstborn," Ella explained. "I never wanted to be royalty anyways. I was just happy to have a family again. But Aunt Celosia keeps me locked in the castle so the people won't find out my father was human. Only Hemnes and Torryn know about my dad. Even Everleigh and Linnmon think my father was an elf. Aunt Celosia thinks the people would despise me if they knew what I am."

Tears brimmed in Ella's eyes, threatening to spill over. "The mission in Haderra was supposed to earn my freedom. My wedding with Linnmon would have been called off, and I would be traveling the worlds with Hemnes and Torryn. Wherever I go, they go. I have one last chance to prove myself to my aunt. I won't fail. I can't. Because if I fail this, I'll fail everyone, and we'll be miserable for the rest of our lives."

She buried her head in her hands. Her shoulders shook with silent sobs. So many years of pain. All she wanted was to prove herself and be loved. Philip could understand that. He just didn't know how to articulate it.

"Gosh, Ella..." Philip didn't know what to say. He felt incredibly insensitive, which wasn't something that would have normally bothered him.

He shifted to sit beside Ella. Instead of pushing him away, she buried her head in his shoulder and continued to cry. His posture automatically went rigid, but he couldn't let his discomfort show. His aversion to emotions and physical contact would have to be shoved aside. Just for a moment.

This level of human connection was completely foreign to him. Never before had he been a literal shoulder for someone to cry on, especially not for a girl. He could barely handle his own emotions, much preferring to file them away and never think of

191

them again.

Ella was so open and vulnerable about what she felt. She'd known him for less than a week, and though he hadn't given her any reason to trust him, she'd been willing to share her story with him. This was new. This was uncomfortable. But this wasn't about him. This was about her, and right now, she needed him to listen to her. To be there for her.

After a few minutes, her sobs reduced to a few stray tears. With a weak laugh, she wiped the tears from her cheeks. "Look at me, crying and telling you my life's story while you're stuck in a strange world with no guarantee of getting home."

Panic shot through his mind. How had she managed to turn this back to him?

Ella continued. "I can imagine how much you miss your family. Your friends too. Maybe even a girlfriend." She nudged him gently with her shoulder.

Philip tensed. Of course, this was how things worked. She shared her story, and it was only fair that he should share his. He should tell her about his life in Queens. He should tell her about his workaholic father and his too-busy mother. He should tell her about Marius's constant, painful 'teasing'. He should tell her how much hatred and anger boiled under his skin. He should tell her how he learned to turn sarcasm and annoyance into armor. He should tell her how he was too afraid to feel things, to let people in.

Instead, he said, "Yeah. The sooner we get home, the better."

Disappointment flickered across Ella's face. He had brutally killed the moment.

"Well," she said after a moment, "we'll get you home before you know it. We should probably get some sleep now. We have a long walk ahead."

"Goodnight," Philip murmured, hating his cowardice. Turning his back on Ella, he settled on the hard, uneven ground. He cocooned himself in a blanket before the chill of the night air could reach him. Stars glittered above him, peeking through the trees. His eyes grew heavy as he gazed at the beauty above. Before he knew it, he drifted to sleep.

Chapter 17

Dash wanted to vomit.

He stood awkwardly at the side of a podium, fiddling with the gold cuffs of his silk jacket. An orator gave a not-so-brief introduction to a crowd of people.

Rhett always said public speaking was a ridiculous fear. But no matter how many times Dash had to stand in front of a crowd and speak, butterflies fluttered in his stomach. The thought of hundreds of eyes staring at him, judging him, and remembering his every mistake sent a shudder down his spine.

If he messed up today, his mistakes would torment him in the dead of night for years to come.

Applause rose from the audience, and Dash's heart rate skyrocketed. Was it time already? He wasn't ready. His palms were sweaty and his head spun and his mind raced... and the orator continued speaking.

He let out a breath of relief. He could have sworn all the fair folk in the first two rows noticed and took mental note of his nervousness.

From the back of the room, Nathan and Adrian caught his attention. They shot him encouraging smiles and thumbs-up, but it did nothing to calm his nerves. If anything, it set him more on edge.

The two of them had been disappearing frequently this past couple of days. They seemed to be avoiding him, though he couldn't figure out why. Whenever he asked about it, they assured him they were just busy with their new royal advisory jobs.

He couldn't shake the feeling they were hiding something. Perhaps they were planning a surprise for his coronation, or a charity event for the Fair Lords. Whatever they were keeping from him could be any number of things. Secrets weren't always bad.

Wincing, Dash could practically see the skeptical raise of Rhett's eyebrow. *'Secrets aren't all bad?' Really, Dash, I taught you better than this.*

Dash sighed; Rhett wouldn't understand. He was too cynical and isolated, unwilling to give any one a chance. Maybe he would be happier if he allowed himself to relax every once in a while. Maybe if he were happier, his magic would be restored more quickly.

That thought made him perk up. He would suggest it to his brother. Any idea of how to restore Rhett's magic sent a surge of hope through him. Even if Rhett was beginning to give up and stop searching for solutions, Dash would never quit. He wouldn't stop searching until his brother had every last drop of magic back to its full power.

The two of them would make it through this. They'd been through far worse together, and Dash wasn't about to let either of them give up now.

With a start, Dash realized the orator was finally bringing the introduction to a close. His throat constricted. His mind scrambled to remember why he was there.

"People of Haderra, I present Prince Dash, your soon-to-be Sovereign Prince and Gold Lord." Applause burst from the audience at the orator's words.

Dash froze, completely caught off-guard. His future title just didn't sound right. Hearing it aloud was like hearing a cat bark.

Not that there were cats in this world. Or dogs, for that matter.

Clearing his throat awkwardly, Dash took his place at the podium in the middle of the stage, where everyone had a good view of him.

He tried to say 'hello', but it came out more like a strangled croak than a word. Heat rushed to his face. His heart plummeted as he saw Nathan and Adrian wince and exchange a worried glance.

He couldn't do this.

There had to be another way.

Why did he have to make an address to the entire government? His business was with the Fair Lords, not everyone else. But this was the standard procedure. Without this address, nothing could get done.

Dash let out an even breath and tried not to think about the hundreds of pairs of eyes that blinked up at him.

This was for them.

He had to do this to keep his kingdom from crumbling to pieces.

With a new resolve, Dash squared his shoulders and gripped the sides of the podium. His tongue was like sandpaper. His breathing came in ragged gasps, but he could do this. He would win over his people. He would convince them of his plan. He could save his kingdom.

"Hello," Dash began with only a slight waver in his voice. "Thank you for gathering here today. As many of you may have heard, I would like to propose a plan that requires your support."

It was too late to turn back now. Without further introduction, he launched into the explanation of his plan. This was the easy part. He didn't relax, but at least he felt confident in the words he spoke. He had spent hours rehearsing this proposal with Rhett. He heard Rhett's calm voice in his head.

Keep your back straight, but not rigid; you want to look imposing, not uncomfortable.

Fold your wings; you shouldn't look like you might fly away at any point in the speech.

Speak slowly and clearly; even the elders in the back should be able to hear you.

Try to smile; the fair folk love beauty and charm.

Hold your head high; soon enough, you'll be their sovereign.

At that moment, Dash would have given anything to be like Rhett. He didn't have his brother's unearthly beauty. He was as ordinary as any regular human. He had too many freckles, a slightly crooked nose, too-large eyes, and messy curls. He didn't have Rhett's sparkling eyes, sharp features, high cheekbones, and tall, slender figure. He certainly couldn't win over a crowd.

Why couldn't Rhett have been the one to speak today? If he were giving this speech, the fair folk would leap to their feet with applause and adoration. They would agree with whatever he had to say before he even uttered a sound.

But Rhett wasn't here. It was just Dash in front of a crowd of fair folk that would soon be his subjects. It was just him with a crazy idea that might be the only thing to keep his kingdom from falling apart.

When Dash finished speaking, the crowd remained completely silent for three, excruciatingly long breaths. Then, they leaped to their feet, hollering questions. Their words crashed down on him, filling his head until he couldn't hear himself think.

Holding his hands out in a placating gesture, he tried to plead with them to settle down. He saw the orator's mouth moving as she called for order, but no one could hear anything over the noise.

Dash's heart thundered louder than the roar of the crowd. This was the worst-case scenario. The people hated his plan. They hated *him*. Why had he ever thought this was a good idea? Why had he believed his people would stand with him? Why—

Nathan and Adrian seized his arms and dragged him from the stage, interrupting his train of thought. The moment he was out of the crowd's line of sight, he sagged and let Nathan and Adrian bear the dead weight of his body.

They took him to a private room and spilled him into a plush chair. Nathan found a cool, damp cloth and draped it over his forehead, while Adrian paced, a green hand resting on the hilt of his sword.

Dash's ears still rang from the crowd's uproar. He barely felt the cloth against his brow, or Nathan trying to get him to drink from a crystal glass, or Adrian's incessant muttering as he paced.

"What happened up there?" Nathan asked.

Dash's words felt clumsy on his lips. "I can't do this."

"If you don't believe in yourself, how do you expect the rest of the kingdom to believe in you?"

Dash blinked at Nathan. "Do *you* believe in me? Do *you* think I'm the best sovereign this kingdom could have?"

Nathan hesitated. He *hesitated.* In the split second of silence that passed between them, Dash's eyes welled with tears. Even his best friends didn't think he could do this. He was better off abdicating and letting the Fair Lords scramble for power. If he abdicated, he could move to the countryside and start an apprenticeship as a healer.

Dash's scrambling thoughts screeched to a halt. If he wasn't royalty, he would just be starting his apprenticeship. That was a sobering thought. But no. Here he was, desperately trying to save an entire kingdom before a crown even sat atop his head.

What was he doing?

What was he *thinking*?

Of course, the Fair Lords would never side with him. He was a child. Why would they put the fate of their kingdom in the hands of a half-human boy who didn't even know how to use his magic until a few years ago?

This was a lost cause.

Nathan must have read Dash's crestfallen expression. He opened his mouth—most likely to offer some pathetic, halfhearted assurance—but before he could speak, the door burst open.

All six Fair Lords filed into the room. Dash shot up in his seat, his sudden posture change popping his spine. He swiped at his cheeks and tried to emulate Rhett's commanding presence. Mercifully, the Fair Lords humored him and pretended not to notice the tracks of tears down his blotchy cheeks.

"Your Sovereignty," The Red Lord said, sweeping a gracious bow. The fluttering, bell-shaped sleeves of his red silk jacket brushed the ground. "We wish to speak with you about your proposal."

Dash searched the Fair Lords' faces for any emotion, but they each wore impassive masks of stone. He had only met the Fair Lords in passing, during balls or banquets. Elliott usually occupied their time and attention, and Dash was usually spared the discomfort of facing them alone. These six were the most powerful fair folk in Haderra. A part of him wondered why they didn't just dethrone him now and establish a bureaucracy. The people would most likely support them.

Instead, they bowed before him. Though they looked down their noses at the child playing sovereign, they still bowed. Was the royal blood that flowed through his veins *that* important to them? Did they care about preserving tradition so much that they would accept him as their Sovereign instead of taking the throne for themselves?

Adrian cleared his throat, and Dash started. The Fair Lords stared expectantly at him.

"Pardon?" Dash asked, trying not to sound like a complete fool.

"We were impressed by your proposal." The Orange Lord said for what Dash guessed was the second time. His rough voice crackled like logs over a fire.

Dash didn't quite believe what he was hearing. His eyebrows drew together in confusion. "You—you were impressed? *I* impressed *you*? I mean, um, my proposal impressed you?"

The Yellow Lord stepped forward, her mustard yellow hair swishing around her shoulders as she nodded. "We are curious to hear more of this plan of yours."

This didn't make sense. With the uproar his proposal caused, Dash had expected a scolding from the Fair Lords. After all, they were supposed to represent the wishes of the people. He imagined the wishes of the people most likely entailed his head on a pike or his banishment to the human world.

The Green Lord folded her green hands into her leaf-green sleeves. "Tell us as much as possible about this plan. Before we take this to our people, we wish to know all of the facts."

"You have great courage to propose such a thing when you have not yet been crowned Sovereign Prince of Haderra," the Blue Lord said, stroking his cerulean beard.

Dash gaped at the Fair Lords in disbelief. "You're not angry?"

"We wish to know more," the Red Lord said. The rest of the Fair Lords expressed their agreement.

Out of the corner of his eye, Dash glimpsed Nathan and Adrian exchanging a look of surprise. He took a deep breath and held it for a count of ten. He believed in this plan. It was the best change their kingdom had for survival. All he had to do was convince the Fair Lords. He could do this. If not, he would be able to look Rhett in the eye and tell him he gave it his best.

"It will all start the day after my coronation..." he began.

Chapter 18

Early-morning sunbeams peeked through the trees. Sweet, fresh dew flavored the air. Birds singing and squirrels chattering combined with the steady rushing of the river created a sort of wild, untamable music. Philip savored the quiet, natural peace. It was something so completely foreign to him, yet it just felt *right*.

Bracing himself for his inevitable caffeine headache, he sat up and rubbed the sleep from his eyes. He stretched his sore back, and a bit of tension escaped his stiff rib cage. He slipped out of his blanket as quietly as he could, grateful that Ella, Max, and Vinnia remained asleep.

Vinnia slept in kelpie form. The early morning sun struck her silver bridle, which glinted like a knife. Her hind leg twitched while she made a small whinnying noise, apparently caught in the middle of a dream.

Philip hesitated as his eyes caught on her needle-like teeth. Though she seemed small and innocent, she was dangerous. She could kill them all in an instant. Her magic could be useful, but was it worth the risk of trusting her?

Before Vinnia could wake up to see him staring at her in dismay, Philip turned away and grabbed his boots, which lay by the remains of the fire. While the once-simple task of getting dressed had become increasingly difficult thanks to the loss of his arm, he could at least strap on his boots without much difficulty.

Something cool and smooth moved beneath his heel as he slid his foot into the left boot. Releasing an embarrassingly high-pitched shriek, he dropped the boot and scrambled away.

The others bolted upright at the sound of his scream. Vinnia morphed back to human form in an instant.

"What's happening?" Ella already had her knife in hand.

Philip froze in terror.

A blood-red snake slithered out of his boot, hissing menacingly. It had three conjoined heads, each of which sported a vicious mouthful of curved fangs. Spines covered its body from the crests of its heads to the barbed tip of its tail. All three heads glared at Philip with glowing yellow eyes.

It lashed out with impossible speed. Three heads sank their fangs into his thigh. He screamed in agony. It felt as if someone had driven white-hot nails into his flesh. A stiff, burning sensation slowly began to spread through his leg.

The snake's forked tongues flickered as it recoiled, preparing to strike again. It lashed out at him again but never made contact.

Vinnia plucked the snake out of the air like it was nothing more than a stray scarf caught in the breeze.

The snake writhed in her grip and sank its fangs into her arm, but she didn't bat an eyelash. Confused by her lack of reaction, the snake hissed and jabbed its barbed tail into her side.

Vinnia's pupils shrank to slits, and she stuck a forked tongue out at the snake. The snake recoiled. Without a second of hesitation, she ripped the heads off the snake's body and tossed them to the dirt like broken toys. They continued to hiss for a moment, before finally falling still.

Philip, Ella, and Max gaped at Vinnia, who rolled her eyes, more annoyed by the ordeal than anything. She discarded the snake's body and wiped her bloody hands on her pants. "Medusa Basilisks can be so dramatic."

The burning in Philip's leg began to spread up to his waist.

"That was a Medusa Basilisk?" Ella's eyes widened in shock, "They're monsters. They're supposed to be trapped on the Island Corvus, not here in the Pixie Forest!"

Vinnia shrugged. "You'd be surprised how many monsters find their way here."

"But they're dangerous!" Ella protested, "A bite from one— oh stars... Philip your leg!"

In one swift movement, Ella used her knife to slice open Philip's deerskin trousers. She gasped in horror as she peeled the bloody fabric away.

Craning his neck, Philip bent forwards to see what was wrong. He immediately wished he hadn't looked. The skin around the puncture wounds on his thigh turned concrete grey. Philip's hand flew to the grey skin, which was as cool and solid as stone.

Philip pressed a hand to his mouth to keep himself from vomiting.

"What's happening to him?" Max asked.

"A Medusa Basilisk's venom turns its victim to stone," Vinnia answered.

Panic seized Philip. He was turning to stone. This wasn't possible. Snake venom was supposed to contain specific toxins. Those, at least, could be explained by science. People didn't just turn to stone because of a snakebite. Granted, the snakebite was from a three-headed snake, but things like this weren't *normal*.

"How do we fix it?" Max asked frantically.

Vinnia's voice stayed casual. "It's supposedly irreversible."

"Supposedly?" Ella demanded.

Vinnia examined the snakebites on her arm, which were also beginning to turn to stone. She placed her fingers against the stone and closed her eyes. Though it was a struggle for Philip to keep his gaze away from the stone that spread down his leg, he watched as Vinnia began to sing. Her voice was thin, raspy, and off-key. At the sound of her singing, the stone stopped spreading and began to recede. Within seconds, her arm was back to normal. The stone had completely disappeared, and the puncture wounds from the snakebites were perfectly healed.

"You—did you just…?" Ella was at a loss for words.

"Mixie magic is more powerful than you think. Now, move over." Vinnia edged Ella out of the way and knelt next to Philip. She placed her hands over the stone on his thigh and began to sing. Just like it did on her arm, the stone stopped spreading and began to recede at the sound of her voice.

The strange wrongness of magic twisted in Philip's abdomen. Something about Vinnia's magic felt different than any other magic he had experienced. This magic left a salty tang on his tongue as if he'd swallowed a mouthful of seawater.

He coughed and sputtered, but Vinnia didn't remove her hand or stop singing. The salty taste stung his tongue and overwhelmed him until even his nostrils were filled with the sharp tang. When Vinnia finally stopped singing, he didn't even bother to examine his leg. He snatched up the canister of water and drank until the taste of saltwater washed away.

Vinnia sat back on her hands and studied him. "Sorry about the salt. It's a side effect of mixie magic."

Philip ran a hand over the skin on his leg, now perfectly soft and smooth. Six scars down his thigh remained as the only evidence of the attack. The stiff, numb sensation of turning to stone had been replaced with the warm, flexible feeling of flesh.

Ella gripped his elbow and supported him as he stood. A rush of dizziness made his caffeine headache spike. He inhaled sharply and hesitated a moment before putting his full weight on his leg. It was as if nothing had happened; there was no pain, no stiffness at all.

"You're welcome, by the way," Vinnia said, stretching like a cat, "Stars, I've been living in a forest most of my life, and my manners are still better than yours."

As much as Philip wanted to ignore her jab or make a sarcastic comeback, he sighed and said, "Thank you."

The corners of Vinnia's lips quirked into a small smile. "Don't mention it. I'm just glad I got a chance to show you how useful my skills can be."

With that, she stood and strode to the side of the river with Max at her heels. Philip watched them go, tilting his head as he studied Vinnia. Something was unsettling about her, but he couldn't put his finger on it. The ever-present suspicion and mistrust that lingered in the back of his mind screamed at him to be wary of her.

He hated the unpredictable air she exuded. She offered to take them to the Elder Tree in exchange for what? Companionship? That was laughable. She had healed him. So what? She had rescued them from the kelpie too. That still didn't mean he had to trust her.

"What she just did shouldn't have been possible," Ella said quietly. Untying the scarf from around her head and untwisting the coil of braids, she shook out her thick braids. They cascaded down her back like a waterfall. She turned her back to give Philip privacy as he changed into fresh clothing.

Philip struggled into yet another pair of deerskin trousers. "What do you mean?"

"Mixie magic is only good for shapeshifting. They're not supposed to be able to do anything else. What Vinnia just did—healing you, I mean—was merfolk magic. But merfolk can't use

206

their magic outside of the water. It doesn't make sense…" Ella trailed off.

"What do you think it means?" Philip asked. He knew nothing about magic, but if Ella said something wasn't possible, he believed her. If she was puzzled, that was cause for concern.

"I don't know," Ella admitted. "I've heard rumors about mixie magic being strange, but I've never met a mixie before now. I wouldn't know what a normal mixie is capable of, let alone an unusual one."

Philip rolled his eyes. "And rumors are *always* reliable."

"Don't I know it," Ella said with a bitter laugh of irony.

After a beat of silence, Philip spoke. "We should get moving. The sooner we find the Elder Tree, the sooner we can get out of this cursed forest."

Ella hesitated. "Are you sure you're feeling well enough to walk? You were just bitten by a Medusa Basilisk."

"He's fine." Vinnia appeared next to Philip. "I healed him, so he should be as good as new and ready to leave."

"Were you eavesdropping?" Philip demanded.

Vinnia shrugged, "Maybe."

Philip shot Ella a wary glance.

"Anyway," Vinnia continued, "If we want to reach the Elder Tree by today, we should start walking."

When no one objected, Vinnia scooped up a roll of blankets and shoved them unceremoniously into the nearest pack. Ella knelt to help her and, with a sigh, Philip did the same.

As soon as the campsite was packed, Vinnia beckoned for them to follow her. She walked along the river, heading downstream. The morning sun was at their backs as they walked. A cool breeze rushed through the forest, offsetting the sun's unrelenting warmth.

While they walked, Ella doled out a meager breakfast of bread and dried fruit. Only Vinnia refused, claiming that mixies survived off a strict diet of fish. Philip found slight consolation in the fact that they didn't have to alter the rations to feed her.

Max skipped alongside Vinnia, spouting nonsense as usual. Philip and Ella hung back, walking side-by-side in silence.

"So mixies only eat fish? Do you eat raw fish or cooked fish? Raw fish is gross unless it's in sushi. I like sushi. Do you like sushi? Do you even have sushi here? I guess if they don't have sushi, you can't have a sushi-pinion. That's a word I made up just now! It means an opinion about sushi. I like making up words. Do you?"

Philip quickly grew exasperated by his brother's incessant chatter. Vinnia humored him, though, and responded to each ridiculous question. At least Max wasn't complaining about the length of the walk. It was nice seeing Max back to his usual self. The stress and emotion of being trapped in this world weighed heavily on him. A carefree kid like him shouldn't have needed to bear that weight.

As they walked, Philip observed his surroundings. He didn't have much experience with forests in general, especially not magical forests. Sunlight illuminated the sunset-colored trees so they glowed like the multicolored fire his chemistry teacher loved to demonstrate in her lab. Birds with lavish, iridescent plumage swooped through the air on brightly colored wings. Squirrels and chipmunks scampered across the ground and bounded from tree to tree, gathering exotic-looking berries and nuts. A heavily perfumed scent enveloped the forest, though there wasn't a flower in sight.

"You know," Ella said, breaking the silence that hung between them, "this forest is one of the few places in this world that feels truly *magical*."

Oddly enough, Philip understood what she meant. Haderra

and Elvenmar were beautiful in their own ways, but this place had an unearthly sort of beauty. It was as if the forest had a pulse or a life in the heart of the trees. The sensation of magic hung in the air, like a bad memory lingering at the back of his mind.

It was strange how quickly he had grown used to magic. The absence of technology constantly plagued him, but he was fascinated by the way people had compensated for the lack of technology with magic.

Sharp, dark movement caught in the corner of his eye, distracting him from his train of thought. A bird swooped to perch in a tree and let out a throaty caw. Its sleek, black feathers contrasted vividly against the tree's lavender leaves. Unlike the rest of the birds he had seen in the Pixie Forest, this bird was familiar.

"Is that a crow?" Philip asked.

Ella followed Philip's gaze and nodded. "I always found it strange that crows were the only ones that existed in both the magical world and the human world."

The crow tilted its head, studying them with intelligent, beady eyes. Philip tilted his head in mimicry of the bird. He'd always liked the birds that frequented the skies in Queens. Most people found New York City's pigeons and starlings to be annoying pests, but he had always felt a sort of connection to them. It was ridiculous and illogical, but anytime he passed a bird, he found himself watching it. It fascinated him to see them hop about their lives, so oblivious to the large role they played in the ecosystem. They had no idea they were irreplaceable gears in a large machine.

"You know," Ella mused, "that might be one of the King's crows."

Vinnia whirled around, amber eyes wide. "What?"

Ella gave Vinnia a strange look. "They say the crowds gather information for the King and report back to him on Corvus. We

209

see the King's crows every once in a while. It's not a big deal."

Vinnia let out a colorful string of swear words. Max's face lit up in the devious expression of a child getting away with something naughty.

"It's nothing to worry about." Ella kept her voice steady and calm.

Vinnia didn't seem to hear her. She glared up at the crow. "Leave me alone!"

Ella rested a gentle hand on Vinnia's shoulder. "Vinnia, what are you doing?" she asked cautiously, "The King will hear you."

"Good," Vinnia shook Ella's hand away, her attention still fixated on the crow. "Go tell your master that he can take his prying, snooping spies and shove them up his—"

"Vinnia!" Ella exclaimed, clamping a hand over Vinnia's mouth. "Excuse her, Your Majesty," she apologized to the bird, "she doesn't mean to insult you."

The bird tittered—an eerie, jarring sound—before spreading its inky wings and taking to the air. Philip gazed after the bird until it disappeared. Its strange call echoed in his head like a siren's song.

When the crow was gone, Vinnia let out an angry breath. "I hate those stupid birds," she muttered.

"You can't just say things like that!" Ella hissed. "The King isn't one to be trifled with. He could do anything to you."

"I'm not afraid of the King," Vinnia snapped, "Nothing he can do would be worse than what's already been done to me."

Ella's expression softened. "Vinnia, I—"

"Let's keep walking." Vinnia didn't wait for an answer as she turned on her heel and marched away.

Chapter 19

Rhett was growing weaker day by day.

He slept more, ate less, and a constant headache plagued him throughout the day. His purple veins stood out dramatically against his translucent skin. Anytime he thought about it, anger roiled in his chest.

Fair folk magic was meant to be used. The more it was used, the more powerful it became. The opposite was also true; unused magic would wither away like an atrophied muscle until it became impossible to summon. Of course, most fair folk likened practicing magic to practicing a religion or enjoying a hobby; they did it often enough, but not so often that it took over their lives.

What Rhett wouldn't give to live like them. *Their* magic could be used safely. *Their* magic wasn't feared by everyone in this world and the next.

Purple magic killed and destroyed. It shook the foundation of the worlds, shattered bones like glass, and split entire kingdoms in half. The more Rhett used his magic, the more powerful it would become. If it weren't for the island that kept him imprisoned until the end of his days, he could set the worlds on fire just to watch them burn.

He wasn't simply imprisoned on the island; he was tethered to it. He was the living sacrifice to atone for the sins of the rulers of the past. The barrier around the island leeched the magic from his veins, fueling it through his very existence. As long as he had magic, the barrier would remain, keeping the monsters trapped.

211

The monsters provided just enough chaos and destruction to feed his magic for a while. But a while wasn't long enough.

As Rhett grew weaker—as his *magic* grew weaker—so did the island's magic. He would wither away, taking the barrier down with him. When the barrier disappeared, the monsters would be free.

Unlike Rhett, the monsters wouldn't show restraint if they got the chance to devour the worlds.

The ache in Philip's feet refused to cease. It worsened with each step until his legs were leaden. Tension lingered in his back. His stomach grumbled in pain.

They had settled into a routine as they walked. Vinnia led the way and set the pace with Max at her heels. The two of them exchanged meaningless banter to keep themselves occupied. Philip and Ella hung back a few feet, walking side-by-side. Conversation between them ebbed and flowed; sometimes they held in-depth discussions, while other times, they remained silent. In the quiet, Philip found himself scanning the sunset-colored trees in search of more crows.

The sun crept higher in the sky, and the day grew hotter. When the sun hung directly overhead, Ella handed out lunch rations. There would be plenty of food to last them the remainder of the journey, though eating the same three things—dried fruit, dried meat, and stale bread—quickly became tiresome.

"Are you sure you don't want something to eat?" Ella asked Vinnia, "I haven't seen you eat a single thing since we met."

"Mixies only eat once a week," Vinnia replied, "I've had plenty to eat. Don't worry about me."

Ella, looking unconvinced, frowned at the chunk of bread in her hand. "All right. If you change your mind, we have plenty of food to share."

They ate in silence as they walked, the only noise being the crunching of leaves beneath their feet. Even Philip grew bored by the monotony. His mind drifted, his thoughts always circling back to the crow. No matter how hard he tried, he couldn't get its caw out of his mind. What was it about that bird that left such an impression on him? Was it the glint of the sun against its midnight wings? Was it the intelligent glint in its beady eyes? He didn't know, which only made him more puzzled.

"Adventures look a lot more exciting in the movies," Max grumbled after a while.

"What is 'the movies'?" Vinnia asked.

As Max launched into a poor explanation of what a movie was, Ella leaned closer to Philip. She spoke in a low voice. "So, I've been thinking…"

"Oh boy," Philip teased, rolling his eyes.

"Kelpies and basilisks are monsters."

"And?"

"And," Ella said, "all the monsters in this world are supposed to be banished to the Island of Corvus. For some reason, the kelpie and the basilisk were here in the Pixie Forest, which is nowhere near Corvus."

She had said something similar when he had been bitten by the Medusa Basilisk.

"Didn't Vinnia say there are more monsters here than we'd think?" Philip recalled.

"Yes, and that's what I'm worried about," Ella replied. "There have been rumors about the King letting monsters out of Corvus. Some people think he's doing it out of spite, others think he's doing it because the monsters are running out of food."

The thought of hungry monsters roaming the world

unsupervised sent a shiver down Philip's spine; he had far too much experience almost becoming a meal for monsters. He still wore the scars from his near-misses with the manticore, the kelpie, and the Medusa Basilisk.

"What do you think it means?" Philip asked.

Ella shook her head. "I don't know, but I'm worried. I get this foreboding feeling whenever I think about it…"

Philip didn't quite understand what she meant, but he nodded anyway. "Has anything like this ever happened before?"

A strange look passed over Ella's face like she was trying to recall a distant memory. "I—I'm not sure. No one knows how long the King has ruled Corvus. People say he's just… always existed. It doesn't make sense, but something like this could've happened a long time ago. Vinnia might know something about it."

Ahead, Vinnia listened intently to Max's rambling about the latest superhero movie. With her large eyes, delicate features, and tiny frame, she looked so harmless and unassuming. She had been living alone in the Pixie Forest most of her life, but she seemed normal. It was as if the wildness and danger of the forest were lost on Vinnia; like she hadn't realized the nature of the cursed place she called home.

What exactly did she know about the monsters that roamed the Pixie Forest? Neither the kelpie nor the Medusa Basilisk fazed her. Now that Philip thought about it, he realized the crow, of all things, had been what made her act strangely.

As if Ella could read his mind, she voiced these same questions aloud to Vinnia, who glanced back and studied them suspiciously. Her eyes narrowed.

"It's pretty common to see them here," she said finally. "Why?"

Ella made a vague noise in her throat. "Do you have any idea why they're here?"

"How should I know?" Vinnia defended. "They show up, and I scare them away. For the most part, they leave me alone, and I do the same."

"Aren't you concerned about the monsters in the forest?" Ella asked, "What if one of them attacks you, and you can't defend yourself? Aren't you afraid of dying here?"

"Am I afraid of dying and being trapped inside my own decaying body?" Vinnia gave a short, harsh laugh. "Not really."

Philip and Ella exchanged an incredulous look. What kind of person didn't fear such a brutal death?

Ella tilted her head, "But—"

"Oh look," Vinnia interrupted. "We found it."

She stopped in front of a tablet-shaped rock that towered over the river. The rock was twice Philip's height and as wide as Vinnia was tall.

Max stared up at the rock in confusion, "*This* is the Elder Tree?"

Philip wanted to smack his little brother upside the head. Critical thinking wasn't one of Max's strengths.

"Of course not," Vinnia said. "This is where we cross the river."

In one fluid motion, she morphed into a kelpie. Rearing back, she slammed her front hooves into the rock. It crashed down with a deafening thud, creating a makeshift bridge over the river.

She climbed on top of the rock and trotted across the flat surface. When she reached the other side of the river, she morphed back to her normal self and beckoned for them to follow. "Come on!"

Max surged forwards, eager to do anything dangerous and "exciting." He skipped across the surface of the rock as if it were nothing more than a game of hopscotch. As if he weren't crossing a river of swift, poisonous water teeming with monsters.

Ella nudged Philip with her shoulder. "You're next."

"Ladies first," he replied.

Ella threw him an exasperated look and stepped onto the rock. She strode across the surface, never losing her footing. When she reached the other side, she shot him an encouraging thumbs-up.

Philip took a deep, steadying breath and followed Ella. Though the surface of the rock was perfectly flat, he crossed slowly, putting one foot in front of the other. His ruined center of balance, which hadn't been the same since he lost all feeling in his right arm, caused him to teeter dangerously close to the edge.

It took ages for him to reach the other side of the river. When he did, he stumbled to solid ground, dizzy and lightheaded.

Vinnia barely waited for his feet to touch the ground before turning and leading them away from the river. Max, as always, trotted at her side. Ella, at least, waited for Philip to regain his footing before following.

As they walked with the river at their backs, the sound slowly faded away, leaving an eerie silence in its absence. The change in the forest was gradual but distinct. First, the vibrant colors of the sunset leaves dulled to gentle pastels, and a strange hush fell over the wildlife. The trees thinned out, and the leaves morphed from soft pastels to metallic silver.

A hollow silence filled the air as they walked through the silver trees, which glinted like mirrors fogged by steam. Beneath their feet, metallic leaves crunched not like regular leaves, but like tinfoil. Any sign of life had completely deserted this part of the forest. Every breath Philip took sounded too loud, like an invasion of sacred ground.

Vinnia stopped abruptly in her tracks. "We're here."

A gasp escaped Philip's lips when he peered through the trees, following Vinnia's gaze. The silver trees formed a sort of wall around a perfectly circular clearing. In the middle of the clearing grew the largest tree Philip had ever seen. Its silver leaves rustled in the wind, tinkling like wind chimes when they clinked together. Streaks of silver wove through the dark brown bark and whorled neatly around the gaping hollow in the tree's center.

"The Elder Tree," Ella breathed reverently.

A pixie ruler's sacred boughs. This was it.

Philip's attention was quickly pulled from the majesty of the Elder Tree to the four, terrifying figures that paced the clearing. Each figure stood over six feet tall and wielded a different weapon.

The first figure held a flaming sword. Its eyes glowed white against its simmering, molten-lava skin. Long, thin wings jutted from its back, flickering like tongues of fire.

The second figure clutched a bow nocked with a feathered arrow. The air whirled around its shifting, translucent form. A phantom wind whipped the figure's white hair around its face. Its wings were made of the wind itself.

The third figure gripped a battle-ax in its crumbling fingers. Clumps of dirt and chunks of stone made up its massive form. As it stalked around the Elder Tree, bits of dirt and rock rained from its limbs. Stone wings were stabbed into its back like knives.

The fourth figure coiled a whip around its forearm. Its body was a swirling, churning mass of water that moved like waves on the sea. Its wings—two waterfalls of dense mist—erupted from

217

its shoulder blades.

Philip shrank back into the trees.

"What *are* they?" Max asked, eyes wide in amazement.

"Those are pixies," Vinnia said, "This *is* the Pixie Forest, after all. Who else should guard our sacred tree?"

Philip refused to believe it. The figures in the clearing couldn't be pixies. Pixies were supposed to be tiny, harmless creatures who could hardly lift a stone. They were *not* supposed to be hulking, six-foot-tall figures that carried deadly weapons.

"We have to figure out a plan," Ella said. "All we need is a couple of leaves."

"Hey, guys!" Max exclaimed, "Look at these cute squirrels!"

"Not now, Max," Philip dismissed his brother without a glance. "How are we going to get past the guards?"

"We'll need a distraction," Ella said.

"Hey, guys," Max said, "Look…"

"Not now, Max," Philip repeated firmly.

"I can morph into a kelpie and distract them while the three of you sneak to the tree," Vinnia suggested.

"That might work," Ella said. "But wouldn't it be easier if only one of us sneaks to the tree while the rest of us cause a distraction?"

"Whoever sneaks up to the tree will need someone to cover them," Philip added.

Ella tapped her chin thoughtfully. "So, we split off into pairs?"

"Maybe we should—"

"Guys!" Max screeched. "The squirrels!"

Philip whirled around, irritation surging through him. But when he saw Max, he froze, all the annoyance draining out of him.

Max perched on top of a large rock, practically folded in on himself. About twenty golden squirrels surrounded the rock in an unnaturally perfect circle. Their beady eyes blinked up at Max with a hungry glint.

"I just wanted to pet one." Max whimpered.

Philip kept his voice low and steady. "Don't move."

One of the squirrels inched forwards, setting a paw on the rock. Max sucked in a sharp breath. The squirrels stilled for a beat. Then, in unison, they leaped onto the rock, swarming him.

Shrieking, Max tumbled from the rock and swiped furiously at the squirrels. They only held on tighter as they clung to his arms, latched onto his neck, and dug into his legs.

Philip and Ella rushed forward to help, but Vinnia reached Max first. She morphed into a kelpie mid-bound and descended on the squirrels. She ground the rodents into the forest floor with her hooves and ripped them off of Max's body with her razor-sharp teeth. When she had destroyed every last squirrel, all that remained was Max, curled into a tight ball. She morphed back to normal and knelt next to him with surprising protectiveness. She set to work healing the bloody bite marks that covered Max's body.

Before Philip could race to his brother's side, Ella seized his arm and yanked him behind a tree. He craned his neck to see Max, but she didn't release her iron grip on him.

The air around them grew hotter. At first, it was barely noticeable, but within seconds, sweat dripped down Philip's forehead and plastered his shirt to his chest. The heat was as stifling as an oven, and its waves radiated through the air.

Wiping sweat from his eyes, Philip peered around the tree. Ella's grip tightened on his good arm. When his gaze found Vinnia and Max, he inhaled sharply; they were surrounded.

219

Chapter 20

This couldn't be happening. They hadn't even put together a semblance of a plan, and already, they had been discovered. As far as Philip knew, the pixies hadn't seen him and Ella, but that was little consolation when Max was being held at sword point.

The fire pixie hovered above them, its flaming sword inches from Max's head. The earth and water pixies flanked the fire pixie on either side. Wind rustled through the leaves, signaling that the wind pixie was nearby.

What was the next logical course of action? Philip had to reach the Elder Tree, which was roughly one hundred yards away from where they stood. What resources did they have? Philip and Ella had swords and knives. Vinnia had magic. And Max... Max was vulnerable.

Vinnia, the first of the two to realize they were surrounded, stood slowly, shoulders back, eyes blazing. She lifted her hands and held them in front of her, not in a placating gesture, but in a fighting stance.

An uneasy shift passed through the pixies. Sure, Vinnia was threatening in her own right—especially if the pixies recognized she was a mixie—but the reaction was unnerving nonetheless.

"Iva?" The earth pixie rasped in a voice like gravel.

Vinnia gave a curt nod, still standing defensively over Max.

The guards shrank away from Vinnia as if she had just declared she had a contagious, life-threatening disease. Her expression hardened. She shifted her stance, and the pixies took a step back.

What was it about Vinnia—tiny, girlish Vinnia—that struck fear into the guards of the Elder Tree? Did they fear mixies that much? Or was it something to do with the word the earth pixie had spoken? *Iva.* What did it mean?

"*Haaf,*" the fire pixie's voice crackled and hissed like wet logs over a fire.

Vinnia clenched her jaw and nodded again, her expression clouded over.

The pixies backed even farther away from Vinnia, trying to gain as much distance from her as possible, while still surrounding them and protecting the Elder Tree. Philip and Ella shifted around the tree, avoiding the retreating guards.

Philip didn't have a clue as to what those words meant, but it was clear they didn't mean anything good. The pixies watched Vinnia like she was a ticking bomb that could explode at any moment.

She began to speak slowly as if she were trying to hypnotize them, but Philip didn't hear a word she said. He curled his fingers around the hilt of his sword and slid it out of the leather sheath. Ella looked up at him with frantic, imploring eyes, but he pressed his lips together and shook his head.

He pressed his back to the rough bark of the tree and gauged the distance to the nearest tree. It was about two feet to his right. Two feet closer to the Elder Tree. Sucking in a deep breath, he darted to the next tree. The split second in no man's land sent his heart thundering.

Ella appeared next to him mere seconds later. Philip gave her a grateful smile, surprised by the relief he felt at having her by his side. The two of them darted from tree to tree as silently as possible. Vinnia continued to talk, and the pixies' focus remained on her.

By some miracle, they reached the edge of the clearing undiscovered. The Elder Tree was only about thirty yards away. If they ran for it, they might be able to make it before the pixies realized. But would it be safer to sneak to the tree? That way, they would make less noise. But what if they were caught sneaking halfway to the tree? They would be out in the open and...

Ella pressed her lips against Philip's ear and whispered, "You go right, I go left. On the count of three, we run for it."

Philip nodded as Ella held one finger up. Then two fingers. Then, on three, he sprinted into the clearing alongside Ella. Their footsteps thumped too loudly, and from the unearthly noises that erupted behind them, he knew they had been spotted.

With every bound, Philip drew nearer to the Elder Tree. The air around him grew stiflingly hot. He gritted his teeth and pushed himself to run harder.

Ella's shriek split through the air.

Philip risked a glance over his shoulder and immediately regretted it. The fire guard was mere feet behind him. Raising its arms like a crescendo, the air pixie sent a gust of wind that swept Ella off her feet. Vinnia hurled walls of water at the water pixie, who countered with larger and stronger waves. Max darted through trees as the earth pixie hurled boulders at him.

This wasn't going to end well.

Pain exploded in Philip's side. He cried out and sprawled face-first at the base of the Elder Tree. Fire roared through his veins. Behind him, the fire pixie held a ball of fire in its hand. The smell of burnt flesh filled his nostrils. Through his tear-blurred vision, he could see the waves of heat radiating from the pixie's body.

He abandoned his sword and used his hand to grip the base

of the Elder Tree. The dark bark and silver metal of the tree's trunk were slick under his sweat-coated palm. Using the Elder Tree for support, he staggered to his feet. He clutched his side and braced himself against the tree, anticipating another attack.

The fire pixie hovered a few yards away from the Elder Tree, a ball of fire in one hand, a flaming sword in the other. It moved closer, but seconds later, sprang back as if it had been burned. The fire pixie let out a frustrated hiss like water being poured over a bonfire.

Philip wiped the sweat from his brow. Why did it have to be so *hot*?

Then, it struck him; the fire pixie couldn't get close to the Elder Tree without catching it on fire. Though parts of the trunk were metal and the leaves appeared to be metallic as well, he guessed the Elder Tree would burn almost as thoroughly as any other tree. As long as he stayed close to the tree, he would be safe. Ironic that the very being that protected the tree could set it ablaze in seconds.

Adrenaline surged through him at the realization. He reached up and snapped a small, low-hanging branch off the Elder Tree. Despite the razor-sharp edges of the silver leaves, he clutched the branch to his chest.

The fire pixie shrieked in rage, catching the other pixies' attention. Philip froze, his back pressed against the Elder Tree as all four pixies whirled to face him. He was like a rabbit surrounded by a pack of wolves. Or one of the nerdy kids at school when the jocks decided to have some "fun" between classes. Or an unsuspecting teenager when their extended family members ambushed them with the inevitable "what are you going to do with your life?" question. Or... or maybe he needed to get out of his head and focus on the situation at hand.

Vinnia took advantage of the shift in the pixie's focus. She sent a wall of water hurtling towards the fire pixie, who noticed it a second too late. The water crashed over the pixie with a deafening hiss. Dropping to its knees, the fire pixie wailed as its molten lava skin steamed and hardened into a black, rocky substance. It collapsed, completely immobilized.

With the shrieks of the fire pixie echoing in his ears, Philip barely registered the rumbling beneath his feet. When thin fissures split the ground beneath him, he snapped out of his trance. He dove out of the way right before a sinkhole opened up where he had just been standing.

The sharp edges of the leaves dug into his chest like tiny knives. He rolled to the side, narrowly avoiding a boulder the earth guard hurled at him. A cloud of dust exploded in his face. His lungs constricted against the dust that filled them with every breath. As he scrambled to his feet, a coughing fit overtook him.

A gust of wind blew away the dust, providing momentary relief. A second gust lifted him off his feet, then slammed him to the ground with bone-crushing force. The air whooshed out of his lungs. He could have sworn he felt a few ribs crack. The branch from the Elder Tree flew from his hands.

Someone started shouting, but through the pain-induced haze, he couldn't tell who it was. He couldn't move. He couldn't breathe. He couldn't think. His vision went white with pain, his head throbbing with a sickening rhythm.

A familiar face appeared in his clouded vision. Vinnia stood over him, her dirty, blood-streaked face set with grim determination. Her hands whipped this way and that, sending waves of water crashing in every direction. She didn't have the branch from the Elder Tree.

Philip wished he could see where Ella and Max were. Were

they okay? Did either of them have the branch? Were they even alive? This would all be for nothing if they didn't escape with the boughs *and* their lives.

Vinnia continued sending wave after wave until words boomed over the rush of the water.

"Come hither."

The words echoed in Philip's head, sounding hollow and far away.

Vinnia froze, eyes glinting like knives. "What?"

"Come hither," the wind repeated.

This time, Philip was less sure he'd heard the correct words. It sounded more like, "Commander," but that didn't make any more sense than, "Come hither."

Vinnia lowered her hands and spoke in a low voice. Her quick, sharp words were unintelligible.

"Come hither."

There it was again. The same, strange words like distant thunder.

Vinnia took a step forward. The air shifted as if the wind itself bent away from her. She took another step. The shift happened again. She threw out her arms and sent out two blasts of water more powerful than a firehose. Everything fell silent.

Vinnia's face was set in an unreadable mask as she knelt next to Philip. Her words slurred together in his head, but after a few moments, he understood.

"Can you stand?" she repeated.

Managing a faint nod, Philip braced himself and struggled to his feet. Though he doubled over in pain, he managed to stand. Vinnia draped his limp arm over her shoulders and began to walk.

Philip limped alongside Vinnia, not daring to ask what was happening. None of the guards pursued them. Not even with a spiteful gust of wind. The two of them simply walked into the trees.

Vinnia said nothing. She refused to meet his eyes. She clenched her jaw and stared resolutely ahead.

Philip couldn't form a cohesive sentence to ask Vinnia what had happened, where they were going, or where Ella and Max were. He forced himself to take one step after another, trying not to lean on her for support. As much as he wanted to curl up and sleep away the pain, he still had *some* dignity left.

They walked and walked and walked until Philip couldn't take it any longer. His knees buckled beneath him, and he collapsed against a tree. Vinnia tried to have him back to his feet, but it was no use. He sagged against the tree and clutched his side, pain and confusion crashing over him like one of Vinnia's waves.

"We have to keep going," Vinnia said, her voice raspy.

Philip shook his head. "Please. Just for a minute."

After a moment of conflict, Vinnia relented. She couldn't hide the relief that crossed her face as she sank to the ground. Philip shrugged his pack off, feeling one hundred times lighter without its weight. With numb fingers, he rummaged around in his pack until he found his nearly-empty canister of water. He handed it to Vinnia before taking a swig himself.

"Where are Ella and Max?" Philip managed to ask.

"We'll meet them by the river. They have the bough." Vinnia said between gulps of water.

"How did we escape?"

"I immobilized the pixies."

"How?"

"Enough questions. Keep walking."

Vinnia's dismissal of his question made Philip suspicious,

226

but the pain took away his will to argue or protest. He forced himself to put the canteen back and don the weight of his pack. His ribs screamed in pain, but he had to ignore them.

His feet were leaden as they walked. Each step only worsened the pain in his side. He had spared a glance at the wound while they rested and immediately regretted it; an angry, oozing burn covered the right side of his abdomen. Seeing the wound almost seemed to make the pain worse.

Vinnia was somber as they walked. It would have been easy for her to morph into a kelpie and trot off without him, but she didn't. She kept a slow pace and allowed him to rest when he needed it—though he suspected the frequent breaks weren't only for him.

By the time they reached the river, the sun hung low over the horizon. They collapsed by the water, panting from exertion and dizzy with fatigue. But no amount of weariness could have kept Philip's heart from practically leaping out of his chest with relief when Ella and Max rushed from the trees to greet them.

Max let out a sob as he collapsed to the ground next to Philip. He threw his arms around him. "You're okay," he cried over and over again.

Wincing in pain, Philip leaned into Max's hug. He wanted to pull away, but his little brother needed the embrace. A sense of groundedness washed over him. He and Vinnia were alive. Ella was unharmed. Most importantly, *Max was safe.*

The energy from their reunion quickly fizzled out, though, and exhaustion sank in. No one waited to unpack anything. They collapsed on the grass and fell asleep instantly.

Chapter 21

Philip woke to the sound of soft singing.

For a moment, he couldn't remember where he was. His brain replayed the events of the previous day with surprising clarity, recovering from and compensating for his shock.

The pain in his side was completely gone. He sat up and lifted the singed remains of his shirt. The burn from the fire pixie's fireball had been completely healed, leaving nothing but mangled scars across his skin. His broken ribs had been healed as well.

Vinnia glanced up from her position bent over Ella's body. She continued to sing, a warbling sound that Philip couldn't believe was the source of such powerful magic.

"You healed us," Philip kept his voice low. "Thanks."

"Don't mention it." Vinnia shrugged. Her eyes still had a hard edge, but otherwise, she showed no signs of injury or fatigue.

Philip's gaze found the branch from the Elder Tree, which lay by Max's head. Gently. He lifted the branch, admiring how the sunlight bounced off of the mirrored leaves with blinding, iridescent light.

"All this pain for a little branch," Vinnia murmured, "What would you three do without me?"

What *were* they going to do without Vinnia? They couldn't take her with them for the rest of the quest, could they?

As if she'd read Philip's mind, Vinnia pulled a piece of parchment from her pocket. "I found this in the front pocket of your pack. Is it important?"

Philip snatched the paper out of Vinnia's hand. "You went through my pack?"

"Only to find water. So, what is it? It looks like some list of riddles."

"It's nothing."

"Well, it's obviously *something*," Vinnia huffed, "We almost died back there for a branch of the Elder Tree. The third item on that list is *'A pixie ruler's sacred boughs.'* The Elder Tree is the pixie's sacred tree. This isn't a coincidence."

"So?" Philip snapped in annoyance. To be fair, it was mostly towards himself for not hiding the list in a safer spot.

"*So*, this list is important. It means something. And I want to help find the other items. I already know the next item on the list. *'A mermaid ruler's precious armor'*. I know exactly what that is. I can take you to the merfolk kingdom and help you find it."

Philip pressed his lips together, considering her offer. So far, Vinnia had been an invaluable asset. There was no question about it; without Vinnia and her magic, they would be dead. She had risked her life to save them time and time again. She had a soft spot for Max and prioritized his safety above all else. She was a formidable opponent. All things considered, why was Philip hesitant to let her help them?

Was it her blatant refusal to answer his questions? Her frustrating dismissal of what happened at the Elder Tree? Or maybe... maybe it was the fact that the pixies guarding the Elder Tree had been so afraid of her. Maybe it was the fact that she killed with frightening ease. Maybe it was the fact that she was too unpredictable.

Maybe Philip just refused to admit Vinnia scared him a little.

Looking down at her slight, five-foot-nothing frame, Philip

told himself it was ridiculous to be afraid of her. But he remembered the cold expression she wore as she tore the heads off the Medusa Basilisk. He remembered the bitterness with which she had snapped at the crows belonging to the most powerful man in this world and the next. What could have happened to make such a young girl so callous?

"All right," he said finally. "You can help."

Vinnia's face broke into a triumphant smirk. He had a feeling she'd known he would give in.

"Now, are you going to tell me what you think the next item is?" he asked.

Vinnia's grin turned devilish. "I'll tell you on the way to Mermaidia."

"Mermaidia?" Philip raised a skeptical eyebrow. "Seriously?"

"It's not like *I* named it."

"Fair enough."

"What's fair?" Ella asked groggily. She pushed herself into a sitting position and rubbed the sleep from her eyes.

"I know how to get the next item," Vinnia replied.

"Really?" At those words, Ella was wide awake, "I had no idea what the next item could be. How did you figure it out so quickly?"

"I happen to know the merfolk ruler," Vinnia said, shrugging casually.

Philip and Ella exchanged a glance.

"You just happen to know the *exact* person we need to find for the next item on the list?" Philip eyed Vinnia suspiciously. This was too convenient to be true.

Vinnia avoided Philip's gaze. "About that..."

"Wait a minute." Realization crossed Ella's face. "There are

230

rumors about the merfolk dictator. They say he used to have a pixie lover, but that would mean…"

Merfolk *dictator*? Philip couldn't believe what he was hearing. Mermaids were supposed to be beautiful, half-fish creatures that had long flowy hair and wore seashell tiaras. They weren't supposed to be power-hungry creatures who had complicated politics and overthrown governments.

But Ella's point wasn't about the dictatorship.

Philip turned to Ella. "You don't mean—"

"Okay, let's cut the drama and mystery. My dad is the dictator of Mermaidia. So what?" Vinnia's defenses shot up.

"So what?" Ella was incredulous, "Your father is Jaxel Haaf. Now everything makes sense! Your ability to fight, the pixies' fear when they said 'Haaf'. But they said 'Iva' too. Iva as in…?"

"The pixie president," Vinnia finished miserably. "I'm the child of a merman and a pixie. A dictator and a president."

Philip didn't want to think about how *that* happened.

"Is this why you live alone in the Pixie Forest? To get away from your parents?" Ella asked gently.

Vinnia gave a slight nod. At that moment, she was like a small, vulnerable girl burdened by the weight of the world. "Neither of them had time for me, and when they did, they were just trying to brainwash me. I couldn't take it anymore."

"I'm so sorry, Vinnia." Ella wrapped her arms around the mixie, "I understand how hard it is to feel unloved by your family."

Philip felt a twinge of sadness; he knew what it was like to be overlooked, to feel like your parents didn't take the time to truly know you. On the rare occasion his workaholic parents were home and weren't taking phone calls or replying to emails, they didn't think to take time for their middle son.

Whenever Marius had struggled in school, his parents immediately sat him down, lectured him about the importance of academics, and offered to find him help. When Max would win a trophy from his elementary soccer team, his parents would pat him on the head and display the trophy for everyone to see. When Philip had started an entire business from his locker, his parents hadn't noticed until almost six months afterward. Then, they'd grounded him for going behind their backs.

And they wondered why he was so prickly all the time.

That version of himself seemed so far away as he sat by the river in the middle of a magical world with people he would dare to call his friends. What would things be like if they returned home? Would he be changed by these experiences, or would he revert to how he was before? Would he try to forget his time in the magical world and pretend like it never existed? Or would he remember every moment and cling to them like a fading dream?

This train of thought caught him off-guard. Since when did he care about personal growth? Normally, he only cared about the growth of his business.

Maybe Ella was rubbing off on him.

"Okay, that's enough bonding," Vinnia said, giving a halfhearted laugh as she pulled away from Ella. "We should get going. If we leave now, we can make it to Mermaidia by this afternoon."

"How are we going to get there so quickly?" Philip asked. It had taken them almost two days of walking to get to the Elder Tree. Surely, they couldn't reach Mermaidia so quickly.

"The Elder Tree is a lot closer to the coast than pixies like to admit. This river flows directly to the Sea of Mermaidia."

"More commonly known as the Sea of Corvus," Ella added.

232

Vinnia ignored Ella's comment. "If we make a raft, I can get us to the sea in half the time. But before we do that, there are two things you should know…"

Philip turned to her, wary of the sudden reluctance in her voice.

"First, Mermaidia is completely underwater. I can breathe underwater and morph my legs into a mermaid tail, but it won't be as easy for you. I'll have to use magic on you to allow you to breathe underwater, and it will be painful."

Okay. Philip didn't savor the idea of painful magic, but he would do whatever it took to get home.

"Second," Vinnia hesitated, "My dad thinks I'm dead."

Preparations for the gilding and coronation were going about as smoothly as Dash expected. On top of the regular ceremonial rituals, each of the Fair Lords had certain traditions they expected to be included in the ceremonies.

The Yellow Lord started the most recent meeting's usual sparks by suggesting the Great Healing—a tradition in which fair folk with yellow magic heal everyone in attendance of the ceremony—should be held first instead of third, as per usual according to rainbow order. She explained that since Dash had yellow magic, it was only logical for the yellow fair folk to be first in line. While the Green Lord and the Blue Lord didn't seem bothered by this, the Red Lord and Orange Lord were scandalized. A heated argument erupted among the Fair Lords and, yet again, remained unresolved.

Dash finally made a split-second decision to keep the usual rainbow order. The Yellow Lord would sulk for a few days, but she would get over it soon enough. Dash had other more pressing matters to worry about. One person couldn't handle everything

233

at once.

In addition to the drama with the Fair Lords, security measures increased drastically, which brought more challenges. Dash hadn't been left alone since Elliott's murder. At least six guards surrounded him at all times. He understood why they needed to be so cautious, but their presence was suffocating.

What he wouldn't give for an hour to spend with Rhett. Whenever he had a problem, he would immediately turn to Rhett. But now, he was hardly allowed to leave the palace for fear of another assassination.

He couldn't keep living like this.

Between meetings about the gilding and the coronation, Dash met with the generals and colonels of the army. *His* army, which Elliott had left in shambles. Rebuilding in such a short amount of time wouldn't be easy, but if his plan succeeded, recruits would come flooding in, eager to serve their kingdom.

If his plan *didn't* succeed... well, he would become the most hated sovereign in the history of Haderra.

The rioting and protests in the city had only increased and become more violent. When Elliott had ascended to the throne at the age of twenty-one, some people had suggested he was too young, too inexperienced. Those people had only made up a small majority.

But now that Dash—the sixteen-year-old, illegitimate child of a playboy prince and a human—was ascending to the throne, those suggestions from the minority had turned into enraged outcries of the majority.

Dash understood why the people didn't want to accept him. His very existence was an embarrassment to the kingdom. He and Rhett were proof of his father's recklessness and flippancy. While he had been lucky to be blessed with yellow magic, Rhett's

234

purple magic was a curse.

The kingdom saw the two of them for only part of what they represented. They pointed out the negative parts—the illegitimacy of their birth, the squander of noble fair folk blood. But Dash saw the parts they missed—the intense, passionate love his parents had, a love that bridged the gap between the human world and the magical world.

He had never fit into either world. In the human world, he had to squander his magic. In the magical world, people scorned him for his human blood. Long ago, he'd accepted the fact that he would never belong entirely to one world.

Now that he would be sovereign, he had a chance to show his people that being human wasn't a fault. He could show them how to accept humans and bridge the gap between the worlds. He could be the start of a new age of kindness and peace that stretched beyond kingdoms and worlds.

If only the people would listen.

Philip didn't particularly like being in charge.

In school, whenever he was forced to be a part of a dreaded group project, he shut his mouth and let other people take charge. It didn't matter if he was working with complete geniuses or the most careless idiots. He never took charge. He had simply completed his part of the project and let others take the credit or the criticism.

But as he was the most educated person in the group and the resident science expert, the vote to put him in charge of building the raft was unanimous. Of course, he didn't get a vote, but it wouldn't have made a difference.

It had taken almost an hour to find enough dead trees and strong roots to start assembling the raft. Under Philip's direction, the others arranged the trees and lashed them together with the roots. They made slow progress, especially since the roots kept snapping. When they finally finished the raft, Ella murmured some sort of elven incantation for good luck. They heaved the raft into the river and, by some miracle, it stayed afloat.

Philip held the rope that kept the raft from floating downstream while Ella, Max, and Vinnia scrambled on. He boarded last, taking a seat in the top left corner to keep the weight balanced.

Vinnia spread her hands over the water, and the tang of salt filled Philips' mouth. The current of the river turned from a steady rush to a rapid roar. Max squealed in delight as the water propelled them down the river.

Philip gripped the raft as tightly as possible, silently praying it wouldn't break apart. Water sprayed him from all sides, drenching him thoroughly.

As they traveled, Vinnia explained her idea about the next item. "I think 'precious armor' means mermaid scales. Our scales are virtually indestructible; they're fire and waterproof, and not even the sharpest blade can cut through them."

That made sense. If mermaid scales were impenetrable, they could be considered a sort of armor.

"Do you have any ideas of how we're going to get scales from the military dictator himself?" Ella asked. "Sure, he's your dad, but he's probably not going to just give us his scales."

"I have a few ideas, but it's not going to be easy." Vinnia sighed, "Our scales are embedded into our tails like fingernails. As you can imagine, they're painful to remove. We're going to have to find a way to incapacitate my dad and cut the scales from his body."

"We have a long ride ahead of us," Ella said. "That should

236

be plenty of time to come up with a plan."

The ride to the sea turned out to be much shorter than Philip expected. With the help of Vinnia's magic, they reached the delta at the mouth of the river by the time the sun hung directly overhead. They only had enough time to come up with a half-baked plan that Philip didn't like one bit.

Having lived in New York his entire life, Philip wasn't unfamiliar with water. They would occasionally drive to the beach on long weekends during the summer to escape the crowded city. But wading in the shallows of the Atlantic Ocean was nothing compared to floating onto the open sea in a hastily crafted raft held together with fragile tree roots. Though they had flown over this same sea when they left the Island of Corvus over a week ago, Philip wasn't prepared for the dread he felt at the sight of the flat, endless waters.

What could be lurking in the depths of the Sea of Corvus? There would be kelpies, no doubt, as well as other dangerous creatures that would be eager to feast on them.

Vinnia continued to propel them farther from shore until it was no more than a dark line on the horizon. She scanned the waters as they floated, leaning farther over the edge of the raft than Philip liked.

Finally, she stopped the raft and turned to them with a grim expression. "Well, this is it," she announced.

Philip glanced around, seeing nothing but water for miles around.

"We're directly above Mermaidia," Vinnia elaborated, apparently noticing his confusion, "It's time to drop by and say hello to dear old Dad."

Chapter 22

Max peered into the dark water. "How are we gonna get down there?"

"Magic, obviously," Vinnia responded. Without another word, she dove into the water. Her legs morphed into a shimmering, lavender mermaid tail. Lavender streaks colored her short, dark hair. Gills striped the sides of her throat, just under her ears.

A strange look passed over Ella's face, but it was so brief that Philip wasn't sure if he'd imagined it.

"Well, what are you waiting for?" Vinnia asked.

Max didn't need to be asked twice. Before Philip could stop him, he plugged his nose and leaped into the water, tucking his legs into a cannonball.

Philip's stomach dropped as Max hit the water with a splash. Max knew how to swim, but even the most experienced swimmer couldn't tread water for long. They couldn't just dive into strange waters because Vinnia told them to. It wasn't safe. What if they drowned? What if they were devoured by vicious sea creatures? Vinnia couldn't protect them from everything.

Ella swung her legs over the side of the raft. Her boots flooded with water and her deerskin trousers clung to her calves. She gracefully slipped into the water, not even bothering to remove her pack, her sword, or the pouch at her hip.

"Come on, Philip!" Max's chin dipped under the surface, and he was met with a mouthful of water.

"Absolutely not," Philip said. He positioned himself in the

middle of the raft to keep it balanced.

There was no way he would trade the relative safety of the raft for the uncertainty and danger of the churning waters beneath him. He only had one arm. He wouldn't be able to tread water nearly well enough to keep himself from drowning.

"Don't be such a spoilsport," Max whined. "This will be fun!"

The possibility of drowning didn't strike Philip as 'fun.' He shook his head resolutely. *"No."*

Ella opened her mouth to protest, but Vinnia cut her off. "Suit yourself." She slipped under the surface, disappearing in the murky water.

Moments later, a gigantic wave rose from nowhere. It loomed over Philip for a terrifying moment, before crashing down on him and smashing the unstable raft to pieces. He was thrown into the sea without a moment to brace himself.

Sputtering and gasping, he desperately paddled to keep himself afloat. The heavy pack strapped across his back weighed him down, threatening to pull him under.

Vinnia surfaced holding three, iridescent conch shells. She blinked innocently at Philip. "Oh, you decided to join us after all."

Philip shot her a withering glare.

"What are those?" Max eagerly eyed the shells in Vinnia's hand.

"These will allow you to breathe underwater, resist your natural buoyancy, and withstand the pressure in the deep. They only last for twelve hours, but that should be plenty of time for us to get in, get the scales, and get out," Vinnia explained, distributing the shells.

Philip looped his arm around a bundle of wood from the

remains of the raft to stay afloat as he took the shell from Vinnia. Already, his body ached from exertion. Now that he was in the water, there was no going back. Following Vinnia's instructions, he held the shell over his mouth and nose like an oxygen mask and inhaled a deep breath.

His throat and lungs constricted instantly. He dropped the shell and clutched at his throat, overwhelmed by panic. It was as if the air had turned stale; no amount of oxygen was enough to satisfy his body. He couldn't breathe. He couldn't stay afloat. He was going to die. A violent coughing fit shook his body. A thick, salty foam frothed in his mouth and bubbled over his lips. He gagged and convulsed as the foam left a filmy coating inside his throat and mouth. No matter how many gulps of seawater he took, the film remained.

"It's much easier to breathe underwater," Vinnia said. She sank below the surface, beckoning for them to follow.

Max plunged his head into the water and sucked in a deep breath. Moments later, he resurfaced with a grin. "It works!"

Philip wanted to throttle his brother. What kind of person *willingly* tried to breathe underwater? What if the magic hadn't worked? How did he just do things like that without thinking of the consequences?

Ella turned to him imploringly. "We have to do it too. We're running out of time. It's now or never."

He would have preferred never, but he had to think about the big picture. If he didn't do this, they wouldn't be able to get home and Ella would be stuck marrying Linnmon.

Bracing himself for the worst possible scenario in which he drowned without another word, he released the remains of the raft. Everything in his body rebelled as he sank below the surface and held his breath. He forced himself to open his eyes, surprised when his vision was as clear as if they were above water. Seconds passed, and his lungs felt as if they were going to burst. If it weren't for Ella's hand in his, he would have clawed his way to the surface by sheer force of will.

His vision blackened around the edges. He was convinced death was near until his brain jolted his body into action. He sucked in a deep breath of water against his own will.

It was as if he were breathing for the first time. Though his lungs filled with water, he was alive. Breathing underwater was like breathing crisp, autumn air. Logically, it made no sense. But this was magic. Since when did magic ever make sense?

Beside him, Ella pressed a hand to her lips, then moved it to her throat, then moved it back to her lips. Her eyes were wide in shock.

"This is awesome!" Max exclaimed. The sound of his brother's voice was distorted and muffled by the water, but still audible and comprehensible.

"How do you feel?" Vinnia asked. The gills on either side of her throat rippled, flapping open and closed in a steady rhythm.

Ella took a shaky breath. "This is weird."

"You'll get used to it pretty quickly," Vinnia said. "We don't have time to tread around. The palace is this way."

Without waiting to see if any one was following, she flicked her tail and sped towards the seabed. Philip and Ella exchanged a glance and followed her. Philip struggled to keep Vinnia's pace with only one arm and two human legs, but Ella stayed back with him. As usual, she didn't make him feel like a hindrance or an annoyance. She simply swam beside him in silence.

As they neared the floor of the sea, a city arose from the murky depths of the water. Mermaidia was carved into the blueish rock that made up the seabed. Bright coral and brilliant anemones covered the rock like flowers, blooming in an array of shapes and colors. Seaweed and other strange plant life rippled in the water and gave the illusion of a slight breeze. Shoals of colorful fish darted around the city like birds.

A palace loomed over the city like a foreboding watchtower. It was a jigsaw of stone, mother-of-pearl, sea glass, seashells, and other random materials that found their way to the bottom of the sea.

If it weren't for the eerie fact that there wasn't a mermaid in sight, Philip might have called the city beautiful.

"Where are the mermaids?" Max wondered aloud.

"Mer*folk*," Vinnia corrected, "and they're not allowed out of their homes past curfew."

"If there's a curfew, who will enforce it?" Ella asked, glancing around the empty streets. "I don't see any soldiers."

Vinnia shook her head. "That's what the krakens are for."

She gestured to what Philip had initially mistaken as a large rock. Tilting his head, he noticed it was slightly greyer than the rocks around it. Like a flashlight being flicked on, a massive, glowing yellow eye snapped open in the middle of the 'rock'.

Philip shoved himself away from the eye, which followed him intently. A guttural shriek emerged from the kraken while shed its camouflage, unfolding a barbed tentacle. It was as if the motion of the water itself stopped when the kraken began to move.

Vinnia swam in front of Philip and addressed the kraken head-on. "I command you to stop."

The kraken froze. Its eye blinked down at Vinnia, looking slightly surprised, if such a thing were possible. Instead of lashing out or shrieking with fury, it retracted its tentacle and curled back into itself. Closing its eye, it camouflaged itself to

242

the rocks surrounding it once again.

Ella and Philip exchanged a wide-eyed glance. What just happened?

Max gaped at Vinnia with awe. "How did you do that?"

"The krakens know me," Vinnia answered, shrugging as if that explained everything. With a flick of her tail, she swam towards the palace as if nothing had happened. Max paddled after her, peppering her with questions about krakens and merfolk and pirates. Ella made a wide arc around the kraken as she followed Vinnia.

Philip swam close behind, not daring to break his gaze away from the kraken. He noticed several camouflaged krakens hidden throughout the empty city. Some opened their glowing eyes to watch them, but none of the krakens moved to stop them.

As they neared the palace, he caught his first glimpses of merfolk. There were subtle signs—a flash of dull color in a window, crude tools scattered across a doorstep, muffled cries echoing from a house—but it was enough to settle the strange, deserted feeling that haunted the city.

The strangest sight of all was the larger-than-life marble statue of a bearded merman that stood in the middle of the city. It was an imposing monstrosity that reminded Philip of an idol worshipped in ancient civilizations.

"That's my dad," Vinnia said casually, as if having her dad's godlike statue erected in the middle of a city was no big deal, "He likes to think of himself as the city's savior. Apparently, putting hundreds of statues of himself all over the kingdom is the best way to remind the people how glorious he is."

"Whoa." Max marveled at the statue. "I wish *my* dad had a statue of himself in the middle of the city."

Philip most certainly did not agree.

Vinnia rolled her eyes. "Trust me; it gets old quickly."

After seeing the statue of Jaxel Haaf, Philip began to seriously doubt their plan. He gnawed on the inside of his cheek as he mulled it over. How were they going to cut the scales from the dictator of Mermaidia? If the statues bore any likeness to Vinnia's father, they were in more trouble than they thought.

When they reached the palace gates, Philip almost wished he had stayed back with the kraken. The palace crawled with heavily armed merfolk guards clad from head to tail in bronze armor. They swam in militant formations as they patrolled the exterior of the palace.

Vinnia didn't bat an eyelash at the sight of the guards. She swam right up to the embellished palace gates like she owned the place. Which, Philip supposed, was partially true. The guards positioned on either side of the gates crossed their mother-of-pearl spears in front of her, blocking her path. Their stoic gazes were as unyielding and intimidating as the harpoons strapped across their chests like machine guns.

"Excuse me." Vinnia folded her arms and glared up at the guards. "Let me in. I'm here to see my father, Jaxel Haaf."

The guards exchanged a suspicious look. "General Haaf's daughter is dead."

"Is that what he's telling everyone?" Vinnia feigned surprise. "Well, I'll be sure to tell him about the two guards who kept me from returning home from my visit to my mother in the Eabith."

After a moment of hesitation, the guards lowered their weapons, moved aside, and drew open the gates. Vinnia breezed past them, leaving Philip, Ella, and Max to follow.

The interior of the palace reminded Philip of a strange sculpture at an art festival. It was a collage of random materials that had been molded together into a vaguely distinguishable shape.

Vinnia knew exactly where to go as she led them through a series of winding hallways. At each turn was a new regiment of guards who broke their stony expressions to gape at them.

When she reached a pair of bronze doors, she stopped short. Max crashed into her, his momentum out of balance in the water. Vinnia didn't pay any attention to him. "I demand to see my father." She spoke in a deep, commanding voice to the merfolk guarding the doors.

"General Haaf has requested not to be interrupted unless there is a dire emergency..." The first guard's voice trailed off uncertainly.

"*I* would consider the reappearance of the general's supposedly dead daughter to be a 'dire emergency', wouldn't you?" Vinnia said.

The guard nodded. "Yes. Of course. Absolutely."

Vinnia didn't wait for the guard to stop speaking. She swam forwards and shoved the bronze doors open with surprising ease. They slammed against the walls with a startling *bang* that caught the attention of everyone in the room.

A merman who could only be Jaxel Haaf himself sat rigidly at the head of a bronze conference table surrounded by merfolk. The statue in the city was an exact likeness. His bronze body was sculpted with impossibly large muscles that tapered off into a midnight blue tail. Spikes of sea glass and seashells were woven into his midnight blue hair, jutting from his head in the shape of a crown. Vinnia had inherited her father's sharp, amber eyes, though she had been spared his heavy brows and wide features.

Jaxel Haaf's hard eyes narrowed as he took in the sight before him. When he saw Vinnia, a gasp escaped his lips. He rose and swam forwards almost hesitantly, like he expected her to disappear any second.

"Vinnie?" His voice rumbled through the room like thunder. "This is impossible. You're dead. I watched the life drain from your eyes."

Vinnia kept her distance but spoke with authority. "My death was greatly exaggerated."

"After all this time, you've finally come home," General Haaf murmured, "Has your brush with death allowed you to make a decision?"

Vinnia stiffened. "That's what I'm here to talk to you about."

General Haaf's attention shifted from Vinnia to the others. A frown settled over his eyebrows. His gaze pierced Philip like a harpoon to the head. "Does your return have anything to do with these humans?"

"How crazy do you have to be to bring humans to Mermaidia?" a turquoise-haired mermaid muttered.

"Who dares speak in my presence?" General Haaf roared. The walls of the palace shook at the sound of his booming voice. Everyone in the room shrank away from him, their terror almost palpable.

The mermaid tried to sputter an apology, but it was too late. General Haaf turned his furious glare on her. "Take her away."

Bronze-clad guards surged forwards and seized the mermaid, ignoring her desperate pleas. They swiftly and dutifully removed her from the room. The mermaid's screams echoed through the palace. When the doors slammed shut behind them, her cries were silenced instantly, leaving the room in fragile, horrified silence.

"So," Vinnia said as if nothing had happened, "I want to speak with you. Alone."

General Haaf glanced down at his daughter, before turning

246

to address the rest of the merfolk seated around the conference table. "This meeting is adjourned."

The merfolk wasted no time in scrambling out of their seats and fleeing the room. Vinnia crossed her arms and slouched her posture, looking the part of the perpetually annoyed teenager.

When the room had been cleared of all the merfolk except the guards positioned in front of each pillar, Vinnia spoke. "Could we speak in *private*?"

"You of all people should know this is as much privacy as a general can have," General Haaf said.

"You say 'general', I hear 'dictator,'" Vinnia muttered.

"'Dictator' is a harsh word," General Haaf shook his head as if he were disappointed in his daughter. "'General' makes the people feel safe andprotected. Like they're under the leadership of a hero. You'll learn that soon enough, Vinnie."

Vinnia folded her arms, treading water with her tail. "I'll learn that *if* I decide to accept your offer."

Philip shifted uncomfortably, feeling like an intruder in this argument. This reunion wasn't what he'd expected, but at least they weren't dead yet,

"Which is why you've come here, is it not?" General Haaf responded, "Most merfolk your age are just beginning their military service. It's time you do the same."

Before Vinnia could respond, a knock sounded. General Haaf froze and snuck a furtive glance at Vinnia before gruffly ordering the guards to open the doors. When a pink-haired mermaid swam into the room, Vinnia's eyes narrowed. The mermaid planted a kiss on General Haaf's cheek. "You asked to see me?"

"Who's this?" Vinnia posture stayed nonchalant, but Philip noticed the hard clench of her jaw as she knotted her fingers around her necklace.

General Haaf wrapped an arm around the mermaid. "Vinnie, this is Leiria, my new wife. Leiria, this is my daughter Vinnia."

Vinnia cast her eyes heavenwards and muttered, "May the King grant me swift death."

Of all the sayings he'd heard in the magical world, Philip decided this was his favorite.

"I trust you'll give Leiria the respect she deserves." General Haaf's voice held a stern warning.

"Lovely to meet you, dear," Leiria plastered a fake smile on her hot pink lips. "Your father made it sound like you were dead."

"It seems I was mistaken." General Haaf turned to Vinnia with a suspicious look. "How *did* you survive? The leviathan tore your neck open. I held you in my arms as you died."

Philip turned to Vinnia, curious to know the answer as well. That sounded much more graphic than any ordinary faked death.

All Vinnia said was, "The King had mercy on me."

General Haaf didn't look convinced. "You died almost three years ago. If you've been alive all this time, why come back now?"

Vinnia shot Philip and Ella a furtive glance. They were going to have to carry out the plan much sooner than they thought. Ella slipped her hand into her pack as discreetly as possible and pulled out a knife. She pressed it into Philip's palm. The weight of the weapon was comforting in his grip. The guards behind them were too fixated on the drama of Vinnia's return to notice the exchange.

"I've been living in the Pixie Forest," Vinnia said. "I thought it would be better if I stayed away, but these humans helped me realize I needed to return and claim my birthright as heir of Mermaidia."

248

"You've been living in the Pixie Forest?" General Haaf narrowed his eyes. He advanced toward Vinnia, who stood her ground. "Did your mother send you? Is this some kind of trick?"

"What? No!" Vinnia looked disgusted. "I wouldn't have gone to her if my life depended on it."

"That's what she would have told you to say," General Haaf growled, clenching his massive hands into fists.

"Jaxel, darling..." Leiria gave a nervous laugh. "Maybe we should sit down and discuss this over dinner. I'm sure it's nothing to worry about. Your daughter wouldn't choose any one over you. *You're* the one who cared for her most of her life. *You're* the one who can give her a kingdom."

Vinnia snarled. "Stay out of this, you pink-haired bimbo."

"How dare you!" Leiria shrieked, a manicured hand flying to her thick, pink locks.

"Speaking of hair color, you changed your hair, Vinnie." General Haaf's low, steady voice was as menacing as storm clouds on the horizon.

Vinnia's eyes widened slightly. "That doesn't matter," she snapped.

Philip glanced at Ella for clarity. Her expression was strange and unreadable, which further unsettled him.

Some kind of realization struck General Haaf. He backed away in horror. When he spoke, his voice was hoarse. "What have you done, Vinnia?"

Vinnia's expression darkened. "What I should have done long ago." She threw up her hands and blasted a current of water at General Haaf and Leiria like a gust of wind.

That was the signal. Philip and Ella whirled around to intercept the guards, keeping Max shielded between them. Just as Vinnia had predicted, the guards were armed with mother-of-

249

pearl spears. In such close quarters, the spears were virtually useless. They were betting on the guards' overconfidence; few people would be crazy enough to attack the dictator. The guards didn't need to be experienced or armed with practical weapons. Their job was to look intimidating.

The guards tried to attack Philip and Ella, but their spears clashed together or knocked into their fellow guards. Philip and Ella extorted their clumsiness. With her sword, Ella slashed and parried, targeting the guards' unprotected hands. Philip did the same with the knife, though he moved with considerably less grace due to the resistance of the water around him.

One guard grazed his right shoulder with the tip of his spear. Despite his disgust at not being able to feel the wound, he lunged forward and stabbed the guard in the wrist. The guard's screams were muffled in Philip's waterlogged ears.

Dark red blood floated through the water like cigar smoke as Philip and Ella's blades made contact with exposed skin. Shock and adrenaline set in. He ducked and slashed and parried like he was a part of an elaborate dance. The world blurred around him, moving at a lightning speed. Still, he didn't slow or allow himself to become distracted.

The frantic songs of guards trying to heal themselves floated through the water. According to Vinnia, they wouldn't be able to heal themselves in time to chase them down.

While he fought, he kept himself aware of Vinnia, who battled her father. The addition of Leiria was an unexpected element, but if it meant General Haaf expended more energy in trying to protect her, it worked to their advantage.

With her mixie magic, Vinnia had the upper hand. It was only a matter of time before she incapacitated her father. She sent wave after wave crashing down upon him, keeping him far enough away from her that his spear was useless. General Haaf tumbled through the water as she formed a whirlpool around him and Leiria.

Vinnia's intense gaze was laser-focused. She didn't notice the guard behind her until it was too late. The guard shot a harpoon, spearing her through the stomach.

Philip sucked in a breath, losing focus for a fraction of a second. A guard's spear nicked his cheek, but he couldn't tear his gaze away from Vinnia.

With a ragged scream, Vinnia morphed into a kelpie and reared towards the guard. Something was different about this transformation, but Philip couldn't put his finger on what was wrong. The harpoon still stuck out of her side, but it didn't hinder her as she ground the guard into pulp beneath her silver hooves. It was as if turning into a kelpie had released the floodgates of violence. She stormed through the room in a furious whirlpool of gnashing teeth and pounding hooves. Within minutes, every guard in the room was unconscious at the very least.

Blood tainted the water around them. Gore floated through the murk, tangling with debris. Faint moans came from the unfortunate merfolk who survived Vinnia's wrath.

General Haaf and Leiria cowered behind a pillar, staring up at Vinnia with horrified gazes. Even Max, who was usually enamored by Vinnia, inched away from her. Ella clutched Philip's limp forearm, standing just behind his shoulder.

Philip simply surveyed the room in shock. Though Vinnia had been excessive with the violence, she had gotten the job done more efficiently than they would have if they followed the original plan. He had to give her points for that.

With a toss of her midnight mane, Vinnia morphed back to mermaid form. The harpoon still stuck out of her side, but she

251

tore it out with a flinch. All it took was a muttered song and a wave of her hand for the gaping wound in her side to close. She snatched the knife from Philip and stormed over to her father. Yanking the silken scarf from around Leiria's neck, Vinnia stuffed it into her father's mouth. "This might hurt."

Jaxel's muffled screams echoed throughout the room as Vinnia sliced the shimmering, blue scales off of her father's tail as easily as if she were descaling a dead fish. Ella's knuckles whitened as she gripped Philip's arm. The detached scales drifted through the bloodied water, landing gently on the smoothed rock floors. Vinnia scooped the scales off the ground and handed them to him. All he could do was blink down at them. They'd done it. They had the next item.

Jaxel spat, his teeth red with blood. "You're a monster, Vinnia."

Vinnia's face was full of scorn as she looked down at her father, who cowered on the ground before her. "I'm just following in my father's wake."

In one swift movement, she sent a current crashing down on her father and stepmother, knocking them unconscious. With that, she flicked her tail and sliced through the water, leaving a wispy trail of blood behind her.

This time, Max kept his distance as he hesitantly followed her. Ella didn't release her grip on Philip's arm as she swam after them. Blood stung his eyes and filled his nose and lungs. The world shifted in and out of focus. He fought to retain his alertness, which was quickly slipping away.

Outside the war room, none of the guards moved to stop them as they swam from the palace. Philip almost laughed at the guards' blissful ignorance. The most commanding, fear-imposing merman in their kingdom was bleeding on the palace floors, yet these guards wore haughty, smug expressions.

Once they passed through the palace gates, Vinnia let out a sharp whistle. She hadn't spared any one a single glance since she'd morphed back to mermaid form. Even as she spoke, she avoided their gazes. "My dad will send guards after us soon. We have to get back to dry land. I've called us a ride there. Hopefully, we'll make it before Dad can find us and put our heads on pikes."

Max gulped audibly, "Would he do that?"

"Gladly."

"Vinnia, what happened back there?" Ella's brows furrowed in concern, "After you transformed…"

"Here's our ride." Vinnia interrupted as three massive forms sped towards them in a swarm of bubbles and seafoam. The beasts that materialized before them were a peculiar collage of horses and fish. Though the front half of each beast was that of a horse, its back half tapered off into an extravagant fin. Each beast's front legs fanned out into silver fins where their hooves should have been. A spiny mohawk of silver dorsal fins crested their heads like a mane.

"Hippocampi," Ella gasped.

"Climb on," Vinnia said.

Philip hesitantly approached the nearest hippocamp. It bowed its head and flicked its tail, brushing the back of his calf with its fin. Mounting the hippocamp was more awkward than he would have liked, especially since he only had one hand. He wrapped an arm around the hippocamp's neck and squeezed his knees against its midsection. With nothing to hold on to, he could only pray the ride would be smooth.

Ella and Max followed suit. Ella looked like a princess perched atop a mystical creature. Even in the depths of the sea, she managed to maintain her grace and poise. Her braids floated behind her like a crown.

Max was much less elegant. He clutched his hippocamp with a vice-like grip. The hippocamp didn't seem to mind. Its interest had been captured by the maroon seaweed that rippled in the gentle current.

Vinnia hardly made sure they were mounted safely before she flicked her tail and shot through the water with surprising speed. Philip gasped and held a white-knuckled grip on his hippocamp as it launched itself after her. The hippocamp's muscles flexed under his desperate hold. The sheer power of the beast was enough to make his head spin.

If any of Jaxel's soldiers had attempted to pursue them, they wouldn't recover from the advantage the hippocampi had. Even Vinnia, who swam faster than Philip would have thought possible, struggled to keep up with the beasts. It wasn't long before she gave up and morphed into hippocamp form herself.

The force of the water surged against his body as they shot away from the city. It was almost enough to knock him off of the hippocamp's back. The skin on his face felt as if it were being ripped from his skull. What little air he had in his lungs was sucked away.

Philip knew he deserved the pain; what they had done to General Haaf and his guards was unforgivable. Though Vinnia had been the one to carry out the violence, they all shared the blame. Didn't the end justify the means, though? The fourth item rested safely in his pack. They already had more than half of the items.

Maybe, just maybe, they would be home soon.

Chapter 23

Philip heaved a strangled gasp as they broke through the surface. The air that filled his lungs was stiff and stale like he was breathing from a jar. When his eyes adjusted to the blinding light of the setting sun reflecting off the water, he saw the shore a few yards away.

Vinnia morphed back into mermaid form. "This is as far as the hippocampi can take us."

Philip relaxed his hold on his hippocamp. He made sure to stay a good distance away from its powerful front fins, which churned the water into whirlpools. The hippocampi's whinnies crashed over each other like waves. Vinnia nodded in understanding. Bowing their heads towards Vinnia, the hippocampi disappeared in a swarm of bubbles and foam.

They all paddled quickly, eager to reach the shore. They'd reached the sea through a river in the Pixie Forest, and now, they neared land covered in white sand and leafy foliage. Where were they?

By the time he dragged himself out of the water, exhaustion ached in his bones. Vinnia was already spread out on the sand in normal form, sunning her brown legs. Max shook his head like a dog, and Philip cringed away from him to avoid the droplets that sprayed everywhere. Ella wrung out her braids, safely out of range from the spray from Max's hair.

"Can we take away the water breathing? It's hard to breathe normal air." Max said, clutching his throat dramatically.

"The effects of the magic should wear off in a few hours,"

Vinnia said, "Until then, you'll just have to deal with it."

Philip paused to study Vinnia. She seemed weary. Tired, even. The weight of what she had done settled on her petite shoulders. Her amber eyes held the hardness that came with the forced maturity of someone who had to fight to survive.

After meeting General Haaf, Philip couldn't imagine what Vinnia's childhood had been like. How much brainwashing had she been forced to overcome? How much of her upbringing was still engrained in her thinking? He could see Jaxel's ruthlessness in the way Vinnia killed without hesitation. He saw Jaxel's ferocity in the skill with which Vinnia fought. But despite all that, Vinnia was not her father. She was the mixie who begged them to allow her to accompany them on their quest simply because she was lonely. She healed them time and time again without complaint and protected them at any cost.

"So," Ella's voice snapped Philip out of his thoughts, carrying forced lightness, "we have four of the seven items. What's next?"

"'A giant ruler's guarded treasure,'" Philip recited automatically. There had been plenty of time to memorize the list during their walk to the Elder Tree.

A small voice in the back of his mind whispered a reminder that with every item, they were drawing closer to the final item—the breath of a dying human. Shaking his head, he forced the thought out of his mind. It wouldn't do any good to think about the last item, though it was growing increasingly difficult to suppress his worry.

"Well, obviously the guarded treasure is the beans," Vinnia said.

Philip wrinkled his brow in confusion. *Beans?* Seriously?

"Like 'Jack and the Beanstalk,'" Max said as if it were

completely normal.

Vinnia tilted her head. "What?"

"'Jack and the Beanstalk.' It's a story about a kid and a giant and a bunch of magic beans that grew a beanstalk to the sky!" Max explained.

"There aren't beanstalks that go to the sky, but there *are* magic beans," Vinnia said. "The giants have their most powerful magic encased in solid gold shaped like beans. When they need to use restricted magic, a giant will go to the emperor and empress to request to purchase a bean. The beans sometimes cost everything a giant owns."

Ella nodded. "Of course! The giants keep them under lock and key, so they're guarded treasure."

Phillip sighed. "Naturally, it's going to be nearly impossible to get these beans, isn't it?"

"Probably." A yawn stretched Vinnia's features. "But we'll worry about that tomorrow. Goodnight." She morphed into kelpie form, curled onto her side, and shut her eyes, ending the conversation.

Despite the cool breeze that chilled their soaked bodies, they each drifted to sleep under the starry sky.

They slept for far too long. By the time Philip awoke, the rich pinks and oranges of the sunrise had dissolved into the pale blue of a morning sky. The last traces of dew lingered on the blades of grass. He shivered at the dampness of his clothing, remembering their soaked packs.

He wasted no time in shaking the others awake. While Ella and Vinnia scrambled to their feet and collected their things, Max groaned and dragged his feet.

"Where are we even going?" Max grumbled. "We don't have griffins and we don't have a boat. Are we going to have to walk

257

again? My feet hurt so bad."

"Max has a point," Ella said. "How are we going to get to the giant kingdom?"

"We're already here," Vinnia gestured to their surroundings. "Welcome to Juren, home of the giants."

Glancing around, Philip didn't see any signs of giants. Everything looked ordinary, from the palm trees on the beach to the snow-capped mountains in the distance.

"Are we close to the palace?" Ella asked.

"The palace is on the opposite side of the kingdom in the highest mountains," Vinnia explained. "We couldn't climb them if we tried."

Philip snorted derisively. "So how are we supposed to get there?"

"This is hippogriff territory."

"You can't be serious!" Ella stared aghast at Vinnia.

Vinnia shrugged. "Hippogriffs are wild and dangerous, but I like to think I fall under that same category. Besides, hippogriffs can fly. Riding them would be the perfect way to reach the palace."

"They would be perfect to ride if you didn't mind getting your hand bitten off." Ella countered.

Max laughed at that. "Good thing Philip can't feel one of his hands!"

Rhett was losing patience.

The rush of magic he'd gained from Elliott's death had long since worn off.

How long had it been since the elves killed his cousin? A few days? A week?

The longer he spent trapped on this island, the more distorted his concept of time became. About three years into his imprisonment, he'd simply decided to stop chiseling tally marks into trees.

The only days that mattered were the days Dash visited. Though recently, the visits were less frequent, he understood. Dash would become sovereign. Inheriting the throne from Elliott was no easy task.

Rhett often worried the weight of the world would be too much for Dash to handle, but so far, his little brother had proved himself to be competent enough. If that generous heart of his didn't get in the way, Dash would make a powerful ruler. After the atrocities they had suffered at Elliott's hands, the fair folk needed a good sovereign.

In a few days, Dash would be gilded and crowned Sovereign Prince of Haderra. The Gilding Ceremony was the sacred practice of anointing the fair folk sovereign. Each Fair Lord would infuse Dash with their magic so he had dominion over every color of magic. Rhett heard it described as an "enlightening" experience, but he didn't believe that for a second. Being infused with an unimaginable amount of power wasn't simply "enlightening."

It was earth-shattering.

Once Dash was infused with gold magic, he would transition directly to his coronation. He would become a gold fair folk and a sovereign in the span of a few hours. Rhett knew it would be a harrowing experience for Dash, but he had to believe his little brother could bear it.

Every day, Rhett wore the chains of his confinement. He was shackled and imprisoned because of his magic. Dash would be wearing a different kind of chain. His was the deceptive golden shackles of leadership. When placed around his neck, would these chains crush him?

Rhett hated the doubt that seeped into his mind. But there was good reason for this doubt.

Dash was kind, soft and vulnerable.

Nathan and Adrian were inexperienced. Incompetent. Untested.

The Fair Lords were vicious. Greedy. Selfish.

The people were dissatisfied. Unpleasable. Ungrateful.

He was the only person who could lead Dash in the right direction. The only person who didn't want anything from Dash. The only person who truly loved his brother.

But Dash didn't see that. Instead of ugly sneers, he saw charming smiles. Instead of conniving whispers, he saw the exchange of sweet nothings. Instead of a knife behind someone's back, he saw a bouquet.

Someone needed to protect Dash from the world and himself.

Who was better than his older brother?

Gold was a malleable metal. It simply had to be molded by the right hands.

Philip turned to glare at the others, who hid in the bushes behind him. Unsurprisingly, the three of them had unanimously voted for him to be the one to walk unarmed into the clearing filled with carnivorous half-horse, half-eagle creatures. Once again, he hadn't gotten a say in the matter.

"You have a way with griffins," Ella had told him. "Maybe it will be the same with hippogriffs."

He hated betting his life on a 'maybe', but—like Max continuously reminded him—the majority ruled.

So, there he was, standing on the edge of a clearing as he

watched a herd of hippogriffs graze on the corpse of a winged deer. The stench of the deer's rotting corpse did nothing to help ease his mind.

Steeling himself for inevitable doom, he took a step forward. Then another. The hippogriffs didn't pay any notice to him. Adrenaline coursed through his veins. Every instinct in his body screamed at him to turn around and run. To get away from these creatures immediately. But he had a job to do. If this was what it took to get one step closer to finding the next item, so be it.

When he was only a yard away from the nearest hippogriff, the entire herd snapped their heads up in unison and fixated their eerie, honey-colored eyes on him. His heart thundered as he took in the creatures before him.

There were seven in total. Each hippogriff's bird-like head was crowned with a ruffle of feathers varying from deep chestnut to snowy white. Their unsettlingly sharp beaks were stained with blood and gore from the deer carcass. Massive wings mounted their shoulders, just before the point in which the feathers of their heads gave way to the horsehair on their bodies.

The only comfort Philip had upon seeing the hippogriffs up close resided in the fact that the tops of their heads barely reached his chin. He clung to the hope that they would be strong enough to carry them to Juren, while still being easy to mount in his current, one-armed condition.

Forcing himself to focus on the task at hand, he took another step. This time, however, the hippogriffs skittered away from him. So much for whatever magical bond Ella hoped he would have with the hippogriffs.

Slowly, he raised a clenched fist, signaling the others to switch to Plan B. Whenever Plan A went wrong, it seemed the answer was to have Vinnia morph into some horse-hybrid creature. She'd objected to using this plan first, claiming she needed to preserve her energy for the long flight ahead, but desperate times called for desperate measures.

Moments later, Vinnia trotted into the clearing with her hippogriff head tilted in curiosity. She approached Philip and bowed her head, allowing him to stroke her crown of bronze feathers. The other hippogriffs relaxed at this display. Some approached him, interested to see what Vinnia had found. Others simply dismissed the newcomer's presence and turned back to their meal of deer flesh.

Vinnia let out a throaty caw. The three hippogriffs who focused their interest on Philip turned and responded to Vinnia. They exchanged caws and screeches until finally, Vinnia seemed satisfied. She gave a commanding screech, and the two smallest hippogriffs bounded towards Ella and Max's hiding spot.

The remaining hippogriff blinked expectantly at Philip. Vinnia jerked her head towards the hippogriff as if to say *What are you waiting for?*

"Here goes nothing." He muttered.

The hippogriff stood perfectly still while he attempted to mount it. Thankfully, he didn't need to jump to get onto the hippogriff's back. Kicking his leg over the hippogriff was awkward, but doable. When he was seated on the hippogriff's back, the tips of his toes brushed the ground. He felt every one of the hippogriff's vertebrae under him.

Ella and Max had no trouble mounting their hippogriffs. They rode into the clearing on the backs of the beasts, beaming with triumph and delight.

Vinnia took half a second to ensure the three of them were seated before spreading her wings and taking to the sky with a screech. Philip's hippogriff launched itself after her.

Philip quickly discovered the difference between griffin and hippogriff flight. While griffins flapped their wings in a strong, consistent rhythm, hippogriffs preferred to glide.

This pattern, however even, became painful after a few hours. Each flap of the hippogriff's wings sent a shot of pain through Philip's spine. To distract himself from the pain, he found himself thinking of Treave. Guilt speared him at the memory of her charming smile. With all the stress he'd been under, he hadn't spared a thought during their quest. But that was no excuse. There had been days where they did almost nothing but walk. Most of that time had been spent contemplating their next move. The next item. The next task. The next struggle.

How could he have been so focused on his own problems that Treave had completely slipped his mind? After everything she'd done for him, he didn't even have the decency to think about her. Perhaps he simply didn't want to think about what had occurred between them. What did it mean? What did she want it to mean? What did *he* want it to mean? She'd flirted with him. She'd kissed him. Yet, he felt nothing. Was there something wrong with him? Shouldn't he have felt something? Some kind of attraction or intrigue… *anything*. Really, he felt uncomfortable even thinking about it. Kissing just wasn't an experience he wanted to have again. With any one. Did that make him a bad person? He wasn't used to thinking about things like this…

A screech pierced the air, providing a distraction from his spiraling thoughts. Ahead of them, Vinnia opened her beak and let out another shrill screech.

It sounded like a warning.

Philip's blood ran cold as a shadow passed over them. For a brief moment, the late afternoon sun was blotted out completely.

"What was that?" Max's voice wavered.

"I don't know," Ella said. "We're within the borders of the giant kingdom. It could be anything."

The hippogriffs screeched and dipped towards the ground as the shadow passed over them again. Whatever was causing that shadow couldn't be good.

The third time the shadow passed over them, Philip caught a glimpse of the creature causing it. The creature was a massive patchwork of every bird imaginable. It was as large as a biplane, with an incredible wingspan. A great, sweeping peacock tail sprouted from a ducklike body carried on great wings with the plumage of a songbird. Long, thin legs dangled from its body. Its golden feathered head sat on a slender neck. Its parrot beak curved into a sharp point.

Philip became dizzy just looking at the creature. Griffins and manticores were easy enough to understand. They weren't *normal*, but they weren't completely outlandish. This was something new. Something borderline incomprehensible. His mind scrambled for any reasonable explanation for the existence of this birdlike creature, but none could be found. Its majesty and grandeur were overwhelming.

"What *is* that?" Max shrieked.

"It's a fenghuang. They're not dangerous," Ella assured them, "At least, I don't think they are…"

The fenghuang circled high above them, its movements graceful as if it were floating in the air. It cast its massive shadow over them again and again. Its jade eyes studied them with interest, but it made no move to harm them. Something about the fenghuang's countenance made Philip relax against his better judgment. A tingle in the back of his mind warned him of the presence of magic, but it was quickly silenced by a numb, blurred peace.

When they finally neared the beginning of a mountain range, the fenghuang let out a musical cry and departed in a flutter of massive feathers. Philip gazed after the bird, and when it was no longer visible, the effects of whatever magic it had used on him snapped. All false peace and security fled his mind, leaving nothing but anxiety and dread and fear.

Though the fenghuang's magic hadn't harmed them, it had manipulated them. It had made them feel something that wasn't real. Any creature with that ability was dangerous. Philip would have to keep his guard up even more than usual.

"I hate the way magic feels," Max grumbled.

Ella craned her neck to look at him in bewilderment. "What do you mean?"

"You know," Max said, "Every time someone does magic, it's like someone is crumpling your intestines into a ball."

That was one way to put it.

Ella's eyebrows drew together. "You can *feel* magic?"

"Yeah. Can't everyone?"

"No. I've never heard of anything like that before," Ella turned to Philip, "Can you feel magic too?"

Philip nodded. "It just feels *wrong* every time someone uses magic."

"That doesn't make any sense..." Ella trailed off with a thoughtful look on her face. She didn't speak a single word the rest of the flight, and Philip could see the wheels turning in her head.

By the time they reached the giants' palace, Philip's thoughts were knotted into an impossible web. Not everyone could feel magic like him and Max. What did that mean? Was it some sort of side effect of not being able to use magic? Or was it simply something that came with being human? If Ella didn't know, there would be no way to tell for sure. And if there was no way to tell for sure, there was no use dwelling on it.

Instead of letting his thoughts spiral even further, Philip focused on the physical world. Picturesque, snow-capped mountains spanned the world as far as the eye could see. The sheer magnitude of the mountains dwarfed him. His breath turned to fog in the frigid, high-altitude air.

The giants' palace rested on the very top of the tallest mountain. The size of the palace was incomprehensible. Philip felt like an ant in front of a skyscraper. They circled the palace's gigantic, layered roof made of bright red glazed tiles. Golden ornamentation perched on the dramatic peaks of the roof, red silk lanterns dangling from it like oversized earrings.

They dipped below the roof, around the ornately carved balconies that surrounded the exterior wall of the palace. The amount of detail put into each knob of wood astounded Philip, but it was nothing compared to the lavish grandeur of the entrance to the palace. Countless stories of jade stairs ascended the side of the mountain, leading to the red and gold doors, which were easily as tall as a football field was long. Pillars of jade and gold stood guard like soldiers at the entrance to the palace.

There were no actual guards to be found.

When Philip dismounted his hippogriff, he discovered why. His back was stiff from sitting so long, his legs ached from squeezing the hippogriff's sides, and his cheeks stung from the cool wind. None of that compared to the feeling of magic that writhed in his gut like a warning. Strange magic radiated from the palace.

"This isn't good," he murmured.

Ella appeared at his shoulder, her expression pensive. "What's wrong?"

266

"There's magic here."

"A *lot* of magic," Max added.

Vinnia morphed back to normal and joined them. Her jaw dropped as she took in the palace's exterior. She tipped her head so far back that she nearly fell backward. "How are we going to find the treasure in there? It could take us days to find anything."

"I'm not sure," Ella admitted. "We'll have to come up with a plan."

Philip opened his mouth to suggest they set up camp, but a flash of color in the corner of his eye grabbed his attention. He turned his head towards the movement. A single yellow and green peacock feather the size of a tarp drifted through the air and landed delicately in front of the palace doors.

"What's that?" Philip asked, pointing to the feather.

"That looks like a feather from the fenghuang." Ella said.

Another feather drifted through the air before a gust of wind swept it under the door.

Vinnia's eyes widened. "I think the fenghuang is leading us to the treasure."

Chapter 24

Philip didn't like this.

When they reached the base of the palace doors, they examined the feather. Vinnia verified that it was indeed a fenghuang feather. She and Ella were convinced these two random feathers meant the fenghuang was helping them.

He wasn't buying it. There was no way this bird was leading them to the treasure. Whether or not it was sentient enough to do such a thing didn't matter; no creature offered help for free. This could be a trap. Maybe the fenghuang wanted to toy with them before feeding them to its young.

Ella knelt to peer under the door. "There are more feathers inside!"

More feathers leading to their doom...

There had to be another way to find the next item. They didn't need "help" from a bird. They could figure this out by themselves. But when Philip relayed these sentiments to the others, they refused to listen.

"I know you're hesitant, Philip, but we can't miss out on this opportunity," Ella said.

"We'll do whatever it takes," Vinnia added.

Scowling, Philip wished he could cross his arms stubbornly. "What if this is a trap?"

"Then we fight our way out together," Ella said. Her resolved, unyielding expression told him there would be no arguing with her now.

Philip gave a relenting sigh. "Fine. Lead the way." If this was a trap, he'd warned them as best as he could.

Entering the palace was surprisingly easy. They simply crawled under the gap between the floor and the bottom of the door. Vinnia urged the hippogriffs inside as well, in case they needed a speedy getaway.

Inside the palace, the feeling of magic was twice as strong. It writhed inside him like an angry python. He forced his focus on the world around him to distract from the pain.

The interior of the palace was pristine. Polished jade tiled the floor like crystalline, green marble. Glossy red pillars the size of redwood trees supported the peaked roof, which soared high above. Luxurious ornamentation of red and gold decorated the palace in the form of lanterns, sculptures, and vases. Ancient tapestries of giants hung from the gold-papered walls.

A trail of fenghuang feathers littered the floor. Each feather was evenly spaced from the previous one, creating a perfect path to wherever the fenghuang intended to lure them.

"I think I'm gonna puke," Max wore a queasy expression as he pressed a hand to his stomach. "There's so much magic in here."

"We'll just have to be extra careful in here," Vinnia said, "Now, come on. The sun is going down, and I don't want to be here all night."

Philip reluctantly joined the others as they followed the path of feathers. Each feather was a different size and shape, but they all had the same red, yellow, and green coloring.

The trail took them through the grand entryway and around a corner, where it led to another jade-tiled, pillar-lined hallway. A large tapestry depicting a giantess with a stern face and black hair hung at the end of the hallway. The giantess cradled a fox in her arms. The fox's golden eyes seemed to follow them as they trailed the feathers down the hallway.

They didn't see a single giant as they walked, a fact that unnerved Philip more than it comforted him. The palace didn't have the same deserted feeling as the merfolk kingdom. It wasn't hollow like a ghost town; rather, it was taut with suspense, like any minute, a horde of giants might leap out of the oversized vases.

But nothing happened as they continued to follow the feathers through hallway after hallway. If the fenghuang intended to confuse them or take away any hope of finding their way out of the palace, it succeeded.

Moonlight poured through the rectangular, glassless windows, illuminating the hallways. Red silk lanterns hanging from the ceiling cast warm light on the cool jade, golden tassels swaying in the gentle breeze that drifted into the palace.

Exhaustion tugged at Philip's limbs and filled his body with each leaden step. To keep himself awake and alert, he dug his fingernails into his thigh. The deerskin fabric of his trousers prevented the full intensity of the pain, but it sufficed for the moment.

Ella yawned, her spine popping audibly as she stretched. She winced at the sound. "Sorry."

Max, almost half-asleep, dragged his feet with a horrible scraping noise. Philip's eye twitched every time Max did it, but no matter how many times he asked him to stop, his little brother pretended not to hear.

Only Vinnia refrained from showing physical symptoms of exhaustion. Her amber eyes shifted, alighting on particular, seemingly random objects. She set a brisk pace, and soon, even the hippogriffs couldn't keep up.

Finally, they reached the end of the feather trail. The last feather lay before a pair of red double doors studded with decorative gold spikes.

"Wow. That doesn't look threatening at all," Philip deadpanned. Exhaustion stripped away his ability to bite his tongue.

"It's no more threatening than my dad," Vinnia muttered. "Come on. We're wasting time." She dropped to her hands and knees and crawled under the door.

"Do you see anything?" Ella called.

"I found the treasure…" Vinnia's voice was muffled through the door. "And the guards."

They wasted no time in dropping to the ground and pulling themselves under the door. Ella, with her two functioning arms, made it through first. She seized Philip's hand and hauled him the rest of the way. Together they scrambled to their feet.

They found themselves in a throne room fit for a king. Everything about the room was lavish and expensive, from the gold plating on the soaring ceiling to the precious artifacts lining the walls. An ornately carved pergola stood over a dais containing a loveseat-style throne made of solid gold. Green vines curled over the pergola's wooden slats. Fist-sized pieces of gold hung from the vines like fruit. Philip could *feel* the magic radiating from the gold pieces.

Three, identical women sat beneath the pergola. Their angular, golden eyes peered like owl eyes under thick, dark lashes. Human-sized skulls were braided into their black hair like ornaments. They each wore a form-fitting silk gown embroidered with golden vines. When they stood, they towered ten feet tall at the very least.

The overwhelming feeling of magic wrenched Philip's stomach like someone was trying to rip his organs out. Max

271

dropped to his knees and vomited all over the clean, jade floor.

The women exchanged glances of bewilderment, clearly not used to people vomiting at the sight of them. Clearing her throat, the tallest woman spoke with a clear, melodic voice. "Behold, small ones. Welcome to the Imperial Palace of Juren. I am—"

Max interrupted the woman with another round of noisy vomiting.

Caught off-guard, the woman paused. She regained her composure and started again, "I am Jia, head guardian of Juren's sacred magic. These are my sisters, Lia and Kia."

Philip resisted a sarcastic snort. *Seriously?* What kind of mother named their daughters like that?

"Enough with the pretenses," Vinnia snapped. "What do you want?"

"The real question is: what do *you* want, Vinnia Haaf?" The shortest woman interrupted.

"We're here for magic," Vinnia said.

"Ah, yes. Come collect the treasure you so desperately need." Jia said. She and her sisters stepped aside, gesturing to the vines that covered the pergola.

A wave of nausea crashed over Philip. He stumbled, and the room seemed to sway beneath him. If it weren't for his own stubborn desire to remain upright, he would have collapsed. Another round of vomiting racked Max's body.

Vinnia, ever the daring one, stepped forward first. Nothing happened. No spikes sprang from the floor. No poisoned darts shot from the walls. No trapdoors swallowed her into the ground. She took another tentative step, and again, nothing happened.

Ella slipped her hand into Philip's. Together, they walked towards the pergola, keeping their guard up. Behind them, Max continued to vomit on the floor.

With each step, Philip braced himself. Surely the women weren't just going to let them walk up to the vines and pluck off a bean or two for the road. As they walked, though, the pergola didn't seem to be growing any closer. If anything, it appeared farther away than when they started.

The shortest woman watched them with her eyebrows raised expectantly, "Well? What are you waiting for? The treasure awaits."

"What kind of magic is this?" Vinnia demanded.

Jia blinked her golden eyes innocently. "Whatever do you mean?"

"Fine," Vinnia snapped. "Be that way." Face set with determination, she continued to march forward.

After a few steps, though, her body went rigid. With slow, jerking movements, she turned around as if someone were controlling her like a puppet. Her eyes flashed from amber to glowing gold. An agonized shriek erupted from her as she collapsed. She skittered backward on her hands, gaping in terror at some invisible thing before her. With a strangled scream, she clutched at her neck and clawed at her shoulders.

What was wrong with her? Philip recoiled, exchanging an alarmed glance with Ella.

When their eyes met, however, Ella's posture snapped to attention as if someone jerked her body with puppet strings. Her gaze turned vacant, and her brown eyes glowed gold. She whirled around, searching the room frantically. Panic filled her expression.

"Dad!" she called, rushing past Philip. "Dad, I'm here! Where are you? Dad!"

Drawing away from Ella, Philip retreated toward Max. Her cries and Vinnia's screams echoed in the throne room. Whatever

273

was happening to the girls, he had to protect his brother first.

Then he noticed the worms.

They inched out of vases, through the windows, out of statues' mouths. Their faceless bodies squirmed towards him. Bile rose in his throat, but it had nothing to do with the overwhelming sense of magic churning in his stomach. The worms beelined straight for him. He scrambled away from them, but they were gaining on him with impossible speed. His breathing sped, and panic clawed at him.

Not worms. Anything but worms.

Every kind of worm—earthworms, leeches, tapeworms, hookworms, and countless others—inched towards him. He couldn't get away fast enough. The first worms reached him, latching onto his shoes. Frantically, he tried to swat them off of him, but they simply cling to his hands too. The worms swarmed him in a writhing mass. Their slimy forms crawled beneath his clothing, directly against his skin. They burrowed into his bare flesh, making their way to his organs. A leech on his chest drained the blood from his veins through his heart. Earthworms delved into his skin like it was dirt. Parasitic worms found their way to his intestines.

He was being devoured by worms from the inside out. He wanted to tear his skin from his body. It took a moment to realize he was screaming.

Somewhere beneath the noise of his screams and the squelching of worms, Vinnia and Ella continued to cry out. On her knees, Vinnia shrieked like a banshee and clutched her neck. Ella wailed, calling for her father as she raced through the throne room.

A worm squirmed across Philip's cheekbone, brushing his lower lashes with its slimy body. Squeezing his eyes shut, he swiped at the worms on his face and stumbled blindly.

"No, no, no. Not his eyes. They would crawl into his eyes, fill his eye sockets, and…"

Philip tripped and crashed to the ground, slamming his head against the jade floor. Lights danced before his eyes. Muffled noises sounded a million miles away.

When his vision cleared, his gaze locked on the golden beans hanging from the pergola. *The treasure.* Maybe the magic could get rid of the worms. It *had* to, or else he would be devoured alive.

Already, the worms piled on top of him. The worms crushed between him and the ground were unharmed; they simply squirmed out from under him and joined the mass on top of him.

He was covered, yet the worms still poured into the room like an endless fountain. They covered every inch of the floor and were crawling onto the walls and ceiling. Ella, Max, and Vinnia provided additional hosts for the worms. They too were covered, unable to escape.

With a sob, Philip clawed through the worms towards the pergola. The golden glow of the beans emanated beneath the worms that covered the wooden structure. Each inch he gained was excruciating. His organs burned like fire, infested with parasites eager to feast on him. His gag reflex heaved, but he couldn't seem to vomit.

Finally—*finally*—he reached the pergola. He struggled to his feet beneath the weight of the worms. The writhing ground was slick and unstable, but he managed to brace himself against the structure. A bean dangled just above his head. A thick, fat leech hung from the bean. Ooze dripped from its pulsating body.

Gritting his teeth, Philip closed his eyes and forced himself to snatch the bean, leech and all.

The moment his hand made contact with the bean, the worms vanished. Their writhing, squelching bodies disappeared without a trace. Gasping in relief, Philip collapsed. His head spun, the world tilting beneath him. But the worms were gone, and the twist of magic in his stomach lessened.

What just happened? Was that some kind of illusion? If so, it had been strong; the phantom sensation of worms crawling over his skin still lingered. Why did it stop? Was he protected by the magic of the beans? Or was there something worse yet to come?

Snatching the bean from the vine, he didn't have much time to ponder these questions. The middle giantesses turned her attention to him, her golden eyes narrowed.

"Release the treasure, human," the giantess commanded.

Philip gripped the bean tighter as if it were his lifeline.

When he didn't obey or respond, the giantess rose. Neither of her sisters noticed, their gazes vacant and trancelike. Philip shrank away, backing deeper under the cover of the pergola. He snatched a few more low-hanging beans on his way.

The giantess's lip curled as she advanced. "You know not what trouble you bring by stealing our treasure."

Philip continued to back away, but this time, he altered his trajectory. A short distance behind him, Vinnia keeled over on her knees, cradling her torso as she shrieked. He drew nearer to her, keeping his gaze focused on the giantess. When he reached Vinnia, he angled his body so the giantess wouldn't see him slip a bean into her lap. Two beans accidentally tumbled from his one-armed grasp, but he didn't have a moment to pick them back up.

Vinnia's screams silenced when the beans touched her body. She curled herself around the beans, cradling them to her chest. The giantess didn't notice, but Jia snapped out of her trance with

276

a furious growl. She shot to her feet and marched towards her sister.

Philip quickened his pace and changed course towards Ella, who still wandered the throne room. Her cries for her father turned to frantic screams. She moved fast, but he was faster. He turned from the giantesses and bolted towards her.

Behind him, the giantesses sped up, but thankfully, their sandals and long robes prevented them from running.

Philip reached Ella and thrust a bean towards her. When it touched her, she slumped forwards, as if someone had cut invisible puppet strings. Her eyes faded back to brown, and she swiped tears from her eyes.

"Wha—what happened?" her words slurred together.

There was no time to explain. The third giantess awakened from her trance. With all three giants advancing toward them, Philip and Ella were trapped.

"Crush it!" Vinnia hollered.

Confused, Philip glanced towards her just in time to see her throw the bean to the ground and stomp on it. With a blinding, golden flash, she was gone.

"Go," he told Ella, "I'll get Max."

"Will you be okay?" Ella's forehead creased in concern.

"Don't worry about me. Just go!"

Ella didn't argue. She dropped the bean and stomped down, disappearing with a flash of light.

Philip was left alone, cornered by three giantesses who stood between him and his brother. Max, still curled in the fetal position, lay near the hippogriffs in the middle of the throne room.

"Your friends may have escaped, little human, but we will be sure to give their punishments to you." Jia threatened.

277

Philip's back pressed against the wall. He had two beans left. Letting out a sharp whistle, he prayed for a miracle.

"Foolish human. You cannot escape us," Jia shook her head in mock pity. "We will make you relieve your worst memories," she continued, "your deepest fears, and your hidden horrors. We will make the monsters of your nightmares a painful reality."

"That sounds great and all," Philip retorted, "but I'll be going now." As soon as the words passed his lips, his hippogriff swooped from above. Philip hooked his elbow around the beast's neck and pulled himself onto its back. They were back in the air before the giantesses could even react.

The hippogriff swooped towards Max, and Philip took his opportunity. He hurled one bean to the ground with enough force to make it shatter like glass. Max and the other hippogriffs disappeared.

As Philip was about to crush the bean for himself, Jia swatted the hippogriff out of the air. Philip flew from its back. Everything slowed as if it were happening in slow motion. The world blurred around him. Sounds faded to a high-pitched ringing. Everything snapped back to real speed as he landed with a sickening crunch. The air whooshed from his lungs. His entire body throbbed.

He had just enough strength to slam the bean against the ground, crushing it to dust. Blinding light turned the world painfully white. Beneath him, the jade floor opened and swallowed him whole.

Chapter 25

One day.

One day until Dash became Sovereign Prince of Haderra.

One day until he would be in charge of an entire kingdom.

Growing up in poor, run-down Nowheresville, West Virginia, he could never afford to dream big. Rhett had frequently reminded him that they were different. Other kids could dream of being doctors or lawyers or CEOs, but Dash was destined for something much different.

When Rhett had said 'different', Dash always assumed he meant 'less.' Maybe he would struggle to work three part-time jobs as their mother had. To him, that wasn't necessarily less—if he was happy, it didn't matter what he did for a living—but the disgust and condescension in Rhett's voice told him otherwise.

Ruling a kingdom was definitely 'different' than what most teenagers were destined for. He didn't mind the path life put him on, but sometimes he allowed dangerous thoughts to slip into his mind.

What if he *had* been destined for 'less'? What would life be like if his father had never shown up to whisk him and Rhett off to the magical world?

He liked to imagine he would have had a group of friends at his high school. Maybe they would have hung out at the local diner every day. They could have spent hours laughing and joking and doing homework together. Maybe one of his friends would have been a sweet, shy girl with flowing hair and eyes like a summer sky. Maybe they would have fallen in love.

These fantasies, which used to be occasional, now plagued him more frequently.

What would Rhett say if he knew?

Dash supposed it didn't matter. He was going to be sovereign. Whatever human wishes he had no longer mattered. His kingdom would be first. Always. Once he was gilded and coronated, his plan would begin. There would be no going back, especially since the Fair Lords supported him completely.

If Rhett could give up his life for the good of the worlds, Dash decided he could do the same for the good of the kingdom.

Philip gasped and bolted upright in the snow. A fit of coughing overtook him as he inhaled snowflakes and frigid air. The temperature change shocked his system like the time Marius had thrown him into a freezing lake during the winter.

Scrambling to his feet, he turned in a slow circle. The freshly-risen sun hung above the horizon in a blindingly blue sky. Snow blanketed the mountains that surrounded them as far as the eye could see. A brisk wind cut through his sparse clothing, sending a shiver down his spine. He couldn't sense even the barest twinge of magic.

Ella, Max, and Vinnia were nowhere in sight.

He had to find the others. They couldn't die out here. Not after everything they'd been through.

With near-frozen hands cupped around his mouth, Philip began to holler. "Ella! Max! Vinnia!"

The rabid howling of the wind rendered his voice nearly useless. He stumbled through the knee-deep snow, shouting anyways. If the others responded, he had no way of knowing.

A hollow shriek rang across the mountaintop. He froze in his tracks, heart thundering. Whatever creature made that noise

280

didn't sound friendly. The shriek echoed again, this time sounding much closer.

He glanced up just in time to see a dark form hurtling through the air towards him. He dove into a snowbank, narrowly avoiding the form as it crashed. A throaty squawk escaped the form as it twitched like an injured bird.

From his position in the snowbank, Philip peered down at the form. A pair of golden eagle eyes framed by slate-grey feathers blinked up at him. He rushed to Max's hippogriff, relief washing over him.

The hippogriff perked up at the sound of his voice. It replaced its pitiful squawking with affectionate cooing. It staggered to its feet and shook itself like a dog. Snow flew off of its sleek feathers, showering Philip. His teeth chattered, and he scowled at the new round of shivering that overtook his body.

They had to find the others before he froze to death. *If* the others had even been transported to the same area. For all he knew, they could have been dumped into the human world. From the mountains surrounding him, he assumed he was still in Juren, but there was no way to be sure.

Swinging himself onto the back of the hippogriff, Philip prayed the others were close by. The warmth of the hippogriff's body helped thaw his frozen legs. When they launched into the air to search from an aerial view, the cold, thin air chilled him to the bone. He realized he'd never known true cold before this.

As they flew through the falling snow, Philip scanned the ground for any sign of Ella, Max, or Vinnia. The ominous black clouds on the horizon threatened him with a looming blizzard.

His gaze caught on an uneven trail through the snow sloping down the side of a mountain. He steered his hippogriff towards it, trying to quell the hope that bubbled in his chest. It could be nothing. It could be the tracks of a monster.

But it could be the footprints of the others.

When he spotted Ella, a gasp of relief escaped his lips. She was kneeling in the snow, digging in a snowbank. Their other two hippogriffs huddled together behind her in a grey and brown mass of feathers and fur.

Philip circled Max's hippogriff around and landed it next to them. The moment he dismounted, Max's hippogriff huddled with the others, making relieved clicking noises.

"Ella!" Philip's voice scratched his raw, dry throat, but he hardly noticed.

Ella's head snapped up. She whirled around and let out a sob when she saw him. They stumbled towards each other, fumbling with frozen limbs as they collided in an embrace. Ella tucked herself against his chest, her closeness a desperately needed source of heat and comfort. He closed his eyes against the prickle of tears in his eyes, which most definitely came from the harsh wind stinging his near-frozen eyeballs.

Ella was alive. Freezing, but alive and *here.*

"Have you seen Max?" he asked at the same time she asked, "Have you seen Vinnia?"

"I found Max. He's safe in the burrow I was digging." Ella didn't pull away from him as she spoke. Her voice rumbled against his chest.

Philip could have laughed with relief. Max was alive and safe.

"Is Vinnia with you?" Ella asked.

Philip's heart sank. "She's not with you?"

Ella pulled away, taking her warmth with her. "We have to find her!"

"She's out there somewhere," Philip said, trying to convince himself as much as Ella. Somewhere on one of these snow-covered mountains, Vinnia Haaf was stumbling through the snow searching for them. She had to be.

Ella and Philip wasted no time in pulling Max out of the burrow and mounting their hippogriffs. They swept low over the mountains, searching through the snowflakes that fell in thick, heavy gusts. The wind only grew harsher and colder as the search went on.

Vinnia was nowhere to be seen.

They searched high and low, examining every tree, every rock, every lump of snow. Whenever they found the occasional animal, they descended upon it immediately, thinking it might be Vinnia. They were disappointed each time when it was nothing but a simple six-legged goat or a frost-furred snow leopard.

After hours of searching, they found the first signs that Vinnia could be anywhere nearby. A trail of scarlet blood dribbled through the snow until the point where it dropped off the edge of a fifty-foot cliff.

"Vinnia!" Ella's scream cut through even the harsh wind. She urged her hippogriff over the edge of the cliff.

A wave of dread crashed over Philip when he saw Vinnia's body lying spread-eagle at the bottom of the cliff. Dark blood seeped from her body like a juice stain on a white carpet. A golden bean rested in the dark, bloody snow.

Behind Philip, Max let out a heartbroken sob. "She's dead!"

"We don't know that," Ella said, but even coming from her, the assurance sounded empty.

Philip followed Ella as she landed her hippogriff and scrambled to Vinnia's body. She dug a handful of powder from the pouch that somehow remained at her hip. Forcing Vinnia's mouth open, she poured the powder directly onto the mixie's nearly frozen tongue.

"We have to get her to warmth," Ella said, turning to address Philip. "You have the most body heat. Can you carry her while we fly?"

Though Philip doubted his ability to keep both himself and Vinnia on the hippogriff's back with only one arm, he agreed; Vinnia's life was on the line.

Ella scooped Vinnia into her arms and passed her to him once he mounted his hippogriff. Finding a secure way to hold Vinnia's limp body proved to be a difficult task. He propped her against his chest, letting her head lean back against his shoulder while he wrapped a steadying arm around her waist. His knees squeezed the hippogriff's side for balance, but his center of gravity misaligned with Vinnia's weight and his inability to balance properly.

When they shot into the air, balance became nearly impossible. The hippogriff's alternating pattern of flapping and gliding did nothing to stabilize either of them.

Thankfully, Ella steered her hippogriff southward, away from the black clouds on the horizon.

Vinnia's stone-cold body lay limp against him. Not for the first time, he was struck by the delicacy of her tiny yet powerful frame. Wherever Ella planned to take them, he hoped they arrived soon. Otherwise, Vinnia might not make it.

They flew for hours, the snowy, mountainous terrain of the giant kingdom stretching on below them. Cold set into Philip's bones, turning his veins to ice. His fingers turned blue, and his entire shivering body went numb. As they flew south, however, the harsh weather mellowed. The sun sank low over the horizon, giving way to the moon and stars. The jagged, grey mountains bled into rolling hills. Though the gradual change in weather thawed Philip's frost-nipped limbs, Vinnia's body remained cold and unmoving as if she were carved from ice.

Ella pushed her hippogriff faster and faster, setting a brutal, urgent pace. Philip recognized his helplessness mirrored in her face, but she disguised hers well with the determined set of her jaw. He didn't dare sleep, too terrified to close his eyes for even a moment in fear of plummeting off the hippogriff's back.

When the sun rose the following morning, the lush greenery that spread over the giants' land began to thin. It was hardly noticeable at first—a dead bush here, a bare patch there—but the land gradually morphed into a dry, barren desert populated with shrubs and dry grasses. Cracked red clay stretched on as far as the eye could see. Every so often, they would fly over a gaping hole in the ground that plunged into black nothingness.

Dry, suffocating heat hung in the air. Sweat beaded on Philip's temple as the early afternoon sun beat down on him without respite. Slowly—painfully slowly— Vinnia's body began to defrost. Her blue-tinged fingers regained a bit of color. The temperature of her body rose little by little until she no longer felt like an ice sculpture. Her snow-dampened clothing clung to her tiny frame.

Philip kept his arm wrapped around her waist despite the sweat that drenched him. Even in the middle of summer in New York City, where most apartment buildings didn't have central air conditioning, and people had to rely on weak electric fans for relief from the heat, it didn't get this hot.

This heat was something different altogether. The stiflingly hot air sat unmoving in the absence of a breeze. Waves of heat radiated from the parched ground. Any moisture had been zapped from the world, leaving nothing but dust and thirst.

A faint groan resonated in the back of Vinnia's throat. She

stirred in Philip's grasp, but her eyes remained closed. Her breathing kept its deep, comalike rhythm. The tips of her frigid fingers twitched against his knee.

"Hey." Philip craned his neck, searching her face for any more signs of wakefulness. "You're going to be okay. Just hang in there."

He kept a secure arm around her as Ella steered her hippogriff towards a cavern-like hole in the ground. Vinnia's head lolled forward, and she nearly slipped from his grasp. Sweat slicked his skin, but he managed to hold on to her.

When they finally landed, he and Ella rushed to spread Vinnia out on the hot ground. Her wet clothing sizzled against the scorching clay. Sweat beaded on her forehead, though her skin was clammy and cool to the touch.

"Can't you just use some more powder to wake her up?" Max asked.

Ella shook her head. "That's just a basic herbal blend to prevent infection from her wounds, but it can't heal her."

Philip frowned. "Her wounds?"

"Didn't you see the gash on the back of her head?"

Philip knelt and rolled Vinnia to her side. Blood darkened the hair at the nape of her neck, but there were no open wounds to be found.

"Huh…" A crease formed between Ella's eyebrows. "Maybe she healed herself unconsciously?"

Max opened his mouth, likely to ask yet another question, but was interrupted by Vinnia, who bolted upright with a strangled gasp. Immediately, her body began to shiver.

"What happened? Where are we?" Vinnia asked through chattering teeth.

"Shhh." Ella pressed a hand to Vinnia's forehead, gauging

286

her temperature, "We're safe now. I brought us to Enan."

"Enan?" Vinnia's face contorted in disgust.

Philip gave a halfhearted smile. Vinnia managed to be herself, even in the face of near-death.

"You need to rest," Ella said, her expression full of concern. "Besides, what's wrong with Enan?"

Vinnia swatted Ella away. "I'm fine. Mixies heal much faster than everyone else. *Besides,* Enan is the dwarf kingdom."

Ella leaned back, humoring Vinnia. "So?"

"*So,* the dwarves helped my dad take over Mermaidia. They sat and watched while he killed thousands. Stars, they *supported* him while he did it! Once my dad took over, the dwarves claimed their spoils of war and burrowed back underground into their little dirt holes while my dad ran his kingdom into the ground."

"You can't judge an entire race simply because they supported your dad."

"Dwarves can't be trusted," Vinnia insisted. "They're greedy and selfish and stupid. Believe me, I've had my share of mishaps with them."

"Well, you're just going to have to put your prejudices aside. The next item is here, and we need your help to get it."

Vinnia gave a relenting sigh, though her lips twisted with displeasure. "What's the next item?"

"'*A dwarf ruler's heart of stone,*'" Philip recited.

Max scrunched his nose. "What do you think that means?"

"I've given this some thought, and I think I have an idea," Ella said, "What if it's a literal heart made of stone?"

Understanding dawned on Vinnia's face. "Do you mean the Yakta?"

"What's a Yakta?" Max asked, tilting his head in confusion.

"Dwarves live in a network of underground tunnels called

burrows," Vinnia explained. "Each burrow can stretch on for miles, but there's always one central room the tunnels branch off of. That room is called the heart of the burrow. It is customary for dwarves to keep a stone carving called a Yakta inside the heart. Every burrow has a different Yakta representing their familial house. Hence, the 'heart of stone.'"

Philip supposed that made sense. It was better than what he'd come up with, which was absolutely nothing.

"How are we going to get to the heart?" he wondered aloud, peering down into the darkness of the cavernous hole.

"Don't worry," Vinnia assured them. "I can morph into some kind of animal, burrow down to the heart, and take the Yakta without any one knowing. It will be easy."

A crease formed between Ella's eyebrows. "Are you sure you're strong enough to do that? You nearly died in Juren, and what happened in the throne room…"

"I'm fine," Vinnia snapped, cutting Ella off. "The giants didn't show me anything I haven't seen before."

A heavy silence fell over them. The phantom sensation of worms squirmed against Philip's skin. He shuddered, reminding himself that it wasn't real. Whatever had happened had just been an illusion of some kind. What illusion had the giants shown Vinnia and Ella? From the somber expressions on their faces, he guessed they weren't too eager to share. That was fine with him; they had every right to keep the horrors to themselves.

Finally, Ella gave a relenting sigh. "If you're sure you're okay, I suppose it wouldn't hurt to try."

Vinnia paused, her face contorting into a strange look. After a moment, nothing happened. Her strange expression turned into one of panic. Her breathing sped. "Something's wrong," she gasped. "I can't morph."

"What do you mean you can't morph?" Philip demanded. Morphing was part of her magic. It wasn't possible for magic to simply stop... was it?

"I don't know!" Vinnia snapped. "If I knew, I would fix it."

Ella set a gentle hand on Vinnia's shoulder. "You've probably pushed yourself too hard. It's okay to need time to rest. Please take it easy for a while. Your magic will most likely return before you know it."

"It's not—*ugh*, never mind." Vinnia stopped herself with an exasperated sigh. "My magic is complicated. But we don't have time to 'take it easy.' This is almost the last item. We're so close."

Philip stiffened at the mention of the last item. *A human's dying breath.* What were they going to do about *that*?

"If Vinnia can't morph, we're going to need another plan..." Ella trailed off, chewing her lip as she thought.

After a painfully long stretch of silence, Vinnia spoke. "I have an idea."

Chapter 26

Dash didn't particularly like the color gold.

There was something about it that just screamed superiority. Maybe that way of thinking remained because Elliott had flaunted his gold magic at every chance. Maybe he only thought that way because of the kingdom's inherent association with gold and wealth.

Ever since the first fair folk ruler founded the kingdom of Haderra, the rulers had been blessed with gold magic. The gilding ceremony in just a few minutes would infuse him with every color of magic—well, *almost* every color—consequently blessing him with gold magic.

On a day like today, Dash would have given anything for Rhett to be with him. But, as purple magic wasn't part of the gilding ceremony, Rhett had to stay locked away on his island like always. Not that he could have left the island even if it were important to the ceremony...

As a servant helped him into a gold silk jacket, Dash couldn't help but feel he was playing an elaborate game of make-believe. He caught his reflection in the mirror and frowned; these past few sleepless nights were catching up with him. Dark circles lined his eyes. Weariness was etched into his expression.

He was struck for the first time in his life with the thought that he resembled Rhett.

Pushing that thought aside, Dash forced himself to concentrate. In a few minutes, he would become the Sovereign Prince of Haderra. He needed to be as alert and focused as possible if he wanted to put his best foot forward, especially since he was asking so much of the people already.

Movement in the corner of the room pulled his attention from the mirror. Nathan and Adrian entered, looking stately and imposing in their gold-accented uniforms. They had taken to their new advisory roles with impossible grace and determination.

"Are you ready, Sire?" Adrian asked with a wink.

This time, the formality didn't bother him. It took him back to the days when Nathan and Adrian could be nothing more than his friends. The days when they'd tease and jostle him around like any of their other friends. Those days were long gone, but at least he still had memories. For the rest of his life, memories would have to be enough.

The servant made the final adjustments on Dash's jacket and stepped away to let him see the entirety of his reflection. Dressed head to toe in gold, he simply stared at himself, unsure what to think.

Was he ready?

Glancing back at Nathan and Adrian, he set his expression with determination. It didn't matter if he was ready or not. This wasn't about him. This was about his kingdom.

His kingdom was ready.

If only he could feel the same.

Vinnia's plan was outlandish and risky, but it was all they had.

Ella was the designated plan maker for a reason, and when a problem stumped her, it was serious.

They descended into the darkness of the underground dwarf palace. As they walked, Philip began to have serious doubts about their plan. He exhaled slowly, reminding himself to stay calm. The rope binding his wrists dug into his flesh. The cool, pitch-black interior of the cavernous hole turned out to be the entrance to a tunnel. Being below the ground provided much-needed shelter from the relentlessly glaring sun. They followed the tunnel as it sloped underground and narrowed. At one point, the ceiling hung so low that even Vinnia, who stood taller than Max only by a few inches, had to crouch while she walked.

Max let out a grunt as he walked into the cavern wall yet again. "How do dwarves see where they're going down here?"

"Dwarves can see in almost complete darkness," Vinnia explained.

"Cool! I wish I had night vision. Did you know bats aren't blind? Ooh! I wonder if there are any bats in this cave…" Max proceeded to ramble about bats to no one in particular.

Just as Philip opened his mouth to tell his brother to stop talking, two unfamiliar voices rang through the darkness.

"Who goes there?"

"State your business."

Vinnia spoke from beside Philip. "I am Vinnia Jaxel Iva Haaf, emissary of the merfolk. I come bearing gifts for your queen from my father, General Jaxel Haaf."

Flint struck against metal. A torch blazed to life, illuminating two, heavily armored dwarves that guarded a round, intricately carved stone door. They wore identical expressions of confusion.

"Vinnia Haaf has been dead for years," the dwarf to the left said, his voice low and rumbling. "The merfolk kingdom and its allies mourned her loss together."

Vinnia stepped forward, straightening militantly. She planted her feet, puffed out her chest, and lifted her chin. "I am Vinnia Jaxel Iva Haaf, daughter of General Jaxel Haaf, heir to the throne of Mermaidia and I am very much alive," she snapped. "I come bearing gifts for the dwarf queen."

The dwarf to the right stroked his beard, appearing perplexed. "What gifts do you bring?"

"My father has sent your queen a tribute: three young servants we captured on the southeastern shores," Vinnia stepped aside and gestured to the rest of them. "These are two humans and an elf, none of whom can perform magic of any kind."

"What's the point to them if they can't do magic?" the dwarf to the left demanded.

Vinnia's lips curved into a malicious grin. "They can't escape."

Philip caught Ella's eye and couldn't help but marvel at the irony of it all. Just a few days ago, they had escaped a dungeon and now, they were willingly walking into one. If Vinnia's plan didn't work, they were going to be in trouble.

"Ah yes," the dwarf to the right said, rubbing his hands together. "The queen will be delighted by these gifts."

"Come," the dwarf to the left, "We will take you to Her Excellency."

The dwarves turned in unison and pressed their palms against the circular stone door behind them. After a moment, deep silver veins in the cave began to glow. The doors opened with the sound of stone grinding against stone.

Behind the door, a silver light welcomed them into a vast cavern. Glowing silver orbs floated around the stalactites like stars. Minerals sparkled in the stone that surrounded them, making up the floor, walls, and ceiling. A pathway wound around stalagmites that ranged from the size of traffic cones to the size of pillars.

"Now that we have entered the burrow, we must introduce ourselves," the dwarf to the right said. "I am Klin of House Pyrite."

"And I am Malm of House Baryte." The dwarf to the left added.

Vinnia dipped her chin in a nod of acknowledgment. "Pleased to make your acquaintance, gentlemen."

After that, they walked in silence, the militant clicks of the dwarves' boots echoing in the cave. Vinnia strode ahead with the dwarves, hands clasped behind her back like a general. Ella and Max followed close behind, gaping at their surroundings. Philip shuffled after them, focused on the press of rope against his wrist. His left wrist stung, raw and chafed from the ropes, while he felt nothing in his right wrist. The skin on his right wrist was just as irritated as the skin on his left wrist, yet he could feel nothing.

"Here we are," Klin announced, stopping in front of a circular stone door carved with an elaborate crown design. Two more dwarves stood guard in front of this door. They nodded at Klin and Malm and drew open the doors, letting them into a massive cavern illuminated by more glowing, silver orbs. What appeared to be a petrified human heart was suspended above a throne-shaped rock formation. Two guards flanked the throne, and, consequently, the stone heart.

A frail, elderly dwarf woman sat on the throne, looking like a doll in an armchair. Deep wrinkles cut through her sharp face, and her emerald green eyes glinted like knives. An elaborate stone crown rested on her head. Philip worried the weight of it might crush the old woman's skull or break her neck.

The dwarf queen glanced up from the group of dwarves cowering before her. "What is the meaning of this interruption?" she snapped.

"Queen Soma, Vinnia Haaf has come bearing gifts on behalf of General Haaf," Klin reported.

The queen lifted a quizzical eyebrow. "The general's

daughter is dead."

Vinnia stepped forward and folded her arms. "As I keep telling everyone, I'm very much alive."

The queen's eyes widened. "Impossible," she breathed.

"For you, maybe, but I've become more powerful than you could ever imagine," Vinnia said.

The doors to the throne room burst open, banging against the stone walls with a deafening crack. Six heavily armed guards brushed past Vinnia wordlessly. Though they only stood as tall as Max, they managed an intimidating front. They marched up to the queen and bowed.

"The prime minister is here with an urgent message, Your Excellency," one of the guards said.

The queen narrowed her eyes. "What could be so urgent as to interrupt my audience?"

The guards didn't respond. They snapped to attention and pivoted to face each other in two parallel lines, creating a clear pathway. An immaculately dressed dwarf woman who could only be the prime minister herself strode into the room. She gave the queen a curt bow and began to speak. "Queen Soma, may we have a word in private?" Her eyes flicked towards Philip as she stressed the word 'private'.

"Don't mind them, Tyda," the queen said with a flick of her hand. "Deliver this 'urgent news' at once."

"This is a matter of national security, Ma'am," the prime minister said in a measured voice.

The queen folded her hands and raised her eyebrows pointedly. "Proceed."

The prime minister sucked in a deep breath and held it for much longer than necessary. She had the look of someone who was just barely maintaining her composure.

"Very well," she sighed. "We just received word that Dash Calloway has been gilded and crowned Sovereign Prince of Haderra. His first act as Sovereign was to declare war on Elvenmar. As we speak, the fair folk are marching to attack the city of Velsailia. We believe this is direct retaliation for the murder of Prince Elliott III."

Philip couldn't believe his ears. He glanced at Ella, who stared at the prime minister in horror. *"No,"* she whispered, eyes filling with tears. She turned away from the prime minister and buried her head in his shoulder, her body shaking with sobs.

Hadn't he seen this coming? Hadn't Treave assured him that the fair folk would celebrate Elliott's death?

"How can this be?" the queen demanded. "A war will tear our kingdoms apart."

"Precisely." Prime Minister Tyda pressed her lips together. "Parliament has already voted to declare neutrality. You must make an address to the people and state our position immediately."

"Bring the parliament here," the queen commanded. "*I* wish to speak with them, as *I* am their queen."

"There is nothing more to discuss," the prime minister insisted. "The vote has already been passed."

Queen Soma raised her chin, locking eyes with the prime minister. *"Bring them here."*

After a moment-long standoff, the prime minister broke her gaze away and gave a relenting sigh. "They're on their way, Your Excellency."

The dwarf parliament flooded the room moments later. About fifty dwarves conversed frantically, their voices echoing off the stone to create an unintelligible din.

Klin and Malm swept Philip, Ella, and Max back to the

corner of the room. Vinnia maneuvered through the crowd, taking a place to the right of the throne.

"Ladies and gentlemen, quiet please!" Prime Minister Tyda hollered over the roar of noise.

If the dwarves heard her, they paid her no attention.

She tried again, "Settle down. Settle down!"

When her voice fell on deaf ears, she growled in frustration, *"Silence!"*

The dwarves continued to shout over the prime minister.

But when Queen Soma rose from the throne, the crowd of dwarves quieted immediately. The prime minister's lips tightened into a thin line.

"I have called you here to discuss the recent vote about Enan's response to Sovereign Prince Dash's declaration of war," Queen Soma began. "This is a matter of great urgency. The prime minister claims you have come to a decision, however, I believe—"

The queen paused as a rumble shook the ground beneath their feet. Bits of stone rained from the ceiling. The dwarves glanced around nervously, murmurs echoing through the cavern.

Philip caught Vinnia's eye over the sea of dwarves. She shot him a furtive smirk and glanced pointedly at the petrified heart above the queen. Taking the hint, Philip crouched and inched towards the throne. Whatever was going to happen, he wanted to be as close to the heart as possible. Klin and Malm didn't notice him slip past them, creeping along the wall.

Queen Soma cleared her throat to regain her composure. "As I was saying. I believe, despite the prime minister's claims, that the decision requires further—"

Again, the queen was interrupted by an earthshaking rumble. The ground shook beneath Philip's feet. Dust and stone fell from the ceiling. Fractures split in the stone walls. This time, the rumbling only grew more intense, until, with an earsplitting crack, the ground burst open. Geysers shot through wide cracks in the stone cavern. The dwarves burst into chaos as they panicked and rushed to flee the cavern before it filled with water.

Philip barely made it to Vinnia's side before her eyes rolled back into her head. She collapsed like a ragdoll in his grasp.

Chapter 27

Rhett would have traded a limb to be with Dash on his gilding and coronation day. This was supposed to be the most important day of his little brother's life, and he could do little more than send a short note wishing him luck.

According to the information he'd received, Dash's ceremonies had gone smoothly. Immediately after the coronation, Dash had announced his declaration of war on the elves. He demanded retribution for Elliott's murder, and though the elves tried to deny it, there was little they could do.

The Fair Lords kept up their end of the bargain and supported Dash completely, and because the Fair Lords supported him, the people—predictably fickle as they were—supported him too.

Yes, there would be people who opposed the war, but those people were only a small minority. At least, they only *appeared* to be a small minority.

Word of Dash's declaration had spread like wildfire to every kingdom, and each kingdom was quick to declare neutrality. For now, Dash would be on his own.

Rhett would do almost anything to help his brother fight this war, but being trapped on the Island of Corvus, he was virtually powerless.

After so many years of imprisonment, though, he found ways to adapt. With a flick of his wrist, he summoned a piece of parchment in a burst of purple flames. He ignored the instant headache that shot through his brain.

If he couldn't go to Dash, then Dash would have to come to him.

Philip sloshed through the knee-deep water, which poured into the cavern, filling it rapidly. Vinnia slumped in his one-armed grasp, but he didn't let her go. If he did, her unconscious form would slip beneath the rising water and drown.

In the chaos, the guards abandoned their posts to usher Queen Soma and Prime Minister Tyda to safety. They barked orders at everyone else to move aside for the queen and prime minister, but the dwarves pushed and shoved, prioritizing themselves over everyone else.

The petrified heart remained completely unguarded and unnoticed. Philip waded towards it, but Ella ushered him towards the exit.

"I'll get it. Just go!" she yelled over the roar of the water.

Philip kept a tight grip on Vinnia and forced his way towards the jammed exit. Along the way, Max grabbed onto his limp arm, clinging to it with desperation. The water reached Max's chin, and he struggled to stay afloat.

When they reached the doors, dwarves elbowed and shoved their way out of the cavern. Philip could only wait for everyone to evacuate before him. Ella would likely have enough time to grab the heart and reach him by the time the exit cleared.

She climbed on top of the throne, just above the water. She lost her footing on the wet stone but caught herself against a stalagmite. Stretching as far as possible, she barely reached the petrified heart. She grasped at it with wet fingers, but it slipped from her grip and plunged into the swirling waters below.

Without hesitation, she leaped from the safety of the throne and disappeared beneath the surface of the water. Philip lost sight of her.

"Ella!" Max shrieked. His head barely bobbed above the water, but he let go of Philip's arm. He paddled towards the throne with determination. Philip shouted for him to stop, but with Vinnia in his grasp, he couldn't grab his brother and pull him back to safety.

When Max was completely out of reach, a current swept him under. He didn't resurface.

No, no, no. This couldn't be happening. Philip yelled his brother's name, straining to see him in the raging waters as he struggled to keep Vinnia's head above water. With only one arm, he couldn't swim while holding her. He couldn't pull Ella and Max out of the water. He couldn't reach them. Couldn't save them. He was forced to choose; risk his life and Vinnia's to search in vain for the others, or save himself and Vinnia while he still could.

Nausea roiled in his stomach, threatening to tear him apart. He couldn't do this. He couldn't make this decision. But he had to.

Tightening his grip on Vinnia, Philip turned towards the door and waded through the water that now reached his chin. Numbness spread through his body as he abandoned the two people he cared for most in this world and the next.

The crowd of dwarves finally made it through the exit. Philip followed close behind, clutching Vinnia desperately. Outside the throne room, water poured into the tunnels. Guards ushered hundreds upon hundreds of dwarves down a wide tunnel. Philip became swept up by the crowd. He could only hope they were all rushing to the exit.

Sure enough, the tunnel veered steeply towards the surface and dumped them into the scorching daylight. A mob of dwarves stood in the heat, their panicked roar of conversation muted in Philip's ears.

Unable to think about what he'd done, Philip deposited Vinnia onto the ground and tried to find her pulse. When he couldn't find one, he tipped her head back and began CPR.

Though it was nearly impossible to perform proper CPR with one hand, Philip had to try. His one-handedness couldn't cause him to lose any one else. Following the steps he learned in first-aid training, he alternated between two breaths directly into Vinnia's mouth and thirty compressions on her sternum.

He took all of the anger, pain, and self-loathing swirling in his body and poured the energy into CPR. Tears blurred his vision, but he couldn't spare a moment to brush them away.

This had to work. It just had to.

He lost track of how long he continued to perform CPR. It didn't matter if it took five minutes or thirty; he refused to give up. His muscles ached from exertion. He flinched every time Vinnia's sternum popped. Sweat dripped into his eyes, but he didn't stop.

Finally, with a gut-wrenching *crack* to her sternum, Vinnia's eyes flew open. She sucked air into her lungs with a painful gasp, then keeled over, coughing up mouthfuls of water. Philip patted her back until all the water had been expelled from her lungs. She clutched at her chest and dry heaved until she collapsed with exhaustion.

"Stars," Vinnia groaned, shoulders hunched to ease the pain of her broken sternum. "What did you do to me?"

He tried to reply, but he couldn't get his lips to form the words.

Vinnia splayed her hand over her chest and healed herself with a sickening *pop*. "It doesn't matter. I'm alive, and we have

302

all of the items. The fair folk are marching to attack the elves, so let's get you and Max home before things get messy. Come on." she glanced around. "Where are Ella and Max? We have to go."

Philip's body was completely numb. "They didn't make it out."

"What?" Vinnia unclogged water from her ears. "I can't hear you."

"They didn't make it out!" His words came louder and more forcefully than he'd intended.

Vinnia's expression went slack. "No, that—that's not possible."

Philip couldn't meet her eyes. "They're gone."

"Philip, I flooded that entire burrow. If they didn't make it out…" realization crashed over her like a wave, "This is all my fault."

This wasn't her fault. If anything, the fault belonged to him. He could have tried to save them. Instead, he chose to save himself and Vinnia. If Ella and Max were dead, the weight of that would rest squarely on his shoulders.

Vinnia buried her head in her hands. She sat perfectly still, her lips moving in silent prayer. Though Philip didn't know who or what she was praying to, he bowed his head as well. The two of them sat together in the heat of the day, each praying for Ella and Max.

Philip expected to feel the crushing pain of grief. He expected his body to be heavy with defeat and hopelessness. Instead, hollow numbness spread through his chest. It was as if he were watching himself from someone else's eyes.

Only when shouts erupted from the crowd did he lift his head to see what the commotion was about. A team of dwarves in white uniforms carried a pile of bodies on a tarp. Gasps and wails

303

arose from the crowd when they laid the bodies out for everyone to see.

Vinnia's head snapped up, her eyes sharpening like an eagle. Without warning, she sprang to her feet and bolted through the crowd towards the line of bodies. Philip scrambled after her, the crowd parting for him like the sea.

When Vinnia reached the bodies she immediately rushed to Ella and Max's unmoving forms. Philip caught up to her as she knelt next to Ella.

"—gonna kill me," Vinnia muttered under her breath.

She planted both hands firmly on Ella's chest, but paused, determination faltering. Quickly, she reached down Ella's shirt and pulled out the dwarves' petrified heart, which she had hidden over her own heart. By some miracle, the dwarves hadn't found it when they recovered her body. Vinnia passed the heart to Philip, who stuck it in his pack.

Closing her eyes, Vinnia pressed down hard on Ella's chest and began to sing. The water in Ella's lungs erupted through her mouth and nose. When she didn't move, Vinnia tried again. It took four more tries for Ella's fingers to twitch, and six more tries for her eyes to fly open.

Ella filled her lungs with heaving gasps like she'd never tasted air before. Philip's heart could have burst with relief. He wrapped his arm around Ella's shoulders, allowing her to lean against him for support. For a moment, they simply sat and breathed together. Then, Ella began to sob.

Vinnia barely spared Ella a glance before she moved on to Max. This time, it took only five tries until the water was expelled from his lungs, and he opened his eyes. He immediately threw his arms around Vinnia, who swayed, just on the verge of passing out. Somehow, she managed to cling to consciousness enough to

304

return Max's hug.

"We were dead!" Max exclaimed, "We were dead, but you healed us!"

All around them, dwarves were too preoccupied with their sobbing and pleading to pay any attention to the magic Vinnia had just performed. Some begged their dead family members to come back to them. A few dwarves desperately tried to revive the bodies. None of the dead dwarves miraculously recovered.

Ella continued to sob in Philip's embrace, her cries mixing with the wails of the dwarves around them. But he knew Ella cried for more than a few dead bodies. She cried for her kingdom, which was on the verge of war.

After a few moments, Ella pulled away. "We have to get to Elvenmar before the fair folk. This war will destroy our kingdom. The fair folk will murder my family. We have to leave now!"

Philip and Ella scrambled to their feet. Together, with Max and Vinnia, they hurried through the crowd to where the hippogriffs still waited. Tears slipped down Ella's cheeks, but she set her face into a mask of determination as she swung herself onto the back of her hippogriff.

Vinnia, who could barely stand on her own, was still too weak to morph. She and Max mounted the smallest hippogriff. Neither of them looked alert enough to fly, but they didn't have time to spare.

As soon as Philip mounted his hippogriff, they took into the air. He dug his knees into her side, urging her to fly faster. She screeched in acknowledgment and flapped her wings harder.

Ella set a brutal pace. She steered them southwest, and the setting sun shone directly into their faces as they flew. She leaned into her hippogriff as if she were willing it to go faster, but her shoulders shook as she cried against her hippogriff's neck.

The sun sank below the horizon, and the moon took its place. Stars glittered overhead, but Philip simply didn't have the energy to admire them like he did most other nights.

In a single week, he had seen more death and pain than he had in his entire life. Until the past twenty-four hours, he'd always thought he would be fine if a loved one died. Sure, he would be sad. He might cry a bit. Maybe he would be too numb to feel anything. Sooner or later, though, he'd assumed he would be perfectly fine.

But the last item—*a human's dying breath*—tugged at the back of his mind. Fear constricted his heart. He'd never been afraid of death, but after so many near-misses, the idea of dying was no longer something abstract and intangible. He'd almost lost Vinnia, Ella, and Max in a single day.

An ominous feeling told him he was next.

Dash sighed as he looked out over the campsite. The army camp spread over the hills as far as the eye could see. Fair folk with orange magic sustained campfires that dotted the land like freckles. Soldiers huddled around the fires, anticipation for battle and bloodshed boiling inside them.

The night air at the Haderra-Elvenmar border was just cool enough to send a chill down Dash's spine. With his new gold magic, he could light a fire to warm himself, but in the hours since his gilding, he'd been hesitant to use his new magic. What if he couldn't control it? What if it was addictive? Once he began to use it, would he ever be able to stop?

Magic swirled beneath his skin. Boundless energy burst in his chest. Summoning magic was easier than ever. Golden flames sprang to life and danced across his fingertips.

Warmth spread through his body. Magic sparked from the

soles of his feet to the tips of his hair. It was electrifying and soothing, energizing and calming, thrilling and comforting. Before the gilding, he'd never dreamed magic could feel so good.

For the first time, he understood Rhett's terror when faced with the prospect of losing his magic. Rhett's magic had always been more powerful than any magic alive, including gold magic. Maybe that's why Elliott had hated Rhett so fiercely.

Magic had always been part of Rhett's life. From the moment he was born, he'd used his magic, though their mother had loathed him for it. For him, losing his magic would be like losing a limb.

Dash, however, hadn't always been able to use his magic. Ever since he was little, Rhett had told him to keep his magic hidden. Whenever Dash would heal himself, Rhett would panic and cover his glowing fingers.

"Don't let Mom see!" Rhett had always said with panic in his violet eyes.

It wasn't until Dash came to the magical world that he began using his magic. He never tired of the feeling that came from using magic, but it didn't feel like *this*.

He had to admit, the changes in his appearance didn't thrill him. His strawberry-blonde hair turned the color of gold leaf. His sun-kissed skin shimmered with a golden pallor. His blue eyes were now the color of liquid gold. It was a small price to pay for the new gold magic that flowed through his gold veins, though.

To keep himself grounded, he repeated the incantation he clung to. His new magic made him powerful, not invincible. Yes, it felt good to use, but magic couldn't solve everything.

Magic couldn't solve the problem of this war.

Now that they were on the warpath, he began having serious doubts about the plan. Was there a weakness he hadn't spotted in the formations? Were there blind spots the enemy could extort? Would the violence and bloodshed be justified by the result?

Footsteps crunched in the grass behind him. Dash straightened, extinguishing the flame in his palm.

"It's just us," Nathan said in that deep, reassuring voice of his.

Dash's posture relaxed. Tension seeped from his shoulders at the comfort his old friends brought.

Nathan and Adrian had supposedly joined him to offer him advice and moral support as they charged into battle. In reality, they were there to help lead the attack. Dash had known he wouldn't be much help in battle—his training in the sacred art of swordsmanship had only lasted a few months, and even that had been a failure—but the Fair Lords expected him to lead the charge as any good Sovereign should. Worst of all, the Fair Lords expected him to kill Queen Celosia in retribution for Elliott's death.

Dash's stomach turned inside-out at the thought of killing someone. He wouldn't—no, couldn't—kill another person. Yellow magic healed, not destroyed. The fact that his yellow magic was gilded into gold magic didn't mean he'd suddenly lost the mindset of a healer.

He could be a good Sovereign without killing someone… right?

According to the Fair Lords, the answer was no. But the Fair Lords didn't dictate what kind of ruler he was going to be. If they saw him as a bad sovereign simply because he refused to kill Queen Celosia, so be it.

"We have bad news," Adrian said.

Of course, they would have bad news. Why would anything go smoothly for him?

Dash's eyes didn't leave the campground as he asked, "What's wrong?"

"Our spies have been surveying the elven castle for the past few days," Adrian reported, "We just received word that the city has been evacuated. The elven royal family escaped to the Island of Corvus with their advisors, castle staff, and a large portion of the army. We think they know about the attack."

Dash's heart sank. The element of surprise was supposed to be their advantage. "How did they know we were coming?"

"We can still catch them off-guard," Nathan said. "We just declared war this morning. I can't imagine fleeing to Corvus with so many people was a smooth process. The amount of magic they'll need to protect themselves from the monsters will be tremendous. They will be completely unprepared."

Nathan was probably right. The fair folk still held the upper hand. Dash let out a steady breath. Worry wouldn't change the situation.

"Have you confirmed this information?" he asked. "What if it's a trap? Is the entire royal family *actually* on Corvus?"

"Yes," Adrian hesitated, "However, according to our spies, Elestren disappeared a week and a half ago. No one knows where she is, not even the queen herself." Adrian had a slight twinge in his voice when he said Elestren's name. According to them, she had been the one sent to murder Elliott. Dash didn't want to believe it, but why would Nathan and Adrian lie about something like that?

"All right," he said, drawing himself up into what he hoped was a regal posture. "We need to change course. In the morning, we fly to Corvus and attack the elves directly."

Nathan and Adrian humored his attempts to be commanding. "Yes, Your Sovereignty." They swept exaggerated bows and marched to inform the generals of the change of plans.

Once he was sure they were gone, Dash pressed the heels of his hands to his eyes until he saw an explosion of colors on the backs of his eyelids. It made sense for the elves to evacuate to Corvus. Everyone knew the dangers of the monsters that prowled the island, and everyone held the King of Corvus in a position of reverence and fear.

The elves were playing a dangerous game.

Would the fair folk attack the island and risk adding monsters and the King's wrath to the complicated equation of warfare? Or would they admit defeat and retreat to Haderra?

Little did they know, Dash knew the Island of Corvus well thanks to his visits with Rhett. He'd faced off with plenty of monsters before and lived to tell the tale.

The elves thought he was weak. They mistook his youth and inexperience for skittishness and incompetence.

While Dash didn't thirst for blood and vengeance like his people, he would fight with everything in him for the good of the fair folk.

Even if it cost him his life.

Chapter 28

They reached Elvenmar by the time the sun began to rise. The sunbeams bathed the forests of Elvenmar in rich pinks, fiery oranges, and foreboding purples like the trees in the Pixie Forest. Just days ago, they had set foot in the Pixie Forest for the first time, believing they would find the objects quickly and be home before dinner. Now, they raced against an army, knowing if they arrived too late, the worlds would be plunged into chaos.

Philip didn't know what Ella planned to do once they reached the castle. Did she have some sort of plan that would cause both sides to lay down their weapons and sign a peace treaty? Or did she simply want to be there with her family while the fair folk lay siege to the castle?

A small part of him wished she would send him and Max home before they got roped into the mess of a war. Wouldn't it be easier for her not to have to worry about two humans while her kingdom defended itself against attackers?

They still had the matter of the seventh and final item to worry about, but maybe it was something simple they had yet to think about. Both he and Max had reached the point of near-death in the past week and a half. Maybe that counted as the part of the last item.

It didn't matter. Philip knew he couldn't Ella to abandon her family to try and send them home first. This war was a storm they would just have to wait out.

The sun had fully risen by the time the city of Velsailia appeared on the horizon, but something was wrong. The towering walls surrounding the city were vacant of their usual guards. Empty crossbow stands lined the walls, abandoned and neglected. Unlit lanterns swung in the trees above.

Philip saw his concern magnified in Ella's apprehensive expression.

"They've probably just moved the outer defense closer to the castle," Ella said, clinging to desperate hope. "Maybe they want to let the fair folk think the posts are abandoned."

Not a single elf could be found in the city. Every lantern, both indoor and outdoor, remained unlit. Silence rang throughout the city, louder than any voices.

Ella dipped her chin, hiding her expression beneath a curtain of braids. Philip imagined her blinking tears from her eyes and clinging to shreds of hope.

When they reached the castle, confusion replaced any hope they may have had. The castle was just as deserted as the rest of the city. They landed in front of the griffin stables to feed and water their hippogriffs, but even the griffin stalls stood empty and abandoned. The musky smell of manure hung thick in the air, though there wasn't a feather to be found.

Ella swung down from her hippogriff and began to pace frantically. "I don't understand. Where is everyone? The entire city is deserted." Her voice cracked under the strain of preventing tears. "Did the fair folk already attack?"

"Maybe your aunt knew about the attack and evacuated the city for the citizens' protection," Vinnia suggested. "It's exactly what my mom would have done, and the opposite of what my dad would have done."

"Yeah," Max added. "Someone probably left you a note or something saying where they went."

Ella chewed on her bottom lip. "If any one left a note, it

would have been Hemnes. We used to leave secret notes for each other in the North Tower when we were younger."

"You three go check for a note," Vinnia said. "I'll stay here and take care of the hippogriffs."

Ella spouted a rushed *'thank you'* to Vinnia before sprinting into the castle. Philip and Max followed as she made a beeline for the familiar stairwell that led to the North Tower. They raced up the many flights of winding steps, their feet barely touching the ground. Philip's thighs and calves burned from exertion, but he didn't slow; they didn't have a moment to spare.

They reached the top of the North Tower and emerged into the circular room. Books and pillows littered the room haphazardly, just like Philip had last seen it. Only the round wooden table in the center of the room had been swept clean. Someone had removed every piece of parchment, quill, and bottle of ink from the table. All that remained was a small, handwritten note.

Ella snatched the note from the table and scanned it. As she read, her anxious expression melted into one of relief. "The citizens have been evacuated to the nearest city, but my family and their servants have set up a secret camp on the Island of Corvus. They have half of the army with them too."

"Is that a good thing?" Philip didn't remember his time on the Island of Corvus with particular fondness.

"Yes!" Ella half-laughed, half-spoke. "Don't you see? The fair folk don't know where my family has gone. We can reach them before the army reaches the city. *And*, Corvus is where we have to form the gateway to get you two home. We're striking two crows with one arrow. By the time the fair folk find out what happened, I'll be with my family, and you two will be safe at home."

This was almost too good to be true. Hope squeezed Philip's chest. He couldn't help it; he hadn't slept in over twenty-four hours and was far beyond suppressing his emotions.

Today. They could be home today.

They rushed back to Vinnia, who waited at the griffin stables, arming themselves with swords and knives on the way back, just in case. They found Vinnia sagged against the stable doors, exhaustion evident on her face.

"Good news?" Vinnia asked upon seeing Ella's expression.

"We have to get to the Island of Corvus," Ella replied. *"Now."*

"What?" Vinnia recoiled, "Why?"

"My family is there." Ella shoved various knives into her pack. "We have to hurry. The fair folk will be here any minute."

Vinnia didn't seem the least bit surprised at this information. "Of course, they're on Corvus," she muttered.

Philip wasn't sure what she meant by that, but they didn't have time to ask questions.

Though the hippogriffs were exhausted from hours of flying, they took off immediately. They kept a slower pace, but Philip was grateful they even left the ground at all. Since Ella didn't seem to have the urgent need to rush to the island as fast as possible, no one pushed the hippogriffs.

After their visit to Mermaidia and their near-death experience with water in the dwarf tunnels, Philip's stomach dropped at the sight of the sea. Water had never been a source of fear before—he wouldn't exactly call his apprehension 'fear'—but he had a newfound respect for the sheer power it held.

The clear blue water merged almost seamlessly on the horizon with the eye-achingly blue sky. As they drew closer to the island, the water grew darker and murkier. Steep waves rose from the once-calm surface. Multiple times, Philip could have sworn he saw a dark form pass through the water.

The Island of Corvus soon appeared as a spot of green on the blue horizon. From a distance, it appeared serene and tranquil. This image clashed violently with Philip's memories of roaring beasts and blinding pain. His image became a reality once more as they neared the island.

They were too late.

Griffins swarmed the skies and clashed against each other in furious blurs of claws and beaks. Their riders fought viciously, swinging their weapons in deadly arcs. Arrows whizzed through the air and exploded like flak.

Below the griffins, a camp spread across the rocky beach along the shore. Canvas tents embellished with the elven crest littered the beach in a compact circle. The smoldering remains of bonfires peeked out from between them. The campsite would have been peaceful if it wasn't a battlefield.

Fire devoured the canvas tents. Battle cries and screams of agony arose from the clash on the beach. Fair folk and elves fought mercilessly. While the armor-clad fair folk carried swords and shields, many elves didn't even have shoes. Some elves wielded real weapons, but the majority fought with whatever object they could get their hands on—rocks, rope, pots, and pans...

This wasn't a battle; it was an ambush.

Bodies littered the camp. Griffins, elves, and fair folk lay bleeding together, staining the rocks with their blood.

Most of the fighting centered around the largest tent. Elven guards surrounded it like a living wall, or, more accurately, a meat shield. From a tactical perspective, putting the queen's tent in the center of the campsite had been smart. But the enemy possessed wings and descended upon the tent from the skies.

Ella's shriek rang through the air as her hippogriff plummeted to the ground. An arrow stuck out of its shoulder. It managed to spiral away from the fighting, towards the trees bordering the beach. Philip urged his hippogriff after Ella.

Her hippogriff crashed into a tree, throwing her from its back. Philip leaped from his hippogriff before it touched the ground. His knees buckled, but he ignored the pain and raced to Ella's side. She slumped against a tree. Blood dripped from a gash on her forehead.

"Ella?" Philip shook her, "Can you hear me?"

"I'm fine." She staggered to her feet. "Do you have your sword?"

Nodding Philip placed his hand over the hilt of the sword he had taken from the castle in Elvenmar. "Where are you going?"

"We are going to defend my family," Ella said. Her expression was set with determination. Her resilience never failed to amaze him, but at the moment, she was determined to march into the middle of a battlefield and run towards the thickest part of the fighting. They could *die.*

"I'll stay here and protect Max and the hippogriffs," Vinnia volunteered. "We're far enough away from the fighting that we shouldn't have any trouble, but I can keep us safe if anything happens."

Ella looked apprehensive. "Aren't you going to come with us?"

Screeched arose from the trees behind Vinnia. She shot an irritated glare to the trees, which writhed with hordes of crows waiting to pick over the bodies of the dead. Turning back to Ella, she shook her head. "I'm still too weak, and this island is too dangerous."

"All right," Ella conceded. "Philip and I will just have to do this ourselves."

"Ella, think this through," Philip began. He struggled to contain the terror that arose in him at the thought of running *toward* the violence. "We can't just charge into a battlefield. We'll be killed. Trained soldiers are dead on that beach. What makes you think we won't be joining them?"

"You would do whatever it takes to get Max home. I'll do whatever it takes to protect my family," Ella said resolutely. "They could die out there. For all we know, they're already dead. If I die on that battlefield, I'll be with the people I love. I'm going to find them no matter what. You don't have to follow me."

Everything in Philip screamed at him to turn and run far away from this mess. He could save himself. He could save Max and Vinnia if they ran with him. But they wouldn't. *He* wouldn't.

After everything Ella had done for them, he owed this to her. He would fight for her, though he might die trying.

He mustered any courage he could find. "I'm coming with you."

Ella's expression broke with relief. *"Thank you."*

If this was to be his final goodbye, Philip wanted to make it count.

He knelt and pulled Max into a hug. "Be brave for me, okay?"

"Okay." Max buried his face in his neck.

Philip swallowed past the tightness in his throat. "I don't know if we'll get home soon, but if you make it back without me, eat some tembleque for me."

"Okay," Max sniffled.

Crushing his little brother to his chest one last time, Philip forced himself to let go. He moved on to Vinnia, but she didn't

317

wait for him to hug her first. Her arms wrapped around his waist, and her forehead pressed against his chest.

"Whatever it takes," she whispered.

Philip nodded and echoed the sentiment. "Whatever it takes."

Vinnia kept their goodbye brief. No tears dripped down her cheeks. Her chin didn't quiver. Her voice didn't waver. She kept her shoulders back like she knew how the situation would end and had already resigned herself to the outcome.

"All right." Philip set his mouth in a grim line and turned to Ella. "Let's go find your family."

Drawing her sword, Ella charged onto the beach. Philip followed at her heels, ready to watch her back.

Out in the fray, he severely regretted leaving the safety of the trees. The battle raged all around them. Fair folk and elves screamed and shouted for comrades to cover them or watch out. The ringing clash of metal against metal made his head throb. He stumbled over the body of a young elf whose curly hair was stained crimson with blood.

To his right, a fair folk soldier stabbed an elf through the chest and yanked the knife out without a second glance. The elf crumpled to the ground, dead the moment his head hit the rocks.

Philip's throat and chest constricted. He had to stay alert. As much as he wanted to block out the carnage, he couldn't pause for even a moment. The moment he lost himself in the chaos would be the moment he lost his life. Adrenaline fueled his body and made his thoughts frantic, yet his focus was acute. His senses were heightened. Everything happened in a blur. His hearing was simultaneously muffled and sharpened.

Ella stumbled backward and crashed into Philip as a fair folk soldier plummeted to the ground in front of her. She caught herself on his shoulder, gripping harder than necessary. Philip saw his terror and confusion mirrored in her eyes.

Somehow, they managed to press on.

The wrongness of magic hung heavy in the air, rolling over Philip in waves of nausea. Some magic tasted like burning, while others smelled like thunder. Flames erupted around them. Vines lashed out like probing tentacles. Flashes of powder collided in brilliant explosions.

Philip flinched as blood splattered onto his forehead and dripped down his face. He didn't spare a glance to see where it came from. Out of the corner of his eyes, he glimpsed a bright red blur headed straight towards them. He dropped his sword, grabbed Ella, and yanked her to the ground just as a red fair folk flew over their heads towards an ax-wielding elf.

"We're almost there." Ella panted.

Philip snatched up his sword as they scrambled to their feet. Sweat and blood slicked his palms. He struggled to keep a grip on the sword. His lungs ached from breathing heavily, while his heart thundered against his sternum. He had to keep moving.

They wove through the fray as fast as possible, conflict meeting them at every turn. The loose rocks beneath them provided no traction and were slick with blood and gore. Bodies littered the beach. Griffins, elves, and fair folk dropped from the sky like meteors.

When they reached the heaviest part of the fighting, Philip's body froze against his will. His thoughts repeated in a single loop: *I'm going to die*. Elves had stacked packs and supplies into a makeshift fortification around the queen's tent, but it wasn't nearly enough to keep the fair folk at bay. They swarmed the tent like flies on rotting meat. Though the elves fought desperately, it was only a matter of time before the fair folk overwhelmed them.

Ella plunged into the fighting, oblivious that Philip wasn't right behind her. He tried to follow, but it was like his feet had solidified into cement. His body refused to move. He stood frozen in the middle of a battlefield. This was bad. He had to move. He couldn't move. He *needed* to move.

The moment a blue fair folk locked eyes with him, Philip knew he was dead. The fair folk charged at him with his sword raised. This was it. This was his final moment.

Just before the fair folk reached him, someone leaped between them and parried the attack. With a jolt, Philip recognized the glossy, dark braid and leather riding gloves. Though grime and blood covered her skin, Treave's eyes blazed with the rush of battle.

She defended him from his attacker like her life depended on it. Her teeth grit as she fought the heavily armored attacker who stood almost twice her height. The attacker used his blue magic to drench her with relentless bursts of water, but she wasn't fazed. Staying light on her feet, she ducked, dodged, and parried with a bloody knife in each leather-clad hand.

When she knocked the sword out of the attacker's grip, her eyes gleamed triumphantly. Enraged, the attacker roared and seized Treave by the hair. Bile rose in Philip's throat as the attacker slammed his armored head into her forehead. Treave's eyes rolled into her head, and her knees gave out. Her knives clattered to the ground. She crumpled to the ground, unconscious and defenseless.

For a moment, time stopped.

Philip pictured Treave's charming grin. He heard her laugh as she ran her fingers across Ochre's feathers. He remembered how her dark eyes glittered that night in the courtyard when they stole the first item. He felt the press of her lips against his.

She'd saved his life. Now, here she was, unconscious in the middle of a battlefield. Blood streamed from the gash on her forehead.

Before Philip could turn and run, a blast of water met him in the face. It was as if someone sprayed him in the face with a firehose. His head snapped back. His eyes stung. His sinuses filled with water. This magic felt sloshy as if he'd drank too much water too quickly.

The next blast knocked the sword out of his hand. The blast after that barreled into his chest, slamming him to the ground. The attacker planted a foot on his sternum.

"What's a little human like you doing here?" the attacker snarled. "You should have stayed in your world."

The attacker pressed down on Philip's chest. Air squeezed out of his lungs. His hand snaked out, groping around the rocks for any possible weapon. His fingertips brushed the blade of Treave's knife. He curled his fingers around it.

With a grimace, he plunged the knife behind his attacker's knee. The attacker howled in pain and lifted his foot to stomp on Philip's chest. Rolling to the side, Philip scrambled to his feet and landed a kick between the attacker's legs. The attacker collapsed but refused to give up. He raised his hand and sent a spray of water at Philip. But this time, the water didn't spray from his hand. It poured from his mouth, ears, and nose.

Horrified, Philip scrambled away from the attacker as endless streams of water poured from his body. What was happening?

He thought back to when Adrian tried to use green magic on Corvus before the manticore attack. Nathan's words echoed in the back of his mind. *Magic doesn't always work here.*

Somehow, the attacker's magic was malfunctioning. Water

poured from his body like something from a scene in a horror movie. Finally, the attacker's eyes rolled into the back of his head, and he collapsed, water still streaming from him.

That image would never leave Philip's mind.

Turning away, he knelt by Treave's side. His body trembled with adrenaline, preventing him from feeling her pulse. Instead, he held the blade of the knife just below her nostrils. When the blade fogged with her breath, he exhaled in relief.

Treave was alive.

Somehow, he had to get her off the battlefield, where any one could crush her skull while they ran for their lives. The tree line lay about fifty yards away. If he could make it to the trees without being killed, he could find a place for Treave to regain consciousness in safety. Then, he could return to the battlefield and find Ella.

Ella. Where was she? Had she found her family? Had she met her fate, mistakenly thinking he would be there to protect her?

One thing at a time. He would worry about Ella once Treave was out of harm's way.

Tucking the knife into his belt, he tried to scoop her into his arms. In the rush of the moment, he'd forgotten that he had only one working arm. He could barely lift her into a sitting position. With a growl of frustration, he sat back on his heels.

So, he couldn't carry Treave to safety. He could drag her to the tree line, but the rocks would cause her to bleed even more. With one arm, he could only do one thing at a time. If someone attacked him while he dragged her, he wouldn't be able to defend both of them.

In the wrecked remains of the camp surrounding him, he searched for anything he could use to get Treave to safety. His gaze landed on a smoldering piece of canvas about the size of a bedsheet. It would suffice.

He snatched up the canvas, spread it out next to Treave, and rolled her onto it. He moved awkwardly, jostling her around, but desperate times called for desperate measures.

Taking hold of the corner and dragging the canvas like a stretcher towards the trees, he prayed no one would attack them. Arrows whizzed by, and a griffin nearly landed on top of them, but his prayers were answered.

Once he reached the tree line, he could have collapsed with relief. But he didn't stop there. He dragged her deeper into the forest until he could no longer see the battlefield.

When he was far enough from the fighting, he sagged against a tree. He took deep, heaving gasps as he tried to catch his breath. His muscles shook from exertion. He ached with exhaustion and sleep deprivation.

Wiping sweat from his eyes, he knelt next to Treave and propped her against the trunk of a sturdy pine tree. Her head lolled to the side. He brushed her hair out of her bruised face. The gash on her forehead bled everywhere, turning her once-white tunic crimson. Her bottom lip swelled black and blue. She looked like death, but she was breathing.

Crows swarmed the branches overhead. Philip covered her prone body with the piece of canvas. It wouldn't do much to fend off the monsters, but they would be too preoccupied with the hordes of bodies on the beach to worry about a single elf.

As much as he wanted to stay with Treave—to curl up next to her and sleep away his pain and exhaustion and weariness— he had to find Ella.

He limped back towards the battlefield with nothing but a knife to defend himself. His entire body throbbed. Sweat rolled down his forehead and dripped into his eyes. He was drenched in blood. All he wanted to do was fall asleep and never wake up.

What was he doing here?

How had his life changed so drastically in the span of a few days?

Nearly two weeks ago, his biggest concern had been surviving his crazy family during the reunion. When they'd ended up in the magical world, his goal had been simple: find the items and get home. Now, he was practically crawling back towards a battlefield where he would most likely die.

Why did he agree to follow Ella into a warzone?

Why did he agree to this stupid quest?

Why did he have to lose his arm to a manticore?

Why did he agree to explore the woods with Max in the first place?

Resentment welled up in his chest. If it weren't for Max and his stupid idea to run off into the forest, they would be safe and sound back home. He would still have his arm. He would still have his hopes and dreams for the future. He would have been safe and clean and, most importantly, not in the magical world marching to his death.

He shook his head and tried to snap back to reality; this was just the exhaustion and pain speaking. He could do nothing to change the past. He had a job to do and promises to keep.

He had to make it back to Ella.

The roar of battle grew louder as he neared the beach. Griffins shrieked in the air. Explosions flashed in the distance. Metal struck metal. Bows twanged. Arrows whizzed through the air. Blades pierced flesh. Elves and fair folk screamed as they died. The burn of magic roiled in Philip's stomach.

He wished everything would just *stop*.

As soon as the thought passed his mind, the noise in the distance died as if someone had pressed a mute button. The world fell into an eerie silence. Philip froze; strange magic swirled in the air. It was hot and cold at the same time, and it tasted bittersweet.

"Hello there," a voice said. It was velvety and sensual like a caress.

Philip whirled around, brandishing his knife in front of him.

"There's no need for that." The voice sounded amused.

It belonged to a young man who stood before Philip. Clear, sparkling wings spread behind him. Dark eyes gleamed from underneath a plume of midnight hair. Fine clothing accented his lean frame.

Philip stared at the man, disarmed by his unearthly beauty. Never before had he seen someone so ethereal. He fumbled for words. Finally, he managed, "What do you want?"

The corners of the man's lips quirked up. "Come with me."

"Why?" Philip peered at the man, unable to mask his suspicion. If he recalled correctly, most fairytales said never to trust a beautiful stranger in the woods.

"I can send you and your brother home right now. Come with me, and I'll strike you a deal. We can discuss it over a cup of coffee."

Those words hit Philip like a blow to the gut. They were honey to his ears. Hope welled in his chest. This stranger was offering him the impossible. They wouldn't have to worry about the last item. They wouldn't have to get involved in this war. *And coffee.* What he wouldn't give for a steaming cup of the strongest black coffee known to man...

He glanced towards the now-silent battlefield. If he were to return from the fray, his chances of survival were minimal.

Ella was out there somewhere. He'd promised to stick with her through this battle, but he'd broken that promise the moment they were separated. It would be too late to go back and find her. She was either reunited with her family or dying on the rocks. There was nothing he could do about that.

He turned back to the man, who studied him with an unreadable expression. The man's eyebrows lifted in what almost looked like interest. When Philip met his eyes, the hot and cold feeling of magic spiked in his chest. Something tugged at him, drawing him towards the man. There was something magnetic about him as if the very air was drawn to him.

The man tilted his head ever so slightly to the side like a bird. "So?"

Taking a deep breath, Philip nodded. "Lead the way."

From the satisfied expression on the man's face, Philip had the sinking suspicion the man knew he would say yes all along.

The man turned away from the battlefield and motioned for him to follow him deeper into the forest.

"Wait," Philip hesitated, "Who are you?"

The man turned over his shoulder to look back at Philip. Sunlight streamed through the branches overhead. When it struck his wings, they glittered iridescently, framing his elegant silhouette. A slow grin spread across his face.

"I'm the King of Corvus."

Printed in the USA
CPSIA information can be obtained
at www.ICGtesting.com
LVHW071317011023
759824LV00003B/8

9 781800 745711